THE
WIDOW

Since *The Firm* in 1991, John Grisham has published a number one bestseller every year. His books have been translated into 45 languages and have sold over 350 million copies worldwide. Nine have been adapted to film, including *The Firm*, *The Pelican Brief* and *A Time To Kill*.

His first work of non-fiction, *The Innocent Man*, was adapted into a six-part Netflix docuseries; his second, *Framed*, written with Jim McCloskey, highlights work with organisations dedicated to exonerating those who have been wrongfully convicted.

He is the two-time winner of the Harper Lee Prize for Legal Fiction and was distinguished with the Library of Congress Creative Achievement Award for Fiction.

John lives on a farm in central Virginia.

JOHN GRISHAM

THE
WIDOW

HODDER &
STOUGHTON

First published in the United States in 2025 by
Doubleday, a division of Penguin Random House
First published in Great Britain in 2025 by Hodder & Stoughton Limited
An Hachette UK company

The authorised representative in the EEA is Hachette Ireland, 8 Castlecourt
Centre, Dublin 15, D15 XTP3, Ireland (email: info@hbgi.ie)

1

A CIP catalogue record for this title is available from the British Library

Hardback ISBN 9781399703413
Trade Paperback ISBN 9781399703352
ebook ISBN 9781399703390

Printed and bound in Australia by McPherson's Printing Group.

Hodder & Stoughton policy is to use papers that are natural, renewable
and recyclable products and made from wood grown in sustainable forests.
The logging and manufacturing processes are expected to conform
to the environmental regulations of the country of origin.

Hodder & Stoughton Limited
Carmelite House
50 Victoria Embankment
London EC4Y 0DZ

www.hodder.co.uk

THE
WIDOW

CHAPTER 1

The clients drawn to the quaint little law office at the corner of Main and Maple brought problems that Simon was tired of. Bankruptcies, drunk driving charges, delinquent child support, foreclosures, nickel-and-dime car wrecks, suspicious slip-and-falls, dubious claims of disabilities—the stock-in-trade of a run-of-the-mill street lawyer whose law school dreams of riches had faded so dim they were almost gone. Eighteen years into the grind and Simon F. Latch, Attorney and Counselor (both) at Law, was burning out. He was weary of other people's problems.

Occasionally there was a break in the misery when an aging client needed some estate work, like an updated last will and testament. These were almost always uncomplicated matters that any first-year law student could handle, regardless of how somber Simon tried to make them. For only $250, he could write, or "draft" as he preferred to say, a three-page simple will, print it on heavy gold bond paper, get it notarized by his "staff," and convey the impression that the client was "executing" something profound.

The truth was half of them didn't even need a will, regardless of how simple, though no lawyer in the history of American jurisprudence had ever said so to a paying client. It was also true that the $250 fee was a rip-off because the internet was filled with free simple wills that were just as binding. It was also true that Mr. Latch would hardly touch the will. Matilda, his secretary, filled in the blanks and printed the important documents.

The current client was Ms. Eleanor Barnett, age eighty-five, a widow who lived alone in a modest suburban home she and her late second husband had purchased ten years earlier. She had no children, though Harry Korsak, her last husband, had two sons from a bad first marriage and had tried for years to convince Eleanor, his beloved second wife, to adopt the pair for various reasons, none of which appealed to her because, as she confided to Matilda during their lengthy second phone chat, she loathed the boys. They were nothing but trouble.

"And do you have a mortgage on your home?" Matilda had asked, politely interrupting the beginning of what promised to be a windy narrative about the two sorry sons.

No. The house was paid for, as was the car. There were no debts. Harry Korsak had been quite frugal, a child of Depression-era parents, you know, and simply hated the idea of debt. Between phone calls, Matilda did her usual internet checking and learned that the home, as assessed by the county for $280,000, was indeed free of liens, and the car, a fifteen-year-old Lincoln, was also unencumbered. Digging a bit deeper, she found a rap sheet for Clyde Korsak, the elder of the two un-adopted sons. Decades earlier he had been caught peddling cocaine and spent four years in prison.

Ms. Barnett would not discuss any more financial matters over the phone, said she'd rather wait until her meeting with Mr. Latch. She arrived promptly at 2 P.M., dressed like a mildly affluent old lady on her way to church. Matilda had seen a thousand of them come and go, and she sized her up immediately as she poured coffee into a fine china cup she kept around for the old gals. Most clients got paper cups. Ms. Barnett walked just fine, no cane, no tottering, a good stride and nice gait, and she sat properly in a reception chair and sipped her coffee, pinkie in the air, a clear sign of either good manners or a trace of snobbery. From all outward appearances, she was in good shape physically, probably had another decade to go before her new last will and testament would be called into action.

After a few minutes, Matilda announced that Mr. Latch was finished with his "judicial conference call" and would like to see her. She led Ms. Barnett down a short hallway and into the conference room where the dark walls were lined with thick law books Mr. Latch hadn't touched in years.

Simon's goal was to be rid of her in thirty minutes. Add another thirty next week when the new will was properly signed, and he would earn, in theory, his hourly rate of $250. A good friend from law school was currently billing four times that much in a Washington tax firm, but Simon tried not to think about such things. Over the years he had almost convinced himself that his quality of life in the small town of Braxton, Virginia, was far better, money be damned.

He turned on the charm, as he always did with the older women, and knew right away that she was smitten. "That's a lovely necklace," he said, fawning.

She smiled and flashed a mouth full of natural, yellow teeth. "Why, thank you."

"I see from the notes that you are single, live alone, and have no children or grandchildren. Two husbands, both deceased." He scanned Matilda's report as if reading the Magna Carta.

"And you kept the name Barnett after you married Mr. Korsak."

"Well, not exactly. After Harry died I decided to go back to 'Barnett.' I never really liked the name Korsak, you know? Between the two of us, I enjoyed Vince Barnett a lot more than Harry Korsak. Vince and I were childhood sweethearts, you know, married young and sort of grew up together. We were younger and more romantically active, know what I mean?"

Simon knew exactly what she meant and had no desire to explore further. "Do you have a current will?"

"They don't expire, do they?"

"Well, no, they don't."

"Yes, but I have doubts about it. I'd like to do a new one, and I want to hire you as my attorney for other matters. On a retainer."

"What other matters concern you?"

"Oh, well, one never knows, especially nowadays with so much fraud and scamming out there. Senior citizens are the favorite targets. It's just awful how many of them lose everything. I want to be protected, and I want you kept on retainer to review things for me. My friend Doris always keeps a lawyer on retainer."

At the moment, Simon could think of nothing worse than being at the beck and call of an elderly client who thought she was being scammed. But if she insisted, then $1,000 might be a fair arrangement.

"How much is her retainer?"

"Oh, not much. She says you can get one pretty cheap."

Simon took a deep breath and tried to get the consultation on track. "Let's get back to your will. It's important that I take a look at your previous one."

"Yes, I know. Matilda out there mentioned it over the phone but I forgot to bring it. Seems like I'm forgetting more and more these days."

Goes with the territory. If they were over eighty, he assumed a few marbles were missing. He and Matilda would confer later and decide if Ms. Barnett had sufficient mental capacity to understand what she was doing. But the first impression was good, and for $250, he was willing to worry only so much.

"Could you possibly drop it off in a day or so?"

"Yes, no problem. Sorry to be a pain."

"Quite all right. We need to talk about your assets and liabilities."

"There are no liabilities. Not one penny of debt. Harry, my late husband, despised debt. Wouldn't even use a credit card. We lived free and clear."

Simon loved the sound of those words and could only dream

of one day clawing his way out of debt. "That's admirable," he said piously, as if she needed his blessings. Everything he owned was heavily mortgaged.

"But I got one after he died. A Visa card."

He scribbled something meaningless and said, "Okay, what about assets? Do you own your home?" He knew she did but most older clients enjoyed bragging about the things they had accumulated. They were proud of their frugal lifestyles and that after decades of pinching pennies they were financially secure.

"I certainly do."

"Any idea of its market value these days?"

"Well, not really, but the county has it assessed for two hundred and eighty thousand, I think. Something like that."

"Okay, that's close enough. The home is usually the biggest asset in a person's estate."

"Not in my case," she said sharply, as if mildly offended.

He kept scribbling and absorbed the first hint that this little will might not be so simple. "Do you own other real estate? A vacation home? Rental properties?"

"Oh no. Harry didn't like real estate. Said it was too much trouble."

Then what, please, did Harry like? "I see. Do you have other investments?"

She took a deep breath and suddenly looked worried. "I can trust you, right, Mr. Latch?"

"Of course. I'm your lawyer, duty bound to keep everything confidential." Simon noticed a slight flutter in his intestines, as if some truly wonderful and unexpected facts might be in the works. He'd had a few surprises in the past eighteen years as a pseudo estate lawyer, but nothing significant.

"Well, you see Mr. Latch—"

"Please call me Simon."

"Simon, what a nice name. You see, Simon, Harry worked for almost forty years as a district sales rep for Coca-Cola. I think that's what killed him. He got his blood sugar up, had a stroke at sixty-nine, never recovered. We always had plenty of Coke, the real thing, not diet, in the fridge and he drank too many, at least in my opinion. Anyway, he qualified for stock options, a few at a time, and he bought every share of Coke he could get his hands on. Never sold a share, just enjoyed watching it pile up. And boy did it. Then about thirty years ago, he began selling Coke products to Wal-Mart and became fascinated with the company. It was selling a lot of soft drinks. Harry began buying stock in Wal-Mart and he never sold a share. When he died suddenly, he was wondering what to do with all that stock. He didn't want to leave it to his boys, because they were nothing but trouble. Still are. And here's the thing, Simon, the boys don't know about the stock. Harry never told them, never told anyone but me. He thought it was funny that we lived quietly in our modest little home and no one knew we were worth millions."

Millions? Simon managed to keep scribbling on his yellow legal pad but his handwriting, illegible on a good day, quickly deteriorated into nothing more than chicken scratch. At that moment, he could not remember a single will he had ever drafted for a person worth a million dollars, excluding the real estate.

He maintained a lawyerly frown as if thoroughly unfazed. "What, uh, did he do with all that stock?"

"He left it to me, along with everything else. What's it called—'the marital deduction'?"

"Yes, that's it. You can leave everything to your spouse free of estate taxes. Harry must have been a smart man."

"Funny thing, he never claimed to be smart. He was quite modest, worked hard, paid his debts, saved his money, bought his stocks, then left it all to me. He wanted to do something to help his sons, and, frankly, he tried everything. But if they had known about his portfolio they would have driven him crazy. So, he never told them. Then he died suddenly."

It was rare for a client seeking a simple will to throw around words like "portfolio" and "marital deduction." Simon's radar went up another notch or two.

"What's the value of the portfolio?"

She actually put a hand over her mouth as if she couldn't say. Then she rubbed her eyes and looked frightened. She lowered her voice and said, "And all of this is strictly confidential, right?"

"We've already established that, Ms. Barnett. If you want me to draft a proper will, then I have to know what's in the estate. A simple will may not be what you need." He could almost feel the new document growing thicker by the moment. And the retainer was growing too, now up to $5,000.

"If people only knew. My friends, Harry's boys. No one knows, Simon."

Simon flashed a comforting smile, as if to say, *You can tell me anything*. Instead, he said, "These walls are made of steel, Ms. Barnett. Nothing leaks through. I'm ethically bound to keep all your secrets."

Fortified, she gritted her teeth and said, "As of last week, the stocks were worth slightly more than sixteen million. The market goes up and down, you know?"

Simon scribbled down the number while managing to keep a solemn poker face, as if this was nothing out of the ordinary.

She leaned in closer and asked, "That's a lot, right?"

"It is."

"Is it pretty unusual?"

"I'd say yes. I rarely get a client with this type of net worth." *Rarely? How about never?*

"And I don't know what to do with it all?"

Oh, the questions. And the suggestions.

"Uh, well, how much of the estate is in Coke stock?"

"About ten million. About six or so in Wal-Mart."

"And the dividends?"

"Well, as you know, Wal-Mart doesn't pay squat for dividends, pennies per share. But Coke, well that's a different story. It's paid four percent a year forever."

"Four percent of ten million annually?"

"Thereabouts. It's a bit over four hundred thousand a year. And it just piles up, you know? I don't know what to do with it. Can you help me, Simon?"

"I'm sure we'll think of something, but this will not be just a simple will, Ms. Barnett. This will take some time."

"Could you please call me Netty? It's my old nickname, but only a few people use it. If you're Simon, then I'm Netty."

He gave her the sappiest smile yet and said, "Of course," as they grew closer. "I guess with that type of income you must have substantial cash in the bank."

"Yes, I do."

A pause. "Okay, how much cash?"

"Almost four million."

"And it's in, well, what type of accounts?"

"Checking, savings, and certificates of deposit. But the bank's not here. Harry wouldn't dare bank with the locals. He was always afraid prying eyes would see our accounts and, well, you know how people love to gossip. So he banked with East Federal in Atlanta, one of the biggest."

"Atlanta?"

"Yes, we lived there for years. Coke's headquarters, you know?"

"Of course." Simon had no idea where Coke was headquartered. He scribbled away as his mind spun in circles. He flipped the pages of his legal pad and started on a blank one. He wrote down the number $10,000, followed by "Retainer."

"Just curious, Netty, in your last will, who did you leave your assets to? The stocks and bank accounts?"

She sighed as if it might be too painful to talk about. "Well, Simon, that's one reason I'm here. I don't like my current will. I signed it weeks ago and I haven't had a good night's sleep ever since."

"Who drafted it?"

"A lawyer across the street. Wally Thackerman. You know him?"

"Oh, sure. I know all the lawyers in town."

"Do you trust him? Is he a good guy?"

"Yes, no, sort of, maybe. Wally is nice enough, but I wouldn't call him a friend. Do I trust him? I'm not sure. Why? Do you trust him?"

"I did, but now I don't know. You see, Simon, I wasn't sure who to put in my will. Who gets the stocks and the money, you know?"

"Uh-huh."

"So Wally convinced me to leave it all to him, in trust. When I pass, he'll sell the stock, put the cash in a trust of some sort, I really never understood it, and then he would have the authority to give the money to my favorite charities."

"And what are your favorite charities?"

"I don't have any."

"None?"

"No. You see, Harry didn't believe in giving money away. He had the attitude that no one gave him money when he was broke and hungry, as a kid, so why should people expect him to give them something? I wouldn't say he was stingy, but maybe he was. Whatever, we just never got in the habit of giving."

"What about after he died and you inherited everything?"

"Well, there was this one charity I liked, or at least I thought so. Years ago I saw something on cable about the spider monkeys in Uganda and how they were starving to death because of some chemicals the government was spraying. Poor things were just shriveling up and dying by the hundreds. It was heartbreaking, so I sent a thousand dollars to the Spider Monkey Trust, had an address in Boston. They said thanks, sent me a calendar and all, made me a member of one of their boards, then asked me for more money. I sent another check, then another, and they kept asking. Wanted to send an executive out here to meet me and have lunch and so on. Then they sold my name and address to somebody else and before long my mailbox was jam-packed with letters from folks trying to save whales and buffaloes and chee-tahs and Canadian wolverines. I sent them nothing. Got so bad I changed my mailing address. Then the FBI busted the Spider Monkey Trust, whole thing was a scam. Got me for eleven thou-sand. So, no, Simon, I don't fool with charities."

Simon managed to listen while his mind raced around that little weasel Wally Thackerman across the street, putting his name in the will and controlling everything. It was highly unethical and grounds for disbarment, but then who needs a law license when you're drowning in cash?

She was prattling on. "Ever since I signed that will I've worried about it. Doesn't seem right for the lawyer to be able to get his hands on everything, right, Simon?"

"I need to see the will, Netty."

She pulled a tissue out of a pocket and was tapping it on her cheeks. "I'm sorry. This is so confusing. I never really felt right, you know, leaving everything to Mr. Thackerman, a man I don't really know. That was not very smart, was it?"

Of course not. Downright stupid. But with the client in tears and vulnerable and sitting on a fortune, Simon grew even warmer. "We'll take care of it, Netty. Trust me. This is easy to fix. Sometimes proper estate planning requires a significant portion of the assets to be placed in trust, and the attorney is often named as the trustee."

"Legal gobbledygook."

"Yes, I'm sorry, but the law can get complicated. Let me take a look at the will and we can go from there."

"Okay."

Simon was dizzy with rapid thoughts. He closed his legal pad, put the cap on his pen, and said, "Look, tomorrow I have some business in Fairhaven close to where you live. Let's meet at that new Starbucks on Millmont Street. You know where it is?"

"I think so, but I really don't mind coming downtown."

"No, I insist. Same time, two P.M. tomorrow. And I'll look over your will."

"I guess."

"And here's something sensitive, Netty, something I can tell only you. Matilda out there is not the most discreet person I've ever hired. We've had issues over her ability to keep secrets, and this is just the type of gossip that she might repeat to the wrong person."

"Oh dear."

"Right. I'll have to terminate her soon enough. A lawyer cannot have a blabbermouth in the office. In the meantime, though, not another word to her. If you need me, just call my cell phone." He slid across a business card.

"Oh dear." She was feigning surprise but also enjoying the intrigue.

"It'll be okay, trust me. I can prepare the will myself and she'll never see it. It's best that way."

"If you say so."

"Trust me. Two P.M. tomorrow at Starbucks."

He followed her down the hall to reception, chatting the whole way about the weather. Netty glared at Matilda as she walked by but said nothing. Simon opened the front door and stepped outside with her. As she wandered off and got in her car, the old Lincoln, he stared at the law office across Main Street.

LAW OFFICES OF WALTER J. THACKERMAN. What a slimeball.

Back inside, Matilda said, "Nice little lady. You have the questionnaire? I'll do the will right now."

Simon stopped and looked out the front window as if there was trouble. "Might have a problem. She could be crazy, really off her rocker. I think she's being treated, gotta be careful. And she's not sure what to do with her house so she wants to think about it for a few days. Could be a real pain."

"I thought she was rather lovely."

"We'll see. Do I have any other appointments this afternoon?"

"Yes, the Pendergrasts. Their bankruptcy is causing problems."

"Great."

CHAPTER 2

The rest of the day was shot. He couldn't stomach the thought of sitting for an hour with Mr. and Mrs. Pendergrast as they squabbled over who was to blame for their financial problems. Simon's speciality was bankruptcies and they were often more trouble than divorces, which he loathed. He called the Pendergrasts and canceled with one of the many standard lawyer fibs used to duck and weave: he said he was suddenly needed in federal court. But he really wasn't needed anywhere. The most pressing file on his desk involved the purchase and sale of an ice-cream shop down the street, a $20,000 deal for which he might earn a fee of a thousand bucks or so.

Suddenly, every file seemed so trivial. An elderly client with $16 million in stocks and more in cash had just left his office with a current will that left her fortune to a rat-faced little lawyer across the street. Simon could think of nothing else. As soon as Matilda said goodbye promptly at five, he left ten minutes later and drove to a watering hole in a motel bar out near the interstate. It was favored by lawyers and judges who didn't want to be seen drinking too much in town, though there were some who drank openly and excessively. Luckily, none of them were there, and Simon nursed a beer in a dark corner and tried to sort out his thoughts.

First things first. He had to see the will to verify that his dear
Netty was telling the truth. It was still hard to believe that a lawyer, any lawyer, would be brazen enough to insert himself in a will
and have unfettered access to an entire fortune. But the fact that
he, the Honorable Simon Latch, was thinking of doing something
very similar to that made him realize it was indeed possible. Upon
Netty's death, there would certainly be a massive legal brawl with
lawsuits flying, but the only named trustee, at the moment one
Wally Thackerman, would be in the driver's seat.

Of course the fortune wouldn't be $20 million. Last time he
checked, the state and federal estate taxes were 40 percent, almost
all of which could be avoided with the marital trust. However,
since Netty had no husband, her estate would be on the chopping
block and fair game for the tax collectors. Eight million in taxes
up in smoke. He actually grimaced at the thought of paying so
much to the government.

But $12 million was still more than he would earn working for
thirty years at the corner of Main and Maple. Then he remembered something he'd read in a newspaper. Congress had been tin-
kering with the tax rates before its December recess. He couldn't
recall the details and usually did a half-ass job of staying informed,
because his clients never worried about gift and estate taxes.

He called a buddy from law school who practiced in a prestigious tax firm in D.C., an hour away. After the usual chatter, he
got around to business. Dirk, his friend, laughed and said, "Come
on, Simon. You haven't heard the big news?"

"I guess not."

"Congress adjourned without repealing the amendment."

Simon wasn't sure what that meant so he kept quiet. Dirk liked
to talk anyway. "Those clowns dropped the ball big-time. The
estate tax deal fell through, no compromise, no tax. Zero, zilch,
nada. For the next twelve months there will be no federal estate
taxes, and, since most states follow the Feds, now is the perfect
time to die. So tell your geezer clients to get their shit in order and
get ready to pull the plug. Have a big Christmas this year, then it's
adios. Their kids and grandkids will love them for it."

"Right! I saw that. What a screw-up."

"Par for the course these days."

As the conversation drifted dangerously close to politics, Simon switched gears and asked about another law school classmate who was battling cancer. Since both were busy lawyers, they managed to wrap up the conversation with promises to get together soon.

Back to $20 million! Simon got another beer and thought about the conversation for a long time. Later, he would go online and do some research, try to find out why Congress allowed the estate tax provisions to slip away. As if one might be able to understand anything Congress did.

CHAPTER 3

Simon and his wife, Paula, had not filed for divorce because they could not afford one. Both desperately wanted out, but since they were barely afloat financially with one household they could not imagine trying to maintain two. Both wounded and scarred, they were tired of fighting and had settled into a somewhat sustainable coexistence that allowed them to pass the days in muted suffering as their three kids grew up. Fortunately, the two older ones were teenagers who were struggling through the usual strains of puberty and adolescence but not yet causing serious problems. They seldom left their bedrooms and never allowed themselves to be caught offline. A device was always in hand. The youngest, Janie, was nine years old and still a sweet kid.

To avoid conflict and keep the tension away from the children, Simon usually slept at the office. He had remodeled a small suite upstairs, knocked out a couple of walls, and configured a small pad where he survived with a tiny bathroom and narrow bed. When talking only to himself he called it The Closet. It wasn't nice but at least it was away from Paula.

She was out this Tuesday night, the monthly book club gathering where wine seemed to be more important than literature. It gave him the green light to cook his favorite Italian sausage meatballs with pasta and hang out with Janie in the kitchen. They talked about school and soccer and life in general. She caught him off guard by asking, "Where do you go at night?"

"Well, I often work late and just sleep at the office."

"That's weird. Why don't you just come home? It's not that far away."

"I don't want to wake up everybody. Mom's a light sleeper and needs her rest."

"Buck thinks you and Mom are getting a divorce."

Buck had always been a nosy brat and too mature for his years. Simon managed a smile while realizing that it was the first time the word "divorce" had been uttered by one of the children, or at least to his knowledge.

He said, "No, we're not getting a divorce, Janie. Mom and I are both working too hard and don't have a lot of time for each other, but that's not unusual these days. Everything will be okay. Tell Buck to stop talking like that."

Divorce had been on the table for at least three years but they had been careful around the kids. Buck was sixteen and missed nothing. Danny was fourteen and going through puberty with his head in the clouds. Janie was a little girl who loved both parents. The thought of leaving her was painful.

"It seems weird that you would sleep at the office when your bedroom is here in the house with us." She watched him as she said this, as if she knew the truth.

"Everything is okay, Janie, I promise. The pasta is ready, so go get your brothers."

The only time Buck and Danny left their rooms was to eat. Both had insatiable appetites, along with awful table manners. Paula had given up on the rules. Danny ate with earbuds and an iPad with some dreadful acid rock band screeching away, barely audible but loud enough to be annoying. Buck had earbuds and a cell phone. Simon asked them to unplug things and talk about their school days. They looked at him as if he were a trespasser and flagrantly disobeyed. At that point, Simon could slap the table, raise his voice, make a scene, start a fight he could not win, and create even more bad blood. Paula would hear about it and weigh in on behalf of her children. It was easier to ignore their behavior, another act of cowardice that had become routine around the Latch household.

So Simon chatted nonstop with Janie as the boys ate like pigs. The sooner they finished, the sooner they could escape to the safety of their rooms. They left their plates on the table, more rules violations, but Simon just ignored them again. After dinner, when the kitchen was spotless and the house was quiet, Simon kissed Janie on the forehead and said he had to get back to work. She wanted to say something but didn't. He locked the doors, made sure the house was secure, and left a few minutes before ten. Paula would be home soon, and the less he saw of her the better.

In earlier years he had parked his car, a leased Audi that needed to be swapped for a later model, in front of his office on Main Street when he worked early and late, a bit of free advertising intended to impress others with his formidable work ethic. These days, though, he hid it in an alley around back at night to quash rumors that he had moved out and was living at the office. He suspected those rumors were already making the rounds, because a couple of Paula's friends had big mouths and didn't like Simon anyway. He was almost certain that the book club girls spent more time sipping wine and bitching about their husbands than discussing the hottest bestseller.

He parked in the alley and, instead of taking the rear stairs up to his pad, he walked three blocks to the basement of an old bank building. Chub's Pub had been a part of his life for many years. He had been there as Chub transformed it from a seedy low-end beer hall, known for its illegal poker and bookmaking, to a mid-level sports bar with a dozen widescreens and a less violent clientele. Gambling was still rampant because Chub was the biggest bookie in the area, but it was kept quiet and out of the way. The vice squad made a perfunctory visit once a week but only because it was expected. Most of the cops hung out in Chub's when off duty. He even paid a few of them to work the door on weekends.

It was a Tuesday night in early March and the place was not crowded. Simon went to his spot at the end of the sweeping bar and settled in before a screen that offered video poker. The bartender, Valerie, soon appeared with a bourbon and ginger ale, along with a fake smile and the same greeting, "What's up, Lawyer Latch?"

"All's well, Valerie, how are you?"

"Just living the dream." Then she was gone. They didn't have much to discuss because Simon had handled two of her no-fault divorces, at cut rates, and she wasn't pleased with the outcome of the second one. With time they had settled into a respectful standoff that required a forced pleasantness but nothing else. Sort of like his marriage.

The drinks were free as long as he was playing video poker, which was still illegal in the state, but Chub was smart enough not to get caught. His machines were hot-wired to a file that kept a running balance of each gambler's wins and losses. No money changed hands in public. The vice squad could see nothing illegal above the table. Simon and the other players received monthly statements from the pub and settled up in cash whenever Chub said so.

Cal Poly was playing UC Irvine and Simon had $500 on the game, his standard bet. He watched it on a screen hanging above the racks of bottles as he sipped his drink and occasionally looked at his poker screen. He knew nothing about either school, so why would he place a substantial wager on a game thousands of miles away? He once asked himself such questions, but stopped doing so because the answer was clear. It was all about the action. March Madness was right around the corner, and, in preparation, Simon needed to watch as many games as possible. The Big Show still got him excited, especially after last year when he mopped up in the Sweet Sixteen and won $4,000.

He did not have a gambling problem. He was certain of that because he had two friends who did and betting had wrecked them financially. He had watched them slide into a black hole playing risky games and wagering more than they could afford to lose. Simon didn't earn a lot of money; therefore, he didn't have much to lose. And after a decade of sports betting he had convinced himself that his wins were slightly more than his losses. He was too cautious to get into trouble. And too afraid of Paula. She knew nothing of his secret little hobby because Simon, and Chub, kept it all in cash.

Chub walked up behind the bar holding, as always, a bottle of beer. "Who you got?" he asked as he reached over for a quick handshake.

"Irvine plus seven," Simon said. Chub knew exactly who he "got." They had made the bet at ten that morning, on the phone. No texts or emails, nothing to leave a trail. Chub had been busted once by the Feds for bookmaking and came within a whisker of doing time, but a slick lawyer, not Simon, worked a deal and kept him out of jail. He went straight for twelve months, with ninety hours of community service, umpiring softball games, then eased back into the business.

"I like Cal Poly," he said and took a swig from his bottle.

He worked both sides of the Vegas line and didn't care which side his customers chose because he collected 10 percent on each bet. For Simon to win $500 with his Irvine bet, he had paid $550. The extra, the "juice," went into Chub's ever-deepening pockets.

Valerie called Chub from the other end of the bar. He offered his standard "Good luck," and waddled away. As always, he wore a fancy tracksuit, this one bright red, with designer sneakers, as if he had just come from a long run. He had not. Someone had stuck him with "Chub" in the first grade and he had never been able to shake it, nor had he been able to shed excess weight as he grew up. Sadly, he was, at forty-five, still growing.

Simon usually stopped at two cocktails. He crunched the ice from the second one as Irvine choked down the stretch and lost by five. But they started the game with an extra seven, so Simon had a spring in his step as he left the pub. He waved at Chub across the room, and Chub waved back with a look that said, *Nice win, I'll get you next time.*

The $500 Simon had just won was more than the legal fees he'd earned that day.

But tomorrow held such promise.

CHAPTER 4

The Starbucks anchored one corner of a strip mall at the edge of a suburb fifteen minutes from his office. It was busy when he arrived half an hour early to scope out the place and look for privacy. He sipped dark roast at four bucks a cup and moved quickly when a corner table opened up. He toyed with his laptop, same as all the other customers, and watched the endless line of cars creep through the drive-thru. Then he saw the old Lincoln turn a corner. Netty couldn't find a spot and parked far away, straddling a yellow line. She drove like a ninety-year-old who'd been a lousy driver seventy years earlier. As she entered, he stood and waved and helped her to her seat. She seemed ill at ease and glanced around.

"Figures," she said. "I'm the only senior here."

"Would you like coffee or tea?"

"Just some water, please."

Simon left and brought back a bottle of water. She ignored it and asked, "Can we really talk here? I mean, it's not very private."

The nearest person was ten feet away, hunched over a laptop with wires running to ears that were invisible under a red hoodie. "Oh, it's very private. No one can hear a word we say because their ears are plugged."

"These young people."

"I know. Addicted to their phones and laptops. What's the world coming to?"

"I guess." She unscrewed the cap and drank some water.

Finally, Simon said, "We were going to talk about your will, the one prepared by Wally Thackerman."

"Yes, I'm just not comfortable with it."

"Did you bring it?"

She reached into a large handbag and retrieved an envelope. As she handed it to him she glanced around again.

"Please relax, Netty. These kids are totally self-absorbed and have no interest in anything we're talking about."

Simon wanted to rip open the envelope and scour the will for the scandalous language, but he managed to take his time and keep smiling at her. It was only four pages long, with the first paragraphs filled with the usual lawyerly crap that he himself charged people for. Then, the juicy part. It established the "Eleanor Korsak Barnett Memorial Trust" and placed all of the liquid assets in it. Her home was to be sold, along with everything else, and the cash added to the trust. All the fancy legal footwork would be done by, of course, the Honorable Wally Thackerman, who was not only the executor of her estate and the sole trustee of her trust, but also the lawyer self-appointed to handle everything. His fees were set at $750 an hour and Simon could almost visualize the thick, padded bills Wally would present to the court for interim payments.

Simon frowned, a grimace prompted by genuine disbelief, but also offered for dramatic effect because Netty was staring at him, waiting. "Is it that bad?" she whispered loudly, then covered her mouth and glanced around again. No one looked at her. No one knew she existed.

"Let me finish," Simon said calmly with a fake smile, as if what he was reading was definitely outrageous but he alone could fix everything.

Moving beyond the hefty fees to come, the worst part was the power granted unto the trustee. In half a page of thick legalese, Wally gave himself the right to do virtually everything and anything with the trust. He could donate to "appropriate" charities and nonprofits, make loans to virtually anyone, hire consultants, appraisers, accountants, and tax experts to help "protect" the trust. After ten years of such shenanigans, he could, in the event any of the money was left, disburse it at his discretion and close the trust.

Simon worked on his poker face. He had to be careful. He could not outright condemn the will, because he was suddenly emboldened to prepare one very much like it. But, he had to criticize it enough to win her support and convince her that he could steer her assets in a safer direction.

"It doesn't mention your two stepsons," he observed, still frowning, reading glasses balanced on the tip of his nose.

"Nothing for them. I thought I told you that."

"Yes, you did, but that could cause problems. If they receive nothing they might get upset and hire some more lawyers to attack the will."

"But they're not entitled to anything, right? That Wally character told me that a person, any person, can exclude a child from her or his will, at least in this state. It that right? And since they're not really my children, they have no claim to my estate?"

"That's correct. You can exclude everyone but a spouse."

"Well, my spouse is dead and he left me everything. Not a dime for those two outlaw sons of his. Nothing. Cut, cut, cut."

She did the cutting with a glow in her eyes, the first sign of possible meanness. Simon was pleased that she was already referring to her soon-to-be ex-lawyer as "that Wally character." He read on, frowning intelligently. When he finished, he took a sip of coffee and said, "I don't like this will."

"I told you so."

"It gives too much power to the attorney for your trust."

"How can we fix it?"

"It'll take a few hours but I'll hop right on it. The obvious challenge here, Netty, is to find a place for the money. I want you to make a list of possible charities you'd like to help."

"Such as?"

"Do you have a church?"

"Yes, sort of. Harry was a Lutheran and we tried to go once a year."

"That's an idea. Think big. There are about a million worthy nonprofits you could help."

"Such as?"

"Such as the Girl Scouts, heart association, orphanages, animal shelters, local library, small colleges, refugees, childhood hunger, environmental groups. You mentioned your work with the spider monkeys."

"That was a rip-off."

"Do you like animals?"

"Not really."

"Okay. Whatever. Sit down tonight and make a list of all the possible groups, causes, and charities that you might want to help."

"What's your favorite charity?"

Simon's lack of generosity was caused by a lack of extra cash rather than an absence of a kind spirit. How could he possibly write checks to help others when he and Paula were underwater and staring at three kids soon going to college? They had not donated more than a hundred bucks in the past five years.

He lied quickly with "The Sierra Club."

"Never heard of it."

"It's not really for you. Have you thought about leaving some money for your friends?"

"My friends, the ones still living, know nothing about the money. If I told them about it they'd drive me crazy and my life would get very complicated. That's what money does, Simon, it really causes problems."

So does the lack of it, he thought to himself but managed to maintain an intelligent frown. He scribbled something on his legal pad and said, "Okay, moving right along. Who prepares your tax returns each year?"

"Why do you want to know?" she snapped, quite defensively.

"Well, because when you die, and I hate to say it that way but that's the real reason we're here, right, so when you die and your new will comes into play, the attorney for your estate will have to work with your tax advisor to prepare your returns."

"Who will be the attorney for my estate?"

"That's entirely up to you, but it's pretty common for the attorney who prepares the will to also act as the probate attorney."

"Kinda like that Wally character."

"Yes, kinda like that."

"What was the question?"

"Your tax advisor?"

"Oh yes, he's this little CPA guy in Atlanta, been doing my taxes forever. One of Harry's old sidekicks. I talk to him once a year, so you don't need to bother him."

"Okay, but it might be important for me to make contact."

"That's what Wally said. Why do you lawyers always want to pry into everything?" Another flash of anger, maybe even bordering on meanness. She was suddenly defensive and Simon quickly changed strategies and backed off. He had done a good job so far of gaining her trust and he didn't want to irritate her.

Pry? Oh yes. What Simon really wanted was some proof that his dear Netty actually owned all that Coke and Wal-Mart stock, in addition to several million dollars just sitting in the bank. He believed her, he wanted so desperately to believe her, but he was also cautious enough to proceed slowly. Clients lied to him all the time. Lawyers, often after a few drinks, loved to tell stories of the outrageous lies their clients had fed them.

He assumed the stocks were held in a brokerage account and a nice, neat, concise summary was sent to Netty each month, same as the bank statements. He gritted his teeth and asked, "Do you have a financial advisor?"

She rolled her eyes as if frustrated and glanced around again, looking for eavesdroppers. She frowned and a ridge of thick wrinkles folded across her forehead. "You mean, like, a stockbroker?"

"Yes, who handles the stocks?"

"Well, it's complicated. You see, Harry did business for years with a firm in Atlanta, then it merged or something with a bigger firm, and so on. After Harry died, one firm got sold to another. I really can't keep up with it all. Now it's all handled by this guy in Atlanta."

"I see. Is there a person I can talk to about your assets?"

"I don't know. Why do you want to talk to someone about my assets?"

"Because the IRS may require proof of assets." Simon had no idea what he was talking about but using the IRS might frighten her somewhat.

She mumbled, "Same thing Wally said." This startled Simon, but he decided to let it go and push later. He pretended to ignore her last comment, cast an important glance at his wristwatch, and said, "Okay, I'll get started on this. Let's meet again in a couple of days and go over a rough draft."

"What's that?"

"It's the first version of your new will. In the meantime, please give some thought to some charities and foundations you might want to include."

"I thought we talked about that. Thought I told you I don't have any favorite charities."

No charities, no friends, no family, no distant relatives. No one to receive the fortune when his dear Netty kicked the bucket. Perhaps that's why Wally Thackerman did not name a single non-profit. His scheme basically left everything in a new foundation that would become his own little piggy bank after her funeral, with at least a dozen ways to siphon money into his own pocket. Simon hated to admit it, but Wally's will was impressive, in spite of its blatant effort at being nothing but a naked grab for money.

Simon vowed to do much better. He capped his pen, pulled his notes together, and said, "There is one thing, Netty. I can't prepare a simple will if I can't verify your assets. For most of my clients, this is not really necessary because they are not wealthy. But you're in a different category."

She was gazing through the window with a blank stare, as if it were time for another nap. She shook her head and said softly, "All this legal stuff."

"I know, I know. But it's important to get this right. Your current will is a mess and will only enable Wally Thackerman to end up with most of the money. That's not right."

She looked as if she might cry. "I feel so stupid."

"Please. I can fix this. But I need to know the name of your stockbroker in Atlanta."

"Buddy Brown."

He repeated the name to himself. For some reason "Buddy" didn't quite fit that profession. He uncapped his pen and scribbled on a paper napkin. "And the name of his firm?"

"Appletree something or other." She was drifting away, her eyelids fluttering, her speech fading as if fatigued. And for the first time Simon wondered about her mental capacity. She was an elderly woman who suddenly looked even older. Hang on, old girl.

Among the many issues roaring through his brain was the challenge of getting her new will witnessed by two people who could attest to her "sound and disposing mind and memory." Normally, it was a routine matter with Matilda and a secretary next door going through the motions. Oh well. It was something else he would deal with later.

He walked her to her car and watched her drive away, on the wrong side of the road and with one foot on the brake.

CHAPTER 5

Simon had a plan, awful as it was, to free himself of Paula, but he was stuck with Matilda. She had worked for him for twelve years and could practice law, or at least his humble version of it, with her eyes closed. She was very good at what she did, tech-savvy, punctual, a real pro at handling their clients and in dealing with lawyers and judges. Contrary to the fib he'd told Eleanor Barnett, Matilda was discreet and had never, at least to his knowledge, breached a meaningful confidence.

They tried to avoid each other's private lives and Simon was saying nothing about his current dust-up at home. They disagreed and bickered occasionally, but always in private and never pushed things too far. She was once a flirt who'd struck out repeatedly with men, and now seemed to have given up on romance. She and Simon never touched each other, not even a little goodbye hug at the end of a long day. There was no physical attraction, to their relief. Indeed, they were determined to keep their distance and show not the slightest interest in anything beyond the employer-employee relationship. In their early years together, Simon had occasionally glanced at her rear end and legs, admiringly, and approved, much the same way he looked at most younger women, but now he tried not to look. She was only thirty-nine, three years younger than him, and she was gradually adding a few pounds per year. In the kitchen fridge she kept an assortment of diet drinks, sugar-free smoothies, protein shakes, meals-in-bottles, herbal flushes, the kind of junk advertised on cable. Evidently, none of it was working, but, of course, Simon only watched with amusement but would never think of commenting.

Tillie, as he called her only in private, arrived each morning promptly at eight, not a minute before, and left each afternoon at five, not a minute after. Depending on how the day was going, she took a flexible hour for lunch to run errands but never to eat, or so she said. Simon admired her for establishing boundaries. She refused to work on weekends, regardless of the urgency, though, truthfully, few of the "open" files on his desk could be considered urgent. She refused to take calls after hours, even from him. She was off on all the federal holidays and planned her summer vacations, ten full working days, in January.

To distance himself from her X-ray vision and constant eavesdropping, and also to prepare for the inevitable showdown with Paula, Simon was creating his own secret world. He was practically living upstairs in The Closet, which he kept locked at all times. If Tillie knew he spent most nights there, she had yet to mention it. He assumed, though, that she knew. She was a massive sponge when it came to gossip. There was a sisterhood amongst the legal secretaries and court clerks in town, and virtually nothing escaped their scrutiny.

He had a post office box in a small town eight miles away and a secret checking account in a small branch bank not far from it. He had a credit card with a $10,000 limit and a small balance, that Paula knew nothing about. A year earlier he had purchased an inexpensive laptop and set up an anonymous email address that only a professional could trace. He used it to place bets occasionally.

At the moment he was using it to track Buddy the stockbroker, who'd worked for Appletree in Atlanta. Netty was correct— Appletree had long since disappeared after having been bought or merged with a regional brokerage firm from Florida, which had then flamed out in bankruptcy and indictments only to be scooped up by a large California discount broker who sold it to a private equity firm in New York who loaded it with debt, almost causing another bankruptcy, before it was sold to a bank in Texas that then sold it to a bank in Atlanta. After numerous name changes and different addresses, it, whatever it was, was now back home. There was no sign of anyone named Buddy. Evidently, he was just one of many casualties of the slick maneuvers perfected by the money runners.

Simon wasted three hours wading through this debris and had nothing to show for it. Reluctantly, he called Spade, a local character who could always find the money. Spade's background was shadier than anyone Simon had ever met. He was an unindicted felon, an unlicensed operator on all fronts, a Houdini-like character who lived in the shadows. He had no office, no website, no business cards, no phone number that was available to the public. If asked by the right people he would say that he was either an investigator or a forensic accountant, but then he studiously avoided the right people. Spade made his money in big divorce cases where the wife's lawyers were hot on the trail of hubby's hidden cash. He could dig more dirt out of the internet than anyone in the business.

"This better be good," he growled as if highly irritated.

"And good afternoon to you, Spade," Simon said. "Sounds like you're having a great day."

"Does it really matter to you?"

"Of course it does. I think about you all the time."

"Lawyers and their lies."

Simon quickly recalled that every conversation with Spade began and ended with insults.

"Right. Look, I'll buy you a beer tonight at Chub's."

"I can buy my own beer, thanks."

"You're welcome. Need to have a chat and as always I can't do it over the phone. Not worried about mine but I assume yours is bugged by some branch of the government, maybe even a foreign power."

"Or an ex-wife."

"Them too. Meet me around ten tonight at Chub's?"

"If I don't get busy. Duke's at Georgia Tech tonight, giving eleven. I see something closer. I'll take Tech for five."

Simon chewed on it for a second and said, "That's a bad bet. Duke's number two in the country and Tech has a losing record."

"You trying to tell me something I don't know?"

"Five hundred, right? Not five grand."

Spade was a high roller who was known to bet big. Simon's max was $500 for any game. "Hundred," he grunted, as if someone really was listening.

"That's an easy one."

"Put up or shut up."

"I'm in. See you at ten and we'll watch the game."

———— •◆• ————

Spade was never on time. When he arrived at ten-thirty, Georgia Tech was up by fourteen and Duke couldn't make a free throw. Chub's had no shortage of dark corners where gamblers and crooks held muted conversations as they drank and watched the widescreens in the distance. Simon had ordered two draft beers, and onion rings for Spade, who was between wives and not eating well. He sat down and the beers arrived. He took a long gulp, wiped his mouth with the back of his hand, and said, "I thought you stayed away from divorces."

"I always try to but it's not a divorce. My client is eighty-plus, single, no kids, says she's got a lot of money. Wants a simple will but things might get complicated."

"Who gets the money?"

"Not sure. First, I need to make sure she's got it."

Spade shrugged as if it would not be a problem. "I'm listening."

"She claims her departed husband loaded up with a pile of stock in Coke and Wal-Mart. Sixteen mil or so. Hoarded the stock and then died suddenly. He has two sons by a first wife, both trouble, or so she says, and they don't know about his assets. No one knows. The old guy was a miser and they lived quietly."

"She's eighty?"

"At least."

"Is she cute?"

"Don't even think about it."

Spade laughed and took another slug of beer. "Keep going."

"The trail is pretty cold. She says he dealt with a brokerage firm in Atlanta called Appletree. I dug around, found nothing. It merged here and there and disappeared. She doesn't want me asking questions about her portfolio."

"I'm sure she gets a monthly statement."

"I'm sure she does but she ain't showing it to me. That's why I'm suspicious. That plus the fact that I've never had a client with such assets."

"Bank?"

"Security Trust, down the street, but just for the small stuff. She draws two thousand a month in Social Security, lives off it. Drives a Lincoln that was built in the last century. House is worth around three hundred thousand max, no mortgage. Claims the old guy hated debt. A Depression boy."

"I've met a few of those. Kinda refreshing, you know?"

The onion rings arrived and Spade dug in. With three minutes to go Duke cut the lead to seven. Chomping away, Spade said, "Duke is Duke. Can't ever count 'em out."

"Yeah, but you got eighteen points to play with." Simon handed over a folded sheet of paper. "Her full name, same for him. Just the basics. Like I said, I didn't find much. Harry died here about ten years ago, but there's no record of probate. Kinda strange, don't you think?"

"Very strange, especially if he had a big estate. Maybe he was still a resident of Georgia. I'll check him out."

"And for your labors?"

"Five hundred, cash of course."

Simon wanted an onion ring but suddenly had a knot in his stomach. Duke hit two straight 3-pointers and Tech's lead was gone.

Spade said, "So, if the old gal is really loaded, who gets the money?"

"We're working on that."

"Just curious."

Duke was fouling and Tech was making free throws. As his bet slipped away, Simon went to the bar for two more beers. With ten seconds to go, and with Tech up by four, Spade held out an empty hand and said, "Five, please."

Simon handed him the cash.

CHAPTER 6

Professional duties returned and required Simon's presence in the courtroom down the street. It was a docket call, an antiquated waste of time wherein most of the town's lawyers gathered in front of an old judge who could barely turn on a computer and dickered about the scheduling of trials for cases that should never have been filed.

As they waited for the judge, the lawyers mingled and gossiped and tried to look important before the crowd of spectators and litigants. They were allowed to drink coffee in the courtroom, but not eat the doughnuts one of the clerks had, for some reason, placed on the stenographer's table.

Simon went out of his way to engage Wally Thackerman in a pleasant conversation about a new shopping center one of Wally's clients was planning. As he chatted on, Simon feigned interest in the shopping center while thinking of nothing but the outrageous last will and testament Wally had written for himself and convinced Eleanor Barnett to sign two months earlier.

That he, Simon, was drafting one very similar did not seem relevant.

What will Wally do when she dies and he sprints to the courthouse to probate his version of Eleanor's last will and testament, only to learn almost immediately that it had just been renounced and held void by a subsequent one prepared by Simon F. Latch, Attorney and Counselor at Law? It was not a pleasant thought.

Wally rattled on about his shopping center. The breathtaking news was that an exciting new chain of sandwich shops from California was near a deal on a long-term lease, one that would certainly attract other classy tenants.

The problem was that Eleanor had no idea what to do with her fortune and needed serious advice, wisdom she was not getting from anyone else. Someone, and certainly not the windbag going on about avocado hoagies, had to help her. There was no one but Simon.

Mercifully, His Honor rallied long enough to make his appearance and get settled behind his bench. Simon managed to extricate himself from Wally's deal-making and took a seat at one of the counsel tables. Salmon Subs? Didn't exactly make your mouth water. Simon shuddered with the thought that some of Eleanor's money might get invested in such ventures. Wally had a reputation for getting tangled up in bad deals.

The judge picked up some papers, frowned, and said good morning. He went through his tired old routine of thanking the lawyers for being such good lawyers and thanking the clerks, and so on. He read the name of the first case and said the trial would start in an hour. He droned on.

Simon nodded off but caught himself. His mind came back to life when he tried to visualize a hot will contest in that very courtroom. He became dizzy at the visual of him sitting at counsel table being gawked at by everyone else—jurors, lawyers, clerks, spectators—all convinced that he had been caught red-handed trying to con an old woman out of her money.

That, of course, would not be true, since the old woman still had her money up until the moment she died, but nonetheless, the case would quickly devolve into a public relations nightmare for Simon. With time, he could endure the nightmare and eventually survive it, if, of course, he had control of the money.

There were too many bad scenarios.

Spade was only fifteen minutes late. Simon was at the bar hovering over a video poker screen and glancing occasionally at a basketball game that held little interest. He ordered two beers and some onion rings and they retired to the same dark corner as the night before.

"Who you got?" Spade asked, nodding at a widescreen above the bar.

"Neither. Tulsa versus Tulane. Not exactly life-or-death."

"So you only play the teams you like. That's a bad strategy."

"Thanks for the advice. About Eleanor Barnett."

"Some progress. Harry Korsak checks out. Born in 1941 in Knoxville, married Betsy in 1965, had two sons, Clyde and Jerry. Betsy died in 1981 and he married Eleanor Barnett in 1989. For decades he worked for Coke, first in a warehouse then got promoted to a district sales job. As such, he qualified for the company's profit-sharing and began buying stock. Retired in 2002, croaked four years later." Spade stopped long enough to take a gulp of beer and wipe his mouth with a sleeve.

Simon said, "Nice, but how much stock?"

"I'm getting there. Truth is we can't know. In 1990, for example, Coke had sixty million common shares outstanding and these were owned by roughly half a million people and entities. Most of it by the big players—mutual funds, hedge funds, retirement funds. They have to report what they own. It's all public record. For example, the Michigan public employees' retirement fund, in 1990, owned eight hundred million dollars' worth of Coke stock."

"That's certainly good to know."

"I'm just trying to explain things to you, Latch, and I'm going real slow, okay?"

The onion rings arrived and Spade began chomping on one. Before swallowing, he continued, "But getting individual names is more difficult, especially when purchased through the company's stock plan. There is a record of old Harry buying the Coke stock from 1965 until he retired, but no record of how much. And, no record of how much he might have sold along the way."

"She says he sold nothing."

"And you always believe your client?"

"No."

"I didn't think so. Think about it, Latch. Today about nine million shares of Coke stock was traded on the Big Board, same yesterday, same tomorrow. It's virtually impossible to keep up with who owns the stock. Same for Wal-Mart."

"How many shares of Wal-Mart were traded?" Simon asked innocently and immediately wished he had not.

"You gotta computer? If you can turn it on, takes about ten seconds."

Simon gave a goofy laugh to deflect his stupidity. He crunched on an onion ring, glanced at the game, and said, "So, we don't know how much stock she might have."

"It would take a subpoena. Here's the interesting part. That Appletree outfit she mentioned got swallowed several times years ago. What's left of it is now known as Rumke-Brown, a quiet little money management firm in an unmarked office in Buckhead. Guess who Brown is?"

"I couldn't begin to guess."

"You could if you tried. Buddy Brown, probably our gal's longtime manager."

"Our gal? You taking an interest?"

"Maybe, because Buddy and his gang don't mess with the common folk. Takes twenty-five million to get in the door."

"Leave her alone. She's eighty-five."

"I know, means she'll croak soon and I'll get a bigger house."

"Knock it off, Spade."

"I know. She's all yours."

"Can we keep things on a professional level?"

Spade laughed as if he were joking and took another onion ring. He washed it down with another gulp and said, "They moved here, bought the house at the bottom of the market. Two months after they moved in, Harry had the big one and checked out. At the time he was still a registered voter in Atlanta, where they had lived for a long time. Get this—there was no probate. Kinda unusual for a big estate, right?"

"I'd say so, but not if all assets were jointly owned."

"Exactly. Everything they had was jointly owned, with survivorship rights, so it all passed immediately to Eleanor without the need for probate. Ole Harry was a pretty slick dude. With the full marital deduction and jointly owned assets, he outfoxed the IRS and she got everything."

"Sounds like he really wanted to keep things away from his two sons."

"And those bloodsucking estate lawyers. No offense."

"Of course not."

Spade was watching the game and said, "I put a thousand on Tulsa minus eight and they're losing by twenty. Remember that cash you gave me last night?"

"It appears to be leaving your wallet. Do we have a next step?"

"I don't think so. We could pay a hacker to take a peek at the firm's books and her account."

"That's a crime."

"Tell me about it. I almost got busted three years ago, remember? I used a hacker in Russia who was about to rat me out when somebody got to him first. Ate a bullet. I ain't going to jail, Latch."

"Nor am I. So, it's fair to say Ms. Barnett is loaded?"

"I'd bet on it, but I wouldn't bet the ranch. Too many unknowns. Did dear Harry sell some stock? Did Ms. Barnett? Is she worth a lot less but Buddy watches her money because he's done it for years? Was she grandfathered in when the firms merged? Safe to say she's got a lot of stock but who knows how much."

"She knows but I doubt she'll show me a statement. I tried once and got a stiff arm."

"Come on, Latch. As charming as you are? Just tell the old gal you can't represent her if you don't know her assets."

"I've tried that."

"Want me to talk to her?

"Hell no!"

"Just joking, Latch. I'd like the rest of my retainer, gotta pay Chub. Tulsa!"

"Always a pleasure, Spade."

CHAPTER 7

Eleanor refused to meet again at Starbucks, said she felt too old there, as if, at the age of eighty-five, there was a place where she might feel young. Simon didn't argue and suggested they meet in his office at 6 P.M. one afternoon, after an alleged long day in court and clearly after 5 P.M. sharp when Matilda clocked out. Any mention of her was now done so in a manner to convey suspicion. Netty admitted that she really didn't trust her. Atta girl.

So far, the last will and testament Simon was contemplating was a complete mystery to his secretary, and it was imperative that it remain so.

Netty sipped sparkling water and said, "I would really like to get this wrapped up, Simon. It's weighing on my mind."

"I understand. Just a couple of things. I've made a list here of about three dozen charities and nonprofits that I want you to consider naming in your will. Your trustee will be given the authority to distribute the money at his or her discretion."

"Who's my trustee?"

"Well, right now it's Wally Thackerman."

"That little crook. The more I think of him the more I despise him."

"I understand. You mentioned a niece and a nephew."

Her chin dropped. Her eyes watered. She suddenly looked very sad. She swallowed hard and said, "I mentioned them only because you asked about relatives. You see, Simon, I have no family. My parents died young. My sister Rose and I were never close. I really never liked her, to be honest. She's dead now and her two kids are my only relatives. It's kinda sad, you know, going through life with no family, no kin folks."

"I know some people who would say it's a blessing," he replied, but the wisecrack went nowhere.

"Vince Barnett and I tried but we couldn't have kids. We were so young."

"Where is your nephew?"

"Oh, gosh, who knows? Last I heard he left his wife and kids and ran off with a college girl."

Simon was suddenly tentative with his questions. "And you have no relationship with him?"

"None. I saw him briefly at my sister's funeral fifteen years ago. He barely spoke to me. We just don't know each other."

"And your niece?"

A long pause as she managed a slight smile. "Maggie. She's certainly a better person than her brother, but I haven't seen her in decades. You see, Simon, their childhood was not good, and Maggie fled as soon as she could. She had to get away from her parents and her brother. She became a veterinarian and moved to Africa where she studies giraffes, last I heard. We've had no contact since she was in college, couldn't even get home for her mother's funeral. Pretty sad family, wouldn't you say?"

"I've seen a lot worse. What if you made a gift to the foundation she works for?"

"To study giraffes?"

"I'm sure they do good work. Do you know its name?"

"The giraffe?"

Simon took a breath as he scribbled something and asked himself if this was one of those moments when the marbles were loose. "No, the nonprofit Maggie works for?"

"Oh no, of course not. I don't even know what country she's

in. And besides, she hasn't bothered to contact me in at least thirty years. So why should I send her a check? I'll be dead, right? You know, when she gets the check?"

"Right, that's the purpose of this will."

"So Maggie gets a check she's not expecting from her dear Aunt Eleanor, who she has obviously forgotten and never really cared about in the first place, and what's she supposed to do, write me a thank-you note? I'll be dead, Simon. Who's going to read the thank-you note?"

Damned sure won't be me, Simon thought to himself, but it was an excellent question. "All right, all right, forget the family. Can you think of any person, a friend, neighbor, anyone, who you might want to leave some money to?"

"No. You've already asked me this. So did Wally. I said no."

"Well, you left a chunk to Wally."

"I did not."

"Yes, Netty, in paragraph fourteen, section A, there is an outright gift to Wally Thackerman for $485,000."

Her jaw dropped and she shook her head. "That little creep."

"He did not explain this to you?"

"Of course not. I don't think so. If he did I don't remember it. Why would he do that?"

Simon had been looking for an opening to bring up the gift to Wally. As he suspected, she was unaware of it because she had not carefully read the will. She had trusted Wally, just as she would trust Simon, hopefully enough to allow him to simply explain the provisions of the will, hitting the high points and skirting by the fine print.

"I can't begin to understand what Wally was thinking," Simon said.

"You're not doing that, are you, Simon?"

"Of course not. It's highly unethical and probably grounds for disbarment."

"Gobbledygook. Please don't take advantage of me."

"There is no gift to me in your will. Period. As the attorney for your estate and for the trust I will be entitled to fees for my services, but all fees must be filed in public records and approved by the court."

She exhaled, obviously relieved. She reached over and touched his hand. "Thank you, Simon."

"Just doing my job, Netty. And part of my job is to protect your estate and prevent trouble. For this reason I want you to leave some money to your two stepsons."

She jerked back her hand and frowned. "Why would I do that?"

"Because they might cause trouble during probate. If they find out how much money you really have, then it's almost guaranteed they'll hire a lawyer and contest the will."

"On what grounds?"

"Oh, lawyers can be very creative when they smell money. They'll come up with all sorts of claims. But, here's the clincher. I'll include in your will a provision that disallows any gift to a person who contests the will. So, say you give each stepson a hundred thousand dollars outright. Now, if one of them contests the will, he runs the risk of losing the gift."

"You are so clever, Simon."

He smiled and almost demurred by saying that such a provision was taught to every second-year law student, but passed on the notion of modesty and in silence took full credit for being so clever. "And, besides, wouldn't Harry want his boys to get some of the money he invested over the years?"

"I suppose."

"Okay. A hundred thousand to Clyde, same to Jerry. Agreed?"

"Yes, if you say so."

Simon was scribbling away as he doled out some of her money. Precious little of it, though. "Now, I know I've asked you this already, but do you want to make gifts to any friends or acquaintances?"

"I've thought about that, yes. Inez Mulberry is an old friend in Atlanta. She's in a care facility there and not doing well. She's ninety-one. Do you know anybody that old who's doing well?" She chuckled at her humor and Simon joined in with a hearty laugh. He wrote down the name and asked, "How much to Inez Mulberry?"

"Uh, let's say, uh, twenty-five thousand."

"Okay. That's not much. Does she need financial assistance?"

"Oh, gosh no. She's loaded. Her husband worked for Coke with Harry and bought tons of stock."

Then why are you leaving her a gift? Simon let it pass. It would be easier just to put Inez in the will and keep going. "Okay, I'll include her at twenty-five thousand. Anyone else?"

"No, can't think of anyone."

"Okay, so moving right along. I asked you before about the firm in Atlanta that handles your portfolio, and you said it was Appletree something or other, right?"

She rolled her eyes in frustration and mumbled, "Here we go again."

Simon pretended to ignore her and continued, "As I said, it is important for me to have a chat with the advisor there who is in charge of your stocks and such."

"Now you sound like Wally, and that's not a good thing."

Simon was being cautious and not about to push. She was proving that she had no loyalty to her estate lawyers and he didn't want to lose her. His dear Netty could be his ticket to an easier, more rewarding life. He could almost smell the huge fees coming his way. "I understand, but to fully take advantage of the tax laws it may be necessary to protect some of your assets. To protect them, I need to know everything about them."

She closed her eyes and frowned hard as if hit by a migraine. After a long, heavy pause she said, "You don't trust me, do you Simon? You don't believe me when I say I have all this money." Her voice was breaking and she was about to cry.

———— ◆◆ ————

The following morning, Simon was sitting in a small courtroom deleting voicemails as he waited to argue a motion in a lawsuit he was destined to lose, when his phone hummed quietly.

Unknown caller, Atlanta. He quickly stepped into the hallway and said, "Latch."

"Good morning, Mr. Latch. My name is Buddy Brown and I run a wealth advisory firm in Atlanta. How are you, sir?" Pleasant voice, proper manners, age between sixty-five and seventy-five.

"I'm fine, Mr. Brown. I appreciate your call."

"My pleasure. Eleanor Barnett has been a client of mine for many years. I knew her husband Harry back in the day. He died too young and left her some common stock in both Coca-Cola and Wal-Mart. I'm not at liberty to say how much, but I can say that Ms. Eleanor is well taken care of."

"Okay, that much I gather. I'm preparing a last will and testament that is not very thick. No heirs, no relatives, everything to charity."

"Sounds like Ms. Eleanor, though I haven't seen her in many years. She knows what she wants. Best of luck, Mr. Latch."

"Thank you, sir."

Evidently Buddy was a man of few words and had better things to do. Spade had found the right man, though the question of Eleanor's real net worth was still unanswered. On the one hand, the call was comforting in that Buddy legitimized her claims of wealth. It was safe to assume that any client with a long history at such an advisory firm would have substantial assets. On the other hand, there was much that Buddy didn't mention and he seemed determined to get off the phone as quickly as Simon got on it.

Simon returned to the courtroom just as his case was being called. He walked to the front of the courtroom, nodded at the judge, and took a seat at counsel table. His adversary, an old pal, began presenting his motion and the judge quickly lost interest. Simon almost chuckled to himself. There he was, quibbling over a useless motion in a worthless lawsuit, while at the same time he had just hooked a client worth $20 million in liquid assets.

Though he had almost no liquid assets and plenty of debts, and his marriage was dangerously on the rocks, and his law office had proven to be a break-even venture over the past eighteen years, he was suddenly smiling at the future. He would continue to build an alternate world and one day soon get lost in it. He would wrangle his way out of his life with Paula while remaining relevant to his children. He would phase out Matilda, though that game plan had not yet materialized. He would wait patiently for Eleanor Barnett to succumb to the years, and as soon as she kicked the bucket he would swoop into probate court and take control of her money.

CHAPTER 8

The execution of the will was carefully planned, or so Simon thought. Since he was not a criminal, he didn't think like one. What was the famous line in the movie *Body Heat*? "When you commit a murder you make ten mistakes. If you can think of seven, you're a genius." Or something like that. Simon wasn't planning a murder, or any other crime for that matter, but he felt guilty anyway. He made lists and charts and diagrams, and when everything seemed to click, he gave it the green light.

It happened on March 27, a day that would find Matilda's birthday lunch far away from the office. As he often did, Simon asked his neighbors for the favor. Tony and Mary Beth Larson ran a mom-and-pop insurance shop next door to Simon's office on Main Street and often stepped over to witness will signings. The law required two people not related to the "testatrix," in this case Eleanor Barnett, to spend a few minutes in easy conversation with her to satisfy any concerns about her mental capacity. As attesting witnesses, they were not expected to read the will—and in this case Simon was certainly determined that they would not—but only to make sure that Ms. Barnett knew what she was doing and was not being unduly influenced.

Simon had written every word of the will on his laptop and printed it in his cramped bathroom, where he kept the new printer he'd paid $150 for at a Wal-Mart. He didn't normally shop at Wal-Mart but suddenly had a keen interest in the company. Coke too. After several drafts, he was convinced it looked almost identical to one that Matilda could have typed. It was five pages long and packed with a lot of dense language that he managed to explain to Eleanor in simple terms that were not altogether forthcoming.

"Legal gobbledygook," she said more than once, exasperated. The gist and thrust was that upon her death her fortune would be placed in a foundation, one not too dissimilar to the trust Wally across the street had devised, and the money would be spread over a multitude of local charities that would do all manner of good things. By keeping the money local, Simon believed the will would be more palatable to a jury in the likely event a big lawsuit erupted later. Food banks, homeless shelters, boys' clubs, girls' clubs, Cub Scouts and Brownies, soccer leagues, senior center, United Way, policemen's fraternal order, a dozen of the town's largest churches of all denominations. The Eleanor Barnett Foundation would make thousands of people smile for years to come, and Simon Latch would be Santa Claus. As executor of the will, and sole director of the trust, as well as the attorney for the estate, he would be in complete control. His fees would be substantial.

Unlike Wally, the greedy little bastard, Simon would not be getting a direct payment of cash upon Eleanor's death. In the depths of the densest and most convoluted paragraph of that will, Wally included an outright gift of $485,000 to himself. A magnifying glass was needed to find the language. The payment was for "accrued services," a vague and unique category of testamentary gifts that, not surprisingly, went undefined. It was absurd to think that Eleanor owed that much money to Wally.

But never mind. It wouldn't matter. Wally wasn't getting squat from the will he drafted or the one dear Netty was signing now in the presence of her two attesting witnesses.

As always, Simon choreographed the execution and asked Tony and Mary Beth Larson if they understood that they were vouching for the mental acuity of Ms. Eleanor Barnett. With enthusiasm, both said yes and eagerly signed their names. There were smiles and even giggles all around. Simon notarized both signatures, and in doing so sealed the fate of the most valuable last will and testament he would ever prepare.

As his way of saying thanks to the Larsons, he usually took them to lunch, and today he insisted that Eleanor join them. The invitation seemed harmless, and though it was made in good faith there was an ulterior motive. Simon, now with one distant eye on future litigation, wanted the Larsons to spend even more time with his client. They had no way of knowing that they were quite likely to be called as witnesses if the whole mess blew up. The more time they spent with Eleanor, and especially on the same morning she signed her will, the more credibility their testimony would have.

Of course Simon did not mention their possible involvement in a will contest. The Larsons had been witnessing wills for years and there had never been a problem. Why bother them now? He did have a twinge of guilt because he couldn't warn them that one day they might get subpoenas, but he forced those thoughts out of his mind for the moment.

Simon pondered these things over chicken salad in a deli two blocks off Main, a hole-in-the-wall seldom frequented by lawyers and the courthouse gang. He did not want Wally to see him out and about with Eleanor Barnett, who was having a delightful time chatting with Tony and Mary Beth. The Larsons were friendly people, they sold insurance, and Eleanor warmed up to them considerably. She seemed to thrive on the interaction and hardly touched her salad.

After an hour of listening, Simon broke up the party with a fib about being needed in court.

The will was done. Properly signed and witnessed and notarized. He had deliberately ignored the matter of the $250 fee, simply because he did not want a check that Matilda might see. Eleanor could keep her money. He had big plans to get it back later, in spades.

———— ◆◆► ————

Back at the office, Eleanor was saying goodbye when she thought of something. "Can we talk for a moment?"

"Of course," Simon said. Whatever she wanted.

"Well, I'm not sure how these things work, but what happens to Wally at this point?"

"What do you mean?"

"Do we tell him that I have a new will and the one he prepared is no longer valid?"

That was the last thing Simon wanted. Wally might react badly and become unpredictable. He might press Eleanor to change her mind yet again. He would certainly come after Simon with all manner of threats, though he probably wouldn't follow through. Sticking his name in her will to the tune of $485,000 cash outright would probably get his license suspended for a year or two, if not revoked. Simon simply did not want to deal with Wally at this point. Their disagreements would erupt later, after her funeral.

He said, "The law does not require one lawyer to inform another lawyer that a client has signed a new will that invalidates a prior one. It's simply not done."

"It seems like we should tell him."

"Not now. Maybe later. The reason it's not done is because a client, you, has the right to change your mind anytime you want. You may decide next month to change something in your new will. You many even decide to have another lawyer prepare a new one." Simon couldn't believe he was uttering such foolishness.

Eleanor grinned and touched his arm. "I would never do that, Simon. I'm in such good hands now. I didn't feel this way with Wally Thackerman. I still can't believe he tried to take my money."

"Let's forget about that. It's history now. I'll keep the original will here in my safe and you take a copy home and hide it somewhere. No one should ever see your will, Netty, do you understand? Friends, stepsons, housekeepers—no one sees your will."

"I understand."

"There's one last thing we have not discussed, and that's your final arrangements. It's a very delicate matter and I think we should do it over lunch in the near future."

"You mean, funeral, things like that?"

"I'm afraid so. You live alone, and there's no family nearby, or anywhere else. Who makes decisions about your health care? Who gets the phone call when you're sick? And, yes, the funeral and burial. Do you have a burial policy?"

"Yes, Harry and I bought one years ago. I'll be put to rest next to him in the Eternal Springs Cemetery. It's a lovely spot."

"I'm sure. I'm happy to help with these decisions, Netty, and some of them could be legal in nature."

"Gobbledygook."

"I know. Let's put this conversation off a couple of weeks and meet for lunch."

"I really enjoy getting out for lunch, Simon. And the Larsons are such nice people."

"Then let's do lunch," he said with a smile. The Larsons would not be invited.

CHAPTER 9

That night, a Friday, was the second round of the Sweet Sixteen. Simon had the bright idea to make a friendly call to Paula and suggest the family dine on pizza and watch basketball. She was lukewarm, but that was a big improvement in their relationship. The kids could stay up late. Simon could sleep on the sofa, and if by chance he was discovered there, he and Paula would laugh and say his snoring was keeping her awake.

They ordered pizza and ate on TV trays in the den in front of the big screen. Simon had prepared brackets for the Sweet Sixteen and each family member had picked winners through the Final Four. Simon had skillfully played the Vegas line and used a few tips he'd picked up hanging around Chub's. Danny and Buck had also done some homework and were already trash-talking about their brilliant picks. Janie, age nine, had chosen her teams based on the school mascots and uniform colors and was undefeated through the first-round games the day before. Paula couldn't have cared less but gamely hung on as if she wanted to win. She picked her winners based on the head coaches' appearances—fitness, good looks, nice suit, well-coordinated necktie. So far she had won three and lost one. Each member put up five dollars for the winning pot, to be determined by who picked the most teams to reach the Final Four.

Simon desperately wanted a beer to go with his pizza, but alcohol had been banned. A year earlier, the school had been rocked by a scandalous party that went off the rails. A group of freshmen had been left unsupervised in a nice home and proceeded to clean out the liquor cabinet. One boy and one girl passed out and could not be revived. An ambulance was called and the kids spent the night in a hospital. They survived but the families were mortified. The school panicked and held meetings for a month. Some of the parents vowed to keep booze out of their homes. Paula, a light drinker to begin with, took a hard line. Simon had no choice but to agree. It was another good reason to live at the office.

Buck, age sixteen, was not at the party but knew most of the kids involved. He assured his parents that he was not sneaking beers, but he would be driving soon, and Simon knew that when he entered that phase of life all bets were off. Paula was convinced they could lead by example, monitor the kids' activities and friends, and protect them from doing the things that all kids wanted to do.

And she didn't like the idea of each one putting up five dollars for the winning pot. It was nothing but a form of gambling.

As the first game was about to tip off, Buck asked Danny, "What's the over?"

Without hesitating, Danny replied, "One twenty-four."

Simon was a bit startled by the quick response, but said nothing. He would listen even harder and hopefully not detect any more signs of fluency in the betting games. Teenage online gambling, especially in sports, was a growing problem.

Paula frowned and asked, "What does that mean—'the over'?"

Buck and Danny froze. Simon decided to jump and try to help them with "Total points scored by both teams."

"I didn't ask you," she replied calmly. She looked at Danny and asked again, "What is 'the over'?"

"Dad's right. The total points by both teams."

"And you can bet on that?"

"If you want to. I never do." He was not convincing.

"Well, I would hope not. I hope you're not betting at all."

Buck stared at the television and said, "We're betting now, Mom. Everybody put up five dollars for the winning pot, so everybody is betting at least five dollars. That's gambling."

The tip-off gave them a chance to take a breath and enjoy some silence. Simon was greatly relieved that the moment had passed, but he was also convinced his sons were gambling at some level. He would think of a way to discuss it with them later. Should he really be that worried? Neither had jobs, income, or savings. Like most teenagers, they watched sports around the clock it seemed, and knew more players, stats, and ESPN gossip than he could ever absorb. What if they were gambling and winning? Sure it was illegal for minors to bet online, but the laws were proving to be thoroughly unenforceable.

What if Buck and Danny could pass along inside tips to their father?

———— ◆ ◆ ————

Janie fell asleep before ten. Around eleven, Paula had seen enough and said good night. Half an hour later, the boys were dozing and Simon ran them off to bed. When all was quiet, he eased down the hall and entered his bedroom. The lights were off. He assumed his wife was asleep. He planned to silently brush his teeth, put on his pajamas, and sneak back to the den.

In the bathroom, he was startled to see a full bottle of scotch next to two tumblers and a small ice bucket. He opened the door just as Paula was flipping on the lamp by her night table.

"There's a bottle of whiskey in here," he said.

"Yes there is. Pour two drinks and have a seat in the chair."

He did as he was told. Five minutes passed in complete silence as they sipped scotch in the dim light and refused to look at one another. Finally, he said, "Thanks for the drink. I needed it."

"You'll probably need more."

"Okay. What's the topic for tonight?"

"It's not divorce. We've had that conversation. I haven't had sex in over four months."

"I remember, vaguely."

"There's not much to remember."

"Ouch. So this is a sex talk?"

"It is. I'm forty-one years old, Simon, and I'm not ready to give up on sex."

"I could do with more of it."

"I want sex, Simon, but not with you."

It was a kick in the gut that he absorbed without flinching. Instead, he gave a slight shrug, then took a long pull from his tumbler. "Got somebody in mind?"

"No. And I'm not looking for a boyfriend. The last thing I need in my life is another relationship. When we finally get divorced I can't see myself ever thinking of marriage again."

"I'm kinda sick of it too."

Each took a deep breath, then another sip.

"So you want one of those open deals?" he asked.

"The marriage is over, we've already agreed on that. Now we're trying to get out of it. Until then, I want the freedom to fool around. I'll be discreet and I'll stay away from married men. I'm looking for fun, not trouble."

Simon would replay the conversation a hundred times in the days to come, and the one feeling that would always surprise him was how little he cared. He had not loved Paula in many years, and he realized at that moment how much he disliked her. The idea of his wife "fooling around" was actually exciting because he would happily accept the same freedom.

He said, "You don't need my approval."

"No, but we have to agree. It wouldn't be fair for this to become an issue when we divorce. Plus, you're a lawyer and I don't trust you."

"Thanks. I've always trusted you."

"And I've always been faithful. Have you?"

"Yes." He rattled his ice, needed some more, and said, "I guess we have no choice but to agree to open things up."

"You don't like it?"

"I really don't care what you do."

"Nor do I care what you do."

"Okay. A deal."

"Pour me some more scotch. I'm not finished."

———————•◆•———————

She finally spoke when the second drink was half gone. "I saw Harriet today."

"Harriet?"

"My therapist."

"Oh yeah. Her. I forgot about Harriet."

"I haven't mentioned her in some time."

"It's great that you're getting therapy, Paula, because I probably need it too. Problem is I can't afford it. They charge more per hour than I do."

"Sounds like a personal problem."

"Aren't we dealing with personal problems here?"

Several years earlier, as things unraveled, they had discussed seeing a couples therapist, an expert to show each one how screwed-up the other one really was and guide them back to true and lasting love. It never happened, primarily because by then both were sick of each other and the last thing they wanted was a lame effort at forced happiness.

Simon had paid $200 for one hour with a counselor whose real objective had been to lock him in for ten more sessions. Matilda gave better advice to their clients as they waited to see Mr. Latch.

Paula said, "Anyway, Harriet thinks we should talk to the children and prepare them for the inevitable."

He took a sip and thought about this. "She's probably right. We can't keep on like this. The kids are growing up and they're not stupid."

"Buck and Danny have us figured out. Janie knows things aren't right. Harriet says it's best to tell them one at a time. The sooner the better."

Another sip, another long, heavy pause. Simon finally said, "Okay, I'll talk to the boys. You handle Janie."

"I think that's best. Let's do it tomorrow afternoon, one at a time, then have another pizza for dinner and watch basketball."

"One happy family."

"When was the last time you and I were happy, Simon?"

"I can't remember."

"Nor can I."

Both took a sip in the quietness. From fifteen feet away he could hear her breathe. She was sitting in the bed, propped up on pillows, covers up to her waist, her fine breasts almost peeking through the sheer nightgown. For a moment, it was difficult to visualize her crawling into bed with another man.

Then he let it pass. "Any changes in the property settlement?"

She took another sip and said, "I don't think so. You?"

"No." They had never disagreed on the terms of the divorce. Joint custody of the children, with them remaining in their home, in their bedrooms, with their mother sleeping right where she was supposed to sleep. Simon would come and go as he pleased, but with no surprise visits. He planned to miss no games, recitals, school plays, graduations. Life would go on as usual. His interest in the house was to be deeded to Paula and he would keep paying the mortgage. No alimony but generous child support. Simon would continue to live somewhere else. It would be as neat and painless as possible, though Simon was fully aware of how many ways things could go wrong. Now that they had the green light to start dating again, it was only a matter of time before one of them fell in love.

He despised himself for allowing the next thought to enter his jumbled mind. He thought of Netty, her new will, and her money. If things went as planned, and he freely admitted to himself that much could go wrong, he would be, in the not so distant future, raking in some substantial fees as the attorney and trustee for her estate. If she really had $20 million in assets—and he had convinced himself that she wasn't exaggerating—it would not be excessive or unusual for the attorney to clip the estate for about 10 percent, over a period of a few years. Not exactly retirement money, but certainly enough to take the pressure off a small-town law practice that was going nowhere.

It was imperative to keep these hypothetical, even fanciful, fees away from Paula.

He managed to shove his dear Netty away for a while. He told himself to savor the moment. He and Paula were taking giant steps to purge each other from their life together, a separation that was long overdue. The kids would suffer but they were also resilient. Hopefully, there would be no permanent damage. Virtually all of their friends were victims of divorce and seemed to be unscarred.

He rattled his cubes again and asked, "Is this conversation over?"

"It is. I'm going to sleep."

"Mind if I get one for the road?"

"I don't care what you do. I really don't."

Simon poured the stiffest one yet, turned off the bathroom light, and left their bedroom.

———— ◆◆► ————

On the sofa, he had trouble sleeping for the excitement. He felt like a frat boy again, dreaming of all the pretty coeds. He started with the single women he knew and explored his chances with each, then, before long, moved on to the married ladies, but only those in unhappy marriages. That route grew complicated and he quickly returned to the singles.

The third scotch finally did the trick and he drifted away. He slept a few hours, woke up feeling great, and single, and rearranged the pillows on the sofa. He went to the kitchen, brewed a pot of coffee, and enjoyed the first cup as he watched the dawn break over the trees in the backyard. At seven, Paula finally emerged from the dark hallway and entered the kitchen. He poured her a cup, and said, "I'm thinking about making pancakes with sausage this morning."

"You'll have to go to the store."

"All right. You need anything?"

"Just a few quiet moments to enjoy my coffee."

"Okay. I don't want to tell the children today."

"Why not?"

"Because this might be one of the few days we are together as a family. We might even have some fun today. Let's wait another week or so."

"Whatever."

She turned and took her coffee back to her bedroom.

CHAPTER 10

Monday morning, Simon stumbled out of The Closet, in his gym shorts and a T-shirt, went downstairs, and sat at his desk. It was not yet seven, so he had a full hour before Matilda arrived and started planning his week. He needed more than an hour. He needed to be in a tiki bar on a beach somewhere, sipping a tall iced drink and watching the waves roll in while his mind went numb with meaningless thoughts.

Aside from having fun with his kids, the weekend had been a tough one. He was still trying to adjust to the fact that his wife was now on the prowl, and he was making progress on that front. The real trouble was the tournament. He was getting wiped out. In the family pool, Janie, sticking with her mascot selections, had won ten games and lost only two. Paula, still picking the best-dressed coaches, was nine and three. Buck and Danny were even. Simon, the serious gambler and true expert, had won four games and lost eight. Last place.

But the five dollars he'd lost at home was nothing compared to the shellacking over at Chub's, where he was down $7,000, a personal record. He was certain he would get it back with the Final Four, but his confidence was wavering.

He sipped strong coffee and checked in with several online gambling gurus who blathered on with piercing analyses while covering their butts—one picked Duke, another picked Kentucky, another Wisconsin. What was a desperate gambler to do? He looked at his daily calendar and saw nothing but the same slog. In fact, for the entire week he could not see potential fees of more than $2,000.

The Final Four. Only three games left in the tournament, the season. At one point, way back in early January, he was up $4,500. He bounced around during conference play and finished the regular season up $3,000. When he was winning he wanted to play more, and when he was losing he wanted to play even more to catch up. But, as always, he kept his focus and knew his limits. At least he kept telling himself that.

The Final Four. Wisconsin, Duke, Michigan State, and Kentucky. None of which he'd chosen two weeks earlier during bracket mania when every single fan was so much smarter. He stopped fretting and stepped back into The Closet where he managed another shower in a cheap glass tube a client had installed for $500. The water was almost warm and barely dripped from a head that was gathering some ominous form of mold. He banged his elbows on the rickety glass panels and was finished in under a minute. He dressed quickly in khakis, a white shirt and a tie, and went downstairs to the office kitchen for more coffee. The Closet was not equipped with a real kitchen.

In the fridge he noticed a new collection of cartons of diet drinks lined up in a neat row on Tillie's side. Seltzers flavored with asparagus and other green vegetables. Weight loss practically guaranteed. Simon smiled and shook his head and almost felt sorry for the poor girl as she battled the bulge.

Promptly at 8 A.M., she was not there. Simon listened for the front door to open and the other familiar sounds of his secretary arriving for work. She was rarely late. At 8:15, he thought about calling her, certain that there was a problem. But he waited, and at 8:30, he heard her noises. She always tapped on his door and said "Good morning, Simon." When she did, at 8:30, he was buried in a document, as if too busy to be concerned with her tardiness.

She walked in and said, "Hey, I know it's eight-thirty, but I have a new schedule. I'll come in at this time from now on and leave at five-thirty."

To make such a decision without asking him was irritating, but he acted nonchalant, as if he didn't care when she came and went. Same with his wife. He was plotting to get rid of both of them. "And the reason is?"

"I've joined a new gym and my class runs from six-thirty to seven-thirty. I need time to run home and shower and such."

In her desperate search for a toned and pliant body, she had changed gyms several times, with no success. "Okay, we'll give it a try," he said without agreeing or disagreeing. For a second she wanted to assert herself and establish her own boundaries, but it was Monday morning, not the best time for a quarrel. She bit her tongue and managed a fake smile, then turned and left his office. As she was leaving, Simon, out of habit, checked her out. Was the asparagus juice working? The new gym? Was it his imagination, or was Tillie actually shedding a few pounds? Or was it that, since he now had the green light from home, he would quite naturally look at women with a different eye.

One thing was certain: On the top-ten list of ways to thoroughly screw up your life, having sex with an employee was somewhere in the first three slots. The laws on sexual harassment were brutal.

Where was gambling on the list?

His thoughts returned to the Final Four, but the phone was ringing now. Wounded and angry people out there needed lawyers.

Ten minutes later, Tillie stuck her head through the crack of his door and said, "Simon, got a minute?"

"Sure." He wasn't working yet, still pondering free online tips from Vegas oddsmakers.

She took a step in and said, "I still have an open file on Eleanor Barnett. She hasn't called in some time. You want to close it?"

Simon thought for a moment as if he really had to make a decision. "Give it a week or so. I doubt she'll be back."

Tillie nodded and disappeared. She returned to her desk and typed notes on her iPad, for personal use only. She had just caught her boss in a lie, one that was probably of some significance, though she didn't know for sure. A friend who worked in a realtor's office had seen Simon in the deli last Friday when Matilda took the day off. He was having lunch with Tony and Mary Beth Larson and an older lady. She called Mary Beth to chat about an insurance matter for one of their clients. They talked all the time and enjoyed the local gossip. Out of the blue, Matilda asked if Mary Beth and Tony had witnessed the execution of a will last Friday. Mary Beth hesitated, just long enough to arouse suspicion, and said yes, they had. For a Ms. Eleanor Barnett, a lovely lady.

Matilda took it in stride as if she was on top of things and ended the call. If Eleanor Barnett signed a will, who typed it? In her twelve years with Simon they had prepared and executed hundreds of wills, and, to her recollection, he had never typed a single one. Nor had he presided over the signing without involving Matilda.

Simon could be a complicated soul and had his flaws, but he was not a liar. When telling stories and spinning yarns he could embellish with the best of them, but on serious matters he would never lie.

Until now.

————◆◆————

During the lunch with Tony and Mary Beth Larson, Simon could not help but notice that Netty was easily impressed with a grilled chicken Caesar that did not appear to be fresh. He suspected her diet was the typical bland fare of an old widow who seldom cooked and ate from a can.

Simon invited her to another lunch. She accepted with great enthusiasm, which was not surprising. He suggested Chinese, then Afghan kabobs, then falafel. She had never heard of the last two and was suspicious of the first. With great patience, he explained that he enjoyed foods from everywhere and wanted her to have the same experience. If they tried something they didn't like, no big deal. They would simply go somewhere else next time. Game on. She couldn't wait to get out of the house. He offered to pick her up at home, primarily because he was curious to see where and how she lived. If her Lincoln was fifteen years old, how about her furniture and rugs? He assumed she had simple tastes, but was it all an act to fake out family and friends and keep prying eyes away from her fortune? Simon spent far too much time pondering these things.

Netty stiff-armed him by insisting that they meet at the restaurant. She was proud that she was still able to drive while most of her friends had had their keys confiscated. Who were these friends? He had so much to learn.

They met at a Greek restaurant Simon had visited before and liked. It was on the edge of town, on the main highway headed toward Washington, far enough from Main Street. He desperately wanted to avoid any chance of bumping into Wally Thackerman at lunch, something that happened maybe once a year. The odds were slim, but weird things happen and he could not imagine the aftershocks of such an encounter. There would be suspicions, then accusations, then fights and so on. Wally would automatically assume Simon was poaching a client, and a wealthy one at that.

They ordered lamb stew with kabobs, rather heavy dishes, with pita bread and water to drink. She wanted to know about his family. She didn't have much of her own and was curious about his. Simon tried to shift the conversation back to her side of the table. He certainly didn't want to brag on his children, nor would he dare discuss the broken marriage. He painted a pleasant portrait of things at home and figured he could be more truthful later. He asked about her stepsons, Clyde and Jerry Korsak, and realized immediately that was out of bounds. Her niece and nephew remained a mystery. It had been at least forty years since the entire family had been together for a summer weekend in the Catskills, a disastrous gathering that ended badly and sent everyone scurrying in different directions, evidently for good.

She had been married to Vince Barnett back then. Vince had clearly been her favorite husband, her first love. They had married young, tried desperately to have a family, traveled a lot because they were childless, and she was devastated when he died suddenly at the age of forty.

After about forty-five minutes, the lunch grew tiresome. Netty seemed to have few interests and seldom left the house. She spent hours watching daytime television as she pieced together jigsaw puzzles. They said goodbye in the parking lot and Simon watched her weave away, one foot on the brake, straddling lanes, oblivious to the angry horns behind her.

As he drove back to the office, he was stuck with the nagging thought that she might live another ten years. Then he was angry with himself for once again dwelling on her demise. It was imperative that he stop thinking about her last will and testament and focus on simply being her friend.

CHAPTER 11

After grappling with a dozen lame excuses to delay the imperative, Simon and Paula finally reached an agreement, a rarity. They would tell the children at the same time, then somehow survive the aftermath. Inflict the pain, have a good cry, then pick up the pieces. They steadied themselves by reminding each other that many of their friends had managed to survive the same dreadful conversations, and then moved on. The kids would be all right.

On a Friday night, Simon took Buck and Danny to a mall to watch a movie, and afterward they ate ice cream in a food court that overlooked a cheesy waterfall. How does one broach the subject? There was no easy way. He cleared his throat and said, "I guess you guys know that Mom and I are not getting along too well."

The boys glanced at each other and their eyes said it all. They knew the inevitable but did not want this conversation. The moment they had been dreading had arrived.

"Is that why you're sleeping at the office?" Buck asked.

"Yes it is." Paula had told the children the truth when it had become obvious. "We have decided to get a divorce."

He let the word hang in the air for a few seconds as he watched their reactions. Danny, the younger, was more emotional and his eyes moistened, though he seemed determined to be tough. Buck would be the harder case.

He said, "Mom says you don't love her anymore."

"I'll always love your mom. We created you guys and Janie and we are extremely proud of you." He had practiced these words many times and they sounded flat and too rehearsed. "But just because you love someone doesn't mean you can get along. Mom and I simply cannot get along anymore." To a sixteen-year-old and a fourteen-year-old, or to any kid for that matter, this sounded like impenetrable crap. All kids want their parents to be together and happy.

"Why can't you get along?" Danny asked.

"Because sometimes people fall in love, get married, have kids, and then grow apart. We got busy with our lives, and, well, things changed."

Buck said, "So you're blaming us?"

"I am not, Buck. I'm blaming no one but myself. Let's make that clear. Your mother has done nothing wrong, neither have I. There's no bad behavior here. We love you guys and Janie and we're determined to support you in every way. We just don't enjoy being around each other anymore."

To put it mildly. Truth was, he and Paula couldn't stand each other. And on the subject of bad behavior, he could only fantasize about who she was seeing on the side. He, certainly, was on the prowl, now that he had the green light, but so far had struck out.

The boys went silent, thoroughly confused. Simon had several boxes yet to check, so he rattled them off: "I'm not going to move away, or marry someone else, or miss a ball game or a practice or a birthday or Christmas. I'll be there for you guys, same as always. And I'm very sorry for what's happening. Your mother and I are both sorry for this. When we got married seventeen years ago we never dreamed this would happen."

A group of girls settled around a table nearby and Buck recognized them. After a long silence, he said, "Can we just go home?"

"Sure."

At home, things were just as complicated. Janie sat on one end of the sofa, Paula the other. Both had been crying for an hour. Janie was heartbroken at the news. Paula felt rotten for breaking it to her and then watching her melt into a puddle of tears. Her eyes were still red and puffy when Simon and the boys returned. Danny ignored his mother and sister and went straight to his room and slammed the door. Buck fell into a big chair by the television. Simon kissed Janie on the top of her head but said nothing. He ignored his wife and she returned the favor. They sat for a long time without speaking, each one staring at the floor or a cushion or anything that didn't stare back. It was a dreadful, painful moment for the family, but Simon knew they would all recover and move on. Paula was certainly eager to gut it out for another hour or so, then go to bed and wake up with a major hurdle behind them.

They could get counseling for the kids. Life had stopped for the moment, but each day would get better. The parents were determined to smother them with love and attention and help them grow up and mature. Or that's what they kept telling themselves.

The parents were equally determined to get away from each other.

Paula finally broke the ice with "How was the movie?"

Buck shrugged and said, "Okay."

"You want to watch another one?"

Another shrug, another "Okay."

Simon stood and said, "I'll make the popcorn."

Chub's was rocking that night. A local pool shark had a big game going in one corner as gamblers looked on, offering no shortage of commentary. Three widescreens were carrying NBA games and the refs were getting cursed by the regulars. A jukebox was blaring in another corner. Simon found a spot at the bar and settled down in front of a video poker screen. Across the way, Valerie nodded at him and soon appeared with a bourbon and ginger ale.

"Who you suing, Latch?" she asked, one of her usual greetings.

"Everybody," he said with a smile. She sauntered away to insult another customer.

Simon needed the alcohol and took a long sip. He glanced at a television above the rows of bottles of booze. Heat versus Rockets, not much of a game and he had almost put $500 on the Rockets and taken the points.

It was important to drop by Chub's at least once a week. He had to give the impression that life was good, that he was still in the game and unfazed by the fact that he was down $6,300. He owed that much to Chub, plus another $1,400 to an online site based offshore and theoretically illegal. His great comeback during the Final Four did not materialize.

Chub eventually appeared, as Simon knew he would, and he worked the crowd as he approached. "What's up, Lawyer Latch?" he asked with a broad smile.

"Same ole stuff, Chub, how you doing?"

"Great. Gamblers are still losing, business is booming. Worried about the Feds, though. If they legalize online betting then I'm up shit creek. You think it'll happen?"

"Who knows, Chub? The gaming world is changing, man."

"Tell me about it. New rules every year. The Vegas boys are spending a fortune to bribe Congress to protect them, but they're facing headwinds. The Indians are outta control with their casinos. You okay with your account?"

Okay with your account? In other words, *Do you realize you owe the house $6,300 and it ain't getting paid?* And, *Do you realize that you've never been in this deep before?*

Simon gave a smile he thought might be comforting but felt as phony as it was. "Sure, Chub, I'm not worried. Are you?"

"If you're not worried, Latch, I'm not worried. But let's make some progress, okay?"

Or else? Simon had never been squeezed before and didn't

like the pinch. He gave Chub a hard look, then returned to his poker screen. Chub said nothing else and drifted away into the crowd. It was rumored that he had a nasty side, had connections with a crime syndicate in New Jersey, had interests in strip clubs in Florida, and so on. Chub kept things private but the rumors swirled around him nonetheless. Most criminals enjoyed an air of shadiness.

Frankly, Simon had always scoffed at the speculation that Chub was some sort of ambitious crime boss. He had met him fifteen years earlier when he opened his first bar only three blocks away, and he had been Simon's bookie ever since. Chub made a lot of money off booking games and video poker, and his clubs were popular. He stayed away from drugs and dabbled in real estate— shopping centers and apartment buildings. Simon knew only the basics because Chub used another lawyer for his legal work. A shady guy Simon avoided.

Simon left the bar, walked to his office, climbed the rear stairs, and entered The Closet at almost 2 A.M. He stripped to his boxers and stretched out on his bed, a cheap one he'd salvaged from a flea market, and stared at the ceiling. The only light was a dim shadow from a street lamp on Main. Downtown was deathly quiet, no traffic at that hour.

———————◆◆◆———————

Eighteen years into a legal career and here he was, reduced to a flimsy bed with a thin mattress, no box springs, and sheets he hadn't washed in weeks. He was hiding in a tiny, makeshift apart- ment because, well, because he owned it and had no place else to go. Perhaps when the divorce was filed and the gossip was con- firmed and the town knew he and Paula were splitting, perhaps then he could find a real apartment and have room for a stove and full-sized refrigerator. Meanwhile, a mile away his family slept in comfort in a nice home he and Paula had purchased eight years earlier, barely qualifying for the hefty mortgage because they were already stretched too thin. Said mortgage had twenty-two years to go, at $2,800 a month, twelve relentless months in a year, and he was about to get stuck with paying every penny of it. He would deed his interest in the house to Paula but continue with the payments because his family was accustomed to such affluence.

Financially, he was wiped out and things were not about to improve.

Was it worth it? Was getting away from Paula and leaving the kids worth a life of poverty? He told himself that it was, that he was only forty-two years old and perfectly capable of a major comeback. Comeback to where? He had not exactly become rich in the first eighteen years of his career. Why would the next eighteen be any different?

He needed another drink. He got up and went downstairs to his office where he kept his bar in a locked cabinet.

CHAPTER 12

Their fourth lunch was at a slightly upscale Korean restaurant that Simon had heard was superb. There were tablecloths and linen napkins and an atmosphere that was more subdued than some of their previous dives. So far they had tasted Greece, Thailand, and Afghanistan, and, though Netty was thoroughly enjoying their lunches, she was not impressed with the wide variety of cuisine. Also, she seemed perfectly willing to allow Simon to pay for all the lunches, which he did while bitching only to himself. Lunch was part of his grand seduction scheme.

She dutifully looked over the menu, thoroughly overwhelmed by it. Simon took charge again and ordered traditional dishes of *mandu,* a pan-fried dumping filled with chopped pork; *japchae* noodles, thin see-through noodles with sliced mushrooms, carrots, and spinach; and, everyone's favorite, Korean fried chicken, made even crunchier after first being rolled in rice flour. Simon made sure the waiter understood that they wanted the tamest version of the chicken. The spiciest was talked about around town.

During the second lunch, Eleanor had made it clear that she did not drink alcohol, so no wine. She encouraged Simon to have a glass if he wanted, but he rarely drank at lunch. Booze made the afternoons sluggish.

When the waiter was gone, Simon decided to get to the point. "We have not discussed your arrangements, have we?"

"What do you mean?"

"Well, when Mr. Korsak died suddenly, who stepped up and made the important decisions about his funeral and burial?"

"Oh my." Her eyes were moist and she looked away. "Is it really time for that?"

"I'm afraid so. As the executor of your will, and in the absence of any family members, I'll have to make those decisions. Unless, of course, you want someone else to do so."

"Oh no, Simon. I'm trusting you to do it."

"Thank you. I appreciate your trust, Netty."

"Which funeral home?"

"Cupit & Moke, downtown. I guess they're still around."

"Oh, they're both dead, but their families run the funeral home. Mind if I take a look at the policy?"

"Why? I'm not even sure if I can find it. Wasn't planning on needing it anytime soon." She cackled at her humor and Simon obliged with a fake laugh. He said, "And your plot is next to Harry's?"

"That's right. Out in Eternal Springs, the cemetery. Nicest one around. I go visit once a month and take some flowers. Well, not every month, but most of the time."

"And the plot is paid for?"

"Oh yes, as far as I know. Haven't seen a bill in forever."

"I'm assuming the policy covers the standard mortuary services, casket, and so on."

"I'm sure it does. Harry's casket was so handsome, made of oak, had to pay extra."

"Again, I'd like to see the policy," Simon said. "There's a trend nowadays away from traditional burials. Many of my clients are choosing cremation. Have you heard of this?"

"I may have read something. Dottie Watson from the poker club passed two years ago and they cremated her, stuck her in a wall in a mausoleum. We thought her family was just trying to save some money."

"My wife and I have chosen cremation," Simon said. "It's easier, quicker, and much cheaper. Plus, it protects the environment. Think of the millions of people who've died and been embalmed and now those chemicals are leaking into the drinking water. It's a looming environmental disaster."

Eleanor was about to take a sip of water and she froze, then set down her glass. Shocked, she said, "I never thought about that."

"It's true. When a person dies, the morticians fill the body with all manner of chemicals, like formaldehyde, phenol, methanol, and glycerin, to preserve things only until the funeral. It's ridiculous, really. About a million gallons of chemicals go into the ground each year. Over time, as the body decomposes, the chemicals start leaking out, regardless of what type of casket is used."

"Well, I never . . ." Her voice trailed off.

"Cremation is the way to go and it's definitely the trend, at least in this country. I'll send you some magazine articles."

"No casket, nothing like that?"

"Nothing like that. Your ashes are put in a cremation urn and it's buried in a mausoleum or a columbarium."

"A what?"

"Columbarium. It's a structure that holds cremation urns."

With thoughts of decaying remains hanging in the air, the mandu arrived on a platter. They were small, round rice dumplings that smelled delicious. Netty said, "Let's change the subject."

"Good idea."

Simon could do a passable job with chopsticks but Eleanor was too inexperienced. He suggested they stick to forks and she readily agreed. The eight small dumplings disappeared in minutes, just as the noodles and fried chicken were served. Eleanor had been lukewarm to the kabobs from Afghanistan and the spicy egg rolls from Thailand, but she devoured the crunchy fried chicken. And, in Simon's opinion, she needed to eat. She was looking thin and frail, not sickly, but she could add a few pounds.

The waiter was a young Korean American kid with a Jersey accent. As he cleared the table Simon asked, "What's a delicious, authentic dessert?"

"Coming right up," he said, with confidence. "Coffee?"

"Of course."

Eleanor asked for spiced tea.

Five minutes later he was back with small plate of sesame honey bars. Eleanor took a bite of one, turned up her nose, and sipped tea.

Simon asked, "Were we finished with the conversation about your arrangements?"

"I don't know. Were we? I'm not sure about this cremation thing. Could I still be buried next to Harry? He and I never talked much about resting peacefully in the same plot, side by side." Her eyes watered again.

Simon listened with a smile. He knew for certain that he and Paula would not spend eternity anywhere near each other. He said, "I'm sure you can be placed next to Harry."

She said, "But there won't be a casket or anything. Just a little vase or box or—"

"An urn. A cremation urn. There are thousands to choose from. It's a much simpler way to go and also cheaper."

"Well, let me think about it."

"There's no rush, Netty."

"I certainly hope not," she said with a laugh that was too loud.

CHAPTER 13

On a perfect spring day in late May, Simon left the office at four with Matilda fighting the phone. He was grateful it was still ringing, though the racket meant there would be a stack of calls to return in the morning. For some unknown reason, his practice had hit a busy cycle after the latest lull and there were some nice fees. But the divorce was looming and would consume money he didn't have. And the situation at Chub's had not improved. Betting on NBA games was proving, once again, to be more challenging than the NCAA.

He really wanted to play nine holes of golf for the first time in weeks, but soccer was calling. Janie's under-10 team, Slash, had yet another game at the sports complex, a place he was learning to loathe. But he didn't dare skip it because Janie would know before the start that he wasn't there. Paula, of course, would arrive early, in part to prove she was the more diligent parent. Who cared? They weren't fighting over custody.

He found the field, one of a dozen, all with games raging, and saw Paula standing alone at one end.

"What's the score?" he asked as he stood beside her without looking at her.

"One–zip. Janie scored a goal in the first thirty seconds. You missed it."

"Chalk up another one for you."

"She's really quite good. Her coach wants her to play on a summer travel team."

Simon's shoulders sagged a bit as he exhaled with frustration. "A travel team? There goes the summer. How many games?"

"Dozens. Six weekend tournaments. Washington, Baltimore, Charlotte, Atlanta, can't remember the rest."

"Great. And I suppose you've already said yes."

"No. She mentioned it for the first time this morning at breakfast."

"How much?"

"Forty-two hundred."

"You must be kidding."

"Nope. Fancy uniforms, travel, tournament fees, the works. Plus, a paid coach."

"A paid coach? She's nine years old, Paula."

"Yes. I know."

They had yet to look at one another. A month or so earlier they had sat together in the bleachers and a little chat grew somewhat testy. It was best if they stayed away from the other fans.

He said, "And I'm sure Janie wants to spend her summer playing soccer."

"I think so. Her therapist says she wants to stay away from the house as much as possible."

"Her therapist?"

"Yes. She's had two sessions."

"Why didn't I know this?"

"You haven't been home. I'm raising the kids now. Solo, it seems."

He wanted to start yelling and cursing loudly but figured that might disrupt the game and embarrass his daughter. Plus, it would only give Paula more ammunition. He had to stay cool at all times. He ground his teeth and made himself smile.

"How much for the therapist?"

"Two-fifty an hour." Same rate as the Honorable Simon F. Latch, Attorney and Counselor at Law. He swallowed hard and asked, with as much sarcasm as possible, "Anybody else in the family seeing a shrink, other than you and Janie?"

"Not at this time. I'm going to protect the children, Simon. Whatever it takes."

"As if I'm trying to harm them?"

"The divorce will do enough damage."

"And the divorce is a mutual undertaking, right? We both want out and have agreed to get a divorce."

"The sooner the better."

The soccer ball bounced nearby, out of play, and Janie scooped it up for the inbounds. "Nice work, Janie! Atta girl!" Simon yelled intensely. Of course, his encouragement was not acknowledged. He glanced at Paula and she rolled her eyes in disgust. What a bitch. He couldn't even cheer properly.

Simon knew that the odds of Janie earning a single dollar playing soccer were about as slim as him winning billion-dollar verdicts against Big Pharma. But his dreams were over. Janie's were only beginning.

"Any comments about the property settlement agreement?" he asked, changing the subject to something other than soccer. Why did he pick the PSA?

She sighed and glanced around to check on their privacy. "Is this really the place?"

"No one's listening. You want me to stop by the house and discuss it in front of the kids?"

"Who prepared it?"

"I did. I told you I would."

"Figures. I'll feel better if I have my own lawyer to review the agreement. And I don't trust any lawyer around here because you know them all."

"Of course I know them all. Sorta goes with being in the profession. And just because I know a lawyer doesn't mean I trust him. In fact, I distrust at least half of the lawyers in town and don't like most of them."

"I'll find one."

"Great. And pay him or her five grand to nitpick a PSA that is straightforward, fair, and includes everything we've already agreed to?"

"You're raising your voice, Simon, please."

The game dragged on as Simon boiled and Paula seethed and both wanted to walk away but neither would be the first to leave. Janie would know instantly if one of them left. Late in the game she scored a third goal. Simon faked a cheer while wondering how much it might cost him. When the ball went out of bounds at the other end, he turned and walked away without another word.

CHAPTER 14

The following week, a rather belligerent gentleman, badly dressed and reeking of alcohol, made a noisy entrance into the reception area of the law office of Wally Thackerman, across Main Street from Simon's building.

Fran, the secretary, who had years of experience handling riffraff from the street, sized him up quickly and asked, "May I help you?"

"I wanna see Wally Thackerman, the lawyer," he demanded.

"Do you have an appointment?"

"Aren't you in charge of appointments? Sure you are, and if you were doing a half-ass job you'd know that I don't have an appointment. And I'm not leaving either."

"Okay. May I have your name and the nature of your business."

"Name's Clyde Korsak and my business ain't none of your business."

"Well, be that as it may, Mr. Thackerman is with a client right now. I'll be happy to make an appointment for tomorrow, say around three P.M."

"Oh how efficient. I'm not coming back tomorrow because I'm not leaving today. I'll see the sonofabitch right now because I'm not going away."

Wally happened to be in his firm's library, which was closer to the front than his office, and when he heard a loud, aggressive voice he inched forward to investigate. "Everything okay, Fran?" He was peeking around from the hallway.

"You Thackerman?" the man snarled.

"Well, yes, I'm Walter Thackerman. And who are you, sir?"

"I'm Clyde Korsak, stepson of Eleanor Barnett, and we need to talk."

———— •◦• ————

Fran hurriedly made fresh coffee, not that Clyde wanted any, but it seemed necessary at the moment. Wally got him situated in the library, at the big table, and managed some small talk as they waited for the coffee.

The man was frightening. He had reluctantly entered his fifties but was still clinging to his thirties, with long, thick, oily, badly dyed dark hair that fell to his shoulders, much like a washed-up 1980s rocker still touring the small venues. Gaudy tattoos covered both forearms, and some sort of green spider was crawling up his neck. He had patches of wrinkles around his red, puffy eyes, and layers across his forehead. Cheap trinkets hung around his wrists. Both ears were adorned with gold crosses. An ancient black leather jacket. Biker's boots.

Wally thought about calling the police before they sat down.

Clyde said, "Momma says you're giving her advice on her will and such."

Momma? When Wally counseled Eleanor Barnett he had certainly quizzed her about children, the usual questions. She had none. Wally could vaguely recall a reference to a child or two belonging to Harry Korsak, but there were no details.

Rattled, Wally said, "Well, I, uh, sir, I don't recall Eleanor saying anything about having children. I'm certain she said she has none."

"You're a damned liar."

"I am not. You said you are a stepson?"

"I am, me and my brother. Momma raised us, with Daddy's help of course." His red eyes glowed at Wally, who was becoming more unsettled.

Clyde said, "Momma says you been working on a will and testament for her. That right?"

Wally puffed up with ethical indignation and said, "Look, sir, I cannot discuss anything Ms. Barnett said to me. It's confidential and privileged. She's my client and I will not discuss her legal affairs."

Clyde seemed ready to explode just as Fran walked in with a pot of coffee, two mugs, and a chirpy "Here, gentlemen. Fresh coffee."

It was awkwardly poured and thoroughly ignored. She asked Wally, "Shall I take notes?"

Great idea. She had never taken notes during a client conference, but this one called for different rules of engagement. Wally might need a witness, or worse, an able body to call 911. Fran sat at the end of the table with her pen ready. Clyde paid no attention to her.

He demanded, "Did you write Momma a new will?"

"Sir, divulging client information is grounds for disbarment. I could lose my law license."

Clyde laughed and sneered and said, "Well, aren't you quite the little smart-ass? How about your teeth? Have you thought about losing some of your teeth? Coupla pints of blood."

Wally managed to deflect the threat, or at least pretended to. "She can tell you but I cannot. Have you asked her?"

"Yeah, I did, but she don't remember, says you put so much bullshit legal talk in the will that she's not sure who gets what. I'm entitled to a chunk of that money because my Daddy made it. He had the brains, not that old bag."

For a split second, Wally made eye contact with Fran and delivered the message: *Call the police.* Fran tapped a key. Help was on the way, supposedly.

From a pocket deep in his leather jacket, Clyde whipped out a pistol, a small, shiny black automatic, and he laid it on the table in front of him without commenting on it. No comments were needed. Wally looked at it and felt faint. Fran tapped the keys again and again.

Oddly enough, she would recall that her first thought was somewhat comforting if purely selfish: he would shoot Wally first, and in doing so might give her a second or two to flee. But, she was immediately embarrassed by such an awful thought and told no one about it.

Clyde said, "I want to see Momma's will."

As calmly as possible, Wally said, "Put the gun away, Mr. Korsak, unless you want to go to prison."

"Ha! I've already been there. Prison ain't no big deal."

"Put the gun away, sir."

"Daddy never told us how much money he made and he damned sure didn't share it with us."

"Please put the gun away."

"Maybe I'm not finished with it. I want to see that will."

"It's not here. I keep my clients' wills in a vault at the bank."

"Oh, how clever. And now the banks are closed, right? So if I come back in the morning you will be happy to walk with me over to the bank and look at the will, right?"

"Sure, if I get permission from Eleanor."

"Got an answer for everything don't you?"

Clyde reached for one of the coffee mugs and seemed ready to take a sip when he suddenly flung the coffee at Wally. The cup was full and the coffee was hot and it splashed across Wally's white shirt and onto his face before he could react. He yelled "Oh shit!" and Clyde yelled "You little son of a bitch!" and Fran screamed "Stop that right now!" But Clyde lunged at Wally and slapped him hard across the nose with the back of his hand, knocking him out of his chair and onto the floor where he tried to scramble but Clyde was all over him flailing away. Both men were in their fifties but Clyde had been in far more fistfights than Wally. Clyde cursed and growled as he pummeled away and seemed determined to kill the lawyer with his bare hands when, suddenly, a shot rang out. It sounded like a cannon and both men froze.

Fran had the pistol and was aiming at the ceiling, where the first bullet had gone.

"Get out of here," she yelled at Clyde, who slowly got to his feet, gawking at the gun. Wally crawled under the table and surfaced on the other side. His nose was bleeding profusely.

"Get out of here," she repeated and sort of waved the gun at the door.

"Gimme the gun," Clyde said, but less forcefully.

"Oh, I'll give it to you all right. You want one between your eyes or between your balls?"

Clyde flinched instinctively.

She said, "Leave now. I'll give the gun to the police when they get here in just a minute. My son's a cop."

He was not but it sounded authentic. Maybe Clyde thought it was true, and perhaps her son had taught her how to shoot a pistol. At any rate, it was time to get out, with everything intact.

"I'll be back," he snarled like a bad actor and disappeared, slamming the front door behind him.

————◆◆◆————

Simon was sleeping as usual at 5:30 A.M. when his cell phone rattled next to his cot. It was Matilda, who had never, for any reason, called at such an hour. She said, "You might want to take a look at the *Gazette* online. Seems your pal Wally Thackerman was assaulted in his office late yesterday afternoon. He's still in the hospital but expected to be released."

"Go on."

"Does the name Clyde Korsak ring a bell? Seems to, vaguely."

"Yes, he's Eleanor Barnett's stepson. You remember her? Came a few months back, looking for a will."

"Oh yeah. I thought we closed that file."

Not quite. "Couldn't make up her mind. Dementia. A widow with two stepsons who want some money."

"Well, he's in jail charged with the assault. Wonder why he beat up Wally?"

"Who knows? I guess it's a dangerous profession."

"Be careful. See you at eight-thirty."

The *Gazette* was the town daily that was thick on shopping coupons and thin on news, not that there was much to report anyway, other than obituaries and football scores. The mauling of a local lawyer was too good to ignore and the headline screamed: "LAWYER ATTACKED IN OFFICE. ARREST MADE."

The word "attacked" was far more sensational than "assaulted." There was an old photo of the Honorable Walter Thackerman taken from a bar directory, but no mug shot of the attacker. He was identified as Clyde Korsak; address, age, employment, all unknown. He was charged with aggravated assault and various weapons violations, as well as public drunkenness and resisting arrest. His bond was $250,000, pretty steep for the alleged crimes, but then the victim was a lawyer and the profession had to protect itself. The accused was scheduled to appear in court later in the day.

Simon put on his robe and went downstairs to the office kitchen where he made a pot of coffee and tried to digest the news. He had to talk to Eleanor but would wait until a decent hour. It was a shocking event that could spiral in many directions. Nothing good could come of the assault.

However, as he listened to the coffee maker hiss and drip, he managed to find some humor. Poor Wally had just had the shit beaten out of him for drafting a will that had now been quietly revoked, and neither he nor his "attacker" had a clue.

Then the humor passed. There would be so many complications.

He poured a cup, took it to his office, turned on his desktop, and began reading the comments to the story.

Jacknut: *"I say we form a mob and attack all law offices. Take up arms, patriots! Gotta protect ourselves from the law and the lawyers!"*

Ole Possum: *"Why such an outrageous bond, for assault? Hell, murderers get less than that. Could it be another case of the legal system bending over to take care of its own?"*

Katty Kate: *"It's about time somebody busted up that little twerp. Ten years ago he screwed my family out of some property in a bad land deal. He should've gone to prison a long time ago."*

Slasher: *"Six years ago I was in a car wreck and made the mistake of hiring Wally Thackerman to sue the insurance company. He forgot about the case and allowed the statute of limitations to expire. We ultimately settled our dispute in a confidential manner that allowed him to keep his license. I wouldn't hire this guy to sweep my floors."*

Finally, Miss Preen wrote: *"Knock it off you people. Wally is a real dear who's been my lawyer for many years. I do hope his injuries are not serious."*

————————

Three cups later, Simon finally called Eleanor, at precisely 8 A.M. By the fourth ring he was once again wondering what she was doing with her cell phone. She struggled with it. Butt-dials were common. It was not unusual to get cut off midsentence, and Simon was expected to redial immediately and apologize for the interruption. She often forgot to wear her hearing aids and yelled into the phone while requiring him to practically yell back. At least half of his calls to her went unanswered, and he had quickly learned to stay away from voicemails.

A weak "Hello" finally came across.

"Good morning, Eleanor, this is Simon. Are you okay?"

"Not really. Have you heard?"

"Yes, that's why I'm calling. Have you seen Clyde?"

"Unfortunately, yes. We need to talk, Simon. I need some help. He's already called three times this morning and wants money, twenty-five thousand, to get out of jail. And he's very mean about it. I think he's dangerous."

Evidently.

He said, "Eleanor, I'm happy to drive over to your house right now and talk about this."

"No. I'll come to your office." She seemed firm about this.

"Very well. Anytime this morning is fine with me. The sooner the better."

"Okay. I'm dressed and ready. I'll be there in half an hour."

"That's fine. Matilda will be here so be careful what you say to her."

"Who's Matilda?"

CHAPTER 15

The last she'd heard from Clyde, he was in Iraq working for the United Nations and trying to clean up the postwar mess over there. He said he was in a real danger zone, heard gunfire every day, and just wanted to check in with Eleanor so she would know he was doing something important. That had been years earlier. As usual, she didn't believe a word of it. A phone call from nowhere almost always led to another one in which he asked for money.

Two nights ago he had called, said he was passing through, and asked to sleep on the sofa. Before she could say no or stall or do anything to avoid him, he was at the front door, banging away. Their history was complicated, filled with tension and distrust, and completely centered on the fact that he was a con man who'd never had a real job, was constantly broke and usually one step ahead of the law, and for the past twenty years had been convinced that Harry, his father, had left behind a pile of money for his widow. He was right about that, though Eleanor had never confirmed it. Harry had been adamant that neither Clyde nor his brother, Jerry, receive a dime of his money.

She fixed him a bowl of tomato soup, which he drank, then two more. As always, he ate like a pig and wiped his mouth with his sleeve. Eleanor told him he could not sleep on the sofa or anywhere else in the house, for that matter, and they argued. She was physically afraid of him and thought about calling the police. Instead, she retreated to her bedroom, locked the door, and spent a sleepless night peeking through the blinds to see if his car left the driveway. It did not. When she ventured out early the next morning, Clyde had made himself at home in the kitchen with a pot of coffee and the morning paper.

They spoke and things were cordial but forced. Then she realized she had forgotten to lock the door to her small study where she kept a desk and some file cabinets. The door was partially open. There were two wills: the first prepared by Wally Thackerman and signed by Eleanor four months earlier, and the second prepared by Simon two months ago. The second revoked and negated the first, though poor Wally had no clue. Both were locked in a fireproof safe, along with the deed to her home, car title, burial policy, disability policy, life policy, and a few other papers that she thought were important. The safe was hidden in the bottom of her closet.

On the desk in her study was a neat stack of current bills and a tray of letters and articles and other papers she had chosen not to throw away yet, though almost all would get tossed in a year or so. In the center drawer was her checkbook, issued by Security Bank, and showing a balance of just over $3,100. The drawer was unlocked and would have been an easy target for anyone nosy enough to be browsing.

She did not offer breakfast, though he mentioned at least twice that he was hungry. She mustered the courage to tell him, rather bluntly, that he was overstaying his welcome and it was time to leave. He asked to borrow $5,000 and she flatly refused. He finally stormed out, and she immediately called the locksmith and changed every lock in the house, with the exception of her hidden safe.

On her desk, in the mail tray, under at least two inches of miscellaneous correspondence and other papers, the majority of which she could not remember why she was keeping, she found the problem. It was a letter from the law offices of Walter J. Thackerman, and it read, in part: "I called twice yesterday and once the day before. Let's meet next Tuesday at three P.M. in my office to finalize your last will and testament."

At this point in her narrative, Simon could not help but interrupt. "Any stray letters from me lying around on your desk, Netty?"

"Oh no. I checked."

He was relieved. He did not want to live the next few months with a pistol in his pocket or within reach.

She went on to explain the obvious: Clyde had searched through her desk during the night and found the letter. After he left, she carefully went through every other piece of paper in her study and found nothing else that might cause problems. Then she threw it all away. "Just junk, stuff I didn't need.

"What am I going to do, Simon?" she asked, pleading. "He's sitting over there in jail and there's no one to help him."

"Let him sit, Netty. He's been there before and he deserves it now. The man is dangerous. He carries a gun and he's desperate."

"Can he get his gun back?"

"I doubt it."

"Will he go to jail?"

"More than likely. Judges take a dim view of thugs who attack lawyers in their own offices. Plus, he's a felon with a firearm. He'll serve some time."

"Well, I guess that's a good thing. He scares me."

"Will his brother bail him out?"

"I don't know. Jerry lives down in Florida somewhere and they're not that close, or at least they were not way back then."

Matilda had kicked off her heels and was tiptoeing around the building, listening in all the good places. However, Simon and Ms. Barnett were in a small conference room with thick carpet and vents in the floor. The voices didn't carry.

Simon said, at low volume, "Don't answer the phone, Netty, and don't go anywhere near the jail. And please don't talk to Wally, should he call."

"Why would Wally call?"

"I don't know, but he's probably quite concerned with the will and the notoriety. If word gets out that he got attacked because he prepared the last will for a client whose stepson is unhappy, then the will becomes an issue. The last thing Wally wants is for anyone to know what's in that will. Don't forget, Netty, that he provided for himself, to the tune of almost a half a million dollars in cash."

"I'm confused. That will is no longer valid, right?"

"It's not valid, it's not invalid. It's just sitting there waiting for you to die."

"Oh dear."

"Sorry to be so blunt. A will is not valid until it is probated after death. The will I prepared for you expressly revokes the will Wally prepared, so his will becomes invalid. Of course, he doesn't know that."

"It seems only fair that we tell him. I mean, he just got beat up over nothing."

"He just got beat up because Clyde is an idiot. No, the law does not require you or me or anyone to tell Wally that you have prepared a new will that revokes the one he prepared."

"It seems awfully deceitful."

"Perhaps, but there are reasons for it. And, sadly, there are plenty of laws that appear to be deceitful but are really necessary."

"If you say so, Simon. I'm trusting you."

———◦◦►———

Simon was desperately needed in court. Not to represent a client and certainly not to help grind the wheels of justice, but to just be there because most of the bar would be there out of curiosity. He knew the lawyers, the courthouse regulars who hung around hoping to pick up a stray client here and there, and while they waited they never hesitated to pass along the latest gossip. In eighteen years, Simon had never heard of anything so sensational—the beating of a lawyer in his own office.

Some twenty years earlier, when Simon was in law school, a well-known divorce lawyer had been caught having sex with a female client on the sofa in his office, his "fee couch." Things spiraled when other women came forth. He lost his license, left town in a hurry, and was last heard of living the good life as a fishing guide in Montana. Simon thought of the guy often, especially during the dreary days when the highlight was another appearance in bankruptcy court.

He could think of no other office drama, though he was sure he would hear of something when he stopped by the courtroom. He had to be there. He had to know if anyone had linked the attacker, Clyde Korsak, to Wally's wealthy client, Eleanor Barnett. Plus, he was curious about Wally's injuries. How badly had he been beaten?

It seemed as though his injuries were not that serious. By the nine-thirty docket call for first appearances in criminal cases, something Simon never attended, the word was out that Wally had been released after an overnight stay in the hospital. Broken nose, some cuts and bruises, slight concussion. "No additional brain damage" was the humorous assessment among his loyal brethren in the bar. The real humor came from the various accounts of Fran grabbing the pistol and firing a shot into the ceiling. One of the assistant prosecutors was spreading the story that the cops heard the shot as they approached Wally's office, and caught the attacker when he stumbled off the porch, drunk as a skunk.

Simon hung around for an hour, long enough to be satisfied that the gossip had not connected Eleanor Barnett to Clyde Korsak. He remained in jail and finally stopped calling his stepmother.

Two days later, Simon was back in the courtroom, milling around as usual, swapping jokes with the bailiffs and clerks, when Clyde was hauled in for his first appearance. Three nights in jail had done nothing to improve his looks, though the orange county jumpsuit was probably cleaner than the clothes he'd worn into the jail. He was unshaven, unclean, unrepentant. He scowled at the judge as if he'd slap her if given the chance, and conveyed an air of being thoroughly unbothered by the jail and the legal proceedings. His young, green public defender stood by his side, but not that close, and told the judge that Mr. Korsak was unemployed, had no money with which to either hire a lawyer or make his bond, and had no real assets, other than his car that had been impounded by the police. His bond was excessive and should be reduced substantially.

"Does he have an address?" the judge asked.

"Your Honor, my client is currently staying with a friend in the Baltimore area."

"That's vague enough. I see he has a criminal record."

"Yes, Your Honor, but that was for a nonviolent crime many years ago. And, it was supposed to have been expunged."

"Well, whatever the case, it has not been expunged."

Clyde decided to help with "The lawyer dropped the ball, Judge. He was a crook."

"I see. The bond will not be reduced at this time. Mr. Korsak, I remand you to the custody of the police."

"Thanks for nothing," Clyde mumbled as the bailiffs led him away. Simon was close enough to realize he wanted no part of the defendant. He had beaten Wally senseless and would enjoy drawing blood from another lawyer.

———————•♦•———————

Eleanor was calling several times a day, always on Simon's private cell phone, and so far he'd been able to keep the conversations away from Matilda, whose radar was on high alert. Eleanor was agitated and frightened and convinced Clyde would soon get out of jail and show up for more trouble. His last voicemails were harsh and threatening.

Simon saw the opportunity to make himself indispensable. He was also worried about Wally. There was little doubt he would reach out to Eleanor and discuss the trouble, and in doing so have another chat about her will. She assured Simon that she and Wally had not spoken in months.

The idea was to get Eleanor out of town for a few days, not far, but to some pleasant location where she would be safely tucked away. Simon knew just the spot. There was a lovely lake in the Blue Ridge Mountains, half an hour from Braxton, near the Maryland state line. Two small hotels hugged Lake Murray and were popular weekend getaways for older couples. The restaurants were okay, as were the spas. It was the perfect place to relax and get lost for a few days. Eleanor loved the idea but was afraid to reserve a room in her name. Clyde might somehow track her down. So Simon used his secret credit card to secure a room at $400 a night.

After lunch in a taco hut, he followed her home, which was an adventure in itself. Netty had no business behind the wheel of a car, but he was not sure how to broach the subject. She rarely took her foot off the brake and never used a signal light. Stop signs were either unnoticed, ignored outright, or taken as mere suggestions. Twice during the ten-minute drive she drew angry horn blasts from some really pissed-off drivers, but seemed not to hear them. When she finally stopped in her driveway and turned off the engine, Simon was able to start breathing again.

Her house was virtually identical to every other one on the street, and the next street, and the next five. Two thousand square feet of cookie-cutter suburban sprawl headed east toward D.C. She instructed him to wait by the lamppost near the front sidewalk as she went inside, determined to keep him out of her house. He found her behavior odd. What was she hiding in there? Given her car, her wardrobe, and now her home, it was obvious Eleanor Barnett had never spent money and perhaps did not know how. Had she and old Harry pinched pennies so long they knew nothing else?

Or, as he'd asked himself before, was it all a charade to keep the money hidden? One thing was certain: If she lived the life she could truly afford, she wouldn't last long in these parts. Staring at the endless rows of identical houses, Simon had to admit he rather admired Eleanor for living such an unassuming life.

CHAPTER 16

Simon loaded her suitcase into the trunk of his car and they drove away. Glancing at the rows of identical houses, he said, "And you and Harry moved here ten years ago?"

"Something like that. I'm not good with dates and such. The house was brand-new and we had just settled in when he suddenly passed. It was just awful."

"I'm so sorry. And you moved here from Atlanta."

"That's right. I never liked Atlanta, too big, too much traffic." Over their series of lunches he had learned that she was from a small town near Nashville and met Harry while vacationing with some friends near Destin. They settled in Atlanta.

"Why'd you move here?" Simon asked.

"Good question. Harry had just retired and we were looking to change scenery. We liked the mountains and a nicer climate. Houses were cheap, or at least a lot cheaper than the other places we looked at."

Cheap. A word she used frequently. Ten years ago when Harry died he was around the age of sixty-nine and had spent a long career working for Coke, where, as her story went, he had secured all the shares of stock available to him and socked them away. Add the Wal-Mart stock. So, as the guessing went, at the time of his death he had substantial net worth. Why, then, would they have been so hung up on buying a cheaper house?

Simon reminded himself that he probably spent too much time analyzing her story and trying to understand her finances. There was an excellent chance that Harry, a "Depression kid," was just plain stingy and cheap, and after twenty or so years of marriage Eleanor had picked up the same habits. She had never referred to herself as being poor as a child. "Modest" was her favorite description. Perhaps she, too, had been raised in a family that was extremely frugal.

And there was always the chance that the money was not there. This thought hit Simon from time to time and made him nervous. However, it was still difficult to understand why a person as modest and unassuming as Eleanor would create the fiction that she was worth millions. What could she possibly gain from such a charade?

There was no answer, but Simon, once again, vowed to keep digging.

Her phone rang. She found it deep in her bag, managed to untangle it, took a look and said, "Oh dear. It's Wally. What should I do?"

Simon knew exactly what to do. He wanted to hear the conversation. "You'd better talk to him. Tell him you're out of town for a few days. Put him on speaker. I'll listen but stay quiet."

She looked thoroughly confused as the phone rang for the fifth time. She tapped it and said, "Hello."

"Eleanor, it's me, Wally. How ya doing?"

"Well, I'm fine, Wally, and how are you?"

"I'm okay. I guess you've seen the news and all that. Had a little scrape with Clyde Korsak a few days ago. Have you seen him lately?"

She looked at Simon who gave a quick nod.

"Why yes. He stopped by the house a few days ago. I haven't seen him in years. We're not close, you know?"

"Right. Well, he came to my office that afternoon, said he wanted to talk about your will, wanted to see it. I explained that

I could not discuss such matters. He was drunk and belligerent, pulled a gun and made threats. It was a bad scene, Eleanor. Then he jumped me and threw some punches."

"I'm so sorry, Wally. Are you okay?"

"I'm fine. He's still in jail. Have you talked to him since?"

"Oh he's called once or twice. I'm out of town for a few days."

A long pause as Wally apparently wondered where she was. "Not a bad idea, really. Here's the question for you, Eleanor. Since I'd never met Clyde before, how did he know I prepared your last will? Did you tell him? I can't believe you would do something like that."

"Oh no, Wally, I said nothing about you. As you cautioned me, my will is top secret. I wouldn't tell a soul." She shot a guilty look at Simon, as if he was somehow to blame for something.

"That's strange. I wonder how Clyde knows that I represent you."

"Beats me. I haven't said a word."

"Okay. Well, be careful. And when you're back in town let's get together and review your will. It's been almost six months."

"Yes, it has."

She ended the call and cradled her phone in her lap. Nothing was said for a long time. "I feel deceitful, Simon. I don't like it."

"Netty, if you tell Wally about your new will, he'll go nuts and demand that the two of you sit down and work things out. He'll call me and make threats. It'll be a disaster."

"I guess so."

Another mile passed in silence. There was so much to say, but the thoughts were scrambled. Finally, she asked, "How long will Clyde stay in jail?"

"Don't know. Aggravated assault carries up to ten years. I suspect, though, that when Wally comes to his senses he may drop the charges."

"I don't understand."

"That's right. The last thing Wally needs is for your will to become public. He did a very bad thing when he included a direct cash gift to himself, and not a small one at that. If that became known, and if you said that you were not aware of the gift, then Wally could face disciplinary charges from the state bar."

"This is all very confusing, Simon. What if I had not signed a new will, the one you prepared? And then I pass on, and then Wally presents, or probates, the will he prepared, with the gift to him? At that point the gift would be made known, right?"

"Right."

"So wouldn't he get in trouble anyway? I don't understand all this."

"Well, it doesn't make sense, really. Yes, Wally would probably get in trouble, but he was willing to roll the dice. He would be the attorney for your estate and the trustee for the trusts he established in your will. He would be in a great position to handle a lot of money. I think Wally just saw the opportunity and couldn't resist the temptation."

Simon tried not to sound pious. He, too, had seen the opportunity and had not resisted the temptation. True, Wally was bolder and greedier, but Simon's will certainly took care of Simon. He tried not to fantasize over the fees but it was impossible not to.

"It's all gobbledygook."

Worse than that, Simon thought.

———— ◆•◆ ————

Robin's Retreat was a small hotel on the shores of Lake Murray. It was nestled at the bottom of some rolling foothills, far away from the busy marina and its bars and restaurants. Simon helped with the check-in and waited in the lobby for half an hour while Netty prepped for lunch. They ate regular American food, on a deck with waves gently lapping the small boats five feet away.

"How's the room?" he asked.

"It's lovely. A beautiful view of the water. Thanks for bringing me here, Simon."

"Stay a few days and let's see what happens with Clyde. I'll keep my ear to the ground around the courthouse, something I do every day anyway. I'll talk to the police and prosecutor and if I hear something important I'll let you know."

"I packed two books to read."

"Perfect. Take it easy, get some rest, go to the spa for a massage if you like. I'm kinda envious."

"You've been here?"

"Once, many years ago. Paula and I had an anniversary and spent two nights here, a great time."

It was not. They fought and bickered and left a day early.

A few more bites and he glanced at his watch, one of those deliberate moves designed to inform the person on the other side of the table that he suddenly had better things to do. "I need to be going, Netty. Gotta big meeting at three."

"I'll be fine here, Simon. You run along."

"Call me if you need anything."

"Thanks so much. You're such a dear."

———————— ◦◦► ————————

He called her twice a day through the weekend and everything was swell. On Monday morning, he took a call from Robin's Retreat about a rather unusual matter. Seemed as though the hotel routinely checked the credit backgrounds of guests who were not regulars. Since Simon's credit card had never been used before at the hotel, and since the guest, Ms. Barnett, was charging everything to the room, the hotel called Visa. With the room rate, plus in-room dining three times a day, plus several visits to the spa, in addition to the hefty occupancy, tourism, and food and beverages taxes, Ms. Barnett was racking up $1,200 day. According to Visa, his limit was $10,000, which she had blown through the day before. The current balance at the hotel was slightly more than $4,100. The card's previous balance was almost $7,000, which included some online betting, which, thankfully, Visa did not reveal.

Simon gasped for breath and tried to explain that he clearly

told the clerk at check-in that all charges were to be paid by the
guest, Eleanor Barnett. His credit card had been used only to
reserve the room. After holding for an eternity, the general manager came back with the report that Ms. Barnett had specifically
instructed the hotel to charge everything to Mr. Latch. This happened after he left.

Simon steamed until noon, and as soon as Tillie left he raced
to his car and headed for Murray Lake. He found her in the restaurant. She was thrilled to see him and invited him to lunch, as
if she were treating. When the check arrived, the waitress, who
was very friendly, said, "Here it is, Ms. Barnett." As if she stayed
there every week.

Simon watched her sign the check, then asked, "Did you
charge lunch to your room?"

A sweet smile. "Why yes. I thought you told me to."

"Okay, but I also told you to use your credit card for all charges.
The hotel manager called this morning and said your bill is over
four thousand dollars. It's on my credit card, not yours."

"But you told me to use your card so no one can find me here.
I'm sorta hiding, right? It was your idea."

It was his idea, from start to finish, and at that moment he was
not sure that he had been perfectly clear with Netty about who
was to pay. He kept smiling and nodding as if everything was fine,
he had plenty of money, the big-shot lawyer. "I'm sorry if I wasn't
clear, Netty, but you can certainly afford to pay for your little stay
here."

"You lawyers. All you think about is money."

"That's not true." But of course it was, especially since Simon
had no money. He had already decided to play it tough because he
was right, and because he was determined not to get bullied into
paying a bill that was pocket change for Eleanor Barnett.

He said, "Why don't you get packed while I talk to the general
manager."

"I have to leave?"

"Yes. It's time to go home."

Her eyes watered but Simon didn't care. When she finally

made it to the reception desk, an hour later, he and a clerk were waiting. Reluctantly, she handed over a Visa credit card. The clerk ran it through as they waited and waited for the charges to clear. Finally, the clerk smiled and Simon grabbed her suitcase.

Another financial crisis averted.

CHAPTER 17

For the next two weeks things were quiet as Clyde remained in jail and Netty fell back into her routine of doing almost nothing. Simon filed bankruptcy petitions by the pound and was busier than ever. He and Paula continued their silent war as they ignored each other and hoped that something would force them to sign the divorce papers.

Each morning, Simon checked with his source at the jail to make sure Clyde was still there. Each afternoon, he checked with a secretary in the prosecutor's office to monitor any activity in the case. The secretary was thirty-five, divorced, and a legendary flirt. She was on his list, if he could ever find the time or energy to chase women again.

The gossip finally died down, without a peep about a suspicious will prepared by Wally. As far as Simon could tell, Eleanor's name had not been linked to the story of the "attack." Nor had his. There was also gossip that Wally's nose was as big as a football and his entire face was rainbow-colored as the bruises matured and blended together. He was hiding, with his cases being continued while he was on medical leave.

Fran enjoyed a brief moment of fame as the fearless secretary who'd fired away and threatened to castrate Clyde with a single bullet. The backstory was that she had been raised with three older brothers who hunted year-round, with or without proper licenses. Any deer was always in season. She had killed her first buck when she was thirteen.

Behind the scenes, though, Wally was working a deal, as Simon predicted. He offered to drop all charges but a simple assault if Clyde agreed to leave town and never return. It would be a misdemeanor, nothing permanent on his record, with one year suspended. No fine. Just get out of town. Clyde jumped at the deal, and after eighteen days walked out. He never answered a question from a cop, never spoke to anyone about the incident. He got in his old car and left town, leaving nothing behind but a few stitches in Wally's face.

———— ◆ ◆ ————

Simon returned to the office after another hectic day in bankruptcy court. He was pleasant enough to Tillie, who, as always, was busy with a mountain of paperwork. He took off his jacket and tie and settled behind his desk to check his phone calls. Tillie walked through the door as she tapped it and said, "You need to call Eleanor Barnett. Says it's an emergency."

Simon looked at his phone, the only one Netty was supposed to call, and saw nothing from her. "What's the emergency?" he asked.

"Something about going to court this afternoon. She didn't say much."

"Okay. Thanks."

Tillie turned and left the office, but not before he noticed that she was losing weight and looking better than she had in years. Evidently, the asparagus and celery shakes were working, along with a full hour in the gym each morning. Go girl.

She closed the door and Simon tapped a key. "It's about time you called," Netty snapped, quite irritated. "I've been calling all morning."

"Hello Netty. I guess my phone is on the blink. It's not showing any calls from you."

"Perhaps you need a new phone," she snapped again.

A new phone cost a thousand dollars and Simon was not ready to spring for one. Besides, the one he was holding was working just fine. He had a hunch why her calls were not coming through, but it was not the time to bicker. "What's going on, Netty?"

"I'm in court this afternoon at four and I think I might need a lawyer."

The only court in session at 4 P.M. on a Wednesday afternoon was the city traffic court. "Okay, what's the case about?"

"Well, this really rude policeman pulled me over and gave me a ticket. I didn't do a thing wrong."

"Why haven't you called me before now?"

"Because I thought I could take care of this, it's all a misunderstanding, you see, but now that I'm here in court it looks like everyone else has a lawyer. Do I need one?"

There were several guys in town who advertised their ability to get traffic tickets reduced or even dismissed, and they usually hung around traffic court hustling people who really didn't need a lawyer.

"What are the charges?"

"I don't know, several. Speeding, I think. Wrong way. Something about an expired license. It's all so confusing. I'm not going to jail, am I, Simon? This is truly frightening."

Speeding seemed unlikely since she drove with one foot on the brake. "I'll be there in fifteen minutes. Don't worry."

The courtroom was four blocks away, in an annex behind city hall. Simon reluctantly put his jacket back on, but not his tie since there was no dress code in traffic court. The judge was a part-timer who had a law license but had never practiced and spent four hours a week refereeing parking and traffic disputes for $500 a month. If he owned a black robe he never wore it.

Simon eased into the crowded courtroom at 3:50 and found Netty in the back row. She was visibly relieved to see him and squeezed his hand. Simon patted hers and whispered, "It'll be okay."

He looked at her ticket and managed to maintain a poker face. Five infractions. It was issued by a Lieutenant Andy Reece, one of several city cops Simon did not know. "Do you see Officer Reece in the courtroom?" he whispered.

"Yes," she said and nodded at a door where several officers were hanging around. "That tall one with red hair."

"Okay, I'll be right back."

Simon walked to the front of the courtroom, spoke to two lawyers he knew, and drifted over to the cops, who were coming and going. He introduced himself to Officer Reece and asked if he had a minute for a chat. Sure. They stepped out of the courtroom and into a hallway. Simon handed him the ticket and he glanced at it. "Oh, her? She's dangerous."

"Can you tell me what happened?"

"Sure. We had radar set up down on Kidder Extended, one way, you know, two blocks behind the Kroger."

"I know the area." It was a notorious speed trap.

"She came busting down the wrong way, clocked her at forty-five in a twenty-five zone. Speeding, reckless, wrong way, no lights, plus expired tags."

"When did they expire?"

"Uh, last week, I believe."

"No lights?"

"Yeah, you see it was raining and her wipers were on. If wipers are on, then lights too."

"Were you solo?"

"Oh, in other words, Do I have a witness?"

"Something like that."

"Yes, I was solo, but I have the video. Dashcam. Slow-motion and living color. Ask me nicely and I'll send you the link."

"Okay. Look, I need to talk to the judge. Any objections if we bump it for a few weeks?"

"No problem here."

It was routine in the city courts to continue cases for a month or so, especially when lawyers got involved.

"Thanks."

"No problem," the officer said. "But, look, has she told you about the other charges?"

"Afraid not."

"Two pending, both moving violations. Ran a red last week, and used a wrong lane two weeks ago. Dashcam, more footage. If this reckless sticks, it's probably time to sell the car."

"Thanks."

Inside the courtroom, Simon stopped by the clerk's desk and filed a short request for a continuance. He and Eleanor left the annex and walked two blocks to a coffee shop where he paid for two cups and they sat in a corner.

With a warm smile, Simon began with "You should've told me about these traffic tickets, Netty. This is more serious than I first thought."

Her eyes watered and she said, "I know. I just didn't want to worry you with them. You've done so much for me. My will, getting me out of town when Clyde was here. I just hate to bother. I know how busy you are."

He kept smiling as he listened, nothing but warmth and understanding. "I'm never too busy to help my clients, Netty. That's what I'm for. Now, who is your insurance agent?"

She frowned, then closed her eyes for a second. "Oh, what's her name? Sells Allstate up north of town, by the mall. I'll think of it."

"I'll find her. This could pose a real problem, Netty. Reckless driving is a serious charge and insurance companies don't like them. Plus you have other charges you never told me about."

"I'm so sorry. Will they take away my license?" The fear was obvious, and Simon felt sorry for her. Mobility was life, and losing it only brought the end closer.

"I don't know but probably not. The bigger problem is losing your insurance. You can't drive if you have no insurance."

"Oh dear."

"But I'll get to work on it. Now, about the expired tags. You've told me that you still pay all of your own bills."

"I do indeed," she bristled. "Every Monday morning, I pay my bills first thing. It's an old habit Harry had."

"I see. So how did you miss the license renewal?"

"I don't know. Something must have fallen through the cracks. It's not a monthly bill, you know?" She was indignant for a moment and tried to seem offended. Then, from nowhere, "Doris wants to do lunch with us. She knows an Indian place out in the country in an old service station. Said the food is great."

Doris was a friend she mentioned occasionally, one of few. Simon wasn't thrilled with the idea of lunching with a stranger. "Is Doris still driving?"

"Oh yes. She's only seventy-nine."

"Married."

"Sort of. Delbert is in a facility, out of it. Hasn't said a word in two years. Really sad. I've told her all about our lunches and she would really like to join us."

"I don't know, Netty. We discuss some pretty serious matters over lunch and there are things we need to decide. Let's wait a while before we include anyone else."

She did not like to be told no and began to pout.

CHAPTER 18

On a glorious Saturday morning in early September, with a chill in the air and the golden leaves falling from the oaks and maples, Simon rose early in The Closet and left to do what he now dreaded: stand away from the crowd and watch his talented nine-year-old daughter chase a soccer ball around the field. Kickoff was eight-thirty, so he arrived ten minutes early to make sure Janie saw him, which she did. Paula had watched the last game. This one was his. The tag-team approach worked because they had no choice.

They had survived the summer travel schedule by taking turns, which meant Simon had spent long weekends in Raleigh, Pittsburgh, and Baltimore. Since Janie was playing in a local recreation league for the fall, all games were at the complex, in the same place. Simon was thankful for small miracles, but it had not been easy. The same guy who'd coached the summer team (at $4,200 per player) was also coaching a fall travel team (another $4,500), with weekend tournaments as far away as Atlanta. Five games guaranteed with dozens of college scouts taking notes as they analyzed ten-year-old athletes. Of course, Janie had been keen to do fall travel, but, in a rare moment of cooperation, both parents said no.

Simon was startled when Paula suddenly said, "I brought you a coffee." She handed him a tall white cup with a lid.

"Thanks. What are you doing here?"

"It wouldn't be a real Saturday without soccer, now would it?"

"I thought you were at a swim meet with Danny."

"He quit."

"Danny quit swimming?"

"He did."

"When?"

"This morning. He wouldn't get out of bed, said he was quitting."

Simon wanted to celebrate. Of all the sports the kids had tried so far, swimming was the worst because it was year-round. Danny had been a fish until he was twelve years old, then the other kids caught up. Now he rarely won a race and was losing his love for the sport.

The ref blew her whistle and the game was on.

"How's Janie's attitude these days?" he asked.

"Who knows? One day she's okay, the next she's in a mood. She's having a rougher time with the divorce than the boys. Our house is a pretty gloomy place these days."

"Then let's get the divorce behind us and move on."

"Move on to where?"

The great question. Where were they going? What was their endgame after splitting the family? Was that supposed to make life fulfilling again? Simon had no answers, nor did Paula, but the only thing they were sure of was that they could not stay together.

She said, "There's something else." Then silence.

Ah, now the real reason for her unscheduled appearance at another soccer game too early on a Saturday morning. He waited without a word, refusing to help her.

"The Glen is being sold, another merger of some variety. I'm not sure what it means for me." She had a master's degree in business administration and earned $72,000 a year as the finance director at a midrange retirement community called The Glen. It

was owned by a large, shifty corporation that changed its name
every three years and had a reputation that was not exactly stellar.

"We had our first round of layoffs yesterday."

"And what are your chances of being laid off?"

"Not sure, but the place is in full panic mode."

The last thing they needed was more uncertainty. Her steady
salary had been the one constant in their otherwise unsteady
finances.

"Any idea when the second round will take place?"

"No. The big boys aren't saying much, probably because they
don't know and they're scared too. The decisions are being made
in San Diego."

"I'm sorry." And he really was. A layoff could only add misery
to what was already a forgettable year. The pressure on him to
produce even more would get ratcheted up. They would probably
be forced to broach the subject of selling their home.

Like clockwork, Janie scored the first goal, a twenty-yard-line
drive that landed high in the net and stunned the other team.
Simon managed to clap his hands together, the proud father. Paula
yelled something that could not be heard.

Regardless of his firm's revenues and expenses, Simon managed to cook the books enough each year to net more than his
wife. It was a matter of pride. He was a lawyer, with seven years
of higher education and membership in an old, honored profession. He was expected to earn big bucks! Never mind the fact that
most of the lawyers up and down Main Street were grunting out a
living and taking home less than a union truck driver.

"Why don't you sign the property settlement so we can get it
filed?"

"Because we need a little cash around the house."

"What else is new?" Simon asked in frustration.

"I will not be reduced to begging you for money, Simon.
These are our children we're talking about."

Kelsey, from the morning coffee club, appeared from nowhere
and went through the silly ritual of quick hugs. She was a horrible

gossip and probably couldn't withstand the temptation to butt into the Latches' latest soccer spat. The rumors of a breakup were rampant and Kelsey, of course, was dying of curiosity and eager to see or hear something she could report to the others. Simon and Paula forced some small talk about the kids and school. Kelsey finally took the hint and said so long.

"They're all watching," Paula said.

"Let's get the divorce filed and be done with it."

"I need twelve thousand dollars, cash."

"For what?"

"Driving lessons for Buck, braces for Danny, piano for Janie, plus a transmission for the car, four thousand there, and a new oven. Give me a check for twelve thousand and I'll sign the property settlement on Monday, at my lawyer's office."

"And who may I ask is your new lawyer?"

"Myrna Covington."

"Never heard of her."

"She's not from around here."

"And how much of the twelve thousand goes for her fees?"

"Can't say. That's privileged."

He mumbled to himself and left. He walked past field after field, game after game, hundreds of happy kids and thousands of proud parents and grandparents, all watching and dreaming of future soccer glory.

Simon didn't have a spare $12,000 lying around, unneeded, in a bank account. He did have a line of credit with a friendly banker down the street, a loyal pal who'd been loaning him small sums for years. Most lawyers in town needed an occasional bump when the fees ran thin, and this banker in particular had always rolled the dice with them.

Ironically, the funds Paula needed equaled almost exactly Simon's current deficit down at Chub's. Saturday was a big day in college football, with showdowns in every major conference, and Simon had studied the board all week. He'd read the game summaries, followed the handicappers in Vegas, or at least the

ones he trusted, pored over gamblers' cheat sheets, and listened
to podcasts, and he was convinced the day was perfect for bold,
unconventional action.

He went online and spread $7,000 over seven games. He called
Chub and put $3,500 on the same seven.

There was no way to lose.

———————•◆•———————

By 8 P.M., Simon was the smartest guy in the world and ready
for a drink. He walked into Chub's with a smile on his face and
took a seat at the bar. He'd won the first five bets and was up
$7,500 for the day, minus the juice of course, with two games to
go. He had never had such luck. Valerie brought him a bourbon
and ginger ale. LSU was at Florida and Clemson was at NC State,
the games side by side on the big screens. Chub, always the good
sport, soon made his way over and said, "Why are you smiling?"

"Might be one of those days, Chub."

"Don't get cocky."

"Not in this business."

"I'll get it back," Chub said with a laugh.

"I'm sure you will."

They laughed and watched the LSU kickoff. Valerie called
Chub away for a business question. The bar was crowded with
drinkers and gamblers. A band played in a distant corner and
dancers lurched around it. Even though it was against the law,
Chub allowed smoking in his club and a thick blue haze hung low
and obscured the lights. The bar was loud, even raucous at times.
It was, after all, Saturday night!

A man dressed like a cowboy took the seat next to Simon and
stuck a twenty-dollar bill into the video machine. Valerie eventually made her way over and he ordered a draft beer. Simon tried
not to speak to strangers in bars and ignored the guy. He was up
seventy dollars in video poker and was quietly relishing his biggest
day ever.

Softly, the cowboy said, "Yolanda says hello."

Simon hesitated for a second but did not look at the guy. In his life he had known only one Yolanda. When Simon did nothing but shrug, the guy said, "We work together."

Yolanda had been a girlfriend in law school where they dated off and on for two years before calling it quits. From there she joined the FBI and moved around. Last he heard, she was in the Richmond office. They'd had no contact since their ten-year reunion. As far as Simon knew, she was married and dedicated to a career with the FBI.

Simon glanced at the guy, who was concentrating on his poker and did not look up. "Nice girl."

"Uh-hmm. Super nice. She asked me to say hello."

Simon took a drink and watched the games. The FBI was there, in Chub's Pub. An old friend had just tipped him off. The small knot in his stomach suddenly felt like a brick. The cowboy, and Yolanda, were doing the unthinkable: compromising an undercover operation. They must consider Simon to be such a small player that he was not really necessary to their plan. They were going for Chub and the big gamblers. Simon was not important.

The conversation was definitely off the record; therefore, the cowboy was not wired. Simon finally said, "Where is she these days?"

"Around."

This guy would give him nothing more.

"Tell her I said hello, and thanks."

"Will do. Don't drag your feet."

Simon's feet were ready to sprint out of the bar and run and hide somewhere. But he played some poker, watched both of his teams fall behind, tried unsuccessfully to ignore the palpable tension emanating from the cowboy, and waited. The guy had not touched his beer, an unprofessional move that would tell anyone watching that he was not a regular and did not belong there. As far as Simon could tell, no one was watching. The cowboy left without another word.

Simon drank a third bourbon and ginger ale to settle his nerves.

At midnight, he was sitting at his desk, in his boxers, in the complete darkness, trying to analyze the situation. Was it possible that he and many others had gambled with Chub for so long, and with no consequences, that they assumed they were safe? Gambling was so pervasive everywhere and at every level that enforcement had become a joke. Look at the billions made legally by casinos in virtually every state. Look at the billions of illegal bets made online at offshore sites.

The disaster scenario was sickening. If the Feds moved in with all their tools—wiretaps, hidden cameras, subpoenas, warrants, press leaks, news conferences, SWAT teams—then Chub and his partners, whoever they might be, along with dozens, perhaps hundreds of good customers, including Simon, would be disgraced, humiliated, or worse. He could lose his license and his livelihood. What would his kids think?

Though he was not a criminal lawyer, he knew quite well the power of the federal government. The FBI could be brutal, unfair, unforgiving, even ruthless. The prosecutors could be unsympathetic, ambitious, and were always fond of publicity. With over five thousand criminal statutes on the books, there were ways to nail just about anybody.

He had to devise a plan but no two thoughts stuck together. Fear overwhelmed every thought. He slept on and off and was up at daybreak with a pot of coffee, still in his boxers, still roaming around his office.

At 7 A.M. his phone dinged and he grabbed it. A text from Paula:

Janie has a soccer game at 9. Rain make up from Wed. Are you going?

You gotta be kidding. Soccer on a Sunday morning? But he knew it was true because it had happened before.

I don't know. Forgot about it.

Of course. She slept with me last night, quite upset. We should be there.

Okay.

He showered quickly—all showers in The Closet were ramped-up—and left his office. He walked down the street, bought a Sunday newspaper, and settled into a booth at Ethel's Diner for eggs and bacon.

He needed to talk to Spade.

———— •• ————

One dark corner of Chub's was reserved each Sunday afternoon for men who smoked long, black, and extremely strong cigars. Spade brought a box of them to share, claimed he got them from a Cuban smuggler. He was sitting with two friends, puffing away, watching three games at the same time. He did a double take when Simon approached, then smiled and asked, "What brings you here on Sunday?"

"Had to get out of the house."

"Want a smoke?"

"No thanks."

"Who you got?"

"Dallas, tonight."

"Same here. Same all around. That's a bad sign."

They laughed, puffed some more, watched the games. Simon was paranoid to the point of breathing erratically, but managed to appear calm. What if some of these guys were wired? What if the FBI was watching with hidden cameras?

When one friend left for more beer and the other stepped away to talk on his phone, Simon leaned in close to Spade and said, "The Feds are here."

Spade took it calmly but his eyes said it all. Simon had his attention. The lawyer was not a player in the underworld but he was still a lawyer, with contacts. And he was a gambler who'd been a regular at Chub's for years.

"Fibbies?" Spade mumbled.

"Yep."

"Contact?"

"Last night. Here."

"You talked to them?"

"No, they talked to me."

Spade drank his beer. Simon whispered, "Can you tell Chub?"

Spade exhaled and rolled his eyes as if that might not work. He shrugged and said, "Don't know. I'll think about it."

The friend with the phone sat down and the conversation was over. But the message was delivered. Simon hung around for another beer, then said goodbye. At the bar he chatted with Valerie. Surely she wasn't wired. He looked for Chub but didn't see him.

It was getting dark when he stepped outside, and looking back he wondered when, if ever, he would be back.

CHAPTER 19

After another restless night that was continually interrupted by nightmares of handcuffs and headlines, Simon went downstairs, in jeans and a T-shirt, and made coffee. It promised to be another dreary Monday. He had a list of eleven unpleasant phone calls that he had carried over from the last unproductive week. First, though, he had to deal with his wealthiest client and her mounting legal problems.

He actually paused for a moment and stared at his phones. Which one should he use? Cell or landline? Since he was such a small-time gambler, would the FBI really have an interest in him? Would Yolanda send him a warning if he were a serious target? And would they really be listening in? Such thoughts had kept him awake all night. He decided to use the old phone on his desk.

Regarding Eleanor's auto insurance, he felt compelled to at least notify the company that she had received three tickets for moving violations. He was careful to point out that he, as her lawyer, was contesting the charges, and that there had been no final adjudication. He was just putting Allstate on notice.

He placed a call to the city prosecutor's office and talked to a secretary. The assistant prosecutors were quite busy, it was after all a Monday morning, but someone would call him back. Half an hour later, a rookie prosecutor called to inform Mr. Latch that she did not have the authority to reduce the penalties for traffic violations. She was stiff and important and seemed to equate bad driving with capital murder. After the call, Simon checked her out online and learned that she finished law school in May and had just passed the bar exam.

His banker finally called him back just before ten, and Simon was forced to sing and dance through the same routine about needing another jolt to his line of credit. The terms of that wretched agreement were clear and did not require him to justify anything. The $25,000 was there for his taking, no questions asked, but he was expected to notify the bank before hitting it again.

He cursed the line of credit every day of his life. The damned thing was not his fault. Five years earlier, he had been working at his desk late one night when he saw a pile of mail Tillie had opened and left in the in-tray on his desk. The friendly solicitation from Union Bank asked, "Do you need $10,000?" In fact, at that moment he did. The first paragraph proclaimed that the money was his because he had somehow qualified. No application. No credit check. No security. No repayments for twelve months. The money was his simply because he was a self-employed lawyer. Cautiously, he signed on for only $4,000. That relieved some pain and was so easy. Within the year he was up to the limit, needed more, and the bank happily raised him to $15,000. His excuse had been a dispute with the IRS, something the bank heard all the time from lawyers. More tax problems followed and the bank finally stopped the bleeding at $25,000.

After the first round of Monday morning phone calls, he was in a dark mood and decided to make matters even worse. There would never be a good time to tell Tillie, and doing so would not be pleasant. So why not do it during an already awful day, as opposed to ruining a good one?

Just before lunch he asked her to step into his office, close the door, have a seat, and ignore the phone. Neither could remember the last time she sat down in his office.

"Paula and I are getting a divorce."

She took it with a sad face but also with a little nod that said she figured as much. Indeed, she had known for some time that the marriage was not stable. "I'm so sorry."

"You've probably noticed that I've been spending a lot of time here at the office."

"Are you living here?"

"Basically, yes."

"I'm sorry, Simon. It must be awful."

"It is, especially for the children. But it's also been awful with the two of us living in the same house."

Tillie and Paula had long since realized that their lives were easier if they remained in their own separate corners. Paula had lost interest in Simon's career years earlier and wanted nothing to do with it, except, of course, the income it generated and what that meant to their ever-straining budget. Tillie had always seen her as aloof, probably because she had a college degree and a professional job.

"May I ask if things are civilized?"

"You may and they are, for the most part. I've prepared a simple property settlement agreement and she's considering it. She gets everything, basically, including the kids. I have liberal visitation. We're splitting expenses, with me paying the mortgage. So far, no fireworks. There are no allegations of bad behavior."

"This is so sad."

"It is, but we'll be okay. I'm determined to get through it and move on to a happier life, hopefully. It should not impact you in any way."

"I wasn't thinking about myself, Simon."

"I know. I appreciate the work you do here, Tillie, and I know I don't say that enough."

"Thank you, Simon. I like my job."

"That's good to hear. And on another unhappy note, I've gone to the bank again because Paula needs some cash. You know how much I hate to do that, but I have no choice."

"Your call, boss." She smiled and got to her feet. "And, if you need someone to talk to, I'm always here. With, you know, the female perspective. Plus, I have one divorce under my belt so I've been through it."

"Thank you."

She turned and walked to the door. Simon couldn't help but admire the view. Tillie was really getting in shape. After she closed the door, Simon pondered something that he should have already noticed. Tillie was a brighter, happier person these days, and she was spending more time not only in the gym but also at the mirror. The clothes, in smaller sizes, were more stylish and flattering.

Could it be that Tillie, after a long dry spell, had found someone new? He certainly hoped so.

CHAPTER 20

Eleanor was getting pushier about their lunches, which she was now describing as their "dates." Simon was suffering through them because they might lead to a pot of gold. However, the culinary adventure had been his idea and he couldn't stop it. Plus, he was getting closer to Netty and she was relying on him more and more. She even let it slip that she "needed" him.

Her friend Doris had eaten twice at the Bombay Oven, a quaint little café in a converted gas station five miles west of town. Eleanor was determined to go there, if for no other reason than to keep up with Doris, who was quite envious that her friend was lunching with a handsome young lawyer. The more Simon heard about Doris, the less he wanted to meet her.

He arrived early as always so he could scope out the parking situation and position himself, low behind the wheel, to study Eleanor's driving ability. It was a county road with little traffic, but Netty managed to find plenty of it. When she came into view, puttering along in the old Lincoln at no more than thirty miles an hour, there were a dozen cars bumper-to-bumper behind her. As she slowed even more and began to pull off the road, the idea of a turning signal never crossed her mind. Horns were blowing as the traffic passed.

He helped her out of her car. She looked great, as always, ready for church in a pretty blue dress, one he'd seen several times, a floral scarf bunched around her neck, dark hose, low heels. As they entered the café, Simon half-expected to smell diesel fuel and axle grease, but the interior was ultra-modern with black and white tiled floors, mirrors, glass, and tables adorned with linen cloths.

So much for a cheap lunch, he thought to himself. They ordered tea and a baked flatbread to get started. The restaurant was quiet and not crowded, the tables spaced reasonably apart. Simon had an agenda but did not want to hurry. These outings meant a lot to Eleanor.

After some chitchat about their complete lack of knowledge of Indian cuisine, they put down the menus. She got serious with "Wally Thackerman called again this morning."

"Again?"

"Yes, he's been calling for a month now, wants me to come to his office to review my estate and such."

At that moment, Simon could think of nothing in his complicated life that was as important as Eleanor's estate. The idea of another lawyer, especially a worm like Wally, getting anywhere near it was quite unsettling.

He gave a nonchalant shrug and asked, "What did you tell him?"

"I'm not a liar, Simon," she said, with a look that implied he thought she would lie.

"Who said you were?" he asked, defensively.

"I told him I wasn't feeling well, which at that moment was a true statement because his calls were upsetting me. But he isn't going away, evidently. What are we going to do?"

Shoot the little bastard, Simon instantly thought, but let it pass. "Well, we could always call Clyde and tell him to come on back and finish the job." Simon was smiling at his own humor. Eleanor was not.

"Sorry, just joking."

"I'm serious here, Simon. I still feel deceitful for not telling

Wally the truth, that I've signed another will and the one he prepared is no good. This just doesn't seem right."

"And you think Wally's been up-front with you? Keep in mind,
Netty, he secretly hid a gift to himself in your will and didn't tell
you about it. Almost half a million dollars. You're not dealing
with an ethical person here. As I have explained, more than once,
you have no obligation to inform Wally about our will. And why
worry, Netty? You have at least ten more years, maybe twenty."

That made her smile. The waitress brought over a platter of
naan with a bowl of spiced garlic hummus. They each took a bite.
She said, "Well, what if I go to his office and talk to him, just to
see what he's up to? I don't have to tell him anything and I don't
have to agree to anything, right?"

"Right. Great idea. Go sit with Wally, talk about his episode
with Clyde, and so on. See what he's thinking."

"That's what I'll do."

When the waitress returned, Simon said, "An Indian friend
recommended the *kofta,* meatballs stuffed with pork and onions
and other things, and your chicken curry."

"I'll take the same," Eleanor said.

The waitress sized them up and said, "I recommend that you
go pretty light on the spices, okay?"

They agreed and she took their menus.

Simon said, "I'd like to finish the conversation about your final
arrangements, if you don't mind."

"That's not one of my favorite topics."

"Understood. But we're talking about dying, Netty, otherwise
you would never have called my office in the first place. As soon
as we can get all the paperwork done, then we can stop talking
about dying."

She crunched on some flatbread and looked like she was about
to cry. "Do you really think I'll live ten more years?"

"Yes, at least ten," he said with a smile.

"And you think I should do the cremation thing?"

"Yes, I really do. It's quick, easy, and more sustainable for the
environment."

"Okay. If you insist."

Simon scribbled some meaningless notes on a small scrap of paper. "What about your funeral service? I asked you to write down some ideas."

"That's ten years away."

"Look, Netty, I really don't want to be doing this. I'm your lawyer, not a blood relative. This is a job for someone in your family, you understand? I don't really care how you want to be buried."

She burst into tears and he felt like a heel for whatever he'd said. She removed her glasses and wiped her eyes. Simon looked around to see if anyone was watching. She put her glasses back on, swallowed hard, and said, "I have no one. I've told you this."

"I'm sorry, Netty. I didn't mean to upset you. But, again, the sooner we get these matters wrapped up, the sooner we can stop talking about them."

"I've made some notes about my service and I'll bring them next time. It will be a small affair in the chapel at the funeral home with the Lutheran minister doing the honors. Just a few friends, that's all. My niece and nephew will never know I'm gone. So sad, isn't it, Simon? To have no one."

She looked as if she might cry some more and he truly felt sorry for her. The chicken curry arrived first in small bowls. The aroma was delicious and they ate in silence for a few minutes.

She took a drink of tea and said, "Well, sorta glad we asked them to go light on the spices. This stuff is hot."

"It's delicious though," Simon said. He drank some tea and decided to lunge forward. There was really no way around it. "There's another matter, Netty, that is somewhat delicate."

"Oh dear. You lawyers."

"Yes, you're spot-on. Lawyers work by the hour. Our time is all we have to sell, and I'm spending a lot of it handling your legal matters."

"Where is this going?" she asked suspiciously. Her look and tone were so cautious, Simon thought he was making a mistake. But it didn't matter anymore. He couldn't work for free.

"I need to get paid, Netty, same as any other lawyer in town. You're my favorite client right now, but all clients have to pay their lawyers. It's that simple."

"Harry didn't believe in paying lawyers."

"Yes, and Harry's been dead for ten years. I'm not being disrespectful, but I really don't care what Harry thought about lawyers. I have an office to pay for and a family to support, and I need to be paid."

"How much?"

What a question. Simon had struggled with it for weeks. If he went high she might be offended and walk out the door. He doubted that would happen, but he did not want to appear greedy. Bigger bucks were around the corner. He had to keep Netty happy. And if he went low, he would not get the fees he had earned and so desperately needed. He had decided to aim for the middle, and said, "Just over three thousand dollars."

She waved him off with a casual flick of the wrist and said, "Is that all?"

What beautiful words. He could always make up later with a heftier bill. "Yes, Netty, my fees are very fair. I enjoy my clients."

What a lie.

"I'll take care of it," she said as she took a bite. "When do we go to court?"

She was thinking of traffic court. Simon had his mind on probate. They were in different worlds.

"Couple of weeks. I'll check the docket." Oh how lawyers loved the word *docket*. It implied important trials and hearings in crowded courtrooms with justice hanging in the balance. But in traffic court it was little more than a sign-up sheet hanging on a clipboard.

The meatballs arrived with an aroma that was even more sumptuous. Netty said, "You promised me I'd meet your family, Simon. I'll bet your wife and kids are adorable."

Not exactly. Janie was a delight to be around, but the others were too troubled. Paula would never consent to meeting someone like Netty, not with the divorce hanging over their heads. She

wanted nothing to do with her husband or his practice. Buck and
Danny were awkward teenagers who had never learned to shake
hands and introduce themselves to adults. They had no desire to
meet anyone over the age of eighteen.

Simon smiled and lied, "I promise, I promise. Everybody is
just so busy. School, soccer, drama, choir, piano, homework.
Seems like every day is booked. I'll try to get them all together
sometime."

Dessert was rice pudding topped with pistachios and sliced
almonds, with strong coffee that Simon needed for the afternoon.
Ninety minutes after they sat down, the waitress placed the check
on the table. Once again, Eleanor, who constantly gazed about
the dining room while eating and seemed to miss nothing, commenting occasionally on other dishes being served, on the decor,
on what another cultured lady might be wearing, was totally
oblivious to the bill.

This was at least their seventh lunch. Simon finally put down
a credit card and paid again. $77.35. An expensive lunch for rural
Virginia. He'd get it back.

Driving to the office, he schemed to rework his monthly bill,
add in a lunch or two, and pad things a bit. She had scoffed at
his initial amount with words he would remember: *Is that all?* He
vowed to send her a more impressive bill.

Truthfully, he didn't care what the lunch had cost because he
and Netty had cleared the air about his fees. He was about to get
paid for the first time in the many months he had known her.

Since it would be impossible to hide the billing and receipts
from his secretary, he met with her that afternoon and described
his business with Eleanor Barnett. Some of it. He was billing her
several hours for two matters: (1) representation in traffic court,
and (2) consultation for estate planning. The bill was $3,650 and
Tillie mailed it that afternoon.

He did not tell Tillie that he had prepared a will for Eleanor,
saying only that they were still discussing her estate, one that had
become more "complicated." Tillie took this in stride, knowing
full well that he was lying.

CHAPTER 21

The line of credit was stretched yet again. Simon received an email notice from the bank informing him that $12,000 had just been deposited in his personal checking account. The money provided several options. The first, and the most sensible and obvious, was to write a check to Paula so she would sign the property settlement agreement and get the divorce filed.

The second was to make a withdrawal, stuff $7,900 in an envelope, try to find Chub somewhere away from his clubs, and pay off his gambling debts once and for all.

The third was to take all the money, pack a bag, book a flight to the Virgin Islands, and disappear. No more fear of being watched by the FBI, no more worries about debts, no more nit-picking phone calls from disgruntled clients, no more stress from Paula, no more sleeping on a bed with all the comforts of a surplus army cot, and no more scheming of ways to get rich off Eleanor Barnett. Drinking on the beach seemed like the perfect solution.

That would last for about a month before the money ran out. But what a great month it would be. Reentry would be another nightmare.

He withdrew $7,900 and went to find his bookie. For a man who lived in the shadows, sipped beer until midnight, and locked the doors to his nightclubs until almost noon, Chub was not an early bird. He stumbled forth around ten and made his way to a greasy spoon on the edge of town. It was a working-class joint with a menu dominated by bleached flour and lard. Chub needed grease every morning of his life. If you wanted to see him before noon, head on over to Bobby's Biscuits.

Simon saw his truck parked on the street. Chub was wealthy but lived a modest life, doing nothing to attract the attention of those dreadful people who carried badges. His truck was a muscled-up late-model Ford with a thick brush guard, huge rims, and tires that could claw up the sides of mountains. Though built for off-road adventures, it was shined and spotless and gave the impression that it never left the pavement.

Inside, the smell of grease greeted Simon like a blast of tropical air. A thick layer of smoke, not from cigarettes, hung close to the ceiling. Chub was not hard to spot because he wore, as always, one of his red, orange, or yellow jogging suits. Today was orange.

He was alone at his favorite table, readers on the tip of his red, bulbous nose, studying a folded newspaper. "Well, well, what brings a lawyer to this part of town?" he asked with a genuine smile. But he knew immediately that something was amiss.

"Mind if I join?" On the off chance that Chub was being wired these days, Simon had planned this surprise visit at a place they'd never met before. If he had a wire, it was still in his truck or his backpack.

"No, not at all." Chub put away his newspaper. Simon could see he had circled some horse-racing results. The sparse remains of biscuits, eggs, and country ham were on his plate. "You hungry? Have a seat."

"No thanks." Simon's mild hunger pains of five minutes earlier had dissipated in the fog of smoke and grease. He sat down as a waitress hustled by and barely stopped long enough to fill the two cups. Simon quickly handed over the envelope and said, "Seventy-nine hundred, cash. Zeroes out my account."

As fast as Simon presented the money, Chub took it and stuffed it into one of many hidden pockets. "You sure that's enough?"

"Positive."

"What's the occasion?"

"I'm retiring."

"Aw, that's no fun, Latch. You've done well."

"Maybe I broke even, if I was lucky. And I'm spending far too much time breaking even."

Chub smiled and took another drink from his cup. "You know, Latch, I always thought you were smarter than the others. It's a fool's game. Nobody wins but the house. The bookies, casinos, lotteries. There's a very good reason they keep building more casinos."

"I've always known that, but, like most players, I've always thought I could beat the house. But it can't be done, can it Chub?"

He smiled and wiped egg off his mustache. "I've never seen it."

"Come on, Chub. Surely you've seen a few guys who were successful at picking winners."

"Maybe one, maybe two. The secret is slowing down when you're ahead and speeding up when you're behind. It's counter-intuitive. I've seen guys have a good run for a year or two, then lose their mojo and give it all back. You're a smart one, Latch. But don't tell anyone I said that."

Simon laughed and said, "I doubt you'll ever see a drop-off. The experts say just the opposite. Studies show Americans gamble more and more each year."

"I hope so."

"Seen Spade lately?"

Chub held his gaze for a moment then looked at his cell phone. "Spade's in twice a week. Why do you ask?"

"No reason. I like him, a good guy. Kinda shady, like most of your regulars."

Chub laughed and said, "You're right about that."

Simon glanced at his watch and said, "Gotta get to the office."

"Don't be a stranger, Latch. Drop in and I'll buy you a beer."

"I will, Chub. I promise."

———— ◆◆ ————

Two days later, Simon drove an hour south on Interstate 81 through the Shenandoah Valley to the college town of Harrison-burg, a trip he made at least twice a month. One branch of the federal bankruptcy court was stationed there and Simon gave it a lot of business. Its docket, a real one, was posted online, so anyone with a computer could follow the court, check the current bank-ruptcies, and see which lawyers were filing them.

Simon had three discharge hearings in the afternoon and fin-ished at four-thirty. As he was leaving the courthouse, he bumped into a delightful memory from his past. Yolanda, his old flame from law school at George Mason. They had not seen each other since their class's tenth reunion.

After some slightly nervous chatter, Simon asked, "What brings you here?"

"Chasing crooks, Simon, that's my job."

"In Harrisonburg?"

"Oh, they're everywhere. Including Braxton."

"I met a colleague of yours the other night."

"You don't say. Hanging around Chub's?"

"That's my spot."

"Where you headed?" she asked.

"To a bar to buy you a drink."

"We shouldn't be seen together."

Simon laughed and said, "Wasn't it that way in law school?"

"At first. Look, there's a steak house on the edge of town, near a truck stop."

"I know it. Not much of a bar."

"I wasn't planning on drinking all night. It's dark. Meet you there."

———— ◆◆◆ ————

By the second beer they had finished with their old classmates and moved on to more serious matters. Landy, as everyone called her, said, "I met your wife at the reunion. Very pretty. Is she still around?"

"Yes, for now, but not for long."

"I'm sorry."

"Me too. Three kids, tons of bills, a lot of stress. The marriage cracked in slow motion, almost before we realized it was too late. I hate it for my kids, but I can't wait to get out."

At some point during their second year of law school, Simon became terrified at the thought of falling in love with Landy. It was his first serious romance and he simply wasn't ready for it. He wanted to finish law school, launch a career in D.C., and establish himself. She had been through a couple of bad breakups and was even more cautious, which served them well in the end. They had never taken time to explore their feelings, primarily because law school was such a grind, but also because sex was a much higher priority. If they were in bed they damned sure weren't talking.

With a grin, she asked, "Excuse me, you seem to be drifting. Are you thinking about sex?"

"Yes."

"Present or past?"

He chuckled because he was guilty, but he knew she was having the same thoughts. "Right now, the past." The tension was odd and palpable. Two former lovers reminiscing about sexual escapades both had never forgotten, and had no desire to do so.

Simon tried to change the subject with "You haven't said much about your husband."

"He's with the agency, like me. In fact, we're equals in every way—rank, salary, responsibilities. They warned us in training to be wary of dating each other, and they were right. Most FBI marriages don't work—too much travel, too many reassignments."

"Is yours working?"

"No. We've grown apart and I've missed my window to have kids. I'm kinda sad about that."

"Kids are overrated. I love mine, but they're so much trouble."

Their beer mugs were empty and two was the limit. She glanced at her watch and asked, "Are you staying here tonight?"

In other words, *Come on over.*

"No, I need to get back. What if we swap phone numbers?"

"Great idea."

He took a deep breath and waded into trouble. "Am I off the hook?"

"That's up to my boss, but I'd say probably so. You're just a minor player, like eighty percent of them."

"Why don't you guys leave Chub alone? He's harmless. He may be the biggest bookie in Braxton, Virginia, but big deal."

"Again, not my call."

"And I know you have bigger fish to catch."

"As in?"

"Oh, I don't know. As in narcotraffickers, cyberterrorists, Russian hackers, to name a few."

"Gee, we never hear that."

"Okay, I won't say it again. But Chub is not a bad guy."

"Call me, Simon. And let's catch up."

CHAPTER 22

When Eleanor finally turned off the engine, her Lincoln was straddling two clearly marked parking spaces in a small lot just off Maple Street. She got out and made her way slowly, somewhat reluctantly, to the row of buildings with awnings over the sidewalk next to Main Street. She stopped at the door of WALTER F. THACKERMAN, ATTORNEY AT LAW, and seemed to hesitate. Then she pushed it and went inside.

Simon watched intently from a dark second-floor window across the street. When the door closed behind her and she disappeared, he shut his eyes and wondered what might transpire over there in the next hour. At times she was so easily influenced that he could see Wally getting under her skin and rattling her to the point of blurting out the truth. Everything could blow up. He waited for the phone to ring, waited for Wally to call yelling and threatening.

Simon and Netty had tried to rehearse the day before but she couldn't concentrate. The efforts convinced him that she was not that reliable.

Fran greeted her with unusual warmth. She declined coffee, tea, and water, and had little to say about the weather. Because she could not dare to do so herself, Fran was hoping Eleanor would bring up the subject of Clyde Korsak's rather memorable visit a few weeks earlier. Fran had told the story to virtually anyone who would listen, and for a while it was a hot topic around town. But with time, the story ran out of gas. Wally warned her not to discuss the incident with their prized client.

Eleanor waited only a few minutes while Mr. Thackerman was "completing a conference call with a federal judge." Fran stood and said, "Please follow me." As they walked down the narrow hallway, Fran said in a whisper, "He's been terribly busy since the shooting." Eleanor gave her a blank look.

Wally met her at the door and led her to a cushioned chair near a coffee table. When Fran left, she stepped into the hallway, where she could hear every word. Wally wanted her to listen. They would debrief after Eleanor left and discuss her mental soundness.

The last will and testament she had typed for Ms. Barnett was signed last January. Wally had instructed Fran to include the language gifting him $485,000, and his story was that the up-front money would serve as some sort of a retainer that he would whittle down in fees once the estate was up and running. In her fifteen years with Wally, Fran had never seen such a clause, or a retainer, and she knew immediately it was a scam. When he knew she was unconvinced, he offered to give her a cash bonus of $50,000, and that made Fran happy. They had a marvelous time divvying up Eleanor's estate before she even signed the will.

Wally decided to deal with the unpleasant matter first. "I've been puzzled by something, Eleanor." She allowed Simon to call her Netty, but not Wally. "How did Clyde Korsak know that I'm your lawyer?"

"You've already asked me that."

"Well, I'm asking again. I'm really curious."

"Oh, I don't know. I really don't. That has puzzled me too, to be honest."

"He's never lived here, knows no one as far as I can tell. Yet, he somehow picked me as your lawyer. How'd that happen?"

"I just don't know."

"Well, did he ask who your lawyer is?"

"I don't recall. He asked a lot of questions. I finally told him to leave the house. He was never invited in, to be honest. I've never liked him or his brother, Jerry."

"Did he ask for money?"

"Of course. First, he wanted to borrow five thousand dollars. I said no. Then he got arrested and demanded twenty-five thousand to make his bail. I said no again. I don't like these questions."

Wally knew it was time to back off, but he had one more: "Do Clyde and Jerry know about the Coke and Wal-Mart stock?"

She took a deep breath and thought for a moment. "Oh, I don't know. Maybe. Many, many years ago, Harry and I were discussing the boys and how much trouble they were causing, and he said something suggesting that he had mistakenly told them about the stock. But I can hardly remember our conversation and I do not know what he told them. It must have been twenty years ago."

Wally took a sip of coffee and frowned as if it was time to get down to business. "Have you read our will, your will, lately?"

"No." Which was partly true. The day before, at a coffee shop, Simon had pulled out the will and summarized it. He showed her the long, dense paragraph where Wally had added the words "four-hundred-and-eighty-five thousand dollars." It was to be paid to him "as soon as practical" upon probating the will. To deflect attention away from the amount, Wally had chosen to use no numerals or dollar signs. Simon was of the opinion that such greed and trickery would lead to serious problems with the bar association if anyone complained.

However, she and Simon had not read the entire will; thus, her answer was sort of true.

"Is there anything in your will you would like to change, or to discuss?"

Other than the money you're raking off? "No, I don't think so." Simon had coached her to say as little as possible. Don't volunteer, don't agree to anything new, pretend as though everything is okay.

She didn't like the pretending. Lawyers and their games!

She did have a trace of sympathy for the poor guy, though.

What a shock it would be when he got to the courthouse with her "old" will, only to learn that Simon had just left after probating her "new" one.

Though it was not yet 11 A.M., Wally suggested they have lunch together, with Fran of course. He knew just the right place, a new sushi restaurant that opened early and was getting rave reviews.

Eleanor thanked him politely. She was caught off guard by the suggestion, but managed to decline with grace, said she had a bit of a stomach bug.

She and Simon had eaten there and had not been too impressed.

They wrapped things up in under thirty minutes. Eleanor thanked Wally for his time, and he thanked her as well. He walked her out of the office and onto the sidewalk, where Simon could see them from across the street.

———◆◆◆———

With 30,000 people, Braxton's exotic dining options were limited. So far, their culinary adventure had led them to sampling dishes from Asia, Latin and South America, Europe, Afghanistan, and India. Nine restaurants and Simon was looking forward to the end of the project. His usual lunch was a cheap sandwich at his desk, often one he brought from home, back when he had a place he could call home.

When Netty called hinting about lunch, he wanted to discuss perhaps taking a break. He knew of no other ethnic places in or close to Braxton. There were thousands in D.C., but that was at least an hour away.

She said, "Let's go back to Tan Lu's. I think that's my favorite."

A victory lap was not something he had considered. "Sure, sounds great."

It was a Vietnamese place with exceptional food, and it was usually packed by 12:15, six days a week.

They arrived at 11:30 and found a table. Tan Lu's did not bother with reservations. The waitress was the teenage daughter of the owners, a star student who had been born in Braxton and was headed for college. She took their orders for pho, the traditional noodle soup with fish and onions in a thick broth. They started with a *goi* salad and ordered shrimp spring rolls as a side.

"And of course the ginger cookies," Netty added with a laugh. The Saigon ginger cookies were so popular that the owners sold them by the box for carryout.

As she prattled on about playing cards with Doris and the girls, Simon was once again hit with the anxiety of being played for a fool. Her assets had not been verified. She refused to show him her bank records and brokerage statements. Was Simon so eager to believe her, and so covetous of her money, that he was willfully missing the red flags?

The waitress served them a plate of colorful raw vegetables with a cucumber dip, and she poured hot spiced tea from a small pot.

Netty said, "We haven't talked about that mess in city court, have we Sy?"

He snapped out of his fog and replied, "No, but things are coming together. I've negotiated with the prosecutor and the city will basically dismiss everything but one speeding ticket. Cost you about forty bucks and nothing will go on your permanent record. I'll go to court around the first of December and take care of it all."

"Do I have to go to court?"

"Oh no, Netty, I've arranged things so you don't have to show up again."

She sighed dramatically and looked as if she might tear up. "Oh, thank you, Sy. I absolutely despised being in that courtroom with all those other people."

"The riffraff?"

"I didn't say that. You know what I mean."

"I know exactly what you mean."

"Thanks for keeping me out of court, Sy."

"Sure, that's my job." A job he apparently wasn't getting paid for at the present time, though he had plans to recoup every single

expense one day. "But slow down, Netty. Slow down and be careful. Follow the traffic signs. Another ticket and I may not be able
to work my magic."

Magic? Any lawyer on Main Street could manipulate traffic
court the way Simon had.

The pho arrived with steam rising from the broth. Both
inhaled the aroma as they picked up their spoons. They ate and
talked about the usual topics, though Netty seemed less interested
in his family. Perhaps she had realized that an introduction to
them was not going to happen. Simon again feigned interest in
her card club, her "poker club," as the gals liked to call it. It met
once a week for a gin rummy tournament at their various homes.
They sipped sherry, ate chocolates, played gin rummy in teams
and gambled a dollar a game, and sometimes watched a movie. It
was great fun and she wished Simon would join them. Simon was
almost asleep.

For dessert, the cookies arrived on small plates with a side of
warm honey for dipping. Netty loved them and asked the waitress
to share the recipe. The mix was whole wheat flower, organic
flour, chopped ginger, milk, and butter, and they were topped
with sesame seeds and frosted brown sugar. They were crunchy
and somewhat messy to eat, but no one cared about the crumbs.
Netty ate four of them and chased them with a small cup of *cà phê,*
an egg coffee with sweet condensed milk.

The bill was almost eighty dollars. Simon got the check.

CHAPTER 23

The call came on his cell late on a Thursday night as he was watching a college basketball game, one of those preseason sleepers where the home team pays good "road money" to a much weaker visiting team that usually gives up at least 90 points and scores half as many. He had no skin in the game and sorely missed his gambling days. It was from Eleanor's cell so he took it immediately. "Mr. Latch?" an unknown male voice said.

"This is Simon Latch. Who is this?"

"Sergeant Pully, Braxton PD. I think we met once in court."

"Oh yeah, I remember." Simon had never met the guy but it was always a good idea to humor the cops, especially when they were calling at odd hours. Something was up and it wasn't good. "What's going on?"

"Well, there's been an accident involving Eleanor Barnett. She's in the hospital with some injuries, but they do not appear to be life-threatening. She asked me to call you, said you were in charge of her affairs."

They had never agreed that he would be in charge of her affairs, but as their relationship had evolved there was really no one else. And that was fine with Simon. "Yes, I am. Can you tell me what happened?"

"Well, sure, but she wants to see you. I'm at the hospital, so come on down and we'll have a chat." It was more of an order than a request.

Twenty minutes later, they were standing outside the ER entrance because Pully needed a smoke. He was saying, "Ms. Barnett was driving and she had a passenger, Doris Platt. You know Ms. Platt?"

"Sort of. We've actually never met."

"According to Ms. Platt, they went to a little Christmas party, a bunch of old ladies, and they played cards, gin rummy I think, and they had dinner and such, and they also hit the sherry pretty hard. They left, with Ms. Barnett behind the wheel."

"She's not supposed to drive at night."

"With good reason. Not supposed to drink and drive either. Ms. Platt said she was all over the road, and they were yapping back and forth when they ran a red light on South Poplar and T-boned another car. The two people in that one are pretty banged up, but nothing fatal, or at least that's the initial report."

"Oh boy," Simon said, shaking his head.

"Happened about two hours ago. All four came in by ambulance and I think they're all stable. I had time to check Ms. Barnett's record. Not good. She has three speeding tickets pending, one is reckless. Her insurance just canceled."

"Say what?"

"Afraid so. Allstate notified the DMV on December the second."

Simon frowned and shook his head. The officer said, "I thought you were in charge of her affairs."

"Not all of them. She pays her own bills, or at least she's supposed to. Are you certain this accident was her fault?"

"We're still at the scene investigating, but there were eyewitnesses who saw her run the red light. Plus, Doris Platt agrees with them."

"And she had no insurance."

"Apparently not. Plus, it looks like she was drinking."

"She doesn't drink."

"Well, she did tonight. Doris confirms it."

Doris needs to shut up, Simon thought but held his tongue.

Pully said, "She gave us a blood sample. Waiting on results."

"You took a blood sample?"

"Yep, she consented, in writing."

"Did she know what she was signing?"

"Yep. Two nurses witnessed it, both said she was lucid."

"Did she ever lose consciousness?"

"I don't think so, but, again, I wasn't there. Her left leg is pretty banged up, not sure about the X-rays. They're still looking her over." Pully frowned and listened to his earphone. "I need to go check something. Why don't you hang out in the waiting room and I'll be back in a minute?"

Simon hadn't smoked since college, but he bummed a cigarette off Pully and said he would stay outside. An hour later, the cop was back. He fired up another and said, "Preliminary blood work shows point-zero-nine. Over the limit. They just moved her to a private room and the doc says you can say hello. She's really upset and wants to talk to you."

"Is she still drunk?"

Pully found that funny and laughed. "Probably got a pretty good buzz. Let's go. I'll take you up there."

————— ◆◆► —————

It was almost midnight when Simon entered the room. Two nurses were fiddling with tubes and checking monitors. Half her forehead was covered with a large gauzy bandage. Her left leg was wrapped in cotton. Her eyes were closed.

Simon could think of nothing else to say so he asked, "Uh, how's she doing?"

One nurse said, "She's been better. Two broken ribs on the left side. Some cuts, plenty of bruises. Her left knee took a hard blow. She's going to be sore for some time."

Eleanor opened her eyes and saw Simon. She stuck out her right arm. Two tubes dangled from it. He gently squeezed her fingers and said, "Hello Netty. I'm so sorry about this."

"So am I," she said, barely audible. "Have you seen Doris?"

He shook his head. A nurse said, "She's down the hall."

The other nurse said, "We're injecting morphine for the pain, so she'll probably slip away for some time. Are you hurting, Ms. Barnett?"

She closed her eyes and said, "A little, I guess. Please stay, Simon."

The thought of spending the night had not crossed his mind and he was suddenly on his heels. A nurse nodded to the only chair in the tiny room and said, "That one reclines. Folks use it all the time."

Simon glared at it. A weird creation designed to ruin lower lumbars.

Pully was listening to his earphone again and said, "Gotta run. I'll be back tomorrow to take a statement from Ms. Barnett."

Simon almost blurted, *She's not making any more statements to the police,* but he let it pass. He would deal with the legal issues tomorrow. He watched a nurse inject the knockout juice into an IV. She smiled at Simon and mouthed the words, *She'll fade away.*

The other nurse said, "Make yourself at home." Both nurses left the room and Simon was suddenly alone with his client. He stood near the door for a long time and tried to absorb the surreal image before him. She looked so tiny and frail in the bed, with a thin white sheet pulled up to her neck, head turned to her left, with a small tube running into one nostril.

How did this person, this nice old lady he met for the first time only nine months earlier, enter his life in such a dramatic fashion? How had she lived for eighty-five fairly comfortable years and reached this point where she had no one to care for her but him? No family, no close friends except for Doris, who she had just practically killed.

He would admit, and only to himself, that greed was the driving force. Months earlier he could have done what she asked him to do, prepare a simple will for $250 and close the matter. And that's exactly what would have happened if she had no money. Matilda would have filed her will away with hundreds of others and forgotten about it.

However, the client was certainly not poor and appeared to be quite vulnerable. His otherwise good judgment was corrupted by greed. He saw an easy way to take control of her money, a fortune that was wonderfully hidden from everyone. Under his clever control, it would remain a delightful secret.

He glanced at a digital clock in one corner of a monitor above her head. The green digits read 12:42.

He analyzed the chair and devised a maneuver to get himself into it without rupturing a disc. Once situated, he managed to lean back with his head resting on a wall. He studied the outline of her shrunken frame under the sheets. He listened to the soft, steady, obnoxious beating of a machine monitoring something. He heard the sounds of the nurses and orderlies shuffling along the hallway. And he wondered how any visitor could be expected to sleep in a hospital. The patients were drugged.

He closed his eyes and tried to breathe deeply.

There were so many issues to fret over. His dear Netty was about to face criminal charges for drunk driving. She was about to be sued by the folks she injured in the wreck. The lawsuit would allow the opposing lawyers to pry into her finances. The criminal charges and lawsuits would be public record.

The more Simon thought, the more problems arose. He opened his eyes and looked at the clock: 12:46.

Gently, he wiggled out of the chair and left the room. He took the stairs down two flights to the ground floor where he followed the signs to the cafeteria. All three of his children had been born in the hospital, but that was before it had been renovated several times. There were new wings and corridors with every visit. The cafeteria was closed, thus forcing him to buy coffee from a machine. He walked outside the building, took one sip, and poured out the rest.

He was contemplating an escape. Eleanor was knocked out and would sleep for hours. Why shouldn't he do the same? He could hustle back to The Closet, sleep until 6 A.M., then shower and return to the hospital. There was no benefit in babysitting a woman who was in another world.

CHAPTER 24

There were a couple of lawyers in town who were known to hang around hospital emergency rooms and hallways waiting to pounce on the families of people injured in car wrecks or on the job. They were throwbacks to an earlier time before the deluge of TV and billboard advertising, back when "ambulance chasing" was frowned upon. They monitored police scanners and bribed tow-truck drivers and used a dozen other tricks to land clients. Simon knew them well and was determined to keep them away from Eleanor, though it would soon be known that she was likely to be a defendant and not a plaintiff.

He returned to the hospital at 7 A.M. and found her still sound asleep. He set up camp beside her bed with the morning papers and a tall cup of coffee, as if he'd been there all night. He coughed and rattled the papers and tried to make as much noise as possible. Eventually, Netty roused herself and opened her eyes. He sat on the edge of her bed and asked how she felt. She wasn't sure. A doctor popped in and did a cursory exam of her bandages. After he left, Simon asked, "Would you like something to eat?"

"No, thanks. It's so good to see you here, Simon."

Wouldn't miss it for the world. "How about some coffee?"

"No, but some water would be good."

He fetched her some in a plastic cup and thought about asking, *How's your hangover?*

She sipped through a straw and asked, "Where is Doris?"

"Down the hall. She's okay. Seems as though she was wearing a seat belt. And you were not."

"Oh my. I really don't remember much."

"You took a blow to the head, got some stitches, a couple of broken ribs."

"Can you tell me what happened?"

He patted her arm and said, "It's a long story, and not a good one."

———— ◆◆ ————

He left a few minutes after nine, and on the way out had a chat with the charge nurse, Loretta Goodwin. Ms. Barnett was not to be questioned by the police or anyone else, and please watch out for other lawyers, insurance adjusters, and the like. Loretta agreed while rolling her eyes. She'd seen it all.

At the office, he briefed Matilda and asked her to hold his calls. He closed his door, stretched out on the sofa, and tried to arrange his thoughts. Eleanor would likely be in the hospital for a few days, a golden opportunity for him to dig deeper into her financial affairs and make himself indispensable. He could petition the court to establish a conservatorship to handle her bills and such, and in doing so have access to virtually everything. The downside was the notoriety. Any court filing would be a public record, and there was no shortage of snoops in the courthouse. So far, in the nine months or so that he had represented her, he had been able to keep his name away from hers. That would all change when she died and he probated her will, but for the moment he wanted the anonymity.

He had just dozed off when Matilda rapped on his door. Without waiting, she barged in with a panicked look. As Simon was scrambling to his feet, she said, "There are two guys here in dark suits. FBI, badges and all. Pretty serious dudes."

"What have you done now?"

"Me? Sorry, boss, they want to see you."

"Send 'em in."

Simon took some deep breaths, tried to relax his face, forced a smile, and met them at the door. Just another exciting day in the life of a small-town lawyer.

Since all FBI agents are special, they introduced themselves as Special Agent Perez and Special Agent Underwood. They wore matching suits and shirts, but their ties were different shades of blue. They sat in chairs at the big desk with Simon on the other side, perched on his executive swivel throne. He showed them his cell phone, pressed a key, and said, "Just for fun, I'll record whatever we are about to say." They shrugged in unison.

After an awkward attempt to catch up on the weather, Simon cut to the chase and asked, "So what's up, guys?"

Underwood appeared to be slightly older, maybe twenty-nine or thirty, and he was in charge. He obviously had more experience with bluster and bravado. "So, you see much of Hubert Nelson these days?"

Simon was perplexed and couldn't respond.

"Also goes by 'Chub.' Owns a few bars in the area."

"Sorry, I've never thought about Chub having a proper name. I've known him for fifteen years and never heard him called Hubert. Plenty of other names, though." Simon thought that last comment was slightly humorous but they did not. "What's Chub done now?"

"We're still trying to figure that out," Underwood said. "The investigation centers around illegal gambling. Our sources tell us that Chub is actively involved. You know anything about that?"

"Well, gentlemen, here are the rules. If I'm a suspect in any crime, then I'm not chatting with you without my lawyer present. Plain and simple."

"Didn't ask about you. What about Chub? You ever bet the games in his sports book?"

"If I did, that would be a crime. So if you're asking me if I've committed a crime, then, again, you'll have to come back when my lawyer is here."

They stood in unison. Underwood tossed a business card onto the desk and said, "Thanks, we'll be in touch."

Simon didn't move as they opened the door and left. He heard them speak to Matilda and leave through the front door. He took deep breaths and tried to reduce his heart rate. He kicked back and put his feet on the desk, as if he hadn't a care in the world. He also put together an excuse for Tillie, who would arrive any moment.

"What was that all about?" she asked, standing in the door.

"Have a seat." His version of the story was that the Feds were investigating Chub's alleged gambling operation. Since his separation from Paula, Simon was spending more time in Chub's and making small bets on games. Nothing serious. He won more than he lost, and so on. All his buddies played the games. The Feds were just tracking down leads.

She said, "I go to Yesterday's occasionally. It's a nice bar."

Yesterday's was Chub's only effort at a legitimate club and attracted singles and young marrieds.

"It's nothing to worry about," Simon said as his stomach flipped. "You'd think they have more important crimes to worry about."

"Is gambling still a crime?"

"Depends on how you do it. But, don't worry. It's nothing."

She closed the door when she left and Simon stretched out on the sofa. Where the hell was Landy? Hadn't she practically guaranteed him he was not a target? After another round of deep breathing, he decided that the visit was nothing but a routine check-in-the-box by a couple of rookies who had to report something to their supervisor. He still refused to believe he could possibly face criminal charges for betting on games. He also knew that the rampant popularity of sports gambling did not make it legal, but why would the Feds choose Chub out of thousands of local bookies? And why would they choose Simon out of millions of casual bettors?

He simply refused to believe he was in trouble.

He snapped out of it, went to his desk, called Tillie and told her to order flowers for Eleanor Barnett, Room 328, Blue Ridge Memorial Hospital.

During lunch, Simon returned to the hospital, and as he parked he wondered how many times he would be doing the same thing over the next week or two. Hospitals were such depressing places.

He tapped her door as he shoved it open and softly said, "Anybody home?"

Her bed was empty; no one was home. There were voices behind him, and he turned to see the door swing fully open. Two young men in hospital garb pushed and pulled a gurney with Eleanor's frail figure tucked under the sheets from the waist down. She sat propped up on pillows, and with a big smile said, "Hello Sy, welcome back." He moved to the side to make way for the gurney.

"These are my new friends," she said, rather cheerily, as if she'd been drinking again. Simon knew immediately it was the meds. "They had to roll me downstairs for X-rays again. Bill and Oscar."

Simon nodded as they hardly noticed him. As they prepared to lift her into her bed, one of the men said, "Please step outside. We'll just be a minute." Simon glanced at the ID badge pinned to his white coat. OSCAR KOFIE.

He hurried outside and bumped into Loretta Goodwin, who seemed to be waiting for him. "Got a minute?"

"Sure," he said.

She spoke in a low voice and glanced around. "The doctors made their rounds this morning and they're concerned about her leg. There's bleeding that might require a little surgery, nothing too complicated. Just took some more X-rays. The problem is that she doesn't have a living will, an advance directive, or a medical power of attorney. And, evidently, she has no family. She lists you as her contact person. Is there anyone else?"

"No, not that I'm aware of."

"Okay, can you talk to her and explain that she needs some paperwork, and, like, real soon?"

"Sure, happy to. When is this surgery?"

"It's not scheduled yet and it may not be necessary. They'll watch her for a couple of days. We, the hospital, just need someone on record as her spokesman."

"Okay. I'll talk to her."

The empty gurney appeared in the door and Bill and Oscar rolled it away.

───◆◆◆───

With Simon dictating, Tillie prepared a power of attorney and an advance directive, giving Simon full authority over virtually every aspect of Eleanor's business affairs and health care. He returned to the hospital where he waited half an hour outside the office of the CEO and chief administrator, a Dr. Connor Wilkes. Once inside, he explained what he was doing and asked for her help. He said, "I want to make it clear that she is signing the power of attorney and advance directive with a thorough understanding of it all."

"There's no family?"

"Afraid not. I'd rather not be doing this," Simon said gravely. "But there is simply no one else."

Dr. Wilkes was reluctant and obviously wary of a lawyer wanting to have important papers signed by a patient who was elderly and drugged. But Simon was convincing and persistent. "Give me an hour to explain it all to my client," he said.

The explaining was made all the more difficult by her mental state. She was horrified at what she had done and worried sick over Doris and the folks in the car she had T-boned. Facing a drunk driving charge was inconceivable. "I'm not going to jail, am I?" she asked several times. Simon assured her she was not, though he wasn't so sure himself. He tried to allay her fears but it was impossible. He was firm yet compassionate, and he truly felt sorry for her.

He said, "Your bills are not getting paid, Netty. I'll handle your paperwork until you get back on your feet. I wish there was someone else."

She wiped more tears and said, "So do I, Simon, but there's no one."

As for the power of attorney, he explained that it was only temporary and could be dissolved anytime she wanted. He would not write a single check without consulting her, but it was imperative that he have access to her checkbook, bills, and other financial records.

She was crying when she said, "I won't be able to drive?"

"No, Netty, your driving days are over."

The advance directive was more complicated. It directed her "health care advisor" to consult with her doctors and so on. If she became completely incapacitated, she was not to be resuscitated. Her life was not to be prolonged by medication, feeding tubes, respirators or other medical devices.

"Am I going to die?" she asked over and over. He assured her she was going to be fine, for now, and that the directive would be used only in some future medical situation. It included language covering her final arrangements.

When Dr. Wilkes arrived she brought an entourage, including Dr. Samuel Lilly, the attending physician. The room was filled with frowning people, all watching Simon with great suspicion. He expected as much and turned on the charm, explaining both documents and repeatedly asking Eleanor if she understood what she was being asked to do. Dr. Wilkes engaged her in an extended conversation, which she managed to handle well enough. It was a fairly thorough grilling and she began to tire, as did the entourage.

When the questions petered out, Simon said to Dr. Wilkes, "We can do this another time if you'd like."

No one in the room wanted to repeat the meeting. Eleanor

seemed to know what she was doing and ended the inquisition with "No, I don't want to do this again. I trust Simon and I want to sign the papers."

She did, and a secretary notarized her signatures. Simon thanked everyone warmly and promised to send copies for the hospital files. After they were gone, Eleanor said she was fatigued, hungry, and tired, and the nurses took over. Simon said goodbye and promised to return later in the evening.

In the lobby, he bumped into Officer Pully and they had a tense chat about the situation. He inquired as to how Simon wanted to handle the arrest.

"Are you kidding? What's the hurry? She's not going anywhere."

"How long will she be in the hospital?"

"She just got here. Give her a break."

"Well, her victims are making some noise."

"Let 'em squawk. There's no rush. When she's able to walk we'll cooperate fully. Just back off, okay?"

"I'd like to take her statement."

Simon bristled even more and said, "You're not speaking to her, got it? Not a word. Back off or I'll call the chief."

"Hey, I don't like threats, especially from lawyers."

"And I don't like pushy cops. Surely you have better things to do than to harass old women in the hospital. Just take it easy and we'll cooperate."

"Damn right you will. I'll see you in court."

"Sir, that's the last place you want to see me." Simon walked away with a swagger, like a real badass trial lawyer.

CHAPTER 25

Simon did not want to be in the house after dark, with a strange car in the driveway. He did not want nosy neighbors ringing the doorbell and asking questions. He did not want to look like a lawyer or a person with authority so he wore jeans and a sports coat. And, he did not want to be rushed.

At 3 P.M. he parked where the old Lincoln once parked and turned off the engine. He had just left Netty's car in the city lot, waiting to be hauled to the scrap heap. It was a total loss, and he considered her lucky to escape with minor injuries. He took some photos for the file but would never need them.

The house had no alarm system. She said Harry didn't believe in them and wouldn't spend the money. Harry had been dead for ten years and she often talked about him as if he were still around.

Once inside the den he inhaled a pleasant aroma, probably the remains of a scented candle. Maybe pine. He switched on lights in the den and kitchen and paused to take inventory. The house was spotless, with everything in order. The kitchen counters were uncluttered, with only a toaster and coffeepot, both at least thirty years old. He wiped a finger across a wooden snack bar. Not a trace of dust. The furniture was fairly modern, nothing ancient, nothing new. The television was a bit dated, though, an old Motorola with two remotes. There was an upright piano against one wall. He could not remember Netty ever saying any-thing about a piano. He stepped into her small study and went straight to her desk, a government surplus throwback from the 1960s with chrome legs and metal panels. As she said, the current mail was in a tray in the right corner.

Her chair was a wicker straight-back that was fragile and shaky and seemed designed for a woman who weighed less than a hun-dred pounds. He settled into it, moving slowly to make sure it would not collapse. The desktop was covered in glass and well organized with nothing out of place. A large cup held the usual collection of pens, pencils, paper clips, etc. Netty was very neat and tidy. There was no computer, no iPad, no devices at all. He took a stack of mail and began sifting through it, at first careful not to misplace anything. He did not find a bill for an internet provider. Perhaps it was packaged with her cable, as was his. He knew that the stack did not include all of her monthly bills. Oth-ers would arrive later.

Though his curiosity was piqued, he felt like some creepy voy-eur looking at the private affairs of an old woman. He kept telling himself that he had no choice. Someone had to do it.

He found the rather abrupt letters from Allstate canceling her auto insurance. He found several other past-due notices and unpaid bills. The checkbook was in the bottom drawer, left side, exactly where she said. It was in a blue leather notebook-style binder, with three checks to a page and stubs that dated back two years. He flipped through the stubs and got a clear picture of where she shopped and what she bought, and nothing was unusual or surprising. She did indeed have a credit card, a Visa, which she had been forced to use when she checked out of the lake cabin two months earlier. But she used it sparingly. In another drawer he found the old Visa statements filed in perfect monthly order. Behind them were the monthly statements from the local bank. The latest was for October and showed a balance in her checking account of $3,100. There was no sign of the past-due bill from his office. An hour passed before he realized it.

In the bottom right drawer was a stack of old magazines—
AARP, Southern Living, Medicare Bulletin, Travel & Leisure. Some
were ten years old and there was nothing to indicate why they
had been kept.

What Simon wanted to find was a monthly statement from
Rumke-Brown, the wealth management firm in Atlanta that handled her stocks. And he wanted bank statements from East Federal, the bank where she allegedly stashed her cash. The fact that
he found neither was troubling. Why would she hide them?

She said her important papers were in a locked safe hidden in
the bottom of her closet. He did not ask for the key and she did
not offer.

When he had gone through every drawer it was dark outside.
He had been there long enough for the first visit, though he had
more questions now than when he arrived.

The doorbell rang and Simon jumped out of his skin, as if he'd
been caught in a burglary. He rushed to the front door, opened it,
and smiled at a couple in their sixties.

"We live next door and saw the car," the man said.

"What are you doing here?" the woman demanded.

"My name is Simon Latch, I'm Eleanor's attorney. She's in the
hospital."

"We know. We heard all about it."

Simon looked them over as they examined him. He said,
"Relax. I'm helping take care of her business."

"How's she doing?" the man asked.

"Okay, I guess. She'll be there for a few days."

"We heard she was drunk," the woman said. "Drinking and
driving, but that doesn't sound like Eleanor."

"I can't comment, sorry."

"What's your name again?" the man asked.

"And what's yours?"

"Frazier, Norris Frazier. And my wife Rose."

"Great. Nice to meet you. I'm Simon Latch, attorney. I'll tell
Eleanor that you checked on things."

"You do that. Can we visit her in the hospital? We probably won't though. Last year Rose was in the hospital for a week and not a word from Eleanor. No sir."

For a second Simon wasn't sure of a response. He said, "Not yet, maybe in a couple of days. I'll let you know. And you'll probably see my car parked here off and on for some time. Feel free to say hello." He was closing the door as he spoke.

Was it Frazier Norris or Norris Frazier? He would have to report it to Netty and he couldn't even remember the name. Rose was the wife. His head was spinning with questions and possibilities and his heart was still racing from the interruption. He needed to get out of the house. Avoiding her fragile chair, he sat on a leather stool near her desk, closed his eyes, and took ten deep breaths. An ugly reality was falling slowly around him as he sunk into a dark gloom.

There was no money, no fortune, no pot of gold filled with shares of stock in Coca-Cola and Wal-Mart, no pile of cash in an Atlanta bank. He was a sucker, the victim of a nutty old woman with a devious mind, a lonely soul who had duped him and probably others into believing she was rich. Rich? He looked around her small study and saw nothing to indicate Eleanor Barnett had the slightest bit of real wealth. Sure, everything was paid for, and given his current state of affairs that was a dream, but she was no richer than many elderly widows whose husbands had been frugal. In the nine months he had known her, he had not seen her spend one dime on anything that wasn't necessary. She wouldn't even pay her bills. She had stiffed him for a dozen lunches. She wore the same clothes over and over. She never traveled, never talked about doing so.

And now she was banged up in the hospital facing lawsuits and a nasty drunk driving charge. Why in hell was he in the middle of this mess?

Greed.

At least he could admit it.

———— ◆◆◆ ————

Dinner was a tuna melt in the rear of Ethel's Diner, four doors down from his office. There was a small aluminum tree by the front cash register. "Jingle Bells" played softly in the background. It would be his first Christmas away from home, away from the kids, which saddened him greatly.

Uglier thoughts, though, were more pressing. It was time to confront Eleanor and demand all of her financial records. And once he had them, and once he knew for sure that her last will and testament was a scam, he would immediately take steps to get rid of her as a client. She was facing enormous legal troubles, all of her own making, and he was not about to get roped in as her lawyer. She wouldn't even pay his first bill for $3,650. If he didn't cut the cord and do so immediately, he could be on the hook for her DUI, normally a $5,000 fee, and the lawsuits from her car wreck. There was no way to calculate those fees, not to mention the damages, when the lawsuits started flying.

He managed to chuckle at the irony of himself, a bankruptcy lawyer, being forced to file a bankruptcy for Eleanor Barnett, a wacky old gal who'd probably gone through life lying about her assets. The humor didn't last. He paid for his dinner and stepped onto the sidewalk. Across the street, carolers serenaded a small crowd in front of the Episcopal church. For a moment, he missed home.

Dessert was a bourbon and ginger ale, the first of the evening, and he needed it because of the unpleasant task at hand. On a small table in the corner of his office, he spread out Netty's monthly bills, current and past due, and opened the bulky notebook that held her checks. He unclipped the three rings and removed the stubs. He flipped to the back to see how many checks were available. There were plenty. In the back binder there was a folder that was almost undetectable. Inside it, carefully tucked away, was a small, thin notebook, eight inches by five. He removed it, opened it, and looked at the first lined page. In the center was the year: 2015. At the bottom, in small, neat cursive was the name: *Eleanor Barnett*. He turned the page. In blue ink, she wrote:

April 4, per BB: Coca-cola at $41, 238,000 shares, total
$9,758,000

WMart at $51, 127,000 shares, total $6,400,000

Per Albert, East Federal Atlanta, cash acct: $362,000

East Fed money mkt acct: $890,000

East Fed jumbo cd: $744,000

East Fed T-bills acct: $501,000

Third Fed 2016 cd: $522,000

East Fed 2017 cd: $1,330,000

Simon stared at the numbers without breathing for a long time, then he tried to tally them mentally. He was afraid to move, but eventually turned the page to July 6. The numbers varied slightly. Evidently, Netty preferred to round things off to the nearest ten grand.

Then to October 7. It was obvious that BB and Albert called her during the first week after each quarter with the updates. He assumed BB was Buddy Brown. He had no idea who Albert was but he worked for East Federal.

He sipped his drink and felt his entire body relax as a mountain of pressure drifted from his shoulders. The bourbon had wound its way to his brain and calmed things considerably.

The notebook made perfect sense. Eleanor was obsessed with secrecy and perpetually afraid that someone would discover her stocks and cash. So, she kept no evidence of them. Rumke-Brown and East Federal did not send her monthly statements because she didn't want them. They did, though, call with the quarterly summaries. Eleanor was a smart woman who kept tabs on her money.

The last entry was December 6, almost three weeks earlier. At the bottom of the page she noted: *Coke up 4% for year; WMart up 2.5%. CD rates still too low.*

Simon could almost see her taking careful notes during the quarterly calls, then sliding the notebook back into its hiding place. It had only twenty-five sheets of onionskin paper, a slightly beige color. He wondered where she hid the notebooks from previous years.

Santa had just arrived and Simon felt a measure of vindication. He hadn't been such a fool after all. His dear Netty was loaded to the max and he would be in charge of her estate one day. He poured out his drink, brushed his teeth, gargled with mouthwash, left his office, and drove to the hospital.

She was watching television in the dark when he eased into the room, tapping on the door. "Netty, it's me. Are you awake?"

Her face glowed with a huge smile and she held out her right arm, IVs and all. He squeezed her fragile, bony hand and whispered, "How are you doing?"

"Much better now," she said warmly and with a voice stronger than he expected. "Thanks for stopping by again, Simon."

It was his third visit of the day. He glanced at the counter near her bed. There were three bouquets of flowers, all sent by his office.

"Any other visitors?" he asked. As always, he was afraid Wally Thackerman or some other lawyer might be slithering around.

"No, no one but you," she said sadly.

"I stopped by your house. Everything is fine. Your neighbors, Norris and Rose, knocked on the door."

"What did they want?"

"Nothing, just saw my car and thought they should check into things. I told them I was your lawyer and things were fine."

"He's okay. She's rather snooty, thinks she's a notch above. They tried to join the country club but couldn't get in."

Simon really didn't care. "They were very nice. Just curious."

"Too curious." She muted the television and said, "Pull up a chair and let's talk. I'm worried sick about this accident, Simon. I don't think it was my fault."

He wrestled the chair over and squeezed into it.

"Are those people okay? The ones in the other car?"

"They'll be fine," he said. Both had broken bones and were missing work. They would hire a lawyer, and when they realized she had no insurance, they would probably file suit. However, at the moment, Simon wasn't worried about litigation, for now he knew the truth about Netty's assets. He could easily negotiate a generous settlement and put the matter to rest. As for the DUI, he couldn't make it go away, but he doubted the prosecutor would be too harsh, given her age. Plus, Simon would offer to pay a huge fine. Money usually allowed the guilty to get off light.

How pleasant it is to have money, he thought.

"How's the food?" he asked.

"Dreadful. Typical hospital stuff."

"Okay, what do you want? How about some egg rolls from that Korean place? Or Chinese dumplings? We've tried every-thing in town."

"What a marvelous idea, Simon. I'll take a bunch of egg rolls, those stuffed with shrimp."

"You got 'em. I'll be there when they open in the morning."

"What would I do without you, Simon?"

CHAPTER 26

Two days before Christmas, Matilda announced that she was leaving an hour early to do some shopping. Since the legal profession was known for loafing through half of December anyway, the office was quiet, and Simon didn't care when she left. He was re-drafting some leases for a real estate client, work that was so dull he'd been putting it off for a month. He was determined to finish it now and not punt it into 2016, a year that promised to be just as tedious and unproductive as the present, unless, of course, some lucrative estate work popped up. Eleanor Barnett's estate. He shook his head as he once again thought of the hours he had wasted dreaming of her death.

When he looked up and saw his secretary he said, "I thought you were gone."

"I was leaving when a man walked in."

"I'm not showing any appointments."

"He doesn't have one."

"Then get rid of him." Simon had learned years earlier that the drop-ins were both bothersome and broke. They never brought their checkbooks.

"You should make time for this guy." She looked uneasy.

"Who is it?"

"Name's Jerry Korsak. Brother of Clyde. Stepson of you know who. I don't think he's leaving."

"Does he appear to be violent?" Simon asked as he quietly pulled open a drawer and glanced at his .38.

"No, actually he's rather polite. Wears a tie."

Simon was not wearing one. He took a deep breath as reality set in. "Okay. Can you break it up in thirty minutes?"

"I'm going shopping, remember?"

"Right. Call me in thirty minutes with some urgent matter."

"Will do."

Simon paused for a second and checked the drawer again. He shook his head and said, "I'll be okay."

"I can't shoot like Fran but I can make some noise."

Both of them chuckled at the legend of Fran. Her threat to blast off Clyde's testicles was still good for a laugh around town. Simon said, "Thanks, but I'm fine."

"Okay. And I'll run by the hospital and see Eleanor. I made her some brownies and have a few other things. Poor lady doesn't see many visitors."

"Thanks for doing that, Tillie. She's a dear old woman in a lot of trouble."

———————— •••• ————————

The necktie was smartly knotted and went nicely with a plaid shirt and wool blazer. Jerry was in his early fifties, lean, cleanshaven, and well groomed. Simon had seen Clyde in the courtroom the day after he slugged poor Wally, and the difference between the brothers was startling.

Jerry said he was living in the "D.C. area" and working for a government contractor, which narrowed things down to around five million people. Simon didn't probe because he didn't want to seem interested, and also, he quickly learned that every answer was vague. As they chatted awkwardly and sipped coffee, Simon tried desperately to figure out if Jerry knew Eleanor was in the hospital,

and if so, then who told him. He referred to her as "Mom." Clyde
had used "Momma." They couldn't keep their lies straight. After a
few minutes of light conversation, Simon was convinced he could
not believe a word Jerry said. He was shifty-eyed, blinked a lot,
and had trouble looking at Simon and holding a gaze.

Finally, Simon asked, "What brings you to Braxton?"

"Oh, well, uh, Mom called last night, told me about her accident, asked me to come check on her."

Simon absorbed this with a hard stare, as if it wasn't true and he
wanted Jerry to know it was a lie. "Who told you I was Eleanor's
lawyer?"

"A nurse at the hospital."

"Really? Which one?"

"Oh, I don't know. Didn't take notes."

"So, you've been to the hospital?"

"Just left. Mom seems to be doing fine, don't you think?"

"I suppose. She got banged up pretty bad."

"I'm thinking of spending Christmas with her."

"In the hospital?"

"No, she says she's going home tomorrow. I figure she'll need
me around the house to help out, you know?"

"She's not going anywhere. She can't even walk yet."

Jerry tried to laugh, his first effort at that, and said, "Well,
someone needs to tell her."

"I talked to her doctor this morning," Simon said, controlling himself. "They'll move her to a rehab unit in a day or so and
start working with her legs. She won't be home anytime soon."
The idea of Jerry in the house was unsettling, though Simon had
removed as much sensitive material as possible. It was all locked
up in a drawer ten feet from his desk.

"Okay," Jerry said, eyes darting even quicker, then he blurted,
"Does she have a current will?"

"You'll have to ask her. I can't discuss client matters."

"She's my stepmother, the widow of my father. You can at
least tell me if she has a current will."

"Why do you want to know?"

"Because my father promised me and Clyde a nice gift in the estate."

"He died ten years ago."

"Right, and he forgot about the gift. We've always figured Mom would make things right in her will."

"How often do you see Eleanor?"

"Uh, well, not much. I've been living down in Florida and it's a long ways off, you know? But we talk all the time on the phone."

Simon had inspected her phone records and checked every long-distance call she'd made in the past year. Another lie. "That's odd, because I've known Eleanor since March and she's never said anything about having a conversation with you."

"Are you calling me a liar?"

"No sir, I am not."

Evidently, Jerry was not as hotheaded as his brother. He shrugged and put down his coffee cup. "Fair enough. I just wanted to say hello and let you know that I'm only an hour away, should you need me."

Simon had a dozen responses but managed to keep it pleasant with a simple "Thanks." He could not imagine any turn of events that would cause him to "need" the man. His sudden appearance was trouble.

After he left, Simon sat for a long time and tried to analyze the visit. Nothing made sense. An hour later, driving to the hospital, Simon decided not to mention the episode. If Eleanor brought it up he might quiz her. If she said nothing about it, he would assume Jerry was lying.

Loretta Goodwin met him in the hallway and said it was a bad time to visit. Eleanor was asleep and had not been feeling well. Her breathing was labored, her blood pressure was erratic, and she needed some rest.

"Has she had any visitors today?" Simon asked.

"I haven't seen any."

"Any lawyers snooping around?"

"As a matter of fact." Loretta pulled a business card out of a pocket and handed it over. "You know this guy?"

Simon looked at the card. It could've been worse. "Yeah, afraid so."

"He left about an hour ago."

"Thanks. I'll hang around in the cafeteria for a while. If she wakes up, come fetch me."

"That's what I live for."

CHAPTER 27

On the morning of Christmas Eve, Simon went to the house he once called home and said goodbye to his family. Paula and the children were packing up for the two-hour drive to Richmond where they would spend a couple of nights with their grandparents. Paula planned to wait until the day after Christmas to break the news about the divorce. Simon was still kicking the can with his mother and stepfather, who he had no plans to see until after the New Year.

The kids were in the holiday spirit and looking forward to seeing their grandparents. Two cousins lived close by and they enjoyed their time together. Simon was delighted to miss the trip.

After they left, he locked the house and went to check on Eleanor's. Ming's Chinese restaurant opened at eleven, and he was the first customer there. For carryout, he ordered two large portions of shrimp spring rolls and a box of crunchy rice cakes. He drove to the hospital and found Eleanor in a wheelchair singing carols with a dozen other patients in the small chapel. A youth minister from the Methodist church was leading them as he banged on the piano. Simon waited in the lobby and checked the Vegas line on football games.

For lunch he pushed her to the cafeteria and found a table with a nice view of the mountains. He unwrapped the spring rolls and poured honey on the side. She took two bites and seemed bored.

Eleanor was not herself. The head bandage was gone and the stitched wound looked awful. Not for the first time, he wondered how much damage the blow had caused. And he wondered how much of a toll the meds were taking. Her left leg was practically useless and would require hours of rehab before she could walk. She fretted over her legal problems and cried at the thought of causing the accident that hurt two others. Her speech was slow, her recall fuzzy. She coughed a lot and made noise when she breathed. Her nurse said they were worried about her fevers and headaches.

She said over and over, "Sy, please promise me I won't go to jail."

"I promise. You have my word."

And she wasn't going to jail. He had talked to the prosecutor several times and they were working out a deal. No one wanted her behind bars. Officer Pully had been reined in and was no longer threatening handcuffs.

She showed a bit more interest in the crunchy rice cakes, and Simon fetched some coffee. She ate one and nibbled on another before giving up. When she said she was tired, Simon pushed her back to her room and waited in the hall while two orderlies put her to bed. She was already asleep when he entered the room and quietly took a seat.

On the table near the bed, there were five floral arrangements, four from his office and one from a person he didn't know. There were four get-well cards, a platter of untouched brownies, and two boxes of Saigon ginger cookies from Tan Lu's.

Her breathing was heavy, even labored at times, but the monitors were not alarmed. Then she became quiet and slept peacefully. He wondered if the only other guest, other than himself and Tillie, had been Jerry Korsak. Did that clown really stop by this room, or was he lying? What was his game?

Simon closed his eyes and could see trouble around every corner.

He couldn't nap in the torture chair and was soon bored with waiting. As he was leaving the hospital, his luck changed dramatically with a phone call. It was Landy, who began with "Ho, Ho, Ho. How's your Christmas?"

"Ho right back. Doing swell, and you?"

"Delightful. Are you making big plans?"

"Not exactly. Paula took the kids to see her family, so it looks like a rather lonely Christmas Eve by the fire. What about you?"

"Same. My husband is in Puerto Rico staking out an arms dealer. Doesn't know when he might be home. How about that for a Merry Christmas?"

"Sounds pretty dull. Where are you?"

"Georgetown. Staying with a friend. You guys file papers?"

"We did. The PSA is on record and we're counting the days to make it official."

"And the kids?"

"Bummed-out but we're making the best of it, so far. Paula's cool. We're not fighting."

She paused for a second and said, "Let's get together, have a little Christmas cheer."

"Now?"

"Why not? I'm only an hour away. Drive over and we'll find a spot for dinner."

"You're on."

"And get a room."

The call was far more important than dinner and sex. It meant that he was no longer a target in whatever gambling probe the FBI was pursuing. Landy would never have a date with someone she was investigating.

Or would she?

They met in a hotel bar, one that couldn't close on Christmas Eve because of guests. Almost all of them appeared to be foreigners and a half dozen languages chattered about. The lobby and bar were draped with ivy and lights and carols hummed overhead. The holiday spirit was contagious, especially after the first drink. Landy had ditched the drab FBI garb and was dressed up in a short, slinky dress and heels. She looked rather fetching and Simon's mind was instantly wandering. They reminisced about their law school days as if they were a couple of geezers instead of two forty-year-olds entering middle age. As they remembered old classmates and difficult professors, both were thinking of the rowdy sex they had enjoyed back in those days.

Simon finally said, "You have to tell me the truth, Landy. About the investigation."

"You think I would be here if you were still involved?"

"No, I don't. When you called, I assumed I was off the hook."

"You are. Justice shut down the investigation. Someone up there ultimately agreed with you and decided we have bigger fish to catch. Small-time gamblers are a dime a dozen and where are the victims? I thought it was a waste of time from day one."

Simon could not suppress a smile. He closed his eyes and said, "Thank you. What about Chub?"

"Free and clear. We don't have the time or energy to chase down bookies."

"Can I tell him?"

"He knows. His lawyer was informed yesterday. Merry Christmas to all."

Simon kept smiling as a heavy, dark cloud disappeared. There were others, but none carried the possibility of a federal indictment.

She said, "But you should be more careful, Simon. When I first saw your name I was shocked."

"How many names were there?"

"Couple of hundred. Chub is a busy boy. At first we thought he was working with some Mexicans and distributing fentanyl, but our sources dried up. Once we realized he was only a bookie we lost interest. He's a big bookie, though, with business up and down the East Coast. I'd stay away from him."

"Don't worry." But Simon was already thinking of late-night visits with a drink or two and the games on the big screens.

"I'm starving. Let's order from the bar menu and stay here."

"Good idea. And the check's on me, a free man."

They ordered sandwiches and fries and had another drink. They talked about their careers and their frustrations. She had been with the FBI for eighteen years, since law school, and, like all agents, would be forced to retire at fifty-seven. She didn't want to wait that long before getting the boot, but she had few options. She felt too old to learn how to practice law.

Don't do it, Simon said. He clicked off a litany of reasons to avoid the grind that had become his life and career. The dinner arrived and the conversation slowly wound around to why they were there. Two married people, old lovers, meeting in a bar on Christmas Eve, indulging in the pleasant pre-game before they hustled upstairs for a romp, one for old time's sake.

She startled him with "I think we should wait before we go to bed."

"Aren't we waiting now?"

"I'm serious. Your marriage is almost over. Mine is a mess. It seems rather foolish to start something now that will only complicate matters."

"When would you like to start?"

"I don't know. You've taken the big step. Curt and I have talked about it. We've drifted so far apart we seldom talk. I haven't seen him in three weeks and don't know when he's coming home. He called four days ago. He's probably seeing someone else."

"It is a mess."

"Give me some time, and I promise it won't be long. I really want to see you, Simon."

"You're seeing me now."

"You know what I mean."

CHAPTER 28

The cough persisted and did not respond to the usual medications. It became more worrisome when Eleanor began spitting mucus. Her fevers and headaches came and went, but always returned with sweating, followed by chills. She complained of a heavy chest and difficulty breathing. Her appetite was gone and she refused everything but the ginger cookies and green tea. She was fatigued but couldn't sleep because of all the coughing. Two days after Christmas, Dr. Lilly informed Simon that she had pneumonia, but it was under control. A few rounds of strong antibiotics should do the trick.

The pneumonia kept her in bed and prevented physical therapy. She had been in the hospital for a week with little improvement. The antibiotics did nothing to help and her breathing became even more labored. When a monitor erupted she was put on a ventilator. On the morning of December 28, Simon and Tillie went to the hospital to check on Eleanor. While Tillie sat by her bed, Simon met with Dr. Lilly, Dr. Wilkes, and two other physicians, and listened as they discussed options. They would immediately begin draining her lungs. She was conscious, most of the time.

Simon was practically living at the hospital, where he camped out in a waiting room. A couple of her girlfriends from the "poker club" showed up, but they were not allowed into her room.

After ten hours on the ventilator, her lungs were filling up faster than they could be drained. Simon whispered in her ear and, for the first time, there was no response. He huddled with Dr. Lilly who said, "She cannot breathe on her own. I'm afraid she's choking. There is virtually no brain activity."

Simon was well aware that what he said and did in the next few hours would probably be reviewed by lawyers, so he said as little as possible.

Then Dr. Lilly said, "Let's wait a few more hours."

Simon mumbled a soft "Okay." He left the hospital, drove to his office, and tried to nap.

Tillie woke him up and said he was needed at the hospital. He asked her to go with him. He might need a witness, though that was not mentioned. As always, he carried his briefcase. In it was the file with the advance directive and power of attorney signed by Eleanor.

Her condition was even more hopeless. Even with the ventilator at full throttle, her frail and aged body could barely breathe. Her brain had already ceased showing any activity, and her lungs and heart were working only with the aid of a machine.

Dr. Wilkes said, "Simon, it looks like the decision is yours."

He had been anticipating this moment and was already shaking his head. "No, I'm not doing that, not going there. It's a medical decision."

Dr. Wilkes said, "The advance directive is quite clear. No resuscitation, no ventilators, no feeding tubes, no device to prolong a heartbeat."

"I know, I wrote it. But I'm not making the decision. I'm not a blood relative and I do not feel comfortable being in this room."

Dr. Lilly tossed the advance directive on the table and said, "Okay, let's meet here at eight in the morning." He walked out of the room, followed by two other doctors and Loretta Goodwin.

The same group reconvened at eight the following morning. Dr. Lilly said, "The patient's condition has not improved, in fact it's only worsened. She can't breathe by herself and the monitors show no brain activity. It is my advice to turn off the ventilator."

Dr. Wilkes said, "Mr. Latch?"

"I'll follow the advice of my client's medical team. Do you all agree?"

Everyone nodded in agreement. Simon retired to the cafeteria and tried to drink some coffee. Ninety minutes passed before Loretta Goodwin walked in and whispered, "It's over."

Eleanor Barnett was pronounced dead at 10:02 A.M., December 30, 2015, at the Blue Ridge Memorial Hospital.

Simon went to the main office to plow through the paperwork with Dr. Wilkes and her staff. She said, "I'm sure you've made final arrangements."

"I have, with Cupit & Moke. When will the body be released?"

"The death certificate is being prepared. A medical examiner will be here in an hour to sign it. We should be finished by one P.M."

————— ◆◆ —————

An informant entered the picture with a tip that arrived not long after the pronouncement of death; 10:26 to be exact, according to the phone records that would be analyzed for months. The person who made the call was thought to be a male, though that was never certain. The anonymous voice was obviously disguised. The call bounced off a tower on top of the hospital. A cheap burner phone, probably tossed in the pond after the call. It was recorded and listened to a thousand times:

"Eleanor Barnett just passed away at Blue Ridge Memorial. The doctors say it's pneumonia. But her death is suspicious. It should be investigated."

The 911 dispatcher called the Braxton Police Department and sent the recording to a Detective Roger Barr. At the moment, Barr was the only detective on duty. If the BPD had a homicide unit, it was Barr. The last murder had been seventeen months earlier and witnessed by four people, so the investigation had been easy. Barr listened to the recording, then listened again with his chief, who shrugged and said, "Give it a go."

Detective Barr called the hospital, talked to Dr. Wilkes, got enough details, and drove to the funeral home of Cupit & Moke. He was loitering in the front parlor when Eleanor was rolled through the back door and taken to the cooling unit. An elderly secretary brought forth Mr. Douglas Gregg, the owner and mortician, in his daily black suit. He smiled and asked, "How may I help you?"

Barr, in his customary battered navy jacket, wrinkled khakis, and worn cowboy boots, said, "Sure, thanks, so what are your plans right now with Ms. Barnett?"

"She is to be cremated and buried next to her husband at Eternal Springs Cemetery."

"Okay, and who's in charge of her arrangements?"

"Mr. Simon Latch, her attorney."

"Heard of him, but don't know him. Look, hold off on the cremation until I find Mr. Latch, okay?"

"Certainly, Officer. We never rush these things. Is there a problem?"

"Don't know yet."

———◆◆◆———

Simon was at his desk examining an egg salad sandwich that had been in the fridge for at least two weeks. Store-bought. Surely there were enough chemicals in it to ward off spoilage, but there was a strange, tangy smell to it. There was nothing else in the fridge, at least on his side. On Tillie's side there was an impressive row of veggie drinks and fruit flushes, all of which were working superbly.

How could he be thinking of her figure at a time like this?

Eleanor Barnett had just died. She had been a huge part of his life for the past nine months and would, most likely, dominate his future. He had warm feelings for her and a great deal of sympathy, a lovely woman who spent her last years with no family and few friends. He was also relieved to be free of the worries and responsibility of her care, though tidying up her affairs might take years. He wouldn't miss the lunches, though some were enjoyable.

He fought off his emotions by telling himself that Netty lived a long, happy life and died with little suffering. He doubted he would see his eighty-fifth year.

Tillie interrupted his solitude by tapping on the door as she entered with the look that only meant trouble. She handed him the business card of DETECTIVE ROGER BARR, BRAXTON POLICE.

"What does he want?"

"Wouldn't say. I'm going to lunch."

Barr settled into his chair in such a way as to reveal a black Glock on his hip. What an amateur. Simon had never met him, but then he tried to avoid criminal work.

Barr's thick mustache covered his top lip. From under it the gruff words came out: "Just left the funeral home. What's the hurry with cremating Ms. Barnett?"

"She died two hours ago. How did you get involved so soon?"

"That's my business, Mr. Latch. Are you in a hurry or something?"

"Not at all. When she was pronounced dead, I called the funeral home. That's what usually happens. Either the family or the hospital will make the call."

"Are you family?"

"I am not. There is no family to speak of." Everything about Barr was irritating. His sudden involvement, his cocky smirk, as if he knew something fishy was in the works. Simon decided to push back. "What's your involvement with Ms. Barnett?"

"Right now, nothing but a lot of curiosity. The death certificate says she died of pneumonia, that right?"

"What's your question?"

"Did she die of pneumonia?"

"Look, I'm not a doctor and I didn't sign her death certificate. If it says pneumonia, then it's pneumonia. Why don't you ask her doctor?"

"Oh, I will. I have a lot of questions. But for now, let's hold off on the cremation, okay?"

"By what authority are you making this request?"

"I'll get a court order. What's the big hurry?"

"There is no hurry. I've never been in this position before. The hospital released the body to the funeral home, and Ms. Barnett's advance directive calls for a cremation, then a burial. I'm just following my client's wishes."

"Got that. I'll get a court order anyway."

Simon was exasperated and trying to think two steps ahead. A court order might mean more publicity, and for some reason that was not what he wanted. He said, "That won't be necessary. I'll call the funeral home and tell them to wait."

"I've already done that."

CHAPTER 29

The year would not end on a quiet note. On Thursday, December 31, Circuit Court Judge Mary Blankenship Pointer was having her morning coffee with her husband at their little breakfast nook, both still in pajamas. They were discussing a small New Year's Eve dinner party they had been invited to but would rather avoid, when their landline rang.

The voice on the other end identified himself as Teddy Hammer, attorney, of the firm of such and such in Washington, D.C. He had an emergency matter that needed to be heard that morning, if at all possible. Judge Pointer explained that she normally kept her office open until noon on New Year's Eve, though there was never much activity. Mr. Hammer explained the nature of his emergency and said he was emailing a copy of his petition for a temporary injunction at that very moment. It was brief, only two pages, and he could be in her courtroom by 10 A.M.

As she waited for the petition to arrive via internet, she checked out Mr. Hammer, a lawyer she had never heard of, but then there were at least a million of them in D.C. The big city was far away from Braxton in so many ways. His firm had ten lawyers with an office on Connecticut Avenue and another one in Arlington. It was a typical lawyer's website, with lots of bluster and self-congratulations.

Mr. Hammer represented Jerry and Clyde Korsak, two step-sons of Ms. Eleanor Barnett, who had passed away the day before. His clients were concerned about the "mysterious circumstances" surrounding her death and wanted to get to the bottom of things. They requested that all funeral and burial arrangements be stopped, or "held in abeyance" in lawyer talk, until an autopsy could be performed. At the bottom of the second page, Mr. Hammer stated that a copy of the petition was being emailed simultaneously to the Honorable Simon F. Latch, attorney for Eleanor Barnett.

Attorney Latch was at his desk studying Vegas lines for bowl games, with his coffee, when the email came across. In one dreadful split second he forgot about football and yelled an expletive. His office door was open but the place was empty. Tillie, of course, had the entire day off. There were no appointments. Simon was still in his boxers.

In the middle of his desk was a small bowl filled with low-fat Greek yogurt, blueberries, and granola, and he had been preparing to dive in. Now, he stared at the food with no desire whatsoever. His stomach churned. He fought off a wave of nausea.

Was this the beginning of the end? Was his grand scheme and scam finally unraveling? What could possibly be mysterious about Netty's death? He had watched her deteriorate as pneumonia set in. The coughing, fevers, labored breathing—all the symptoms were there and he had discussed her condition with the nurses and the doctors. An eighty-five-year-old woman got banged up in a car wreck, couldn't walk, didn't eat much, took plenty of meds, and slowly withered away. Where was the mystery?

Now the vultures were swarming.

Once he had collected his thoughts, somewhat, and the room had stopped spinning, he thought about calling Mr. Teddy Hammer and cursing him. But the more diplomatic and beneficial approach might be to call with a professional hello and dig for information. Either call was a bad idea.

He searched Hammer's firm, absorbed the first image of the man, and loathed everything about him. Age about fifty, expensive dark suit, chubby cheeks, puffy eyes, the cocky smirk of a street lawyer who knew how to hurt you. His firm wasn't much; the usual collection of hustlers trying to portray an image of a blue-ribbon D.C. firm with plenty of connections.

There were so many baffling scenarios, but the one that was most disturbing was the fact that Jerry and Clyde had joined forces. When Simon had quizzed Eleanor about them, she had always given the impression that the stepsons lived in separate worlds and didn't like each other. Now the two outlaws had teamed up with an aggressive lawyer to wreak havoc with Eleanor's death.

⸺•••⸺

When Simon walked into the courtroom at exactly ten-thirty, Judge Pointer was already on the bench and chatting with a clerk. A court reporter filed her nails as she waited, obviously irritated at being called in on a holiday. Simon introduced himself to Teddy Hammer, who was alone. The only spectator in the room was Detective Roger Barr, who sat in the front row and flipped through a magazine.

They were in Courtroom B, a much smaller room and one used for non-jury trials. Judge Pointer preferred it over the larger, grander courtroom because it was more intimate, plus the HVAC system was more reliable. She had been given her judgeship fourteen years earlier by the General Assembly, no messy campaigns to worry about, and she was well regarded by the bar. After a round of all the obligatory pleasantries, she called things to order and the court reporter began recording the proceedings.

Judge Pointer said, "This is an expedited matter that would normally require notice to all parties and some preparation, but, as I understand things, Ms. Barnett died yesterday and there is some concern over what happens next with her remains. Mr. Latch, you are her attorney? Please keep your seat."

"I suppose I am, Your Honor. I prepared her last will and testament and I have a power of attorney over her affairs, but I have not been appointed by the court to handle her estate. I'm sort of in limbo here."

"Okay, let's proceed."

Simon jumped in with "And Your Honor, just to be on the safe side, I suggest that this hearing be closed and the record secured, for now anyway."

Hammer said, "We have no problem with that."

Judge Pointer said, "Well, the only spectator I can see right now is Detective Barr with the Braxton Police. Mr. Barr, do you mind stepping outside? We'll call you if we need you."

Barr was irritated and glared at Simon as he left the courtroom.

Judge Pointer said, "Mr. Hammer, it's your petition. You have the floor."

"Thank you, Your Honor. It's really quite simple. I represent the two stepsons of Ms. Eleanor Barnett. She passed yesterday. It appears as though Mr. Latch is eager to have her remains cremated. Indeed, at this moment she's being held in the cooling unit in the basement of Cupit & Moke Funeral Home, just down the street. We are in no position to make accusations or arouse suspicion, but my clients would like to know the exact cause of death before she is buried. Thus, they request a time-out and an autopsy."

Simon had made the decision years earlier to avoid courtrooms if at all possible. He loathed trial work and had never felt comfortable on his feet. The courtrooms he frequented did not have jury boxes or counsel tables. Most matters were not contested. It was obvious to him that Teddy Hammer was a smooth brawler who had addressed many judges and juries.

Simon replied, "Ms. Barnett was in the hospital for two weeks before she died. She was treated by the best doctors in town. I was there every day. I watched her slowly succumb to pneumonia. Her doctors tried everything, including a ventilator for the final two days. They have no doubt she died of pneumonia. There is no need for an autopsy."

Judge Pointer asked, "And you prepared her last will and testament?"

"That's correct."

"And in that will did she give instructions as to her final arrangements?"

"No, ma'am. Those instructions were given in a subsequent document, her advance directive."

"And when did she sign that?"

"Twelve days ago."

"In the hospital?"

"Yes."

"And it was prepared by you?"

"Yes."

The judge seemed suspicious. Indeed, an air of suspicion seemed to settle in the courtroom. Hammer read it perfectly and said, "Your Honor, my clients believe that their father and step-mother owned a burial policy issued by Cupit & Moke, and it provides for funeral services and a burial next to their father at the Eternal Springs Cemetery. It covers embalming, preparation, a nice casket, a memorial service, and burial. The works. There's nothing in that policy about cremation."

"Mr. Latch?"

"It's simple, Your Honor," Simon said. "Ms. Barnett changed her mind. We discussed it many times. Cremation is gaining popularity across the country and she liked the idea."

"Do you have copies of her advance directive?"

"Of course." Simon quickly handed a copy to the judge and one to Hammer. They took their time and read every word. When they finished, Hammer said, "Your Honor, Ms. Barnett can be cremated next week, after an autopsy, as per her wishes. There's no problem. And there's no rush. It's a holiday weekend. Everybody is off work on Monday. Let the family get the autopsy and have that peace of mind, and if it proves the cause of death was pneumonia, then she can be cremated. No problem."

Judge Pointer pushed her file away and said, "Okay, here's what we'll do. I'll grant the injunction and order the funeral home to transport the remains for an autopsy. In the meantime, I will order that all estate proceedings be held in abeyance until after the autopsy and after the burial. At that time, we will meet again and decide how to proceed with probate. This record of this hearing is sealed, as is the file. All participants are ordered to keep this matter confidential. Understood?"

Both lawyers nodded and agreed. Judge Pointer adjourned the hearing and disappeared. Simon and Teddy stood and shook hands. Simon asked, "So who does the autopsy?"

"The chief medical examiner at the crime lab in Richmond."

Crime? Simon took a deep breath and tried to speak.

Teddy flashed a conspiratorial look that spoke volumes, and said, "Off the record, Mr. Latch, but there's a good chance your client did not die of natural causes."

CHAPTER 30

Detective Barr left the courthouse and drove to the hospital. Along the way he took a call from Teddy Hammer, who told him everything that happened after he was kicked out of the courtroom.

At the hospital, Barr met Dr. Wilkes and followed her to a small conference room where the table was covered with various items collected from the hospital room occupied by Eleanor Barnett. Nurse Loretta Goodwin and an orderly had arranged the items in some order and prepared an inventory. Barr carefully photographed everything, then recorded it all with a video.

There was a disposable aluminum platter with eleven chocolate brownies and some crumbs. From the looks of it, Eleanor was not a fan of chocolate. There were three floral arrangements from the same local florist, all with cards from the law offices of Simon Latch. The flowers were wilted and needed to be tossed. There were four get-well cards from four different people. And there were two decorative boxes for carryout from the Vietnamese restaurant Tan Lu's. Inside one box were two Saigon ginger cookies. The other identical box held nine of them. The restaurant's name and logo were printed on two sides of each box.

Barr was careful not to touch any of the items. Loretta and the orderly were wearing nitrile exam gloves.

He said, "Okay, I'm going to play it safe and wait until I get a search warrant before I take these items. Until then, I ask you to box it all up and store it in a cool place. The food will only continue to deteriorate."

"For how long?" asked Dr. Wilkes.

"Not long."

———— ◆•◆ ————

At 2 P.M. Thursday afternoon, December 31, the body of Eleanor Barnett was placed into a cheap metal casket, loaded into the Cupit & Moke hearse, and driven two hours to the state crime lab in Richmond. It was placed on a rack in the morgue, along with six other bodies, to await an autopsy in a few days.

It was a holiday weekend and the medical examiner was out of town.

———— ◆•◆ ————

For Simon, it was the worst New Year's holiday of his life. He roamed his locked office talking to himself, replaying each day of December, trying to piece together conversations and meetings and movements. He wanted desperately to plunge into the internet and dig for information about autopsies, but he was afraid to touch it. Everything left a trail. He recalled an infamous case from California in which a husband was the suspect in his wife's disappearance. An expert was hired by the police to dig into hubby's internet activities, and he found visits to such sites as "How To Dispose Of A Human Body," and "Killing With No Evidence Left Behind," and "Phantom Murders." Hubby was now doing life with no parole.

Every email, every website, every text message might become fair game at some awful point in the future. So he stayed with the gambling and sports sites, with which he was well acquainted.

But what was he afraid of? He'd done nothing wrong.

He wanted to see his kids but Paula was in a foul mood. If she only knew. His mood was a hundred times darker than hers so he stayed away from the house. When the office walls closed in he retreated to Chub's where he played video poker for hours as Valerie brought one drink after another. With his inhibitions on the wane, he said what the hell and started betting on bowl games. A hundred bucks a pop. He won his first five in a row and upped the ante.

He awoke on Saturday, January 2, with a hangover and cursed himself for being such a loser. As a penance, he packed a lunch and plenty of water and drove two hours to the south end of the Shenandoah National Park. The temperature was dropping and snow was forecast, and snow was what he wanted. He hit the trails, hiking for hours as he went deeper into the park. When they first fell in love, he and Paula had spent hours on the same trails, often hiking until dark when they pitched a trail tent and slept naked together in the same sleeping bag. To keep their backpacks light, they carried little food, just jerky and canned meats, and after three days of hiking and sex they emerged famished and pounds lighter. Their destination was always the same barbecue joint in the town of Staunton.

The snow finally began falling midafternoon, and Simon turned around. Everything ached, from the pounding inside his head to the soles of his feet, but he didn't care. The hike had cleared his mind, if only for a few hours.

CHAPTER 31

In Virginia, fewer than 5 percent of corpses underwent autopsies. There were several reasons for performing one, with a potential homicide the most likely. In those cases, the local law enforcement officials contacted the state medical examiner and sent along the body. The suspected cause of death was placed on a tag and attached to the body.

For Eleanor Barnett, the tag read: POSSIBLE POISONING.

With that warning, the state medical examiner, Dr. Dendra Brock, knew what to look for. She began her work at 9:31 on Monday morning, January 4. With no entry wounds, exit wounds, bullets, fragments, rope burns, or knife incisions to worry about, she concentrated on the organs. She was assisted by Dr. Henry Roster, a forensic toxicologist whose lab assistants were on standby. Among other procedures, they removed the liver, kidneys, heart, lungs, stomach, esophagus, pancreas, and sections of the large and small intestines. They weighed each organ, then dissected them to obtain tissue samples.

After working for two hours nonstop, they returned the organs to the cavity, stitched the corpse, and tidied up.

The cause of death was not pneumonia. It was a clear case of ingesting a highly toxic poison. Six hours later, Dr. Roster called Dr. Brock and reported that the poison was thallium. Odorless, tasteless, colorless, it had been around for decades and had been either used or suspected in dozens of murders around the world. Its production had been banned in the United States since 1984.

The following day, Dr. Brock met with Detective Barr and reviewed her findings. She had no control over what happened to the body but strongly urged the police to prevent cremation. Barr followed the hearse back to Braxton. Along the way, he called Teddy Hammer with the news that they were expecting. He called Judge Pointer, who agreed to stop the cremation. He did not call Simon Latch. He obtained a search warrant and took possession of the items Eleanor left behind in her hospital room. He also wanted to search her home and the judge signed a second warrant. On Wednesday morning, Barr returned to the state crime lab with the items and presented them to Dr. Henry Roster. Since he had a good idea as to what they were looking for, their job was much easier.

According to Nurse Loretta Goodwin, the brownies had been baked by Matilda, who delivered them herself. Eleanor didn't like them and had tried to give them to the nurses and orderlies. Thankfully, they had refused. It was against the hospital's policy to sample food brought to the patients. The brownies were at least a week old by then. The chemical analysis revealed no toxicity.

The Saigon ginger cookies were another story. There were eleven, two in one box, older and stale, and nine in another box. Both containers were clearly marked as being from Tan Lu's. Significant levels of thallium were found in every cookie.

On Thursday morning, Detective Barr walked into Tan Lu's with a search warrant and asked for their sales receipts. The Vietnamese were terrified and overly eager to comply. Within minutes, they found the receipts. The waitress identified a photo of Simon Latch, and even remembered his name.

———◆▸———

Simon had been staring at his phone for days and was a nervous wreck. The landline on his desk. It hadn't made a sound.

The first week in January was usually the slowest of the year and the landline seldom rang anyway. Now, though, he kept checking to make sure it wasn't unplugged. He would make the calls himself if he knew who to call. He had no contact with the medical examiner's office, and even if he had one he couldn't simply call and ask about the autopsy. Such information was strictly confidential, or it was until it got hashed about in a court of law. Simon could call the funeral home but why waste the time? He really wanted to have a chat with Detective Barr, a man who was dominating his thoughts, dreams, even nightmares, but he knew Barr would make an appearance on his own terms.

The waiting was nerve-racking and debilitating. He could not concentrate on anything and his current files were gathering dust.

Detective Barr called just before 6 P.M. on Thursday and asked if he could stop by. As if Simon could say no.

They sat in the conference room with a wide table between them. Barr looked at his notes, of which there seemed to be plenty, and asked, "Did you prepare a last will and testament for Ms. Barnett?"

"I did, back in March."

"Could I see it?"

"I don't think so. It's confidential."

"Well, your client is dead and you have to probate the will, right?"

"That's the plan, as soon as Judge Pointer gives the green light."

"And the probate becomes a public matter, right? So the public can see the will, right?"

"Maybe, maybe not. It's possible to close the file and keep everything confidential."

"How convenient. Did Ms. Barnett have a lot of money?"

"I really can't discuss this right now. Maybe later. What about the autopsy?"

"I can't discuss it."

"Did it confirm the cause of death as pneumonia?"

"I can't discuss it."

"There seems to be a lot of secrets here, a lot of things we can't discuss."

"Yeah, I guess it'll all come out in court," Barr said with a nasty little smile.

"Court? Who's going to court?"

"I can't discuss it right now."

"Why are we having this meeting if you can't talk about anything?"

"I want to see her will."

"Sorry."

"I'll get a warrant."

"Go ahead."

"And I'll need to search your computers."

"Sorry."

"I'll get some more warrants."

"I can't stop you."

"Later." Barr abruptly stood and left the room.

Simon didn't move for a few minutes. When he did, he realized his underarms were wet and his shirt was sticking to his back. He walked into the alley behind his office for a blast of arctic air. He made a call, and an hour later walked around the corner and down the street to the offices of the best criminal lawyer in town, a man few people liked, including Simon.

———◆◆◆———

Raymond Lassiter was a large, loud, boisterous attorney who strove to be colorful. His reputation had been built on a couple of sensational murder trials he had won many years earlier, and he still attracted high-end criminals up and down the Shenandoah Valley. He once boasted of having won seventeen murder trials in a row, but there was no one to verify it. Much of what Raymond said needed verification, but why bother? Most folks enjoyed his act and routine and took him in stride. He was a tough courtroom fighter. Police and prosecutors preferred to avoid him. If you got yourself in trouble and had a little money, he was the lawyer to see. He was in his early seventies and still worked seven days a week. Because of his excessive drinking, his mornings were slow and he seldom hit his stride until his staff left around five. He was known to work until midnight, usually with a bourbon on his desk and a cigar in the ashtray. A strict disciplinarian, he put away the booze when a trial started and became laser-focused. Sobriety made him meaner.

But he wasn't entirely sober when Simon arrived shortly after eight, nor was he drunk. Raymond could drink all day and keep his blood alcohol level around 0.10, a nice buzz but nothing that would distract him. Simon took a bourbon but not a cigar. Raymond propped up his feet on his oversized desk and said, "Tell me your story, but I only want to hear what I need to hear. Not everything, you understand?"

Simon had never shared secrets with a criminal lawyer before and wasn't sure what Raymond wanted to hear. "Shouldn't we sign something, like a representation agreement, you know, with a fee? To make it official?"

Raymond waved him off with his cigar. "Later. My fee is five bucks for the next twenty minutes. I want to hear your story. We'll do the paperwork later."

"So it's now attorney-client?"

"Yeah, yeah, get on with it."

After the basics, Raymond interrupted with "So you don't know what's in the autopsy?"

"No. Detective Barr wouldn't say."

"Barr's a good guy. Not too bright but dogged and tough. I've had him on the stand a few times." Raymond blew smoke as if he had eviscerated Barr and might want to talk about it later.

Simon said, "But Teddy Hammer hinted rather strongly that the death was not natural."

"Hammer's an asshole," Raymond said, blowing more smoke.

I'm sure he's a big fan of yours. Are we making progress by name-calling?

"He seemed quite sure of himself. I have not been accused of anything, Raymond, but I can feel the suspicion."

"Suspicion? It's a PR nightmare. Greedy lawyer discovers nice old lady has a secret fortune so he prepares a will that gives him control of her assets then convinces her, while she's injured and drugged and in the hospital, to sign a power of attorney and advance directive that gives him even more power, including the right to pull the plug, which he does, conveniently on December thirtieth as the clock is running out, and she barely dies last year when there's no estate tax, thus giving said greedy lawyer even more money to play with. Her death was suspicious and the greedy lawyer tries his damnedest to get her remains cremated, his idea not hers, before anybody can ask questions. Did you say *suspicion*?"

Simon had never felt so guilty.

Raymond had him bleeding and on the ropes and went for the kill. "Son, I get two hundred thousand bucks up front for a murder case, not a penny less."

Simon was prepared to be shocked, or so he thought. He had no idea how much a noted trial lawyer would charge for a murder case, but his guess was somewhat lower. He said, "I don't have that kind of money. And I'm not sure I'll be charged with anything. It's just that the cops are sniffing around and I don't want to make the wrong move."

"Smart guy. Look, consider this. I'll cover for you now in the initial stages. When Barr comes back for more, tell him I represent you. Sometimes that scares the cops off, but not always. I'll bully Barr and see how serious it is. And I'll do it pro bono until there's an indictment."

"There won't be an indictment because I've done nothing wrong. I just need someone to talk to."

"Fine. Talk to me and follow my advice. If things get more serious, then we'll have another chat."

A blue cloud hung near the ceiling and the rich smell of fine tobacco permeated the room. Simon was frightened and didn't want to leave. "If the offer is still there, I'll have one of those cigars."

Raymond smiled and said, "Help yourself. I'll pour us another drink."

CHAPTER 32

Friday morning, Simon finally mustered the courage to place a phone call he should have made months earlier. If Eleanor had had it her way, Wally would have been notified a long time ago.

He answered the phone with a warm "Well, good morning, Simon."

After two minutes of the obligatory small talk, Wally said, "I saw the injunction and was told you were in charge of the burial. What's going on?"

"Well, Wally, it's a long story and I'll be brief. Last March, Eleanor came to my office and wanted a new will. She said she was not happy with the one you drafted and wanted to make some changes. I did what she wanted. Her new one was signed two months after the one you prepared. So, your will is revoked, null, and void."

"Sounds like a lawsuit, Latch."

"I was expecting something like that. If I were you I wouldn't get too trigger-happy. Your will is worthless and should be tossed. No one knows about it, Wally, and no one knows about the little cash bonus payable to you that's buried in the fine print. If you try and probate that will, of course there will be a big fight. However, your immediate problem is the gift to you. Outright, payable upon probate, a naked grab for cash by the estate lawyer. From a nice little old lady who trusted you. If you try to probate your will, or object to mine, then I'll file a complaint with the state bar association and send them your will."

"You son of a bitch."

"Cuss all you want, Wally, it doesn't bother me."

He cussed some more, then settled down. "When will you probate your will?"

"Not sure. I'll have to check with Judge Pointer, she seems to be in charge of things."

"I heard about the autopsy. Why bother? She was eighty-five years old."

Simon said, "Wasn't my idea. Looks like Clyde and his brother Jerry hired a big-shot lawyer to gum up the works. You remember Clyde, don't you?"

"Funny, Latch. I guess he beat up the wrong lawyer."

"You'll take him in the rematch."

"Funny. Mind if I take a look at the will you drafted?"

"Not until it's probated."

"Who gets the money?"

"A bunch of nonprofits, nothing to family and friends."

"Did you find the money?"

"Sort of. Did you?"

Wally waited a long time before saying, "Not really. I made some calls to people she mentioned but I didn't dig too deep."

Simon waited just as long, and before he could speak Wally said, "Pretty shitty deal on your part, Latch. You should've told me."

"And what would that have accomplished? Probably nothing more than a knee-jerk lawsuit of some sort."

"You should've told me," he said again, rather sadly, as if he'd just heard the news that a big pile of money had vanished, a fortune he was counting on.

Before he could stop himself, Simon blurted, "Eleanor didn't want me to." It was a terrible lie, but then she was dead and Wally would never know the difference.

Long after he ended the call, Simon still couldn't believe he had lied so easily and convincingly.

———◆◆◆———

Sitting at his desk after another unproductive hour, Simon could almost hear the walls closing in. His building had been built in 1904, so the wall studs and most of the plaster were a century old. They were moving, centimeter by centimeter, slowly toward the center where they would inevitably crunch violently together and slaughter him in the process. There was no way out, nowhere to run, and no one to talk to. Except Raymond, his new free lawyer who was already looking for a way to ditch him if things got hot. And talking to Raymond was a chore. No conversation was complete without at least two war stories about his old courtroom victories. He never said a word about his losses.

At times Simon could hear the floor squeak, the walls moan, the vents contract, the plaster chip, and his latest daydream would be shattered. He was daydreaming a lot because he was tired, fatigued from sleep deprivation. He had no appetite, not for food anyway, but he worried that he was drinking too much. Most mornings he woke up with a cobweb or two, nothing debilitating that would ruin his day, but some little aches in the brain that told him he needed to cut back. What was the old saying? "If you think you might be drinking too much, then you are."

"The Last Will and Testament of Eleanor Barnett" was always somewhere within reach. He had typed it himself some ten months earlier, and was trying to convince himself that he would change nothing about it. Nor would he do anything different.

Why, then, was he losing sleep and weight and drinking too much?

———◆◆◆———

His worst fears were played out in slow motion. Nine days after the autopsy, and with Eleanor still in the freezer, Raymond called with the troubling news that Detective Barr wanted to arrange a meeting to discuss the case. That was not too unexpected, according to Raymond, who'd been through it many times. Barr suggested the meeting take place in Simon's office.

It was immediately obvious that the detective was uneasy around Raymond, probably because of his reputation. But Barr was the investigator and playing offense. He opened the meeting with "I just have a few questions for your client, Mr. Lassiter, and a few requests."

"And we have some questions too," Raymond said smugly.

Barr ignored this and looked at his notes. "First, as you know, we've searched the home of Ms. Barnett, but it was not a thorough search. I'd rather not ransack the place, so I'll ask you what items have you removed from the home?"

Raymond nodded at Simon who said, "As her attorney, I am in charge of her financial affairs. I have a copy of the power of attorney for you. I've taken her checkbook and a stack of bills. I've also removed a small safe from her closet but I have not opened it."

"Where was the safe?"

"Hidden in the bottom of her bedroom closet."

"And what's in the safe?"

"Don't know. I was advised by counsel not to open it."

Raymond chimed in with "We'll wait until you get a warrant and open it together."

"Okay. Do you have a general idea what's in the safe?"

Raymond nodded at Simon who replied, "A burial policy, her last will and testament, property deeds, car title, various insurance policies. That's all she told me."

"Any valuables? Jewelry, cash, the like?"

"Don't know."

Barr stuck his pen in his shirt pocket and said, "Very well, then, I suggest we meet back here at the same time tomorrow. I'll have another search warrant."

Raymond asked, "We'd like to see the autopsy report."

"I'll bring it tomorrow."

"Okay. Last question—Is Mr. Latch a suspect in the death of Eleanor Barnett?"

"I can't answer that right now."

———•••———

The following day, Raymond was back in the conference room, chatting with Simon as they drank coffee and waited for Detective Barr, who was running late. Raymond's cell rang and he answered it. His look became worried and he took a deep breath when the call was over. "Wow. Not good."

"What is it?" Simon asked.

"He's bringing the Cougar. Dammit."

Cora Cook had been the city's Commonwealth's attorney, or chief prosecutor, for over a decade. Elected by the people, she handled the serious crimes in town, of which there were few. Raymond tangled with her occasionally and didn't like her, but then he didn't like most prosecutors. Simon assumed they cared little for him. For a public official, and one who faced the voters every four years, Cora had a colorful reputation as a party girl. She'd been through a couple of husbands, made the rounds in the town's nicer clubs, avoided the church scene, and preferred younger men. Thus the nickname, one that had stuck. She liked tight leather skirts that were always too short and out of fashion, and spiked heels that would make a hooker blush. She kept her job because she was a good politician and a tough prosecutor.

Her arrival darkened the mood considerably and Simon was thankful he had an experienced lawyer on his side. A criminal defense lawyer? What the hell was happening? He had committed no crime! He took a deep breath and closed his eyes as the walls began moving again.

From across the table she slid a document to Raymond and said, "Here's a search warrant for the safe. I assume you have not opened it."

Raymond shook his head smugly as he looked at the warrant without answering her directly.

The safe was sitting on the end of the table. It was a cheap fireproof box with a handle and a key, available anywhere for less than $100. Simon opened it and removed some legal documents: the will he prepared, the will Wally prepared, some insurance policies rubber-banded together, the title to the old car Netty had destroyed while driving under the influence, the burial policy issued by Cupit & Moke, $300 in cash, and a small velvet pouch with some earrings and bracelets. Not a very impressive stash of assets.

Detective Barr photographed it all.

When they were finished with the safe and its contents, Raymond asked, "Is my client a suspect?"

Ms. Cook replied, "Let's say he is a person of interest."

"Oh come on. If a crime has been committed, define it for us. Stop beating around the bush."

Unbothered, she calmly handed over the reports. She said, "The first is the autopsy. The pathologist and the forensic toxicologist found moderate levels of a drug known as thallium, a highly toxic compound no longer on the market but once used in rat poison. It has often been used to kill people because it has no odor, color, or taste. It has a wide range of symptoms, depending on the dosage. These can include fever, nausea, headaches, breathing problems, common symptoms, thus use of the drug can be masked until it's too late."

Simon tried to read the report but the words were blurred. The paper was shaking. He felt like the same symptoms were attacking him.

She slid across another report, one from the toxicologist. "A report of the examination of the food taken from the hospital room of the victim."

Victim? Even in his fog, Simon caught the word "victim."

"Eight chocolate brownies, delivered to the room by one Matilda Clark, who, according to one of the nurses, sort of boasted that her pecan fudge brownies were great. Evidently, the victim felt otherwise and wouldn't eat them. They were analyzed in the lab and nothing unusual was found. There were also eleven cookies, known as Saigon ginger cookies, in two carryout boxes from Tan Lu's Vietnamese restaurant here in town. All eleven had significant levels of thallium. The cookies were delivered on two occasions by Matilda Clark."

Raymond tried to speak, but had to first clear his throat. Finally he said, "Are you suggesting that my client poisoned Ms. Barnett?"

Simon was dumbstruck, stunned, bewildered, and couldn't control himself. "What? I didn't do anything!"

Raymond held up both hands to quieten him. "That's enough, Simon."

Coolly, the Cougar said, "The grand jury meets in the morning and we will present this evidence."

"You gotta be kidding!" Simon yelled across the table. He was wild-eyed and red-faced.

Raymond said, "Please Simon."

Raymond looked at Cora and asked, "What's the hurry here? At least give us time to review these reports, talk to some witnesses, do our own investigation. This is an ambush. The Commonwealth has had plenty of time to dig for dirt, but you've just caught us off guard. There's nothing fair about this."

"I've done nothing, okay?" Simon pleaded.

Cora was closing her file. "We will proceed with the grand jury."

An hour after she left with Detective Barr, Raymond and Simon were still in the conference room, talking in circles while getting nowhere. There was no shortage of urgent fires to put out, but the most pressing one was the need to prevent a grand jury investigation. Raymond knew, as did Simon, that the grand jury was nothing but a rubber stamp for the prosecutor. If Cora Cook wanted an indictment for murder in the morning she would have one by lunch.

They talked about other suspects. Who would gain by the death of Eleanor? Obviously Clyde and Jerry were at the top of the list. They had joined forces and hired a slick lawyer from D.C. That could not have been done overnight; thus, they had been planning it for some time. Jerry told Simon he had stopped by the hospital to see his stepmother.

Wally Thackerman had much to gain by Eleanor's death. He didn't know until after she died that his scheme would not work. Put him on the list.

Raymond got tired of this game and said, "We should concentrate on your defense and not worry about others right now."

"My defense? I can't believe this."

"I need to go. I'll call tomorrow. I suggest you talk to your wife and tell her what might happen."

"What might happen?"

"More than likely you'll be arrested in the very near future."

"Why don't you go tell her?"

"Sorry, Simon."

CHAPTER 33

What do you wear to your arrest? It was one of those questions that one never thinks about, not even hardened criminals. Simon chose jeans, a sports coat, and a white shirt. Raymond said to pack some toiletries, so he filled a paper shopping bag with a few necessities, some clean underwear, and two paperbacks. He took one last look in the mirror and despised what he saw, then turned off the lights in his office with no idea when he might turn them on again.

In the reception area, he fell into a chair and looked at Tillie in absolute defeat.

"What's wrong?" she asked, alarmed.

"About two hours ago the grand jury indicted me for the murder of Eleanor Barnett." The words sounded as if they were spoken by an unseen voice from above. She was stunned and couldn't speak.

"I'm on my way to the city jail where Raymond Lassiter is waiting. I'll be processed like the other criminals and put in a cell. I don't know when I'll get out."

"Murder!" she blurted.

He took a deep breath and said, "Evidently, someone poisoned Eleanor when she was in the hospital. Those damned ginger cookies I sent were laced with poison. All eyes are on me."

She swallowed hard and kept her composure, then wiped her cheeks with tissues and managed to say, "This is ridiculous, Simon. You're not capable of doing something like that."

He nodded his agreement but said nothing. Another long moment passed as they ignored the buzzing of the landline on her desk. She asked, "What about Paula and the kids?"

"Pretty ugly. I told her last night after the kids were in bed. She was horrified, angry, frightened, the works. Our greatest concern is protecting our children, but there's no way. They are about to be humiliated and I can't stop it. I can't protect them." His voice cracked and he couldn't go on. She wiped her eyes again and seemed determined to contain her emotions.

He said, "I'll call from the jail as soon as I can. Lock up the office and stay away. I'm sure reporters will be banging on the door very soon, so lay low."

"I can't believe this, Simon."

"I'm sleepwalking through a nightmare, Tillie, and no one has a clue how it will end. There are so many unknowns. The best scenario for next week is that I can make bond and get out. If so, we can try to keep this place afloat until trial."

"A trial?"

"That's what usually happens once you're charged, unless, of course, you plead guilty. I'm not doing that."

"When is the trial?"

"Who knows? Months."

He stood and thought about giving her an awkward hug, but since they had never done that, he simply said, "Be strong," and opened the door.

"You'll need a coat."

The temperature was in the twenties and the wind was howling. He walked down Main Street, past the shops and offices he knew so well, and tried not to guess what those people would think and say when they heard the gossip, the unbelievable news. He slowed in front of Ethel's Diner, empty at 4 P.M. on a dreary Friday, but Bella, his favorite waitress, was at the counter drying tea glasses and gabbing at someone in the kitchen. Bella would never believe that Simon would do something so awful and would volunteer for jury service if possible.

He crossed the street and walked along Monroe until he came to the courthouse, a neoclassical masterpiece that Braxton was so proud of. A hundred years earlier, the city won a lawsuit against a railroad and wisely chose to put the money into a new monument to itself, with no expense spared. With its grand arches, vaulted ceilings, and marble columns, it was routinely voted the most beautiful courthouse in Virginia.

He thought of all the clerks, secretaries, janitors, bailiffs, lawyers, and judges who worked there, people he had known for almost twenty years, and tried to picture their faces when they heard the news. It was almost too painful to think about. On the second floor, the lights were on in the main courtroom where in a few short days he would be led in, not as a lawyer but as a criminal defendant and facing a judge for an arraignment, his first appearance of many.

He kept walking through the streets of downtown, his town, somewhat aimlessly but in the general direction of the jail.

Sleepwalking.

———◆◆———

There was no crowd waiting at the entrance. No reporters yelling at him. No photographers clicking away. That would come later, but not late enough. He stepped inside and saw Raymond chatting with a uniformed officer. The arrest of a lawyer for murder was a momentous occasion in Braxton, but, thankfully, the police were downplaying it. Simon had feared a gang of cops loitering about, waiting for a glimpse of their new trophy, but there were only a couple trying their best to ignore him.

Raymond handed him a copy of the indictment, hot off the press, and he read it slowly. The chief of police appeared and said, "I'm sorry, Simon." They had known each other for a few years and it was obvious the chief preferred to be elsewhere. "I have no choice."

"I understand. Let's get it over with."

The processing took an hour. Simon handed over his wallet, which contained nothing but his driver's license, and his cell phone. Because his wristwatch had a leather band he was allowed to keep it, for the logical reason that it might be difficult to murder another inmate with a leather band. He posed for his mug shot, then surrendered his clothing. He changed into a pair of bright orange overalls with the words CITY JAIL across the back. He was allowed to keep his socks and running shoes. He was fingerprinted and voluntarily gave a sample of blood. The paperwork took fifteen minutes.

It was a humiliating process, to say the least, and frightening, but he was determined to keep a firm jaw and clenched teeth and act as though nothing they dished out could faze him. He was an innocent man, and once that was proven to the world he could look back and boast, to himself, that he had survived the worst. On his office desk he kept a tall coffee cup filled with pens, pencils, and markers, and on one side was his favorite slogan: WHAT DOESN'T KILL YOU MAKES YOU TOUGHER.

Once officially an inmate in the city jail, he was led, unshackled, to a small room where lawyers met their clients. In eighteen years, he'd been there a few times, but never as the poor schmuck in coveralls.

"You look nice in orange," Raymond said.

"You trying to be funny?"

"No. I just talked to Judge Pointer again and she's not willing to set bond until Monday at the arraignment."

"No surprise."

"I practically begged for a release on recognition, but she wouldn't budge. Didn't seem too sympathetic. Looks like you're here for the weekend."

"I'll be all right. I brought some books. It'll be a good time to think, try to sort things out."

"Good luck with that."

"Raymond, I really thank you for being here. I know it's pro bono and all that, but it means a lot."

"I'm with you, Simon."

"Could I ask a favor?"

"Sure."

"Could I borrow your phone? I need to call my mother."

———•◆•———

The leaker struck again Friday night. He or she sent an anonymous email to Iris Kane, a reporter for the *Washington Journal*. It read:

Breaking news from Braxton, Virginia. Local attorney arrested in poisoning death of wealthy client after revising her will. Simon Latch, 42, was indicted by the grand jury this afternoon and surrendered to authorities at the city jail. Scheduled to appear in Circuit Court Monday morning.

Iris made half a dozen calls and with little progress. Apparently, most sources shut down on Friday night in Braxton. Fifteen minutes later, another anonymous email arrived:

Eleanor Barnett, age 85, was pronounced dead on December 30, at the Blue Ridge Memorial Hospital. Cause of death—pneumonia. But, an autopsy later revealed she had been poisoned. You have the exclusive but act fast. This story has enormous tabloid appeal.

Iris agreed and kept digging online for another hour, again with nothing to show for it. She went to bed early with plans to head over to Braxton in the morning for a long day of investigating.

———•◆•———

The cell was twelve-by-twelve with concrete blocks on three sides and a wall of iron bars facing the hallway. Two bunk beds hung from the wall by metal braces. Fortunately, the top bunk was unoccupied, and Simon had the cell to himself. Directly across the hall, Loomis, a car thief, was also solo, and lonely, and wanted to talk to someone. Actually, he preferred to have someone listen while he went on and on. Two cells away, Carl, an alleged drug dealer who claimed to be innocent, told Loomis more than once to shut up. Others yelled back and forth, but as the night wore on, the talking stopped.

Simon tried to read but could not concentrate. He tried every trick he could remember to keep his thoughts away from his children, but it was impossible. They were about to be subjected to unrelenting embarrassment because of something he didn't do, but the damage would be done before he could be cleared. The damage was just beginning.

The cheap mattress was two inches thick. The blanket was well worn but clean. The temperature was a little on the chilly side, but Loomis said they were lucky because the heat pump had been on the blink. It was snowing outside, though that was hearsay to Simon. He didn't know where the nearest window might be but it wasn't close.

Loomis said men often cried during their first nights in jail, after lights out. He said you could always hear them in the dark, even with pillows over their faces. The pathetic sobs of grown men locked away from everything they love.

When their wing was finally still, Simon knew the men were awake, waiting to hear him cry.

CHAPTER 34

On his first morning of captivity, Simon learned several important things. First, the alarm sounded at five-thirty, according to his wristwatch, which seemed cruel for any day but especially harsh for a cold Saturday in January. Second, breakfast was served fifteen minutes later when a guard slid a tray through a narrow opening under the bars. Third, breakfast was a miserable effort at even the most basic food preparation. The white bread toast was cold and burnt around the edges. The powdered eggs were mush, just as cold, and served on top of three slices of fatty bacon that a dog would only sniff at. The small metal bowl of grits had the smell and texture of caulking compound. The green apple was bitter. The instant coffee was little more than hot water and thoroughly free of any flavor. Fourth, as lousy as it was, it was the best meal of the day, according to Loomis across the hall.

Simon had no idea how long he would be incarcerated but he couldn't survive more than a week before starvation became a factor. Something didn't add up. The food was barely edible but most of the inmates were as fat as the guards. There must be vending machines somewhere in the jail.

When the guard came to retrieve the tray about fifteen minutes later, Simon said, "Wow, thanks, that was delicious. What time is lunch?"

The guard, a thick simpleton who had never missed a meal, frowned and said, "Two thousand calories a day, bud, that's all you get."

Yeah, and you get that many with your morning doughnuts.

Simon reclined on his bunk and braced himself for a long day of boredom and humiliation. He was still hungry. There was one light in the center of the ceiling and it was on. He could not turn it off. He couldn't sleep, couldn't read, and had no desire to begin the day listening to Loomis over there chatter on about the cars he'd stolen.

———◆◆————

Iris Kane had a hunch that the best gossip would be in the coffee shops, and she was right. She trudged through the two inches of snow covering the sidewalks, walked past the City Café, saw the crowd, ducked inside, grabbed a stool at the counter, and ordered coffee and a biscuit. A long, stained mirror offered a good view of the customers. A quick glance revealed that she was the only female customer. The men were layered in flannel and heavy down jackets to stay warm. Every head had a trucker's cap. Half the men had beards. The scene reminded Iris of a logging camp in Oregon she had once covered.

Everyone seemed to be talking. Nothing like a good murder to stir up the locals, though this one lacked the violence and drama they expected from television. Poisoning an old woman? What a cowardly crime.

Within two minutes, any rookie reporter would have been well versed in the story of the day.

"I hear Latch is looking at the death penalty."

"Crooked sumbitch was after her money, plain and simple."

"Anybody ever meet the old gal?"

"No. I heard she's from Atlanta, moved here to retire with a bundle of money."

"God help her if she trusted these lawyers."

"Well, I never trusted Latch."

"He picked her clean, or was trying to."

"He's a tricky one."

"Hang on. I like Simon, known him for years. Good boy."

"Heard he and his wife filed papers. Splitsville."

"Well, she'll get the house and kids now, with his ass locked up."

"When's he going to court?"

"Heard it was Monday morning. He's trying to get out of jail already."

"Can he make bond on a murder charge?"

"Of course he can. He's a lawyer. No judge is going to keep a lawyer in jail for long. He'll be out before you know it and they'll have a helluva time hanging a murder charge on him. Different rules for different folks."

"Heard he's hired Raymond Lassiter."

"See what I mean. Slickest dude in Virginia, never loses in the courtroom."

"Well, he's got his hands full with this one."

Iris tried to scribble notes without getting caught. She was probably the only outsider in the place and if they suspected she was a reporter they would go silent in an instant. She might even get tossed. She found a copy of a local shopper's guide and pretended to read it.

One truth was obvious: Simon Latch and his defense team should demand a change of venue and get the case away from these registered voters. Everyone had an opinion and the clear majority had already decided Latch was guilty.

Iris paid her bill and left before anyone noticed her. The town was coming to life and merchants up and down Main Street were scraping the sidewalk and shoving snow to the gutter. The public library opened at eight and she found a quiet corner. She opened her laptop and began writing down as many of the comments as possible. She searched for Raymond Lassiter and called his office, but got only the recording. It was, after all, Saturday. She found a number for the city jail but the officer on duty would not confirm the identity of any inmate. She went to the archives for both the

Journal and the *Braxton Gazette* and looked at the rather sparse references to Simon Latch. From the county court records, she found the divorce filing, which revealed very little. There was a reference to a recent petition involving Eleanor Barnett, but the file had been sealed by court order. Suspicious?

After two hours of digging, Iris needed to walk. She bundled up and went outside. She found the offices of Raymond Lassiter and knocked on the door. No answer. Same at the offices of Simon F. Latch, Attorney and Counselor at Law. The city police department was practically deserted and the officer on duty clammed up when she said she was a reporter. She walked to the jail to try again, but no one would confirm anything. She drove to the hospital and poked around, but if anyone knew anything or had any authority, they were off duty. She stopped by the funeral home where there were no services scheduled for the weekend. A part-time secretary knew nothing.

She had Simon's home address but chose not to upset the family. His wife had filed for divorce. He was sitting in jail charged with murder. She could not imagine the nightmare they were going through.

For lunch, Iris chose another downtown café, one that was not crowded. She ate a salad as she eavesdropped, but there was no talk of the arrest. She returned to her quiet spot in the library and began putting together a story. Her working title was: "Lawyer Arrested in Poisoning Death of Wealthy Client." She liked it but knew her editor would not. He seldom did.

As if someone were watching, another phantom email pinged. The anonymous source was back with: "DC atty Teddy Hammer represents E. Barnett's heirs. He likes to talk."

The informant was trouble because he or she knew far too much about the case. Which, to Iris or any other investigator, meant the informant was probably involved in the crime at some level. Why did this person want Simon Latch investigated and humiliated? Many questions, few answers.

Iris called the office number for Teddy Hammer and got the standard after-hours recording. She left a message and returned to her notes. Ten minutes later her cell phone buzzed, and it was Teddy Hammer.

"I can't talk on the record," he said. "But I can share some deep background."

Cautiously, she asked, "What is your involvement in the case?"

"Can we agree that I will not be sourced? Can we agree this is deep background?"

Iris loathed using unnamed sources and was always irritated by these situations, but she really had no choice. A prominent lawyer knew the case, had a lot to say, and wanted to talk. At the moment her story had too many gaps, and she had a hunch this guy could fill most of them.

She said, "Okay, you're off the record and now considered deep background."

"I'm recording this conversation and I suggest you do the same."

She tapped a key and said, "I'm recording this conversation with Mr. Teddy Hammer on Saturday, January sixteenth, at 2:20 P.M."

Mr. Hammer immediately said, "There's been no press so far. How did you hear of the arrest?"

"An anonymous tip, by email, last night."

A pause as he mulled it over. "Okay, what's your first question."

"What is your involvement?"

"I represent the two stepsons of Eleanor Barnett, Jerry and Clyde Korsak. Two weeks ago we rushed to court to prevent the cremation of Ms. Barnett only hours after she died."

"Who was trying to cremate her?"

"He's sitting in jail."

CHAPTER 35

At five-thirty the following morning, Simon was actually sleeping for a change when the alarm bells sounded and the guards entered the wing, clanging doors and yelling for everyone to wake up. Breakfast was being served. As if breakfast was something to get excited about. In the break room down the hall Simon had found the vending machines and was currently subsisting on Cokes and potato chips.

Cokes. The same thought flashed through his mind: Netty and all that common stock, and he still wondered if it was really there.

The guard, Mason, worked the early shift and thus had the pleasure of serving two gourmet meals to his boys. Simon had managed to chat him up the day before.

"Mornin', Latch."

"Well, good morning, Officer Mason. So good to see you again. What's cooking this morning?"

"The same."

"Lucky me."

As Simon was picking up his tray, Mason slid a newspaper under the bars. "Might want to take a look at this. Front page, Metro. You've hit the big time, Latch. A real star."

The Sunday *Journal,* two inches thick and packed with cou-pons. Simon knew what was coming so he sat on the edge of his bed and took a deep breath. He thought he had braced himself for the bad PR. It could not have been worse.

Metro, above the fold, a large black-and-white photo of Simon Latch, smiling, jacket and tie, posing for the camera. Someone had borrowed it from the county bar directory published a few years earlier. Beside it was the unrestrained tabloid headline: "Estate Lawyer Accused in Poisoning Death of Wealthy Widow Client."

It covered everything: a brief bio of the accused; same for the victim; the new will that gave him absolute control of her assets; then a power of attorney and advance directive, signed in the hos-pital just days before her death, that gave him the power to turn off the ventilator; which he did; the suspicious efforts to cremate the body a few hours after death; the heroic intervention of the stepsons, who demanded an autopsy; and the fact that she was poisoned, probably while in the hospital. It was a long article with no shortage of innuendos and speculations. Indeed, at every point where one word would suffice but three would seem more sinis-ter, Ms. Kane went with the longer sentence. While not a single source agreed to be quoted or identified, off the record they were babbling away. Simon immediately suspected Teddy Hammer as one of the conspirators. His flattering accounts of the actions by his clients, the stepsons, were a bit over-the-top. Some of the details from the injunction hearing before Judge Pointer had to be relayed by a person who was in the courtroom, a clear violation of the judge's orders.

The article ended with the information that Mr. Latch would appear in court Monday morning at 9 A.M. to be arraigned and request bail, which was discretionary but rarely given in murder cases. The tone was basically an invitation for everyone to come to court tomorrow, have a look at the defendant, and share in the excitement.

Simon wiped sweat from his forehead, realized his hands were shaking, and suddenly bolted for the tiny metal toilet in one corner of his cell. He vomited and retched and gagged until all of yesterday's potato chips were in either the bowl or on the lid.

Across the hall Loomis asked, "Hey man, you okay?"

But Simon did not answer. When the nausea finally passed he stretched out on his bunk and pulled the blanket up to his eyes. He wanted to die. Was it possible to suffocate oneself with a pillow?

Every potential juror reading the *Journal* would quickly vote to convict, and Simon couldn't blame them.

———— ◆•◆ ————

Traffic at the jail was slow on Sunday mornings, and Mason had the front desk to himself. At 9 A.M., another guard put handcuffs on Simon and led him to the front.

"I'd like to use the phone," he said politely.

"Who you calling?" Mason asked.

"My wife and my lawyer."

"Local calls?"

"Yes sir."

Mason nodded at a door and the guard led him into a room with several phones on a long table. The guard removed the handcuffs and said, "I'll be outside." He shut the door and Simon was alone.

He called Paula's cell and she didn't answer, which was not unusual. She rarely took a call from an unidentified number. Simon left the message that he would call back in five minutes. He did and she answered after the first ring.

"How are the kids?" he asked.

"Coping, I guess. It's not easy."

"Have you seen the *Journal*?"

"Oh yes. The story was posted last night online and Matilda called me. By midnight it was all over town. Now it's everywhere. My phone's ringing, lots of emails."

"Have the kids seen it?"

"Are you kidding? Buck and Danny live online and miss nothing. They're locked in their rooms and won't come out. We did a lousy job of monitoring their devices."

"I assume there's a lot of chatter online."

"It's horrible."

"And social media?"

"It's horrible."

She was using the same icy tone Simon had become accustomed to over the years, yet there was an even harder edge to it. He couldn't blame her.

"What about Janie?"

"She's a mess. They're all in shock, Simon. What do you expect? Their father is in jail charged with murder. First our separation, then the divorce, now this. It's front-page news and viral on the internet. The kids are traumatized."

"Have you explained to them that I am not guilty, that I haven't killed anyone?"

"Yes, I've tried and they want to believe it, they really do. They love their father. But it's all so confusing and they're just overwhelmed. Right now there are two television vans parked in the street in front of the house. We can't go out. A city cop is guarding the driveway. We had reporters knocking on the door at eight this morning. These creeps are rude and shameless, Simon, but they're here and they're not going away. We need to get out of town. I'm thinking of sneaking away to my parents'. Forget school tomorrow. I'm not sending them and they don't want to go."

Simon rubbed his eyes with one hand and held the phone with the other. He had never felt so defeated.

She continued, strong and icy, "And this is just the beginning, Simon. Tomorrow you're in court and it will be a zoo, but it's just the first appearance, the first of many, all leading up to a trial that will be a world-class shit show. Those creeps in the street will dog you, and your family, every step of the way."

Simon thought that was a bit over-reactive, but he had no standing to argue. Nor was he hiding in the house, peeking through the curtains at the creeps with cameras.

He said, "Look, Paula, I have to talk to the kids and convince them I'm innocent. They have to know right now, up front, that their father is not a murderer."

"Simon, right now that seems impossible."

Another gut punch.

"The sentiment online is running heavily in favor of guilt and there seems to be no shortage of people who want to know why you're charged with first-degree murder and not capital murder. They want the death penalty."

Another gut punch.

A thirty-second ceasefire ensued as both realized they were getting nowhere. Finally, Simon said, "I need a favor. Could you please call Raymond Lassiter and ask him to be here at the jail at two this afternoon?"

"And who is Raymond Lassiter?"

"My lawyer, for now anyway."

"Oh yeah. I saw his name. How much will this cost you, Simon?"

You, not *us.*

"I don't know. We're still negotiating. There's a good chance he'll fire me this afternoon."

"Then who will represent you?"

"Probably some court-appointed kid fresh out of law school. I'll worry about that tomorrow."

It was apparent that she was not worrying much about him. She had not asked about bail and the prospect of getting out, nor had she shown any interest in the life behind bars. That was fine with Simon. She was concerned only with the kids.

To end the misery, Simon said, "Gotta go now, I'm out of time."

"I don't know what to say, Simon. I'm sorry this is happening. I wish I could help but we are, after all, practically divorced now. My only concern is protecting the children and I'm not sure how to do that right now. Any suggestions?"

"Get 'em out of town."

———— •◆• ————

Simon opened the door and waited as the guard cuffed his wrists. As he walked by the front desk, Mason said, "Hey Latch, got some reporters outside lurking around. What do you want to do with them?"

"Arrest them, put them in the cell next to me and I'll give them a story."

CHAPTER 36

The street was still dark and empty when Paula opened the garage door a few minutes after five on Monday morning. A police cruiser pulled into the driveway, on schedule, and the officer got out and said hello. She herded the three kids out of the house, each carrying an overnight bag and a backpack. They hustled to the car and sped away behind the officer. No one noticed them. One mile past the city limits, the cruiser turned into the parking lot of a convenience store. Paula tapped the horn and never slowed down. She had no idea when she might return.

She had spent the night in her bed with her laptop, never bothering to put on pajamas and with no thoughts of sleep. The story was huge and growing by the hour, though almost no new facts had surfaced in the past twenty-four hours. The news cycle was now spinning what had already been spun and recycling every tidbit of speculation. Simon's face was on every major newspaper's online edition, with print on the way. The story was simply too sensational to ignore. When she saw the headline from a newspaper in Oregon that screamed: "Virginia Lawyer Arrested for Poisoning Rich Client" she knew any hope of fairness was gone. There was no tempering, no throttling, no effort whatsoever to play by the old rules. What rules? Not too long ago any reputable newspaper would try to control itself and cautiously use language like "alleged poisoning." Not now. Now Simon had been caught and declared guilty.

The comments from the average readers were so mean-spirited and scathing that Paula forced herself to stop reading them. She spent hours throughout the night answering thoughtful emails from many of their friends. By phone, she spoke to her boss and informed him she was taking a week of vacation. Getting out of Braxton couldn't happen fast enough.

Mercifully, the three kids were asleep within minutes, and as she drove Paula tried to enjoy the solitude without worrying about being watched. She felt sorry for Simon, but there was nothing she could do at the moment.

———— •••• ————

The chief of police arrived to take charge, and sent for the prisoner. When Simon stepped into the visitation room the chief said, "Look, Simon, you got a packed house today with lots of cameras. Raymond asked for a big favor and I said yes. It might be embarrassing for you to walk into court in your orange coveralls, so take 'em off and put these on again." He nodded at Simon's jeans and jacket.

"Thanks Chief." Simon seemed grateful, but what he really wanted to do was to ask the chief why his jail used bright orange, practically neon orange, coveralls in the first place.

The jail was soon busy with officers. The moment offered excitement and the chief wanted a show of force. Simon wanted to ask why. The victim was an old woman with no family and few friends. Where was the security risk? Who were the cops afraid of?

A pack of dogs waited outside the jail and readied their cameras as the cops filed out. Some couldn't resist the opportunity and yelled such banalities as "Hey, Simon, how much money is in the estate?" and "Hey, Simon, where'd you get the thallium? It's banned in the U.S."

The van was fifteen feet from the back door of the jail and Simon ducked into it. Two motorcycles and a cruiser led the way, with another behind the van. Simon could have walked from the jail to the courthouse in five minutes, but a little parade was necessary. They went down Main Street so everyone could have a look, then circled the square. Simon sat high in the seat and looked through the window. If not handcuffed, he would have waved at his spectators.

Protected by the same security force, he entered the courtroom from a side door and did not look at the crowd. The place was full, and he had no desire to make eye contact with anyone. He took a seat near the jury box and studied his feet, a cop on each side. Raymond bent down and they whispered. When Judge Pointer finished with some paperwork, she called his name. He and Raymond approached the bench. Simon gritted his teeth, looked Her Honor dead in the eyes, and refused to blink.

Staring right back, she said, "Mr. Latch, this is not an arraignment, we'll do that later. There are two pressing issues here, one is your representation, the other is the matter of bail. Mr. Lassiter is here as a matter of courtesy, as I understand the relationship. Will he continue to represent you?"

"No ma'am. If I can make bail, I will find another lawyer. Mr. Lassiter has advised me, pro bono, until now. He is here only as a friend."

Evidently, Raymond was quite taken with the size of the crowd and the number of cameras and reporters. Simon's would be the biggest trial in the recent history of Braxton, and Raymond's office was not far from the courthouse. It would be a shame to miss it, fee or no fee. He said, "Your Honor, if it's okay with you, I will continue to represent Mr. Latch until he hires other counsel. Show me as his attorney of record."

Simon looked to his right, nodded humbly at Raymond, and whispered, "Thank you." Simon, and the other lawyers in the courtroom, knew damned well that Raymond Lassiter was now on the hook for the trial. He could not dare allow another defense lawyer to trespass on his turf.

Her Honor said, "Moving right along. Mr. Lassiter, what are your thoughts on bail?"

"Only one, Your Honor. My client has practiced law in this town and in this courtroom for almost nineteen years now. He is well known in this community. He owns an office building on Main Street. He will surrender his passport and agree to leave the state only with your permission. He is not a flight risk and should be released on his own recognizance."

"And for the Commonwealth, Ms. Cook?"

The Cougar was well aware that public sentiment, for the moment anyway, was running strongly against the defendant. She said, "Your Honor, this is first-degree murder and bail is always required. A high bond should be set for Mr. Latch, same as any other defendant facing such a serious charge. Just because he's a member of the bar doesn't mean he gets special treatment. Releasing him on recognizance would send the wrong message to the rest of the community."

Raymond was quick to jump in with "Bail is not used to send messages to the community, Your Honor. The purpose of bail is to guarantee an appearance in court to face the charges. Nothing more or less. Do you really believe, Ms. Cook, that Simon Latch will skip town and disappear?"

Lawyer Latch was dreaming of skipping town on the first bus and getting off somewhere in Canada.

Ms. Cook said, "Stranger things have happened. I never dreamed he would be indicted for murder."

Judge Pointer raised her hands and said, "Okay, okay. Give me a figure, Ms. Cook."

"Five hundred thousand."

"Mr. Lassiter?"

He wanted to say *Zero,* but then he would not be taken seriously. So he said, "One hundred thousand."

"Okay, here are the terms of bail, Mr. Latch. Turn in your passport, pledge the title to your office building, and post a bond in the amount of three hundred thousand dollars."

Simon nodded in agreement as if he had plenty of spare cash, but he really wanted to scream.

Scheduling was the next issue and the lawyers went back and forth. Judge Pointer finally raised her hands again for quiet and said, "All right. We'll have an arraignment next Wednesday at nine A.M. Anything further?"

Both lawyers shook their heads no. Simon was escorted out of the courtroom after being there for less than fifteen minutes. Judge Pointer tapped her gavel and disappeared from the bench. For a few moments, the spectators didn't move, as if they were waiting for more drama. Realizing there would be none, they slowly rose and began filing out.

———•◆•———

Raymond followed Simon out of the courtroom and asked the officers if he could speak to his client. Simon was handcuffed again and permitted to follow his lawyer. They stepped into the law library, which was always empty, and closed the door.

"How you doing?" Raymond asked.

"I guess I need thirty thousand dollars, right?"

"Yep. That's what it costs to post the bond. I've talked to a good bondsman, one I've used before. He'll meet us at the jail. You said you could scrape together ten grand."

"Scrape is the word. Can you loan me twenty?"

Raymond laughed and Simon managed a grin, a brief one. "Can't do it. Against the ethics. Any equity in your office building?"

"I told you, Raymond. Everything I own is double-mortgaged. I could probably squeeze ten thousand out of our home, but I don't own it anymore. It's all Paula's, as per our property settlement agreement."

"Can you ask her?"

"No. And I can't go to the bank. No one will loan me a dime right now. Can't really blame them."

"All right. What's the plan?"

"I'll call my mother."

"Is she loaded?"

"No, but she'll try. And I'd like to pay you too, Raymond, I swear I would. I'll put the office building on the market and hope for a miracle, and if I can find the right buyer maybe—"

Raymond held up a hand as he shook his head. "We'll talk about it later."

———————————

At 1 P.M., Judge Pointer convened another hearing, a much different one with no spectators. In Courtroom B, she stationed two bailiffs at the door with instructions to allow no one to enter.

Teddy Hammer had filed a petition to establish a conservatorship for the estate of Eleanor Barnett. There were several pressing matters, the most obvious being the burial of the deceased. Her bills needed to be paid and her assets inventoried. Hammer had requested that his client, Jerry Korsak, be appointed to handle everything, on a temporary basis. Jerry was called to the witness stand and put under oath. He began lying immediately when he tried to convince the court that he and Ms. Barnett, or "Mom" as he called her, had actually been quite close over the years. Since she had no children of her own, she had always relied on Jerry for advice on a wide range of topics.

Hammer was careful not to let him go too far. He knew that phone records would be subpoenaed and scrutinized and would show little contact.

Clyde Korsak was not in the courtroom and his brother had no idea where he was.

Judge Pointer was skeptical. She knew the story of Clyde's last visit and his arrest for pummeling Wally, and she had heard plenty of rumors since Eleanor's death. There was no one to cross-examine Jerry, and Judge Pointer was dismissive of his testimony. And, she already had a plan.

When Jerry stepped down, and when Teddy had nothing else

to say, she announced she was appointing a young lawyer named Clement Gelly as conservator. He was a local attorney with a good reputation. Her instructions were strict: There would be no probate until a few weeks passed. The last will and testament prepared by Simon Latch and signed by the deceased would be held in abeyance until further orders. In the meantime, Mr. Gelly would make sure the bills were paid and the assets identified. The file would remain sealed and she would keep it on her desk.

Late that afternoon, Raymond went to the jail and informed Simon of the new conservatorship. He was intrigued by it but had more pressing matters to worry about. He wanted to get out of jail, get out of town, and go see his kids.

After Raymond left, Simon called Paula and they talked for half an hour. She and the kids were at her parents' home in Richmond and felt safe, no one was bothering them. They discussed the hearing that morning, and the ins and outs of bail procedure, but at no time did she offer financial assistance. Simon did not ask for any. In addition to her future as a single mother, she was afraid she was about to lose her job. Her parents were semi-retired. They had worked hard, saved religiously, and had a nice retirement fund that was off-limits.

Simon would waste away in jail before he asked them for help.

CHAPTER 37

As for his own mother, things were just as complicated. She had been married many years to Arn, her second husband. Unhappy years, in Simon's opinion. Arn was a complicated person who had never tried to make her life easier. Simon did not like him and the feelings were mutual. He was a tough guy who'd once owned a successful roofing company and probably had some cash in the bank. They had a nice home downstate in the Roanoke area. The problem was that all of their assets were jointly owned. His mother had no bank account of her own. When Simon explained that he needed to borrow $20,000 to get out of jail, she became emotional and said she would do whatever she could to help. Arn was not sympathetic. When she put him on the phone, Simon asked for the money and promised to repay as soon as he sold his office building. He might as well have asked for twenty million. Arn handed the phone back to his wife and could be heard mumbling in the background. She promised to discuss it and call back the following day.

Knowing Arn, he was reading the newspaper accounts of Simon's mess and figured the boy was going to prison. Thus, the money would never be repaid. The phone call home was a disaster and made a bad day even worse, if that was possible.

During his fourth night in jail, Simon was able to read half a novel. He tried to convince himself that he could survive incarceration now that the shock had worn off. He felt safe. Loomis explained that there was another wing where they kept the harder cases, but on their wing things were civilized. The chief ran a tight ship and violence, or the threat of it, was dealt with harshly. It was a clean jail without too many rules, and the guards were real people who tried to help. Simon also admitted to himself that, for the moment anyway, it was rather pleasant being away from the glare and gossip. The flashbacks of all those reporters and cameras were unsettling. He felt sorry for Paula and the kids and hoped to see them soon. He actually slept a few hours without interruption.

By nine the next morning, his mother had not called. He could not imagine the war between her and Arn and he felt lousy for causing trouble, but he had no choice. He was confident she would prevail and convince Arn to lend a hand. Dammit, her only son was in jail and that was an emergency.

Raymond dropped by midmorning and they discussed the plan to sell the office building. They talked about various real estate agents in town, few of whom inspired confidence. Such a sale, if indeed anyone wanted to buy the building, would take days if not weeks. There would be an appraisal, then a listing, then showings, and so on. Simon could easily envision a drawn-out process.

For two hours each afternoon, the inmates were allowed into the Pit, a break room with a television, pool table, checker boards, and plenty of old magazines. Simon was making new friends right and left, most of them duly impressed because they'd never had a lawyer in their midst. A few wanted legal advice, but were disappointed when he claimed to know nothing but bankruptcy law. He was playing checkers with Loomis late Tuesday afternoon when a guard said he had a phone call. He was certain it was his mother with good news and hurried to the front. It was not his mother. A familiar voice said, "So, you've finally found your rightful place, huh Latch?"

"Hello, Spade. It's almost good to hear your voice."

"Got yourself in a jam, huh?"

"You could say that."

"I just did. Look, is anyone listening to this call?"

In Spade's world someone was always listening or wearing a wire. Simon thought the calls were secure but wasn't sure. He said, "Of course not. It's unconstitutional to listen to inmates' calls."

"And you believe that? Listen, Chub called this morning. His joint is closed for renovations, but he's around and is somewhat concerned. He's seen the papers, called me, asked me to say hello."

"I'm touched."

"You should be. Look, Chub thinks it was you who got the Fibbies to back off. Don't know if that's true, but you gave him the heads-up and he left town. Now it looks like the investigation has lost steam, you know? He's wondering if there's any way to help."

"Damned right. He could loan me twenty thousand bucks for my bail."

"Twenty thousand. Wow."

Twenty thousand was nothing to Chub. "Tell Chub I'll pay it all back when I sell my office building. Every penny."

"He likes you, for some reason. Thinks you're a stand-up guy."

"Well, I am, in spite of my current situation. Better yet, tell Chub I'll sell him my building at a fair price, clear just enough to get me out of here. He likes real estate."

"That he does. I'll see what I can do."

"Thanks Spade."

"I'll call back tomorrow."

———————— ◆◆◆ ————————

Tillie arrived later in the afternoon and they were allowed to meet in the attorney conference room. She brought a printout of their current bankruptcy cases and a schedule of his upcoming court appearances. Even if he made bail and was free to move around, he could not imagine walking into any courtroom for even a routine matter.

After a few minutes, she became emotional. "What's going to happen to you, Simon?" she asked. "I can't believe this."

He thought for a moment and said, "I honestly don't know, Tillie. Looks like I'll be forced to sell everything to get out of here, and that's only the beginning. A trial will be months away. Who knows what happens then. I can't think of any reason to be optimistic in the short term."

"So, the practice gets shut down?"

"Probably. Even if I keep the building it will be impossible to do business. My name is dirt around town. I don't even want to ask what you're hearing."

"Nothing good."

"Everyone thinks I'm guilty, right?"

She nodded as she bit her lip. She wiped her eyes and said, "It's awful. I'm afraid to go anywhere near the office."

"Don't go there."

"I want to leave town but where do I go?" She began sobbing and her hands were shaking. "I'm sorry. I promised myself I wouldn't do this."

In their twelve years together, he had seen her cry only twice, both times in the past month. They had never allowed themselves to become close, primarily because she had been hurt by other men.

She swallowed hard and said, "So, I guess I should start looking for another job."

"Not so fast. Let's get through this week, see if I can spring myself. We'll work together and try to clean up the files. I need you right now, Tillie."

She managed a smile and said, "Okay."

———◆◆———

No calls were allowed after 6 P.M., but Simon was desperate to get out and the guards knew it. He needed to call his mother, and the jailer eventually said yes. He waited until 8 P.M., hoping, of course, that she would call him. When she did not, he dialed the number. Arn answered with a gruff "Hello."

Neither was in the mood for friendly chitchat. When his mother said hello her voice was shaky. Then she barked at Arn, who was apparently standing close by. "Can I have some privacy, please?" A few seconds passed and a door slammed.

"He won't do it," she said. "I've tried everything, Simon, I really have. We've fought and fought and right now I can't stand him. I'm so sorry, but the money is tied up in joint accounts. Pretty stupid, right, but he's always controlled the money. I would give you all of it if I could. I'm so sorry."

Simon listened with his eyes closed. His own mother and step-father wouldn't bail him out of jail.

"I'm going to leave him, Simon, I swear. This time I'm going to leave him. I'm fed up with him."

"Come on, Mom. Settle down. I'll be all right." The idea of his mother walking out and starting over at the age of seventy-three was hard to grasp, but, at the moment, he really couldn't blame her.

"No, I mean it, Simon. This is the last straw. I've put at least eighty thousand dollars in CDs and it's my money. He has no right to control it."

Eighty thousand sounded like a million. "Mom, take a deep breath. Go for a long ride in your car. Let the moment pass."

"I'm so sorry, Simon. I'll keep trying."

"I love you, Mom. I'll see you soon, and I'll get this mess cleared up, okay?"

"I love you too, and I'm so sorry."

Simon followed the guard back to his cell, stretched out on his bed, and tried to read. Hours later he was still awake, wondering if he'd caused another divorce.

CHAPTER 38

Neither Chub nor Spade would ever voluntarily go near a jail, so the details were left to the law offices of Raymond Lassiter, with assistance from Matilda. Chub was in an expansive mood and attacking the new year with enthusiasm, now that the FBI had lost interest. He had big plans to expand his clubs and holdings and rely less on bookmaking. Being investigated by the Feds was a sobering experience. He had collected far too many legitimate assets to worry about a lengthy prison sentence.

On Thursday, Chub agreed to buy Simon's Main Street office building for $41,000 more than the mortgages. It was a straightforward deal without a lot of paperwork, but the banks took their time, as always. Chub also agreed to allow Simon to continue using the office for six months, at no charge. Simon was thrilled with the deal and also relieved not to be homeless.

The money changed hands Friday morning and Simon said goodbye to Loomis. A week after walking into the jail, Simon walked out a free man, for the moment anyway. The chief offered to drive him to his office, but Simon did not want to be seen in another police car. He hustled away on foot, avoiding the busier streets, and even took an alley. His car was where he had parked it, nothing disturbed. He sat at his desk for a long time, taking deep breaths and reminding himself that he had just survived seven nights in jail. He had toughed it out, made the best of it, even made some friends and had some laughs. Prison would present more of a challenge, but he would worry about that later. What he really wanted was a cheeseburger and some fries. Since he wouldn't dare show his face in a café, he drove to a Wendy's and used the drive-thru. He ate at his desk while his cell phone charged.

After lunch, he began calling people. His mother, Paula, Tillie, Raymond, Chub, and Spade. With reluctance, he opened his laptop, stayed away from the news and social media, and read emails. There were hundreds of them, most from friends, acquaintances, and clients, all wishing him well and offering encouragement, but there were also quite a few from idiots he'd never heard of, all wishing him a painful death. He counted twenty-seven emails from reporters. On the whole, it was a depressing exercise.

At 2 P.M., as scheduled, he drove to Raymond's office and parked in the rear, something he would be doing from then on. As usual, Raymond was red-faced and puffy-eyed from another long night, but he was wide awake and bickering with his secretaries.

He growled at Simon, "You hungry? I need some lunch."

The burger and fries had been tasty and filling, but after a week of starvation he could eat some more. "Sure."

"I'll send one of the girls for sandwiches. You should stay away from the downtown joints for a while."

Simon wasn't looking for advice but held his tongue. He handed Raymond an envelope.

"What's this?"

"A promissory note for one hundred ninety thousand. And a check for the other ten."

"I wasn't expecting this."

"You said your fee was two hundred thousand for a first-degree murder case. I'll pay you when I can."

Raymond smiled and put the envelope on his desk. "We have a lot of work to do."

"I know."

At 4 P.M. Friday afternoon, the Cupit & Moke hearse stopped at a maroon and gold burial tent over an open grave at Eternal Springs Cemetery. Four paid pallbearers hauled the faux wooden casket to the tent where a handful of friends and neighbors waited in the cold. Doris, still banged up, struggled with her new walker. Jerry Korsak dutifully represented the family but introduced himself to no one. A rent-a-priest went through the motions, said a prayer, read some Holy Scripture, said another prayer, and tossed some dirt on the casket of a woman he had never met.

Eleanor Barnett was finally laid to rest, intact.

Leaving Braxton behind had never been so exhilarating. He could almost taste and smell the freedom. He refused to look in his rearview mirror. No one was back there.

After seven nights as a prisoner, Simon had made the firm decision that he would never again be locked up. If his streak of bad luck continued, and if he were one day faced with a lengthy sentence, he would either head for Brazil or jump off a bridge.

He pondered such things for two hours as the miles flew by. It was dark when he turned into the driveway on the western edge of Richmond. He braced himself and rang the doorbell. The door swung open, and all three kids grabbed him with bear hugs. There were tears and more hugs as they settled on a sofa in the den. Paula was gracious enough to peck him on the cheek and say, "Good to see you." Her parents had stepped out for a long dinner, so the little Latch family could be alone. When things settled down, Simon got right to the point. He said that he was not guilty, that he would never harm another person unless in self-defense, that he had grown close to Netty and had nothing to do with her death. He had a good lawyer, the best in town, and they were confident they would prevail. He did not know who poisoned Netty but they were putting together a list of suspects.

The police had stopped their investigation when he was arrested, as they always do, so it was up to him and his lawyer to find the killer. In spite of their efforts, his case would move forward and one day soon he would probably be put on trial.

Buck and Danny had a dozen questions. Janie snuggled under her father's arm and just listened. They were in new schools in the Richmond district and struggling to adjust. Paula was desperately looking for another job, one outside Braxton. There was no way she was staying there and subjecting the children to more humiliation.

The pizza arrived and they gathered around a coffee table for dinner. Buck found an old western on cable and the kids grew quieter as they watched it and ate. After an hour, Simon and Paula bundled up and went outside. As they walked down the street, she asked, "So how was jail?" They both chuckled.

"Not that bad."

"No gangs, no violence, great food."

"All of the above. The chief runs a clean operation, but I'm not going back. Seven days is my max."

"I hope you're right."

"How long are you staying here?"

"Not long. The bad thing about living with your parents after twenty years is that you are suddenly faced with all the quirks you had forgotten, and the quirks are far more bothersome now. I guess we forget the bad and hold on to the good. We love our parents and want them to be well-rounded people, but sometimes they don't measure up."

Simon had never considered her parents to be well-rounded. He said, "My mom's filing for divorce."

"She should've left Arn years ago."

"No, she should never have married him in the first place. He caught her on the rebound, a bad one. The final straw was all about money. She had the money in the bank to help me get out of jail, but the accounts are in both names. She couldn't touch it and he said no. Kept saying no. She issued an ultimatum, then walked out."

"I'm proud of her."

"She always liked you."

"Let's talk about something else."

They turned onto another street and ambled along. He asked, "What are your plans?"

"I'm scrambling, Simon, as you might guess. I can't stay here. The kids are in new schools because they have to be in school, right? But they're about to get yanked around again when I find a job."

"No way you're going home?"

"Absolutely not. I'm not sure you realize how bad things are these days, Simon. The press has thoroughly smeared you. Hungry lawyer seduces rich widow then poisons her. You can't find three people in Braxton who believe otherwise."

"You were always blunt."

"Maybe you need some bluntness."

"No, I don't. I know it's bad, believe me. Where are you going?"

"I don't know. I'm on the phone and computer all day looking for a job and there are some prospects."

They walked for a long time in silence, until they were cold. When his car was in sight she said, "It's almost ten. My parents will be home in a minute. You want to say hello?"

"I'll do it tomorrow. Okay if I take the kids out for pancakes?"

"They would like that."

———————◆◆◆———————

He checked into a Hyatt near the campus of VCU and went straight to the bar. Landy was waiting in a dark booth, the perfect spot for a little rendezvous. He had called her on the drive down. She had been expecting another lonely Friday night, with hubby stalking some bad guys in Florida.

They talked about him for a minute or two. She broke the news that she and her husband had agreed, on Christmas Day no less, to split and peacefully go their separate ways. There was nothing left of the marriage, and, thankfully, no children to fight over.

Then they went through the jail talk. As a veteran FBI agent who threw people into jail, she was curious about what it was like in there. Simon downplayed it and refused to whine.

"We're talking confidentially, okay Landy? You're not an agent right now and I'm not a lawyer. Just two old friends."

"Friends and lovers," she said with a wicked grin.

His heart fluttered but he controlled himself. He gave her the facts as he knew them. The autopsy results, the toxicology reports, his visits to the hospital, the visits of others, or those he knew of. He mentioned a few names of his top suspects and described both his will and Wally's.

After they ordered second drinks, Simon said, "I need your help. I didn't do the crime, okay?"

"I know that, Simon. I didn't believe it the first time I heard it."

"Thank you. I didn't do it, but someone did. Someone laced the ginger cookies with thallium. Have you ever heard of thallium?"

"Maybe, somewhere during training."

"Anyway, I have to dig and I need your help. As far as the police are concerned the investigation is over. They have their man. They've closed their case file and given it to the prosecutor. Just like that."

"I'm not sure about this, Simon. We are strictly prohibited from any sideline work. We can't moonlight. We have more than enough cases of our own."

"I get that, but you've got to help me track down the poison. I don't have the money to hire a private investigator, nor does my lawyer. Hell, I'm barely paying him. I'll do the snooping around Braxton—the hospital, the nurses, the orderlies, the janitors, the florists. I can handle that part of the investigation, but I can't find the source to thallium without help. It's been banned in this country for thirty years. Where did it come from and how do you get it?"

She said, reluctantly, "Let me think about it."

The drinks arrived. She sipped wine and he gulped beer.

With a smile she asked, "Want to talk about our divorces?"

"Please."

"Good. After you called, I took a long hot bath, shaved my legs, picked the skimpiest lingerie I own, and dressed for the evening."

"You look great."

"Wait till you see the lingerie. We're going up to your room now, Simon, and I'm not taking no for an answer."

"Who's saying no?"

CHAPTER 39

Raymond convinced Judge Pointer to skip a formal arraignment and allow Simon to enter a not-guilty plea on paper. It was a formality anyway, and given the throng that showed up for the simple bail hearing, Raymond preferred to avoid the attention. The not-guilty plea was recorded, and *Commonwealth of Virginia v. Simon F. Latch* entered the docket. Simon and Raymond agreed that there was no benefit in stalling and decided to request a speedy trial, the speedier the better. Cora Cook was not in a position to object. As the chief prosecutor, it was important for her to aggressively go after the criminals. She had, after all, ramrodded the indictment through the grand jury, then asked for a huge bond in an effort to keep Simon in jail. She could never show weakness, not that she was inclined to anyway. The voters expected nothing less. She agreed to fast-track the case, and joined the defense in a motion to place it on what was informally known as the "rocket docket." Judge Pointer was happy to accommodate both sides and set a trial date of May 23.

The reality was that Simon's was the only murder case in Braxton at the moment, and the town had never seen such attention. Journalists snooped around, digging for unique angles. Every lawyer in town was approached for a comment, though most declined. Two true-crime shows, allegedly from Hollywood but actually from Reno and St. Paul, excited the locals with their equipment trailers and bulky cameras. What they were filming was anybody's guess. At least twice a day a reporter with a film crew stood on the edge of Main Street and shot footage of Simon's office, with its permanently locked door. Tillie was just behind it, always jittery. She was monitoring the story in the press and online, and her scrapbook was filling up quickly. Simon had no desire to look at it.

"Simon sightings" were rare because he seldom left his building. He peeked through the shades upstairs and often saw reporters lurking in the alley. He was isolated, depressed, and frightened about the trial and his future. He seldom ate and Tillie fussed at him about his weight, as she continued to tone up.

He spent hours at his desk writing, by hand—nothing in the computer—and compiling his notes on Netty's final days. He broke down each one, almost hour by hour, with as much detail as he could recall. Her movements, his movements, her auto accident, his trips to the hospital, who else was there, who were the doctors and nurses, and so on. She had been admitted on December 17, and died on Wednesday, December 30. He charted every day and asked Tillie to double-check her calendars and phone calls. She had made three trips to the hospital to check on Netty and take brownies. She took those damned ginger cookies that Simon had bought at Tan Lu's. Who did she see at the hospital? Did she log in at the front desk, as required? Yes, the first time, but not for the second and third visits. The hospital was not strict about monitoring visitors.

The long dreary days of January gave way to more of the same in February. The phone simply wasn't ringing, and for a street practice that depended on word of mouth, the traffic was far too slow. Word of mouth was out there somewhere, but it was not being kind to Simon Latch.

In the second week of February, Paula called with the news that she had found a promising job with a new retirement village in the town of Danville, four hours south on the North Carolina state line. Danville was roughly the size of Braxton, with good schools and even a small college, and about as far away as possible while still being in Virginia. She had found an apartment and they would be moving in a matter of days. Her parents were driving her crazy and the kids were climbing the walls. Yes, it was all quite unsettling, but finally they were making progress. He volunteered to help with the move-in and she invited him to join the party.

Landy's reluctant efforts to find manufacturers, markets, and dealers for banned poisons was not going well. What she had found so far was something she already knew: there were thousands of banned and/or illegal chemicals, compounds, and drugs smuggled into America every year, for every reason, and from every entry point. Billions were spent trying to stop the flood of cocaine, heroin, and fentanyl. Poisons were not a priority and almost impossible to track.

Landy and her husband had filed their no-fault divorce and shook hands on the deal. As career FBI agents who moved frequently, they did not own a home. Their condo lease was up in a few months and she would remain in it until she found another apartment. Simon became a regular guest. He enjoyed being away from Braxton almost as much as he enjoyed the high-octane sex life they had jump-started. It was like a flashback twenty years to law school when they almost flunked out due to extracurricular activities.

But they were no longer twenty, and after a few weeks things cooled off as they slowly realized there was a good reason their old romance had not survived outside the bedroom. In late February, she surprised him with the news that she would be gone for a month on an assignment she could not discuss.

———•••———

On a snowy day in early March, Tillie walked into Simon's office and took a seat. She was obviously troubled and got right to the point. "I think it's time for me to move on."

He slowly put down a contract he was mulling over and said, "Okay."

"I cannot in good conscience keep getting paid when we're so low on cash and the business has dried up. We're fooling ourselves, Simon, if we think things are going to improve. I keep the books. I see the income, what little there is of it. The phones might as well be unplugged. The front door stays locked, and if anyone knocks it's usually a reporter. We get at least two prank calls every day from idiots who want you dead. I can't take it anymore." She was wiping her eyes.

"What are you going to do?"

"Leave town and go find a job somewhere."

"Okay. Any ideas?"

"Maybe. I have a good friend down in Sarasota, a kid from school. She says there are plenty of jobs and I can stay with her for a few months. I'll find something."

"So it's come to this?"

"Afraid so. I'll always cherish these days, Simon, the good ones anyway. There weren't many bad ones."

"You've been wonderful and I don't want to see you go."

"I know. And I know that if you had the income and the business I'd stay forever, but that's where we are. I'm so worried about you, Simon."

"Thanks. Unfortunately, there's plenty to worry about."

They were silent for a long time as they stared at the walls and remembered the good days. She touched her eyes with a tissue and he felt like crying too. Finally, she said, "I'll leave Friday."

"You can always come back, you know?"

"I wish I could believe that, Simon, I really do."

They stood and hugged for the first time, then hugged again for the last time.

CHAPTER 40

With Simon focused on his criminal problems, and with Judge Pointer steadfastly refusing to even discuss Eleanor Barnett's complicated estate, Teddy Hammer quietly pursued his grand scheme. His plan was to attack the will prepared by Simon on the grounds of undue influence. If Simon was convicted of murder, he would go away for a long time and his will would be worthless. If he was acquitted, something no one really expected, then they would have a huge court fight over his actions in preparing the will. Teddy would also attack the will prepared by Wally Thackerman, also on the grounds of undue influence. He was confident he could use the threat of an ethics complaint to bully Wally into backing off.

Once Simon and Wally and their wills were out of the picture, Teddy could reveal his secret. Neither lawyer had discovered that there was a third will, one signed by Harry Korsak in 1988. According to Jerry Korsak, who had a copy of the old will, his father had agreed to leave everything to Eleanor, in trust. Upon her death, the assets would go to Jerry and Clyde in equal shares. Because Eleanor had such strong feelings against the boys, Harry had not told her about the will and she did not sign a similar one at that time.

Teddy at first doubted the story because he had learned to doubt almost everything Jerry told him. However, the old will was straightforward and attempted to protect Jerry and Clyde upon Eleanor's death. The will had been prepared by a lawyer who died years earlier, and it was a near perfect example of legal malpractice. It virtually guaranteed years of litigation. For example, Harry kept his assets jointly owned with Eleanor while at the same time attempting to shield the assets in a poorly drafted trust. Why the old will was not probated at Harry's death was not clear. Teddy surmised that Eleanor knew nothing about it and managed to avoid probate because the assets were jointly owned. He was also certain that neither Simon nor Wally knew about the old will. How could they? There were many unanswered questions, but the bottom line was that Clyde and Jerry were the only blood relatives still around. Eleanor's niece and nephew didn't even know she was dead.

The most pressing matter was the issue of the assets. What was in Eleanor's estate? Jerry was convinced there was plenty. He knew his father owned stock in Coke and Wal-Mart, but some of his claims seemed rather grandiose. Before Teddy invested hundreds of hours of work, he needed to make sure there were significant assets. Otherwise, the case was not worth pursuing. To investigate, Teddy befriended the conservator, Clement Gelly, the conscientious young lawyer who had not asked to be involved. Judge Pointer trusted him and leaned on him for the favor.

Teddy convinced Clement to take a trip together. After getting Judge Pointer's quiet approval, they flew together, at Teddy's expense, to Atlanta and checked into a splendid hotel in the ritzy Buckhead neighborhood. Teddy had learned the identity of Buddy Brown, a principal in Rumke-Brown, Harry's old brokerage house. However, his two attempts to get him on the phone had gone nowhere.

Buddy was fully aware of Eleanor's death and the surrounding drama with her lawyer in Braxton, Virginia. In fact, he had a file with the press clippings and had followed the chatter online. He

knew he would be involved at some point, so when the conservator, one Clement Gelly, called and asked for a meeting, Buddy
really had no choice but to agree.

Teddy stayed at the hotel and kept busy while Clement took
a cab a few blocks away to an office building filled with professionals and firms that seemed to want little attention. Rumke-
Brown's first-floor suite spoke of understated wealth. The walls
and floors were decorated in a minimalist theme, with contem-
porary paintings and strange bronzes on the end tables. The mood
was subdued and quiet with soft background music. There was no
receptionist because the firm did not allow walk-ins or encourage
visitors. An assistant met Clement and led him through the halls
to a large corner office where Buddy Brown was waiting with a
smile.

The firm's website followed the minimalist theme of revealing
almost nothing. There were a few partners and about a dozen
associates, all much younger than Brown. Though his age was not
given, he graduated from Emory in 1962, so he was in his mid-
seventies. Fit, tanned, vigorous, ready for the next tennis match.
No pickleball for him. The same assistant served them coffee
and designer water on the conference table. Brown rolled up his
sleeves, glanced at his watch, and was ready to donate one hour to
the cause, whatever it was.

He said, "Looks like you got yourself a real mess up there."

"Lots of drama," Clement agreed. "I was minding my own
business when the judge hooked me in as the conservator."

"Yes, that's what you said on the phone." In other words, *I've
already heard this.* "Where is the case procedurally?"

"Which one? The murder trial is set for May twenty-third.
The estate mess is on hold until the criminal matters are resolved.
Same judge with both cases and she's very much in control."

"So, what's my involvement at this point?"

"Nothing officially. I'm just trying to verify Ms. Barnett's
assets."

"Okay, I spent an hour with our attorney yesterday and this is
my position. I have, or had, a fiduciary relationship with Harry

Korsak and Eleanor Barnett, both now deceased. It was a confidential, privileged relationship, as with all our clients. However, upon their deaths, the confidentiality became somewhat less
strict, shall we say. I will agree to give a deposition, with my
attorney present, for the record. I will not agree to testify in any
proceeding, unless, of course, I am subpoenaed, at which time I
will comply. Fair enough?"

"I suppose."

"But there are some things I can tell you now, off the record,
and in confidence, that might help you inventory her assets. Are
we off the record?"

Clement wasn't sure what the record was, and he knew he
would immediately debrief with Teddy Hammer over lunch. He
wasn't a journalist working on a story, and he had not traveled all
the way to Atlanta to get stiff-armed. "Sure," he said.

Buddy started at the beginning.

———————◆◆◆———————

He was a stockbroker with Merrill Lynch in Atlanta when
he met Harry and Eleanor. Her first husband died a few years
earlier and she had $50,000 in life insurance. Harry was work-
ing for Coca-Cola and had just qualified for its employee stock-
option plan. They put all their money in Coke and kept buying
shares for many years. They were frugal, saved as much as possible, and for thirty years bought all the Coke stock they could
afford. Later, they began buying Wal-Mart shares with the same
strategy. Both companies grew over the years and split their common stock numerous times. The little Korsak nest egg became a
fortune. Around 1990, they splurged on a vacation and went to
a small Caribbean island few people had heard of. It was called
Montrouge, in the French West Indies, near Guadeloupe. Some
executives at Coke had discovered the place and were trying to
keep it quiet. It was paradise, just a speck of an island with beautiful mountains and white beaches. Harry and Eleanor fell for the
place and bought a nice bungalow for half a million. An Atlanta

developer showed up and saw the potential. The plan was to buy
the entire island, sell off individual lots, put in a resort or two,
and watch the value increase. Sort of like Mustique. Harry, whose
health was not great, was tired of working and began dreaming
of a glorious retirement on the island. He put $5 million into the
development and built a bigger house on the beach. The land was
selling at outrageous prices. A few celebrities moved in and the
prices went even higher. A deal to sell Montrouge for $200 mil-
lion fell through. Harry's piece would have been worth 15 percent
of the total. More financing was needed to finish a third resort,
and Harry put up another $5 million. Buddy voiced his concern
at that point, but Harry was determined. The limited partners
began squabbling and lawsuits were filed. The resorts were doing
well and the property values were through the roof, but there was
discord among the ownership. One group tried to buy another
in a hostile takeover. Harry sided with the losing group. A hefty
loan was in default. Harry put in another $5 million. Almost all
of his Coke and Wal-Mart stock was gone but his real estate protected his net worth. Then, an unbelievable disaster. On the first
day of June 1999, the volcano on Montrouge erupted for the first
time in 240 years. The island was practically blown out of the
ocean and off the map. Over a hundred people, tourists and resi-
dents, were killed, most of them never found. Harry and Eleanor
had been there the week before. Their luxury home was totally
destroyed. The typical insurance coverage on the island protected
the homes and resorts against fire, wind, flooding, and so on. Not
a single one mentioned volcanoes. Big lawsuits were filed by the
owners, and the litigation raged until the owners got tired of losing. The insurance companies won every case.

Harry's bad health deteriorated even faster. He and Eleanor
had nervous breakdowns together and went into therapy. To run
away, they sold their home in Atlanta and moved to the hills of
northern Virginia. Harry died not long after the move.

It was a very sad story.

The obvious question was: How much, if any, of the money
was left?

Buddy dodged the question for a while, then said, "Upon the advice of counsel, I can't give you the exact value of the stocks in the portfolio. I will if a court orders me to, but I can't now."

Clement was frustrated by Buddy's reluctance and said, "Okay, I get that, but I'm trying to anticipate litigation, and it would be helpful if I had an idea, in the ballpark, of the value of Eleanor's stocks."

"I understand. At its peak, the Coke stock was worth a little over ten million. What's left is less than half a million. Wal-Mart was about six mil, and it's all gone."

Clement managed to stifle his reaction. "That's quite a bit less than we thought."

"Substantially less than half a million."

———————◆◆◆———————

Clement left after an hour and a half, returned to the hotel, and found Teddy Hammer at a small desk in the business center. He sat in a chair across from him, smiling as he shook his head, and said, "It's all a hoax."

CHAPTER 41

A month before the trial, Judge Pointer scheduled a closed hearing to address a number of issues, the most important of which was venue.

Raymond had been adamant from day one that the trial must take place far away from Braxton. He really didn't care where, but preferably out of the reach of the Washington and Richmond press. His client had been pilloried and savaged from the day of his indictment and the damage was irreversible. The only remaining question in the press was: Where was the firing squad? Raymond had been a prominent criminal defense lawyer for forty years and had never represented a defendant so thoroughly condemned by his neighbors and townsfolk. His own secretary, a compassionate soul, had quietly said to him several times, "Better get a plea bargain."

Simon had been reluctant at first. For a while he argued that by the terms of the will he drafted for Eleanor, virtually everyone in Braxton would benefit from her generosity. The trust he so cleverly created spread her money to every church, civic club, food bank, scout troop, garden club, and so on. And, more important, the will did not give Simon Latch a dime of her money. He had to earn it! He would be paid $500 an hour and his fees would be impressive, but an hour away in Washington the going rate for the big firm guys was double that. Under oath and on cross-examination he was confident he could justify his billings.

Raymond countered with the argument that the terms of the will might never be heard by the jury. The will was not the issue. Murder was. Oddly enough, motive was not always a factor and did not have to be proven. Simon believed the will would be the Commonwealth's first exhibit, dramatically waved in front of the jury by Cora Cook as proof that the defendant was dreaming of huge fees and profiting from the death of Eleanor Barnett.

He and Raymond argued for several weeks, usually late at night over cigars and bourbon. But Raymond would not budge and even threatened to withdraw, a ploy he used occasionally. The defense filed a motion seeking a change of venue.

During their discussions and arguments, they were joined by Casey Noland, the newest member of Raymond's firm. He was thirty years old and had spent the past three years as a federal public defender. His unabashed goal in life was to become a high-octane, radical, colorful criminal defense lawyer, similar to Raymond Lassiter. While his law school buddies dreamed of the big corporate firms and million-dollar salaries, Casey wanted to be in the courtroom defending clients accused of horrible crimes. He wanted to protect the rights of the worst killers. He wanted to face skeptical juries. He wanted the spotlight.

Casey was also single and worked strange hours. To impress Raymond enough to get a job, he was developing a taste for bourbon and cigars.

For the hearing, Judge Pointer put two bailiffs at the door of Courtroom B and banned all spectators. She was tired of reporters hanging around the courthouse and bothering her secretary. She had called the police on several occasions to get rid of people digging for dirt about the case.

Cora Cook opposed the motion because she was supposed to, but she, too, knew a fair trial was impossible in Braxton. Around her office, the sentiment always leaned toward guilt, but that was to be expected among the staff of a prosecutor. No one was willing to give Simon Latch the benefit of the doubt. Forget about the presumption of innocence. Out of respect, her friends never commented on or gossiped about a case, but she knew they thought Simon poisoned Eleanor. Her current boyfriend thought a conviction was a slam dunk.

As always, the hearing was on the record, but Judge Pointer, as she often did, treated it as informally as possible. The attorneys kept their seats as they bantered back and forth, respectfully. Judge Pointer interrupted when necessary. Simon sat between Raymond and Casey Noland, and passed notes to both, once again thankful that he had not pursued a career as a criminal lawyer. He was still trying to warm up to Casey.

Virginia, like most states, allowed either side, defense or prosecution, to request a change of venue. However, neither side could suggest a preferred alternate. That was within the sole discretion of the judge.

After an hour of discussion, and little argument, it was apparent that Judge Pointer had made up her mind. She said, "I'll grant the motion to change venue and I'll decide on the jurisdiction later. I'm looking at various parts of the state and I tend to agree with the defense that the trial should be moved far away."

The attorneys scribbled notes. No one was surprised. Simon didn't relish the idea of spending a week or two in a cheap motel in a strange town, but the longer he stayed in Braxton, the more he was convinced that he needed to leave.

They then quibbled over discovery matters, with Her Honor lecturing both sides on the rules that required full disclosure. Cora Cook had a stellar reputation as an ethical prosecutor and withheld nothing. Raymond's reputation did not quite match hers but he had nothing to hide.

At noon, Judge Pointer surprised them when she recessed until 2 P.M. There was nothing left on the agenda, not in *Commonwealth of Virginia v. Simon F. Latch,* and the lawyers left the courtroom scratching their heads. What was the unfinished business?

Simon tried diligently to avoid being seen in public anywhere in Braxton, especially downtown where the lawyers and courthouse gang had their lunches. Casey drove them to an old country store where they had sandwiches at a table in a corner. It was one of the few restaurants Simon and Eleanor had not tried.

At 2 P.M. they reconvened and waited fifteen minutes for Judge Pointer to assume the bench. She was religiously punctual and the slight delay was unusual. When she took her place she dismissed the court reporter and settled in for a casual chat with Raymond, Casey, Cora, and Simon.

She began, "My husband is from the Tidewater area and I know it well. From here, it's four hours by car. It's also another world, very different from the Blue Ridge Mountains that we know and love. There are two million people in the area, big towns like Hampton, Chesapeake, Norfolk, Newport News, Portsmouth. Virginia Beach is the largest, with twice the population of Richmond. The *Tidewater Times* has the largest circulation and it hardly covered this story. I found only two reports, while the state's other newspapers were trying to out-scream each other. As you probably know, the area has a strong military influence. The largest naval base in the world is in Norfolk. The population is very diverse and transient. I have no doubt that it will be easier to find impartial jurors. So, I've notified the supreme court that I'm moving the case to Virginia Beach. This will not affect the trial date of May twenty-three."

She took a sip of water and cleared her throat. "I have also informed the supreme court that I am recusing myself from this case. My reasons are as follows. There are two cases, one criminal, one probate. Under our system, the circuit court has jurisdiction of both, and since I'm the senior circuit judge in Braxton, they're on my desk. The facts of one case bleed into another. I could learn something from one case that could affect my judgment in the other. It's best if I turn loose of one. The other reason is that I am facing some medical issues that will require a lighter load for a few months."

The lawyers frowned appropriately. Judge Pointer certainly looked as healthy as ever. There were suddenly plenty of questions, but none were asked.

"My prognosis is good but it may take some time." Another

sip of water. "And there's something else, something that may or may not be relevant in the criminal case. I had a talk with Clement Gelly last week and he informed me, sort of off the record, that he has learned something important. He went to Atlanta and met with the investment advisor for Eleanor Barnett. It looks as though she rather outrageously inflated the value of her estate. Her late husband lost his fortune, some fifteen million, in bad investments. Then they moved here and he promptly died. Clement values her home at two hundred and fifty thousand, about the same for her stocks and cash."

Simon wanted to puke again, but he managed a poker face and nodded as if he'd known this all along, no big deal. It had been a year since he met her. A year since she had uttered, almost in a whisper, the words that wrecked his life: *Ten million in Coke stock, six million in Wal-Mart stock, about four million in cash.*

How could a pleasant old widow who appeared perfectly normal and acted like the other eighty-five-year-olds be afflicted with some weird strain of *insanity*? Nothing else in her life, or at least nothing Simon had noticed, gave any indication of mental illness. The word "sucker" rattled around his brain.

Judge Pointer kept talking, something about the will contest, but Simon heard nothing.

————— •◆• —————

At least three nights a week, Simon found himself in Raymond's law library. He worked on briefs and motions, all designed to aid his own defense. He read dozens of criminal cases involving poison. He studied procedure and began to understand criminal law. He read every report and researched every witness to be offered against him by the Commonwealth.

Raymond's office was down the hall, his door always open, his cigar smoke wafting through the entire building. At least once each night, he would bark, "Simon," as if his client was just another paralegal. Simon always answered the call. It was the least he could do for an expensive lawyer working for free.

On the night of the venue hearing, around 10 P.M., Simon sat down and inhaled a load of smoke. Casey joined, in jogging shorts and running shoes. Raymond walked to the liquor cabinet, poured three stiff bourbons, and closed his door. They clinked glasses.

"Cora called this afternoon to offer a plea deal, sort of a formality."

"It was expected, right?"

"Right. Take a hit for fifteen years, parole after ten, probably, but parole is tough in this state."

"Fifteen years? I'll jump off a bridge first."

"It's not a bad offer, given the circumstances."

"What circumstances are you talking about?"

"The facts, Simon, the facts."

"You still don't believe me, do you?"

"Oh, I do. I've never doubted you. The problem, Simon, is that you look guilty as hell, and I'm not sure how we change that."

"I'll testify. I'll explain everything I did, and I'll make the jury believe me."

"Famous last words. Whether you'll testify or not is a decision we'll make at the last minute."

"The answer is no. I'm not guilty and I'm not pleading guilty."

They worked on their drinks, puffed their cigars. As usual, Casey said little.

For some reason, Raymond began to chuckle. "What is it?" Simon finally snapped.

"Did you really believe the old girl had twenty million dollars?"

"I'm glad you think it's funny."

"Did you?"

"Yes."

"So, what was your first reaction when you were taking notes, the initial consultation with a new client, right, and she says she's loaded, got twenty mil or so? What was your first thought?"

"Well, it was not a good one. Had something to do with greed."

Raymond was laughing and Casey appeared to be amused. After a moment or two, Simon wanted to join them. But he couldn't do it.

He finished his bourbon and left with half a cigar. The only time he walked the streets of Braxton was late at night, usually after leaving Raymond's. During the day he stayed in his office with the doors locked, and ventured out only after dark.

The air was cool and the night was clear, and so he walked. His thoughts were scrambled around the suggestion that he plead guilty, which was ridiculous, and the destructive lies told by Eleanor, and the prospect of being judged by people who lived far away and knew nothing about the case.

At the moment, Simon felt abandoned by his friends. Not a single one had been loyal. Many had sent quick emails after his arrest, but those had all but stopped. Some of his friends were also friends of Paula's and, as in most divorces, they couldn't take sides and found it easier to just ignore the Latches.

The loss of support was crushing. The loss of his children was painful. He called and texted them every day, but they were now four hours away and struggling with their new lives.

And so he walked, for hours.

CHAPTER 42

In the first week of May two events occurred at virtually the same time, and though neither could rescue Simon from the ugly prospect of being put on trial for murder, they provided the first glimmer of good luck he had seen in months.

First, Paula sold the house in Braxton for more than the list price. After paying off both mortgages, she netted $28,000, a windfall no one was expecting. Simon did the paperwork and charged nothing for the closing. At the last minute, Paula told her ex that she would pay $5,000 in legal fees for his services. It was a fine, generous gesture and, after first protesting meekly, Simon agreed to take the money.

Two days later, his mother called with the welcome news that after twenty-seven unhappy years she was splitting with Arn. Things were somewhat amicable, and they had agreed to a division of the assets. With Arn's name off her bank accounts, she was now in charge of her money. She was sending her son $10,000 to help with his legal bills. He accepted the money, called it a loan, and promised to repay it at some undetermined time in the future. He was proud of her for showing the courage to walk away from a bad marriage at the age of seventy-three and take her savings with her. He did not know how much money she had squirreled away and he was not about to ask. Never, ever again would he pry into the financial affairs of a senior citizen. On the phone, she sounded ten years younger and was planning a trip to the Greek Isles with some friends. However, if he needed her to be in the courtroom she would happily postpone the trip. He thanked her and promised to consider it.

Off to the Greek Isles with a pocketful of money. He was headed to a courtroom where he would either be condemned to prison or narrowly escape with nothing but the shirt on his back. He had not envied his mother in many years; indeed, he had pitied her because she was stuck with a turd like Arn. Now, she seemed like the luckiest person he knew.

Simon did not want his mother or his children anywhere near the courtroom. He and Paula had discussed the trial at length. It would be impossible to shield the kids from the publicity. Even if the local news in Danville ignored the story, there would be an avalanche of crap online. On the phone, he and Paula had floated the idea of a nightly recap of the trial with the children. She could review the news stories and hold a discussion that would include the facts as presented by the press. It seemed a slightly better idea than simply ignoring the trial and dreaming the kids might somehow escape it. Simon was not afraid of the truth and wanted his children to know that he was not guilty of anything, other than perhaps a little bad judgment. Still, the visual of him going to and from the courthouse, with a horde following and all manner of sensational coverage by the talking heads, was not pleasant.

When the check arrived from his mother, Simon promptly deposited it in his firm's account and wrote another one to Raymond for legal fees. $10,000. He walked it over to Raymond's office that night and handed it to him. "One eighty to go," he said proudly.

"Where'd you get this?" Raymond asked suspiciously.

Simon told him the story. The lawyer put the check in a drawer.

Raymond had talked to some attorney friends in the Tidewater area and was now firmly convinced that moving the case there was of great benefit to Simon. It was far away from the Blue Ridge Mountains and in another world.

To replace Mary Blankenship Pointer, the supreme court had appointed Padma Shyam, one of three female judges on the Virginia Beach Circuit Court. She was forty-six years old, had been on the bench for nine years, and annually received the highest ratings not only from her colleagues, but also from lawyers who appeared before her.

Simon had a good friend from law school who practiced in Chesapeake, next door to Virginia Beach, and the guy raved about Judge Shyam.

Both Raymond and Simon had fretted over Judge Pointer's recusal. They knew her well and thought they understood her leanings and eccentricities. She was a tough law-and-order judge, but she was unfailingly fair to both sides. Simon was still smarting from the $300,000 bond she had required for his release, not to mention the seven nights in jail, but he had forgiven her and had convinced himself she would give him a break if needed.

Now, though, she was forgotten, at least for the murder trial. Raymond had chatted twice with Judge Shyam and felt comfortable with her. She, too, was worried about publicity and too much press. She had the idea of selecting the jury a week before the announced trial date of May 23. The court clerk could quietly summons fifty or so prospects to an empty courtroom, and the lawyers could grill them about serving on the jury. If more were needed, call another fifty. If they could keep the story away from the press, the majority of the jurors would not know about the case. But if they waited until Monday, May 23, the courthouse would be a circus and the prospective jurors would have to walk through a throng just to get to the courtroom. By then, the story would be front-page. An uninformed and impartial jury would be almost impossible.

Judge Shyam warmed up to her own idea. The lawyers thought it would work well. She had never held jury selection before the actual start date of a trial, but there was no procedural rule against it. She also liked the idea of a gag order to quieten the lawyers and witnesses. Raymond, a trial lawyer who loved to see his name in the newspapers, agreed wholeheartedly. He promised not to say a word about the trial and to keep Simon quiet as well.

Simon had no intention of showing his face outside the courtroom.

———————◆◆◆———————

Through many late-night meetings they had slowly pieced together a defense strategy that was both bold and risky. There was no direct evidence against Simon—no one had seen him buy the thallium and there was nothing to link him to its acquisition. No one had seen him lace the ginger cookies with the poison, nor feed them to Eleanor Barnett. The indirect evidence would undoubtedly be used to create a great deal of suspicion around his actions, but it was not enough to convict. The prosecution would be forced to rely on circumstantial evidence to convince jurors of his guilt.

Raymond had leaned on a friend who knew a pathologist who agreed to study the autopsy for only $1,000, a greatly reduced fee. Dr. Brock, the state medical examiner who performed it, had impressive credentials and experience and would make a believable witness for the Commonwealth. Same for the forensic toxicologist. To attack both would require finding other experts with unimpeachable qualifications who were willing to testify. And they would cost a fortune.

Raymond's friend agreed with the conclusions of the autopsy.

So why bother? Why attack the experts? The smarter approach was to admit almost everything. Admit Eleanor died of thallium poisoning. Admit Simon bought the ginger cookies at Tan Lu's, a place he had taken her for lunch three times. Admit she liked the food there and so did he. Admit Matilda visited Eleanor in the hospital on three occasions, twice taking her ginger cookies and other goodies. Admit the will. Admit the power of attorney.

Admit the retainer agreement. Admit everything that was true and obvious.

But deny vehemently that Simon poisoned the cookies. Obviously, someone did, but it wasn't Simon.

So who did it? That was a problem for the police and prosecutors, not for Simon. He was under no obligation to solve the crime.

His only obligation was to save his own skin.

CHAPTER 43

Monday, May 23.

Simon was awake staring at the digital clock when it chirped at 5 A.M.

It was depressing to begin a day knowing full well that the day would be one of the worst in his life. It was even more depressing to think that tomorrow would be even worse and the following days would only spiral down. He needed strong coffee but there was none in the budget hotel "suite" he had reserved for the next five days. After two nights he was having fond memories of the Braxton city jail.

Perhaps the only bright spot at the moment was the fact that his head was clear; no cobwebs, no dull pain. If Raymond could swear off booze during the trial, then so could his client. He allowed himself five minutes to stare at the dark ceiling and listen to the grind of diesel engines in eighteen-wheelers passing each other on one of the Tidewater's endless six-lane bypasses. Dawn was an hour away but the traffic was already making noise. Where was he and how did he get there? That question had dogged him for months now, and with effort he could almost piece together a narrative. For the much larger question—Where was he going?—there was no answer, only fear.

The awful day was not going away. It had to be confronted,

and if not outright challenged then at least stared down with a faux confidence that he could handle anything the mighty Commonwealth of Virginia threw at him. He kicked off the covers, planted his feet on the cheap carpet, and realized he was already tired. Then he showered quickly and dressed as he had been told. Raymond suggested a dark suit, white shirt, bland tie, nothing that might irritate a juror. As a former gambler, Simon would bet $1,000 on the spot that none of the seven male jurors waiting to judge him would be wearing a tie.

Seven men, five women; nine whites, two blacks, one Asian. Two alternates. He knew their names, occupations, religions, educational backgrounds, and so on. The previous Wednesday, they had been selected in an empty courtroom in less than three hours. Of the forty-eight in the first panel summoned by the clerk, only seven raised their hands when asked if they knew anything about the case. Over half had never heard of Braxton, Virginia. The defense was thrilled with the lack of notoriety. A second panel was not needed. Judge Shyam was a wizard in the courtroom and flawlessly officiated the selection of the jury. Raymond said it was the fairest process he had ever seen in his forty-plus years.

Her Honor was also quite prescient in anticipating publicity. The Sunday edition of the *Tidewater Times* had a front-page story with a stock photo of Simon, complete with all of the sensational allegations against him. It included hints about the mysterious last will and testament, the alleged fortune, the power of attorney signed on her deathbed, the advance directive which allowed him to pull the plug, the fortuitous passing on December 30, the cremation angle, then the proof of poisoning. On page two there were other stories, one filled with random man-on-the-street comments from folks in Braxton. Most hid behind requests for anonymity. Another story traced the history of murder-by-poison in America and used FBI statistics. Thallium has a long and sordid history with murder.

Simon was nauseous when he read the stories, but also grateful the jury had already been selected. Now that it was empaneled, it had been strongly admonished by Her Honor to avoid the press if possible, speak to no one about the case, and, most important, keep an open mind until all the evidence had been presented. She had dwelt on the presumption of innocence and lectured the jury on the basic principle that Simon Latch was innocent until proven guilty beyond a reasonable doubt.

It certainly sounded strong last Wednesday in an empty courtroom. Today, though, the courtroom would be crowded with journalists of every stripe and ilk, along with dozens of spectators and courthouse regulars. Additional bailiffs and guards had been summoned by Judge Shyam.

As he left his room he stopped to examine himself in the mirror. His pants were loose because he was quite a bit thinner than he'd been before the indictment. Landy, his de facto girlfriend, had said more than once that his face was gaunt and he had bags under his eyes. Raymond said it was important for him to maintain a pleasant look on his face, nothing fake or goofy, just an occasional quick smile, maybe a nod here and there, and never a frown nor a look of concern, though, at the same time, never a look of cockiness or indignation.

Thanks, Raymond. Anything else? Any other tricks to try with my face while I'm trying to listen, analyze, and remember every word spoken in court, and also taking pages of notes while stealing glances at the jurors?

It was still dark when he left the hotel and headed toward Virginia Beach, three miles away. He saw an all-night pancake house and stopped for coffee. He bought the Monday edition of the *Tidewater Times,* and once again saw his face on the front page.

———•••———

Raymond had no shortage of trial lawyer buddies around the Commonwealth. Marshall Graff was the king of torts in Virginia Beach and had offered his offices to the defense. They were impressive, a far cry from anything in Braxton. Expensive, ultramodern furnishings, a splendid conference room with twenty leather chairs around a long, wide table, enough offices to house his twenty-five-lawyer team and support staff, and on the third floor a small workroom where Raymond set up shop with a view of the courthouse.

Simon walked in at 7 A.M. and found the coffeepot. Raymond and Casey Noland arrived a few minutes later. Raymond said he was ready, said it was "showtime," said if you weren't nervous the first day of the trial, then something was wrong. He told a couple first-day stories that were hard to follow.

Simon listened as he kept an eye on the street in front of the courthouse. The television vans were arriving and being herded to the proper spots by a small army of city policemen. Barricades were in place to keep the sidewalks clear of reporters and onlookers. The jurors would enter through a side door, away from the press. Simon had his own strategy, one that Marshall Graff had put together with his paralegals.

At 8:30, Raymond and Casey loaded their thick briefcases and walked to the front entrance of the courthouse. They attracted plenty of attention, and a smiling Raymond enjoyed bantering with the reporters while saying nothing. They wanted to know where his client was hiding. Raymond said Simon was sleeping in that morning.

An associate of Marshall Graff's drove Simon to a service entrance, where he jumped out by the dumpsters and entered, unseen. At 8:55, he strode into the courtroom with Raymond and Casey, took a seat at the defense table, and tried not to notice the crowd watching him.

Judge Shyam assumed the bench at precisely 9 A.M. and said good morning. She went through her usual spiel about the trial and her rules governing the decorum in her courtroom. She gave a general outline of how the trial would progress and predicted it would be completed by the end of the week, but there was no rush. She informed the crowd that the jury had already been selected and asked the bailiffs to bring the jurors. They entered, some rather tentatively, and assumed their numbered chairs in the jury box.

Judge Shyam nodded at Cora Cook, who rose and walked purposefully to the podium in front of the jurors. Not a single garment in her closet could be considered conservative, but she was still quite impressive in solid black. The heels were not quite as high and the skirt wasn't quite as tight, but she kept a nice figure and knew how to display it. The jurors looked her over while she smiled and said hello. Then she began with an obsequious opening in which she thanked the jurors repeatedly for their service, and so on.

Simon scribbled on his legal pad, "as if they have a choice???"

Cora got to the heart of the matter soon enough. "This is a case of murder driven by greed." Her words were delivered solemnly, with a nice dramatic flair. Simon could feel the jurors' eyes boring down upon him. He did not look up.

"In March of last year, in the town of Braxton, up in the Blue Ridge Mountains, a lovely lady named Eleanor Barnett, a widow with no children, made an appointment to see a lawyer named Simon Latch, the defendant." Cora paused for more drama and pointed at Simon. He nodded gravely at her finger as if to say, *Yes, that's me but you got the wrong person.*

"Ms. Barnett was eighty-five years old and wanted to make a new will. The defendant had been a lawyer in Braxton for eighteen years, was well known, and had prepared many simple, inexpensive wills. The meeting took place as scheduled on March the tenth in his office on Main Street. At some point during the first meeting, the defendant realized that a simple will would not be sufficient for Ms. Barnett, at least not in his opinion. She was not an average client. Indeed, she said she had millions of dollars in assets, and no debts. She claimed to own stock in Coca-Cola and Wal-Mart and said she kept several million dollars in cash in a bank in Atlanta. Greed entered the picture and the defendant decided on a different course of action. For the previous twelve years, his secretary, Matilda Clark, had typed every will in the office. It's fairly routine legal work. But for some reason, the defendant did not allow Ms. Clark to prepare the will, but rather typed it himself and said nothing to his secretary about it.

From that moment on, the defendant had a scheme to ingratiate himself to Ms. Barnett and get as much of her money as possible."

Simon scribbled, "So far, so good, pretty much on point, got her facts straight. Why am I sweating already?"

Raymond had warned him that most prosecutors try to dehumanize their targets by referring to them only as *the defendant*. Cora was following the playbook.

She said, "Unfortunately, the scheme ended in the poisoning and death of Ms. Barnett." In another effort at high drama, she pointed at him again and said, "Ladies and gentlemen of the jury, Ms. Barnett died at the hands of her own lawyer, this defendant sitting right here."

Cora then made a harmless mistake by talking about the will the defendant prepared and typed himself. She lost the jury for the moment when she tried to explain some of the trusts. Simon watched them and knew they were either confused or bored.

His mind wandered. To be called a murderer and put on trial would be a nightmarish ordeal even for a guilty person. The horror was the potential punishment: death by lethal injection, or decades in prison. But for an innocent man, the entire charade was overwhelming and surreal. Simon kept telling himself that it wasn't really happening, that at some pivotal moment the judge would stop everything, dismiss the jury, admonish the prosecutor, and instruct the defendant to walk out of the courthouse, an innocent man. And, oh by the way, sorry for the trouble. But with each hour of each day, he was quietly growing accustomed to the role of the accused. The grinding machinery of American justice was often slow to start, but once the disparate elements finally came together at one time and in one place—the courtroom— there was no stopping the train wreck.

Cora returned to his scheming ways and the jury perked up. The defendant typed the will, then convinced an insurance agent and his wife next door to witness it, then tried his best to keep it quiet. Because of a quirk in our estate tax laws, it would be greatly advantageous to the heirs if Ms. Barnett died in calendar year

2015. Thus, the defendant had a deadline. He slowly befriended Ms. Barnett, spent more time with her, took her to many long lunches, all of which he paid for. During one outing, the couple discovered a Vietnamese restaurant in Braxton. Ms. Barnett especially liked the Saigon ginger cookies the place was known for.

On a large screen hung from the wall across from the jury, Cora flashed a color photo of one of the ginger cookies. Flat, about two inches in diameter. Then she added a photo of the Tan Lu's box. For $6.25 you got a dozen cookies. The last photo was a small mound of white powder on a lab test tray. It resembled baking soda. She said it was a sample of thallium, a poison no longer produced in America but not illegal to possess. Until recently it was commonly used in rat poison. Most of it came from China and India. It was odorless, tasteless, invisible when mixed with other substances, and lethal.

In a movement that was quite dramatic, Cora walked to the exhibit table near the bench and from a cardboard box removed a standard, plastic hospital tray. Two of Tan Lu's boxes were in the center of it. She held it in front of the jury and said, "Ladies and gentlemen, here's the murder weapon. Eleven cookies. Nine in one box, two in the other, all laced with thallium. The thirteen that are missing were consumed by the victim. All were purchased by the defendant on two separate days last December, then taken by his secretary to the hospital room of Eleanor Barnett. After the cookies were consumed over a one-week period, Ms. Barnett died of acute toxic poisoning. Her death was slow, painful, and agonizing. The state medical examiner will describe the condition of her body."

The courtroom was perfectly still. Everyone watched as Cora carefully placed the tray back in the cardboard box. She handled it as if the slightest jiggle might unleash the thallium and kill her, the court reporter, maybe the judge as well.

She returned to the podium and flipped through her notes. Simon could almost feel the stares from some of the jurors, and they were not conveying sympathy.

"Now, once Ms. Barnett was dead, the defendant tried desperately to cover his tracks, to hide the evidence." She lifted a document and waved it around. "This is called an advance directive. Also known as a living will. Typed up by the defendant, presented to Ms. Barnett in the hospital, probably while she was eating the cookies, and signed by her there, upon his advice."

Raymond startled everyone by standing and yelling, "Objection, Your Honor. Pure speculation. Ms. Cook doesn't know when the deceased ate the cookies."

Her Honor was as shaken as everyone else by the outburst and took a second to react. Raymond thundered away, "Please instruct the prosecutor to stick to the facts, Your Honor." He turned and glared at Cora and said, "Or maybe you do know if she was eating and what she was eating when she signed the document, and if you do know then please tell us, but don't just fabricate facts."

"Order, order, Mr. Lassiter," the judge said. "That's enough. This is an opening statement and great latitude is allowed. You'll get your chance in a moment, Mr. Lassiter. Objection is overruled."

Raymond angrily fell into his chair, still glaring at Cora as if she'd committed a major sin. She had not. She had simply massaged the facts a bit, something that happened all the time and was routinely allowed. Raymond's loud interruption was nothing but drama, an attempt to intimidate Cora and also set the tone for the trial. He would not be pushed around.

Cora was flustered for a moment and lost her place. She shuffled some papers, checked her notes, and lifted another document, holding each by a corner as if they were sticky and odorous. "And this is a power of attorney signed by Ms. Barnett as she was signing her advance directive. Taken together, both documents gave the defendant the power to terminate her medical care with, of course, the advice of her doctors. On Wednesday, December 30, while on a ventilator and showing no brain activity, the defendant, along with the doctors, decided to pull the plug. She died ninety minutes later."

Simon glanced at his watch, though there was no need. A large clock hung on the wall high above the bench. Cora had been going strong for almost an hour, and the jury was still captivated. Simon felt ill and struggled to maintain a look of concerned confidence.

Cora Cook was good and quite effective. She didn't yell or preach or overplay the facts. She stuck to them, probably because they were in her favor. She walked the jury through the actions taken by the defendant immediately after Ms. Barnett died. Within two hours he called the funeral home and arranged to have her picked up from the hospital and whisked away to be . . . cremated!

Burning a corpse, even when done intentionally by a mortician, was such a dramatic visual and Cora banged the drum too long. Simon scribbled, "Enough already!"

What was the killer's motive? Greed, money, absolute control of the estate, huge fees. The will the defendant typed himself and signed by Ms. Barnett gave him complete control of her assets. Her home, her stocks, everything she owned would be sold and the proceeds put in a trust and there was only one trustee—the defendant. He controlled the checkbook. He could play Santa Claus and give it all away. And while doing so he could pay himself rather generously to the tune of $500 an hour. Such a rate might seem low on Wall Street where billionaires and giant corporations sue each other, but for a general practice lawyer doing simple estate work in small-town America, the rate was excessive.

Again, she went on a bit too long as she found the greed angle irresistible. But she seemed to realize it, and moved quickly to the punch line, to the joke, to the hoax. It seemed as if the defendant's scheme to collect huge fees was all for naught. At one point in her life Eleanor Barnett was a very wealthy woman, but the money vanished in bad investments. There was no fortune. Perhaps she was living in the past, still dreaming, but we'll never know.

Cora finally began to wind down. Judge Shyam had not set a time limit and perhaps that was a mistake. Cora read the situation right and rushed through her final comments. She promised the jurors that when all the proof was in, they would have no problem believing the defendant poisoned his client. It would be their sworn duty to return a verdict of guilty.

Judge Shyam recessed for twenty minutes.

CHAPTER 44

Over coffee that morning, Raymond had told Casey and Simon that he was prepared to make one of three opening statements, depending on Cora's tactics. She had a lot of ground to cover and he suspected she might ramble a bit. All in all, though, he gave her high marks for her presentation. The jury stayed with her as she told a compelling story and piled plenty of suspicion upon Simon.

Raymond's approach would be that the defense had nothing to prove and would need only to poke holes in the prosecution's case. Once the jurors had settled into their chairs after the recess, he walked to the podium, with no notes, and offered a charming smile.

"Ladies and gentlemen, allow me to remind you that nothing you just heard from Ms. Cook has been proven, none of it is evidence, all of it just her speculation, her hopes and dreams maybe, of what the Commonwealth might try to prove against Simon Latch. She tells a nice story. She's an experienced prosecutor. The problem is that she has promised too much. She can't deliver all that she promised, nearly two hours' worth, because she doesn't have the proof."

He stepped away from the podium and stuck both hands deep into his pants pockets. "There are so many important facts that she conveniently left out. For example, she said that Ms. Barnett was in the hospital being treated for injuries received in a car wreck. What she failed to include was that Ms. Barnett was driving too fast late at night, ran a red light, and T-boned another car, seriously injuring its occupants. At the time of the crash, she was driving and she was, well, let's just say she was intoxicated. Point zero-nine, over the limit. It seems that she had been out partying with the girls, they had some type of 'poker' club they called it, and it was their annual Christmas party. She got hammered, got behind the wheel, and as her friend Doris rode shotgun they took off down the streets of Braxton at ten-thirty at night. She damned near killed Doris."

He managed to make killing Doris sound almost humorous. Simon was impressed with his oratorical skills. For years he had heard stories about Raymond's courtroom antics and abilities, but he had never seen him in action. With a packed house, an attentive jury, and everything on the line, Raymond was in the center of the ring and completely at home.

"Greed!" he snarled loudly. Then he managed a belly laugh that startled everyone. "Greed. For the simple will, Simon Latch charged Eleanor Barnett the greedy sum of two hundred and fifty dollars. And she never paid him! And for the retainer that she insisted on, he got really greedy and charged her one thousand dollars. And she never paid that bill either! For almost nine months of legal work, and not counting the long lunches she insisted on, nor the coffees, nor the late-night phone calls, nor the hospital visits, not counting anything but the hours spent at his desk tending to her legal matters, over sixty hours of billable time, the defendant, Simon Latch, received a total sum of . . . zero! Nothing, not a dime. Why are we talking about greed?"

Raymond wandered away from the podium, shaking his head at such foolishness.

"Something else Ms. Cook neglected. Mr. Simon Latch, a well-respected member of the bar with no ethics complaints or malpractice suits filed against him throughout his entire career in Braxton, was immediately suspicious of Ms. Barnett's assertions of being rich. How often does a client walk into a law office to meet an attorney for the first time and claim to have twenty million or so in assets? In Braxton, Virginia? It never happens, I can assure you of that. Simon Latch was no fool. He saw the signs of modest affluence—the absence of debt, a nice pension inherited from her husband, a lovely home free and clear—but those things were not unusual. He immediately suspected she wasn't being truthful. He repeatedly asked her for proof, as in periodic brokerage statements or bank records. When she resisted, he became even more suspicious."

And here the fiction began. Only Simon could tell the jury what went on between himself and Eleanor. Only he could reinvent what his thoughts were at the beginning. There was an element of truth in what Raymond was telling the jury, but the fiction was taking over.

"He wasn't driven by greed. The poor woman had no one else. No husband, no children, no siblings, no close relatives. She needed a friend, a counselor, a lawyer to help her through the legal maze. She was eighty-five, single and lonely, and she claimed to have a lot of assets. Perhaps she really believed the money was still there. Perhaps, ladies and gentlemen, Ms. Eleanor Barnett was already a bit off her rocker, as we sometimes say."

Simon had never really believed Netty was unbalanced or losing her mental acuity, but something was wrong. A screw was loose somewhere. To build an elaborate charade and pursue it with such detail was still difficult to comprehend.

"Ms. Cook makes hay from this cremation issue. Again, her facts are wrong. Years ago Simon and his wife signed new wills and advance directives providing for their own cremations and interments in a mausoleum. Nothing new. They were convinced it was a cheaper, more sustainable way to go. Cremation is rapidly gaining popularity across the country, with a thirty percent increase every year for the past ten. Simon recommended cremation to many of his clients. Eleanor Barnett was one. He wasn't trying to destroy evidence by having her cremated. Nonsense."

Raymond spat out "nonsense" as if only a fool could believe such stupidity.

"And the bit about pulling the plug. Oh, that's rich, that's juicy. But, alas, it's not true either. Again, Ms. Cook leaves out some very important facts. You'll hear from Dr. Connor Wilkes, the hospital's CEO, and she will tell you that Simon wanted no part of the decision to take Ms. Barnett off the ventilator. He flat-out told her and the doctors that it was a medical decision to be made by them, and not him."

Suddenly, he was sad and frustrated. He spoke softly, as if confiding in the jurors. "The truth is, we don't know who poisoned Eleanor Barnett. And the Commonwealth of Virginia is going to waste this entire week trying to pin a murder on an innocent man, while the killer laughs at us. The killer could be in this courtroom at this very moment." Raymond allowed those words to settle upon the crowd, then he, a bit too dramatically, paused and gazed at the audience, as if searching for the murderer. As if he knew the person was watching and listening.

He returned to the jurors and said, "At the rate we're going, her murder will never be solved. The police picked the wrong suspect, arrested him, then stopped their investigation. The prosecutor ran to the grand jury, got an indictment, and never considered other suspects. Now we're here, in this courtroom, watching and listening as the Commonwealth of Virginia tries in vain to pin the murder on Simon Latch. He didn't do it, ladies and gentlemen. No one saw him buy the poison. There are no records of him doing so. No one saw him tamper with the ginger cookies, because he didn't. No one saw him feed them to Ms. Barnett, because he didn't. There is simply no proof."

Simon scribbled, "Brilliant, but a good time to quit."

Raymond knew it too. With a look of total frustration, he wrapped it up with "When all the witnesses are finished, and the proof is in, and you deliberate and realize that Simon Latch is not guilty, then you will march back into this courtroom, take your seats, declare his innocence, and go home having done your civic duty, and the real killer will still be out there. Laughing. No doubt, laughing."

———————◆◆———————

Detective Roger Barr was sworn in as the first witness for the prosecution. It was 1:15 Monday, and he was in for a long afternoon. Cora Cook walked him through his training and experience and so on, though he was not testifying as an expert in any field. His task was to present the framework of the case. Others would fill in the gaps and nail down the proof.

His involvement began on December 30 of the prior year, when a dispatcher at the city desk informed him that an anonymous phone call had been received and recorded. A distorted voice said, "Eleanor Barnett just passed away at Blue Ridge Memorial. The doctors say it's pneumonia. But her death is suspicious. It should be investigated."

Ms. Cook walked to the exhibit table where a recorder had been prepared. She got the nod from Judge Shyam and pressed a key. The message boomed from the courtroom's PA system. Ms. Cook waited a few seconds, and played it again.

Detective Barr went through an exhaustive description of the efforts by the state crime lab to identify and track the caller, but it was not possible. The technicians could not agree on the gender of the informant. He or she had used a cheap throwaway phone with a temporary number. The voice was disguised. At any rate, Detective Barr was given the green light to investigate by the chief, and he went straight to the hospital. Referring to his detailed notes, he walked the jury step by step, minute by minute, through his initial actions. The interviews with the doctors and staff, the collection of items from Eleanor's hospital room, the visit to the funeral home to stop the cremation, and so on.

Simon pretended to listen with great interest, but he had read all of Barr's reports. He had read everything in the police files, every exhibit the Commonwealth would throw at him. He had

read and re-read and memorized every detail known to the lawyers, experts, and investigators. So he made notes, the same ones
he had scribbled onto paper a hundred times in the past four
months. Who was the leaker, the informant, the person close
enough to Eleanor to know when she died? His top suspect was
Jerry Korsak, who had been to the hospital at least once and probably more than that. He clearly had an interest in the estate and
had even hired an expensive lawyer to get involved. Jerry was
slippery and evil enough to poison his dear stepmother. He was
broke and crooked enough to go for her money. He was also thick
between the ears and not smart enough to pull it off. The one
great question Simon always confronted when suspecting Jerry
was: How did he know about the cremation? The leaker stopped
it cold. If two more hours had passed, what was left of dear Eleanor would have gone up in smoke.

His next suspect was Tillie, primarily because she handled the
ginger cookies. Simon bought them and put them on her desk
to take to the hospital. Tillie knew about the plans to cremate
because she typed the advance directive. She knew the time of
Eleanor's death. But Simon could not force himself to believe that
a gentle soul like Matilda Clark would commit such a horrible
crime.

Wally Thackerman's name was always on Simon's list, for obvious reasons. Two days before Eleanor died, he checked in at the
hospital's front desk, as all visitors were supposed to do. He visited
Eleanor for half an hour and signed out. Simon was not aware of
his visit until much later when he saw the hospital logs. In Simon's
world, Wally remained a suspect, though not a serious one. If he
was planning to poison her, why would he bother signing in and
out and leaving clear proof that he had been there?

He forgot about his sleuthing when Raymond began bark-
ing. The Commonwealth was attempting to introduce into evidence the last will and testament Simon had drafted for Eleanor.
Raymond objected, but only because he had to. There was no
way to keep the will from the jury. Two weeks earlier, in an all-
day motion hearing, the two sides had fought vigorously over

which documents would be admitted into evidence. The defense took the position that the will was the private work-product of an attorney, and thus privileged and protected. The will had not been probated and was not a matter of public record. The Commonwealth argued that the privilege expired when Eleanor died, so Simon had no right to conceal the will. It was a crucial issue and both sides submitted lengthy briefs. Simon wrote his own, all thirty pages of it. Judge Shyam promptly ruled in favor of the prosecution. The will, advance directive, and power of attorney could be admitted. Raymond was not surprised with the ruling.

Detective Barr explained to the jury how he came to possess the documents, but was not prepared to discuss them. He was not a lawyer.

At 3:30, everyone needed a break, and Judge Shyam recessed until 4 P.M. The courtroom emptied quickly as folks raced for the toilets. Simon remained at the defense table and watched the crowd. He was surprised to see Teddy Hammer, evidently there to keep an eye on things. With the value of Eleanor's estate now greatly diminished, Simon had assumed Teddy would move on to hunt bigger game. Maybe not. Maybe he was still sniffing around, plotting to grab a hundred grand or so in fees from whatever was left. Oh well. The chaos of Eleanor's estate would be handled by someone else. Simon was much more concerned with his own problems.

A ballsy reporter thrust herself toward him and was about to pop a question when a bailiff practically clotheslined her. "No press, no press!" he growled as he shooed her away.

Simon chatted with Casey Noland. "I assume the horde is still out there in full force."

"Oh yes. Dozens of them."

"Have they convicted me yet?"

"That happened months ago."

"Thanks for nothing."

Detective Barr returned to the witness stand and proceeded to answer questions about Eleanor Barnett's driving record and her accident. Copies of her tickets and court transcripts were admitted. Such evidence was not needed nor was it relevant, but Raymond had mentioned it during his opening remarks and Judge Shyam saw no harm in allowing it. Raymond had no plans to criticize Ms. Barnett, may she rest in peace.

When Cora Cook was finally finished with Detective Barr, she tendered the witness for cross-examination. Raymond carried a legal pad to the podium and tossed it down. "Detective Barr, where does one purchase thallium?"

"I don't know."

"You don't know?"

"I don't know."

"Have you tried to purchase it, as a law enforcement officer?"

"No. Why should I?"

"Oh, I don't know. Maybe to better understand the murder weapon. Maybe to better inform the jury. Maybe to gain knowledge that might be useful later on. I can think of several reasons."

"Sorry. Never tried it."

"But you believe that Mr. Latch purchased it, right?"

"I don't know how he got it. Why don't you ask him?"

"I'm in charge of the questions right now, Detective. Certainly you've talked to other homicide detectives, and perhaps toxicologists, perhaps other experts in the field, to gain some understanding of where the poison comes from. Right?"

"Is that a question?"

"It is. Answer it," Judge Shyam snapped, obviously ticked off at Barr's cockiness.

"Well, I spoke with the toxicologist at the crime lab right after the autopsy. We had a general discussion about thallium, but nothing specific."

"Okay. Now, back in January, you asked Mr. Latch if he would voluntarily surrender his laptops and desktop computers, is that right?"

"Yes."

"And did he?"

"Not at first. He was rather reluctant."

"Has it been your experience that most people are reluctant to hand over their computers to a homicide detective?"

"I guess you could say so."

"And did he eventually give you his computers?"

"Yes, after I got a warrant. You were there, Mr. Lassiter. The entire meeting is on video."

"Okay, now why did you want his computers?"

"We were looking for evidence, for any entry or any reference to poisons, specifically to thallium."

"Who examined Mr. Latch's computers?"

"Charles Pettigrew, a tech analyst with the state crime lab."

"Did Mr. Pettigrew find what he was looking for?"

"No."

"Did Mr. Pettigrew find any evidence that Mr. Latch or someone else had erased or scrubbed or in any way deleted files or references from either computer?"

"No, there was none of that."

"So your search of Mr. Latch's computers turned up nothing relative to poisons?"

"That's correct."

"Did you also have a look at Mr. Latch's phone records, both his cell and his office landline?"

"Yes, we got a search warrant and collected those records."

"Searching for what?"

"The same. Any reference to poisons, poisoning deaths, thallium, the like."

"And what did you find?"

"Nothing of interest."

"Not a hint of anything remotely related to poisons in general and thallium specifically?"

"That's correct."

"How long have you been a police officer in Braxton?"

"Eleven years."

"And how long have you been a homicide detective?"

"The past six years."

"How many homicides have you investigated?"

"About half a dozen. We don't have many homicides in Braxton."

"Did any of these homicides involve thallium?"

"No."

"Did you seek assistance from the Virginia State Police?"

"Yes, we normally consult with them in homicide cases, but they were not officially involved in this one."

"Did they have any idea where one might procure thallium?"

"Well, uh, I don't recall the state police having knowledge of other poisoning cases such as this one."

"They knew of no one who might deal in lethal poisons?"

"If they did, they didn't mention it to me."

With a heavy sigh and a frustrated look, Raymond said, "Your Honor, that's all I have at this time. I'd like to reserve the right to recall this witness in the morning."

"As you wish. We are adjourned until nine A.M. tomorrow."

CHAPTER 45

The more "important" witnesses testified Tuesday morning. They were all doctors with busy schedules that prevented them from having to hang around the hallway outside the courtroom and waste time, like the other witnesses. They were given firm dates on which to testify, with approximate hours.

At 9 A.M. sharp, just after Judge Shyam welcomed everyone back and quizzed the jurors about their general health and happiness, Dr. Samuel Lilly was sworn in and took the stand. Cora Cook led him through the preliminaries and established that he was well educated, suitably experienced, and had been the chief of staff at Blue Ridge Memorial Hospital for the past four years. He had also been the attending physician for Eleanor Barnett and described the injuries that brought her to the hospital.

In non-medical terms, she was banged up with cuts and bruises and two broken ribs, but her condition was not life-threatening. However, because of her age, a lengthy convalescence was expected. Referring to his notes, he told the jury that after four days she began to show signs of something else, which he and the nurses thought was pneumonia. Fever, fatigue, nausea, even more aches and pains. But she was stable and there was no sense of urgency.

Dr. Lilly met the defendant the day after Eleanor was admitted and spoke with him almost every day until she died. Dr. Lilly was present when the defendant presented a power of attorney and advance directive to the patient as she sat propped up in her bed. Others were present, including Dr. Connor Wilkes. Dr. Lilly viewed the situation as unusual, but the defendant did a thorough job of explaining the necessity of the documents and, more important, making sure Eleanor understood what she was doing. At no time did Dr. Lilly feel as though Eleanor was being unduly pressured or taken advantage of. However, given the situation, it was obvious she was being advised by her attorney, the defendant.

Earlier, in a private conversation in the hallway, the defendant had admitted to Dr. Lilly that he felt uncomfortable having control over the patient's medical directives, but there was simply no one else to do so. No family, no friends.

As her condition deteriorated, the defendant was close by and appeared deeply concerned with what was happening. The patient was placed on a ventilator, as she could not breathe on her own. During her last twenty-four hours, Dr. Lilly, Dr. Wilkes, and two other doctors, along with the defendant, met to discuss their options. Mr. Latch was adamant that he would not make the decision to terminate care. He said it was a medical decision. Once they were unable to detect activity in the brain, Dr. Lilly decided to remove the ventilator. The defendant agreed, but once again said it was a medical decision. The patient died ninety minutes later. Dr. Lilly and his staff were of the unanimous opinion that she had died of acute viral pneumonia. At no time did they suspect the patient had been poisoned.

During a lengthy and methodical cross-examination, Raymond slowly walked the doctor through the last two days of Eleanor's treatment, and repeatedly drove home the point that Simon Latch had been reluctant to take part in the conversations about her care. He was obviously troubled by what was happening and felt out of place.

When Dr. Lilly was excused and walked out of the courtroom,

Simon and Raymond knew his testimony could not have been better.

———————◆◆———————

The next expert was Dr. Dendra Brock, the longtime medical examiner for the Commonwealth. She was a highly respected pathologist with thousands of autopsies under her belt. She had taught, lectured here and there, and published dozens of articles, even a book. An impressive résumé. As Cora began the stock questions to establish her preeminence in the field, Raymond stood with a smile and said, "Your Honor, if I may interrupt. The defense is perfectly willing to stipulate that Dr. Brock is more than qualified as an expert in her field. Indeed, we feel honored to have her in Virginia and are grateful for her long record of outstanding public service."

Ms. Cook nodded and smiled at Raymond. Judge Shyam smiled at both and said, "Very well, Dr. Brock is hereby qualified as an expert in the field of forensic pathology. You may proceed."

In a Q&A that was obviously well rehearsed, Ms. Cook and Dr. Brock went back and forth to establish the groundwork for the autopsy of Eleanor Barnett. Her body arrived from Braxton on December 31 and was kept in the freezer until Monday, January 4, the day Dr. Brock performed the autopsy. She had been advised by Detective Roger Barr that there was a possibility of poisoning, and she explained in layman's terms how important this was to her work. There were no external signs of a crime, though the body was badly bruised. At first glance, she knew the bruises were several days old and not related to whatever caused her death. She read Dr. Lilly's notes and knew the deceased had been in an automobile accident.

It was standard procedure to video and photograph each autopsy. Eleanor's lasted for two hours and ten minutes. Simon and Raymond had watched it in his office, with Simon barely keeping it together. He swore he would never watch another one.

Raymond stood again and said, "May it please the court, we are stipulating that Eleanor Barnett died not from pneumonia but from acute toxic poisoning. We have never denied this, not denying it now. It is simply not necessary to drag this jury through the details of the autopsy. We know how she died. We know the cause of death."

Judge Shyam agreed and said, "How in-depth do you plan to go, Ms. Cook?"

"Well, Your Honor, we want the jury to get a clear picture of what caused her death."

"But the defense is stipulating that the cause of death was acute toxic poisoning."

"Just some background, Your Honor, if I may."

"We will proceed slowly."

Raymond sat down, but was on the edge of his seat, ready for more objections.

Dr. Brock had testified many times and was completely at ease. She knew her stuff and connected with the jurors by avoiding most of the medical jargon. Working with two assistants, she had begun the autopsy by draining the bladder and collecting urine samples. She drained the blood. The deceased had eaten very little but she was able to retrieve about 11 grams of ingested food. One sample was large enough to be dissected, and it was composed of bleached flour, white sugar, processed ginger root, and molasses. As Cora was preparing to flash on the screen a photo of the remains of the cookie, Raymond stood and, quite exasperated, said, "Your Honor, really? Do we need to subject the jurors to viewing this?"

"No. Sustained. We get the picture, Ms. Cook, please move along."

The urine and blood contained moderate levels of an unusual substance, later identified as thallium. Dr. Brock compared specimens of urine and blood taken from the corpse with those taken upon admission to the hospital, to prove the thallium was ingested while the deceased was a patient. On the screen opposite the jurors, Ms. Cook projected a color photograph of the liver on a lab plate, all two pounds, thirteen ounces of it. The average weight of a human liver is 3.3 pounds, but it varies, Dr. Brock casually explained to the jury. It was generally pink in color, but around the left side there were darker blotches, clear signs, to her anyway, that the liver had been heavily damaged. Next to it, Ms. Cook projected an image of a healthy liver, no splotches. Much like an expert chatting with students, Dr. Brock explained that the liver is where the body metabolizes most drugs and toxicants; thus, they are concentrated there.

While watching the video of the autopsy two weeks earlier, Simon could almost feel a pain in his own liver, and vowed again to cut back on the bourbon.

Other bright color photos followed: microscopic images of liver tissues from both a once-healthy person and from the deceased; the right kidney, weighing in at 1.6 pounds and show-ing darkened areas that, at least in her opinion, proved irrevers-ible damage due to toxins; slides of kidney tissues; then on to the gallbladder with the spleen on deck.

After an hour of gawking at Eleanor's organs, the jurors had had enough. Raymond stood again, even more exasperated, and said, "Please, Your Honor, we're trying to stipulate to the obvious here. Ms. Barnett died of toxic poisoning. Someone poisoned her. The problem is that the Commonwealth has the wrong defendant."

If he sounded like a broken record, it was intentional. Say something over and over and eventually folks will start to believe it. Ms. Cook was tired of the self-serving nature of Raymond's objections and snapped, "Oh, we have the right defendant, Your Honor."

"Please, please," Judge Shyam said, both hands in the air. "How much longer with this witness?"

Ms. Cook lost her cool and said, "Oh, I don't know, Judge. I didn't realize we had a time limit."

"There is no time limit, Ms. Cook. It's just that you have proven what needs to be proven with this witness, and the defense has agreed. Can we please move along?"

"Certainly."

Dr. Brock went through the procedures of collecting biological fluids and tissue samples, labeling and storing them, then delivering them to her preferred lab in Bethesda. The day after the autopsy, a special courier drove the samples to the lab. At each step of the process, the chain of custody was certified.

Raymond said more than once, "Your Honor, we are not questioning the chain of custody. We're not questioning anything pertaining to the cause of death."

———◆◆———

Dr. Henry Roster was a forensic toxicologist who Dr. Brock used whenever he was available. The pair had worked several poisoning cases together, though, thankfully, such crimes were rare. Dr. Roster's résumé was just as thick as Dr. Brock's, and Raymond wanted no part of it. He politely stipulated that the witness was a "preeminent" toxicologist and was willing to believe anything he said.

Dr. Roster began by cautioning the jury that the post-mortem analysis of drugs and poisons was extremely complicated and involved a large number of analytical techniques in special toxicological labs. After a lengthy description of how difficult the task was, Raymond finally interrupted. "Your Honor, I hate to be a pest, but we are willing, once again, to stipulate that the analysis by this esteemed researcher proves without a doubt that Ms. Barnett died of acute toxic poisoning."

"Overruled. We'll see where it goes."

Dr. Roster was not as skilled at testifying as was Dr. Brock. He began by saying that the most commonly used drug screening tests involved techniques known as "immunoassays." Since perhaps three people in the courtroom had ever heard that word, Ms. Cook pressed a key and it appeared on the big screen. Seeing it in print did nothing to help explain it. Dr. Roster tried. Immunoassays are tests that use antibodies to detect reactions with suspicious substances. What's an antibody? A protein produced by the body to provide a defense against an antigen. What's an antigen? Any foreign substance that is injected into the body and stimulates the production of antibodies.

Simon glanced at the jurors. Of the twelve, four had college degrees, two had not finished high school. Three were retired, two were unemployed, one was laid off from a job driving a fork-lift. As a group they were reasonably well read and intelligent and had been attentive so far. Roster had already lost them.

He was explaining the four interpretations of a drug-screening test: a true positive, a false positive, a true negative, and a false negative. He went on and on, trying hard to be interesting while knowing full well that his was an impenetrable subject. One by one, the jurors began looking around, casting about for someone to rescue them. Raymond decided not to help. He had tried repeatedly to speed things along, only to be stymied by Her Honor.

Ms. Cook tried to liven things up with more color slides, and Dr. Roster managed to inch away from the boredom. He drowned, though, when he was forced to confront a "chromatographic detection." Sorry, but the term could not be avoided. Nor could it be suitably explained in under five minutes. It was an analytical procedure used to separate compounds and drugs.

To save them all, Judge Shyam interrupted with "Ms. Cook, it's ten minutes after twelve and the jury is ready for lunch. How much longer with this witness?" Her tone left no doubt that this witness had said enough.

"Oh, not much, Your Honor. Less than ten minutes."

"And Mr. Lassiter, how much time for your cross-examination?"

"My cross? Hell, Judge, I've been trying to agree with everything the expert said, what little of it I can understand."

It was a smart retort and not overly humorous, but in pressurized settings like packed courtrooms the slightest effort at levity or mockery was often rewarded with roaring laughter. The crowd guffawed and bellowed and seemed to savor the moment by blowing off steam. Judge Shyam saw the humor and grinned along, until it was time to call for order. She tapped her gavel and said, "Very well. We'll wrap up this witness and go to lunch."

———— •◆• ————

Raymond enjoyed bantering with highly educated and erudite experts in front of common-folk jurors who were not always that sophisticated. He began with "Now, Dr. Roster, I live in the town of Braxton, population thirty thousand, same as my client, Simon Latch. Let's say I had a problem with rats in my barn and I wanted to get rid of them. Where would I go to purchase some thallium?"

"It's not possible. Thallium is not sold in this country."

"And why not?"

"Well, its production was outlawed years ago. For a while it was used, legally, in rat and mouse poison, but then that was stopped, too."

"Why was it removed from rat poison?"

"Because too many domestic animals were eating it and dying."

"It's very dangerous, right?"

"Oh yes."

"And why is that?"

"Well, in layman's terms, it's tasteless, odorless, colorless, and lethal."

"In fact, Dr. Roster, it has a long and sordid history of being the preferred poison for murderers, correct?"

"That's the legend, sir. I'm not sure that's been proven scientifically. That's a bit out of my field."

"Fair enough. You work for one of the leading labs in the country, correct?"

"We like to think so, yes."

"And does your lab keep an inventory of various poisons, toxins, and so on?"

"Yes, it's crucial to our work."

"How many?"

"I don't know. Hundreds. We have a procurement staff that does nothing but find and inventory compounds, illicit drugs, toxins, poisons, all with approval of the Food and Drug Administration, I might add."

"So you keep a supply of thallium?"

"Yes."

"Where do you get it?"

Dr. Roster thought for a second then shrugged. "I wasn't prepared to answer that question, sir. If given an hour or so, I could contact the lab and get the answer to your question."

"Don't bother. Where does thallium originate?"

"It's a metal that's found just under the crust of the earth and is collected as a by-product to the mining of other metals, such as zinc and copper."

"Okay. Let's say I wanted to poison someone and decided to use thallium. Where would I find it?"

"I have no experience with that, sir."

"Well, if it's been the favorite choice for murderers for decades, both here and abroad, then somebody somewhere has to know where to find it, right?"

Dr. Roster shrugged again, as if playing along. "I suppose."

"So who would you contact to ask around, you know? How would you begin your search for a little box of thallium?"

"Sir, again, that is outside the scope of my knowledge and experience."

"That's kinda bizarre, Doctor, if you ask me. You, one of the premier forensic toxicologists in the nation, if not the world, do not have a clue where to go or who to call to purchase thallium. Is this what you're telling the jury?"

"I guess, Mr. Lassiter. I would not know who to call."

"Then how in the world would a small-town lawyer from Braxton, Virginia, an honest man who's never heard of thallium, know how to get his hands on the perfect poison?"

"I suppose you'll have to ask him."

"You're confused, sir. He's not on the witness stand. You are. Can you answer my question?"

"I cannot."

"I didn't think so. You say you've worked as a forensic toxicologist for twenty-seven years. How many times have you testified in a murder case involving thallium?"

"Twice. This is the third one."

"Where was the first one?"

Cora Cook stood and said, "Your Honor, objection. Relevancy. Are we really going to revisit these old cases that have absolutely nothing to do with this one?"

Before Judge Shyam could speak, Raymond thundered in with "Hang on, Judge. This is a cross-examination! I'm allowed to explore all manner of irrelevant material. The Commonwealth has certainly been doing so."

Judge Shyam patiently said, "Okay, overruled for now. But there are limits, Mr. Lassiter."

Raymond glared at Roster as if he'd caught him lying. "Where was the first one, sir?"

"Ohio, 1998."

"That was the McGregor case, right?" Raymond asked as he looked at the jurors, as if to say, "Aren't I clever?"

"I believe so." Roster suddenly realized Raymond knew as much about the old case as he did, so he added, "Yes, McGregor."

"And he was found not guilty, right?"

"That's correct."

"And where did Mr. McGregor get the poison, the thallium?"

"Well, it was alleged that he stole it from a lab in Cincinnati, but I don't believe that was ever proven."

Raymond turned for his seat and said loudly, "Not guilty. Not guilty on all counts."

CHAPTER 46

A friendly bailiff led Simon to a side exit and he was out of the building before Raymond greeted the reporters on the front steps with his usual banter and no-comments. They had learned by then that he was not about to say anything remotely relevant to the case, but they followed him anyway, in a pack down the sidewalk, taking photos and videos that would look exactly the same as the ones they had taken on Monday. He answered all their banal questions without saying anything. Simon, meanwhile, wearing a green John Deere cap, jumped into the front passenger seat of a black Chevy Impala, obviously government-issued, and sped away with Landy behind the wheel. When the courthouse was out of sight and no one chasing, he sat up and asked, "So how do you think it went?"

"Pretty boring morning, actually. Raymond is smart to agree with the doctors. His steady refrain of 'Yep, she was poisoned but not by my guy' resonates. The prosecutor is not that exciting."

"Few of them are."

"You weren't turned on by her leopard-spotted slingbacks?"

"No. They look ridiculous."

Landy rolled her eyes. "The boys on the jury sure like them."

"Where are we going?"

"There's a seafood joint near the beach. Dark and quiet."

"You do much work around here?"

"A couple of cases a year. Right now we're talking to witnesses in a bid-rigging case. Extremely monotonous. The life of an FBI agent is not always gunfights and car chases."

"Are you here tonight?"

"Is that an invitation?"

"Standing," he said.

"I'll see if I can work you in. Delano doesn't like your jury."

"Tell me about Delano."

"My partner on this job. He watched the first two hours this morning and he knows his stuff. Spent four years in the federal defender's office and did a lot of trial work. Says your jury is not on your side. The first impression was damaging—greedy lawyer sees the opportunity to take advantage of a vulnerable client with no family."

"Do you agree?"

"I saw only the first half this morning, and Delano and I can't hang around this afternoon. Work beckons. But we're in and out tomorrow. Just trying to help, Simon."

"Thanks, but you didn't answer my question. Do you think the jury is against me?"

"They're hard to read, as always. And all the proof's not in. I'd say it's half and half."

Simon took a deep breath and let it sink in. After a moment, he said, "I didn't take advantage of my client. I've earned nothing from all of this. In fact, I've lost everything."

"I know. I'm on your side. But your client is dead and you bought the cookies."

⎯⎯⎯⎯⎯◆◆◆⎯⎯⎯⎯⎯

The Commonwealth called Dr. Connor Wilkes as its next witness, and she took the stand at 2 P.M. Tuesday. Cora Cook quickly established that she had been the CEO of the hospital for three years, and she had met with the defendant on several occasions before Ms. Barnett passed away. Dr. Wilkes described the scene when Mr. Latch appeared in her office with a new power of attorney and advance directive and asked her to review them. He left and she read them. Then she sent copies to the hospital's attorney for his review. He thought the documents were fine but stressed that she, Dr. Wilkes, along with the doctors, had to ensure that the patient was not being pressured to sign anything. Dr. Wilkes met with the doctors and nurses, several of whom were suspicious and did not want to witness the signings. However, it was obvious that there were no other family members present.

They walked as a group to Ms. Barnett's room and met Mr. Latch there. He passed out copies of the documents and answered all questions. Slowly and thoughtfully, he explained each sentence to his client. Though medicated, Ms. Barnett was alert and seemed to enjoy the attention. At least twice, Mr. Latch offered to postpone the signings until some date in the future. However, since she was eighty-five years old and in the hospital, they felt like proceeding. The patient signed everything and Mr. Latch left copies for the hospital.

Yes, it was certainly unusual to sign such documents at the hospital, and Dr. Wilkes could think of only one similar occurrence. But, under the circumstances, she felt as though nothing was wrong. The patient needed the advance directive and power of attorney and knew what she was doing.

As her condition deteriorated rapidly, the defendant visited the hospital several times and met with the medical team. He was obviously concerned about her care and spoke often to the doctors and nurses. He refused to make the decision to remove Ms. Barnett from the ventilator. He said, more than once, that it was a medical decision. She was pronounced dead at 10:02 A.M., December 30.

About an hour later, Dr. Wilkes took a phone call from Detective Barr.

On cross-examination, Raymond drilled away at the heart of

her testimony: At no time did Simon Latch seem even remotely eager to get involved in the final decisions regarding his client's care. He didn't want to be there, but there was no one else.

With that point well made, Raymond caught her off guard by asking if she ever reviewed the visitor sign-in logs at the front desk. No, she did not. He handed her a thick printout and asked her to turn to December 22 of last year.

She found the entries for that date and said, "Okay, sir, I've got it."

Gazing dramatically at the jurors, Raymond asked, "Now, do you see an entry for a man named Jerry Korsak on that date?"

"Yes. He checked in at five thirty-five P.M. to visit Ms. Barnett and stayed about twenty minutes."

"Did you meet him?"

"No, I don't regularly meet visitors."

"Of course not. Do you know who he is?"

"I was informed later that he is the stepson of Ms. Barnett."

"Indeed he is. Now please turn to December 26, around four P.M. Do you seen an entry for a Mr. Wally Thackerman?"

She flipped and scanned and finally said, "Yes, looks like he checked in at four-eleven."

"To visit which patient?"

"Eleanor Barnett. Stayed about fifteen minutes and left."

"Thank you. Now, Dr. Wilkes, does the hospital keep a log of gifts, flowers, candy, cards, that sort of stuff, that is delivered to each patient's room?"

"No, I'm not aware of any hospital that can keep up with all that stuff."

———— •◆• ————

Raymond felt it was necessary to introduce the names of Jerry Korsak and Wally Thackerman to the proceedings. It might be helpful later to argue that Eleanor had other guests. Perhaps there could be other suspects.

The owner and director of Cupit & Moke Funeral Home was Douglas Gregg, a pleasant old gentleman who had been embalming Braxton's dead for decades. If he owned a suit that wasn't black he'd never been seen in it. He took the stand in his mortician's finest and looked petrified.

His testimony was that he had met the defendant for the first time on December 29, the day before Ms. Barnett died, when Mr. Latch stopped by to say hello and check on her burial policy. He showed Mr. Gregg her advance directive, with instructions that she was to be cremated at once and buried in the Eternal Springs Cemetery next to her late husband. The following day he called to say she had passed.

Cora Cook handed the witness a copy of his office phone records. On December 30, at 10:49 A.M., Mr. Gregg received a phone call from the defendant and was told that Ms. Barnett had just died and he should send the hearse to pick her up at the hospital as soon as she was released. In his business, this was quite routine. After the body was brought to Cupit & Moke, the detective showed up and put a stop to the plans for cremation.

About a month later, Ms. Barnett was finally put to rest, intact, next to her late husband.

Only forty-seven minutes from the official time of death to the call to the funeral home. The Commonwealth would repeat that timeline over and over for the rest of the trial to prove that the defendant was in a hurry to get the body cremated, thus destroying evidence of his poisoning.

On cross-examination, Raymond attempted to coax Mr. Gregg into saying that forty-seven minutes was not unusual, but he wouldn't budge. Several hours usually passed before he was called in by either the hospital or the family.

"He did seem to be in quite a hurry," Mr. Gregg said.

Juror number four on the front row was a hard-ass. Nigel Adcock, forty-eight, district sales rep for a steel company, married, three children, Catholic, probably the best dressed of the seven men. Simon didn't like him at first sight and wanted to cut him during jury selection, but Raymond needed his cuts elsewhere. Adcock had tried to get himself excused from jury duty by claiming he had too many deals in the works, traveled a lot, and was a busy man whose boss would not understand if he lost a week in court. Judge Shyam was not sympathetic and refused to excuse him.

By Tuesday afternoon, Simon had stolen enough glances at his jury to read them, or at least he thought so. And he knew Adcock had already made up his mind and was not going to help. Simon had passed notes to Raymond and Casey and they were watching too.

———————◆◆◆———————

The last witness of the day was a roll of the dice for the prosecution. By calling Matilda Clark to the stand, Ms. Cook hoped to prove that the defendant typed Eleanor's will himself and tried his best to hide it from his secretary. His behavior was highly suspicious. The only reasonable explanation was that he wanted to bury the will until it was time for probate.

Matilda looked great—tanned and toned with a smart new haircut and designer frames Simon had never seen before. But, from the moment she swore to tell the truth she appeared reluctant, as if testifying against her old boss was the last thing she wanted.

Ms. Cook led her through the preliminaries—twelve years with Simon, routine legal work with emphasis on bankruptcies, hundreds of wills, the usual work in a small-town law office. Her voice cracked and her eyes were moist, confirming that she hated being there helping the prosecutors.

She remembered Eleanor Barnett very well and recalled their initial phone conversations. A lovely lady with no family. Matilda pried some of the basic client info from her, and later verified that she had a nice pension and no debts. However, Ms. Barnett refused to discuss financial matters with the secretary.

The deceit began immediately, as soon as the client left the office. As a routine matter, Matilda would take the questionnaire, fill in the blanks, crank out a three-page will, and wait a week or so for the client to return and sign it with Mr. Latch. The fee had been $250 for years. With Ms. Barnett, though, Simon kept his notes and said she might be trouble. They would have to wait a few weeks. And so on.

On March 27, Matilda took the day off because it was her birthday. Simon met with Ms. Barnett to sign the will and had it witnessed by two people who worked in the office next door. Matilda found out about the signing and asked Simon, point blank, if he had drafted a will for the client.

He lied and said he had not. Matilda wiped her eyes again, obviously upset by the betrayal of trust. No, in all her years with Simon she could not remember a single will he had ever typed himself. The forms were in her computer and she could spit one out in seconds, nice and customized.

In the weeks that followed, she quizzed him about Ms. Barnett on several occasions. Her file was still open and Matilda ran a tight ship with the files. Simon was always evasive. More betrayal, more tears.

Simon was under a lot of pressure. His marriage was breaking up and he was practically living at the office. He tried to keep this away from Matilda, but secretaries have a way of knowing everything. As a lawyer, he was barely staying afloat. He worked hard and put in the hours, but it was a tough grind in a small town. Through the spring and summer, at least seven other clients hired Simon to prepare their simple wills, which were done in their routine manner. The fee was still $250.

When Eleanor was injured in the auto accident and hospitalized, Matilda visited her at least three times, twice taking her homemade brownies along with ginger cookies from Tan Lu's. Simon explained that he had taken her to lunch there and she loved the cookies. Matilda was certain that neither the brownies nor the cookies were tampered with in any way before she delivered them to the hospital room. Her visits were friendly, but short. Eleanor had never shown much interest in Matilda.

Cora handed the witness a document marked EXHIBIT #8 and asked if she had seen it before. It was the will prepared by Simon, signed by Eleanor Barnett, and witnessed by Tony and Mary Beth Larson on March 27 of the previous year. Matilda said yes, she had been shown a copy a few weeks earlier.

Cora asked, "In your twelve years as the defendant's secretary, did you ever prepare a will like this one?"

"Oh no. We never tried anything like this. It's pretty complicated, with all the trusts and such. Simon was not a tax and estate lawyer, never pretended to be. We just did simple wills."

"What was Mr. Latch's hourly rate for legal work?"

She sort of shrugged and chuckled and said, "I'm not sure we had one. He didn't really work by the hour. He charged flat fees for bankruptcies, real estate closings, small criminal matters in city court, our typical cases. Occasionally he tried to charge three hundred an hour, but the client usually balked at that and they negotiated down."

"This will provides for five hundred dollars an hour. Is that the going rate in a town like Braxton?"

"Oh, I don't know what the other firms charge. But Simon never got paid that much."

"Does it seem excessive to you?"

"I can't say."

"You handled the billing, right?"

"Yes, and the bookkeeping."

"How often did the defendant charge five hundred dollars an hour and get paid for it?"

She thought for a second, but the answer was obvious. "I don't recall a case like that."

CHAPTER 47

After four days of sobriety, Raymond needed a drink. The lawyers retired to one of Marshall Graff's favorite watering holes and ordered cocktails and oysters. They huddled in a corner with their backs to the world and began replaying the day's testimony.

Raymond thought Matilda's performance was a wash. It raised suspicions and portrayed Simon as a sneaky type up to something, but what exactly? Preparing a perfectly legitimate last will and testament for a client? Where was the crime in that? He was on trial for murder, not lying to his secretary. Nothing Matilda said on the stand proved he had poisoned Eleanor Barnett. Sure, he bought the damned cookies, but they were harmless when delivered to the hospital. And he was dreaming of getting paid a bigger hourly fee for his work, not exactly a crime either. If that was illegal, every lawyer in the country would be indicted. Casey usually disagreed with Raymond out of habit, and he thought her testimony was damaging because she seemed sincerely betrayed by her boss. Two of the female jurors appeared to be very sympathetic.

Simon was pleased that Tillie had not done more damage. She knew plenty of secrets, including the countless times he had stuffed cash fees in his pockets with nothing on the books. Of course, he almost always shared the unreported loot with her. But

it was tax evasion on a small scale. "Every lawyer does it," he liked
to say. Tillie could have portrayed the law office for what it really
was—a heavily mortgaged assembly line for cheap bankruptcies
and other mundane legal matters, a practice that was barely afloat.
She could have portrayed her ex-boss as a man who lived beyond
his means and really needed some bigger fees.

After an hour of rehash and two martinis, with a dozen oysters,
Simon left them and made his way back to his dark and lonely
hotel suite. Landy had texted and said she could not drop by for
something more pleasant. Maybe tomorrow night. She was probably working out with Delano, whoever he might be.

At 8 P.M., Simon called Paula and said hello to the family.
He had an image of her, Buck, Danny, and Janie sitting around
the kitchen table, after dinner, perhaps in the middle of homework, having their nightly chat into the speakerphone with their
indicted father. He went through the order of witnesses for that
day and gave his opinions on how they performed. The lawyers
were upbeat. The jurors were engaged. The judge was impartial and fair. The courtroom was still crowded with spectators.
The trial should be over by Friday. No, he would not predict the
outcome.

Simon managed to sound confident, or least to fake it, but it
was not easy. He could not control the terrible thoughts of his
children hearing their father had been convicted of murder. They
had done nothing to deserve such pain.

Neither had he.

———◆◆◆———

Instead of a romp with Landy, he went to bed alone around
10 P.M. The hour did not matter because he could not sleep
regardless. Landy didn't help when she called at 11:17 and said,
"We gotta talk."

"Okay, we're talking."

"Do you think someone might be listening?"

For at least six months Simon had lived with the assumption

that someone was always listening or watching online. "I don't know. Hell, you're the FBI."

"There's a Best Western on Brodnax Road, close to downtown. I'll meet you in the lobby at midnight."

"Must be important."

"You're not going to believe it."

"I'm on my way."

There was no one else in the lobby. Even the desk clerk had disappeared. Simon followed Landy up two floors to her room. She chained and locked the door. Her laptop was on the breakfast table, already open. She said, "We followed Matilda Clark after she left court."

"Didn't know you were working this case."

"I'm not. Just a favor." She pressed a key and said, "She went here and there, zigged and zagged, real suspicious-like, as if she didn't want to be followed. She finally stopped at a Hampton Inn, a half a mile from here."

The dark video showed Matilda in the lobby where she spoke to a man who could not be identified. They disappeared.

"Room 220. Occupied for the last three nights by one Jerry Korsak. You want to sit down."

Simon took a seat.

———•••———

After five more hours of no sleep, Simon showered and changed into the same suit and shirt he'd worn on Monday, drove to the Balfour Hotel, and walked into the lobby at dawn. He found Raymond and Casey in a business-center conference room working on a tall thermos of coffee. A platter of untouched pastries was nearby.

Raymond, red-eyed and haggard but not hungover, said, "Okay, we're listening."

Simon removed a legal pad from his briefcase and looked at the notes he had labored over for the past six hours. "The first time I met Eleanor was March tenth, last year, in my office. She mentioned her two stepsons, Clyde and Jerry Korsak, but insisted on leaving them nothing. I encouraged her to leave a hundred thousand in cash to each one to prevent trouble."

"Nice try," Raymond said, like a real smart-ass.

"Thanks. She signed the will, life went on. On June fifteenth, Clyde came to town and assaulted Wally Thackerman in his office. Another story. Still no sign of his brother Jerry. Weeks pass. About that time I noticed that Matilda was looking pretty good. She was losing weight, going to the gym every morning, eating all manner of greens, dressing nicer. This came and went over the years as she bounced from one bad boyfriend to the other. She's struggled to find Mr. Right."

"You ever touch her?" Raymond asked.

"None of your business but the answer is no."

"The skinnier she got the happier too, and I suspected she had found a new guy. There had been several serious ones and I had learned not to ask. My marriage was in the tank and I didn't want to talk about it. We kept our private lives to ourselves. But it became so obvious that I was tempted to say something, but I bit my tongue. Evidently, about this time, last summer or fall, she met Jerry Korsak."

Raymond said, "His brother's a thug. What's he like?"

"Much smoother. Nice-looking, well dressed, I'd guess about fifty years old. I met him only once. Last December, when Eleanor was in the hospital, he came to town and stopped by the office, said he'd been to see his 'mom,' as he called her. I had no idea he was also seeing Matilda."

"You don't know that he was."

"No, I don't. But it now looks suspicious. Earlier this year, after I got indicted, the law practice had dried up and I had to part ways with Matilda. At the time she said she was going to Sarasota or someplace down there to live with a friend."

"And you haven't spoken to her since?"

"Oh, yes, several times. We're old friends. She worked for me for twelve years."

Raymond was irritated by the diversion. "This is quite inter-esting but it doesn't change a damned thing. We're in the middle of a murder trial and now we learn this. We can't ask for a time-out to chase down your ex-secretary and ask her who she's sleep-ing with. This proves nothing."

Casey wanted to disagree but could think of nothing to argue. In the middle of a trial, it was far too late to discover new evidence that was potentially relevant. If Simon were to be convicted, he might be able to point the finger at someone else on appeal. If he were acquitted, it wouldn't matter, at least not to him.

Raymond munched on a croissant, crumbs scattering around the table. After a long silence in the tense room, he said, "Okay, boys, this is fascinating, but it leads to nowhere, at least not now in the middle of the trial. We have a full day of testimony ahead of us, and witnesses to confront. We'll deal with it later. Let's get our eyes back on the ball."

Casey looked at Simon and asked, "You think Matilda and Jerry are behind the poisoning?"

"As of now, they're the top suspects."

"Later boys," Raymond growled. "Eyes back on the ball."

———— ◆◆◆ ————

As was customary, the Commonwealth had issued subpoenas for more witnesses than it intended to call to the stand. One of them was Wally Thackerman.

The original copy of Eleanor's will that Wally prepared two months before Simon typed one of his own had mysteriously dis-appeared. It was generally thought that it would be with her other important papers, but was not found by Detective Roger Barr. When Wally got his subpoena, he was compelled to appear to testify and instructed to bring his office copy of the will with him. He did not do so.

Raymond and Casey disagreed over whether the Common-wealth would actually call Wally to the stand. When Cora Cook resumed her case Wednesday morning, she announced, "Your Honor, the Commonwealth calls Mr. Walter Thackerman to the stand."

Minutes passed as a bailiff found Wally in the hallway and dragged him in. He took the stand and swore to tell the truth. Weighing his words carefully, he told the story of his history with Eleanor Barnett. She was a widow with no children and needed a simple will. The same story she'd fed Simon two months later. He marveled at her imagination, her thoroughness, and her scheming.

Most of Wally's testimony was objectionable on the grounds of hearsay. He was repeating statements made by a dead person. However, neither side objected because both sides wanted the jury to hear the testimony. The Commonwealth was attempting to prove that because of Eleanor's apparent wealth both lawyers, Wally and especially Simon, were motivated by greed. Because of her assets, a more complicated will was necessary, one that would generate plenty of fees. The defense wanted Wally to portray Eleanor as a nutty old woman still dreaming of her lost fortune.

Cora asked, "And she signed the will you prepared for her on January seventh of last year, correct?"

"That's correct."

"And what happened to the original?"

"The client always keeps the original. I kept a copy."

"Her original has not been found. Do you have any idea where it might be?"

Wally cast a casual look at Simon and coolly said, "I do not."

"Where is your copy?"

"In my office. In Braxton."

"You were supposed to bring it to court today."

"I refuse to do so."

"On what grounds?"

"On the grounds that it is my work-product and therefore privileged. The will has not been probated and is not public record. I have been charged with no crime. Therefore, my work-product is not discoverable."

"Your Honor, I ask the court to order this witness to produce his copy of the will he prepared for Eleanor Barnett."

Judge Shyam had been briefed on the issue by her clerk and did not hesitate. "Your request is denied. The will has not been probated and may never see the light of day. Therefore, it is still considered attorney work-product and privileged. Please proceed."

Wally glanced again at Simon and gave a slight nod, as if to say, *I'll protect you. You protect me.*

The dirty little secret of Wally's gift of $485,000 to himself would remain buried.

Cora was frustrated but kept her cool. She asked Wally if he could describe in general terms how the money would be distributed by Eleanor's will. He launched into a windy summary of trusts and their beneficiaries, but continually scoffed at the notion that the money was actually there. He defended his language that gave himself $750 an hour. Yes, it was on the high end, but the work would be complicated. Furthermore, estate lawyers in Washington and New York were charging more than that. There was even a big firm right down the street in Virginia Beach in which the lawyers were billing a thousand bucks an hour. At times he almost made $750 an hour sound like minimum wage.

Simon was amused and let Wally know it. One day, hopefully, they might be able to have a laugh over a beer.

During a recess, Raymond, Casey, and Simon debated how to handle Wally on cross. Simon said, "Leave him alone. He did nothing to hurt us."

"What about his grab for half a million bucks?" Casey asked.

"Let it go. It doesn't help us."

CHAPTER 48

When Clement Gelly agreed to serve as the conservator of Eleanor Barnett's estate back in January, he was practically guaranteed by Judge Pointer that he would not get tangled up in any criminal proceedings. He certainly did not want to testify against Simon Latch, a lawyer he liked and respected. Now that he was entangled and even subpoenaed, he tried to avoid taking the stand by filing a motion with the court. Said motion was denied. He pleaded with Judge Pointer to remove him as conservator, but she refused. She apologized for the mess he was in, but had no choice because no other lawyer in Braxton would get near the case.

He swore to tell the truth and sat in the witness chair with the firm intention of saying as little as necessary. If at all possible, he would say nothing to harm Simon's defense.

Using real estate tax records, bank statements, and quarterly notices from Rumke-Brown, he quickly laid out the value of Ms. Barnett's estate. The house was unencumbered by debt and appraised last year for $292,000. A checking account at Security Bank in Braxton had a balance of $3,300. There were two certificates of deposit held by the East Federal bank in Atlanta, one for $21,000 and one for $13,000. A money market account at the same bank had a balance of $28,400. The estate owned

6,775 shares of common stock in the Coca-Cola corporation, market value the day before of $271,000. Add another $5,000 for furniture and assorted personal items, and the total value was slightly more than $630,000. No state or federal estate taxes were anticipated.

As Simon scribbled the numbers down and tallied them up, he had to admit that most of the wills he had prepared in his career involved estates with far fewer assets. It was an impressive estate for Braxton, Virginia, but a far, lonely, and pathetic cry from what he once dreamed of. He could not help but remember the first time he tallied up the value of her estate. It had been more than a year earlier, in his conference room, as Netty softly dabbed her eyes with a tissue and lied through those natural yellow teeth. What a smooth and convincing liar she had been. What a gullible and greedy fool he had been.

Relying on brokerage statements provided by Buddy Brown, Clement gave a succinct summary of Harry Korsak's investment history and the accumulation of wealth. Because he could not verify the story, he skipped the best part, the volcano that blew Montrouge out of the Caribbean and off the map, and said that Harry had lost most of his money through bad investments. It was a colorful subplot but thoroughly irrelevant.

Clement showed the jury the mysterious notebook Ms. Barnett kept partially hidden in a check binder, but refused to speculate on why she did so. The jury would have to speculate too. Apparently, the old gal lost her marbles not long after she lost her money, and still pretended she was loaded. In great detail, she had lied to two lawyers and kept her fiction straight.

Simon thought of the hours lost with her, primarily eating in ethnic restaurants and discussing strange food. And all on his beleaguered credit card.

She never offered to pay for the first meal.

The estate was liquid and would provide a nice windfall for someone, probably Jerry and Clyde Korsak. There was enough money to keep a bigshot like Teddy Hammer sticking around. He was back in the courtroom for the third day, second row from the rear, left side, a regular vulture. Praying for a conviction to keep Simon on the sideline for years to come.

The Commonwealth wanted to use Clement to further its theory that Simon became convinced his client was wealthy; thus, the motive to use her estate as a vehicle to collect some fat fees. In Simon's opinion, that motive had already been established.

The next witness piled on. Dirk Wheeler had been subpoenaed by the prosecutor and reluctantly took the stand. Cora established that he was a lawyer in D.C. and had gone to law school with the defendant. They were old friends who kept in touch.

"Mr. Wheeler, on March the tenth of last year, you received a call on your office phone from the defendant, correct?"

"Simon Latch called me, yes."

"According to your phone records, the call lasted for almost fifteen minutes."

"Is that a question?"

"Let's say it is."

"You have my phone records, Ms. Cook, and Simon's as well. You know exactly how long the call lasted."

"What did you talk about?"

"The weather, college basketball, life in general, a law school friend who has some medical issues."

"What prompted the call?"

"Simon placed the call. You'll have to ask him."

"What did he want?"

"Well, among other things, he said he had a client with a substantial net worth and wanted some off-the-cuff tax advice."

"And you're a tax lawyer, correct?"

"Yes, estate and tax."

"What kind of off-the-cuff tax advice?"

"Rates, primarily."

"Can you explain this to the jury?"

"Yes, I can."

After an awkward pause during which Cora glared at the witness and the witness never blinked, she said, "Then please do so."

"We never got into the current rate structure for estate taxes because there were no estate taxes for last year. It was a loophole Congress overlooked. I explained this to Simon."

"He didn't know it?"

"If he had known it, he wouldn't have called and asked me."

"Wasn't this rather basic knowledge at the time?"

Dirk snickered as if she was an idiot and said, "Absolutely not. Very few lawyers were aware of the loophole last year. It's a tax issue, and most lawyers stay away from tax work. It's all I do."

"How often does the defendant call you for advice?"

"I don't log my personal phone calls, Ms. Cook. Simon and I talk all the time. Last year I had a bankruptcy question so I called him. Back and forth. That's what lawyers do. There was nothing at all unusual about the call you're referring to."

Dirk was believable and Cora was on her heels, six-inch ones. Actually, lawyers, or at least the ones Simon knew, rarely relied on one another for legal advice. To do so would be to admit ignorance. But Dirk was scoring points for the defense and the Commonwealth was losing interest.

On cross-examination, Raymond asked, "Mr. Wheeler, what's the going hourly rate for estate tax lawyers these days in Washington, D.C.?"

"Oh, they vary, same as most legal fees. The big firms with the big clients are charging fifteen hundred an hour. Smaller tax firms are trying to catch up."

"May I ask how much you charge per hour?"

"Sure. It's no secret. We post all of our fees for any new client. Right now my rate is nine hundred an hour."

"That sounds like a lot of money?"

"It is indeed, but we deal with wealthy clients with many assets, often in different countries. They owe a lot in taxes and prefer to avoid them as much as possible. These are complicated situations that require a high level of skill."

"Do you think five hundred an hour is a fair rate for the legal work involved in Ms. Barnett's estate?"

"More than fair."

Simon glanced at the jury box and made eye contact with

Number Eleven, Mindy Rutledge, a thirty-four-year-old mother of three whose husband had just been kicked out of the Navy. The disgusted look she gave Simon meant only one thing: *How dare you expect me to believe that anybody is worth five hundred dollars an hour?*

———•◦•———

During lunch, they hustled back to the offices of Marshall Graff and met in the "war room," as they called it. They were standing and eating cold sandwiches when Landy arrived and shut the door behind her. "This meeting never happened, okay?"

They agreed and gathered around her laptop on the table. She pressed a key and the video began. Landy narrated, "At eight-oh-four this morning, Matilda Clark left the Hampton Inn. That's her in front, behind is Jerry Korsak. They stopped, said goodbye, quick peck on the cheek, and they got in separate cars."

She froze the video for a close-up of Tillie. Simon, Raymond, and Casey leaned in closer.

"Ms. Clark drove three hours to Fredericksburg, Virginia, where she parked in a lot next to an apartment building in a large complex. Unit 614 has been rented by Jerry Korsak since February of this year. About an hour after she entered the building, a repairman knocked on the door, she answered, and he apologized, said he had the wrong place. He works for us and verified her identity. Meanwhile, Jerry returned to the courtroom and found a seat on the back row. He's wearing glasses and may be trying to disguise himself."

Simon said, "I saw him. He's been here every day."

Casey: "I guess he's an interested party."

Simon said, "His lawyer, Teddy Hammer, is back there too. They smell blood."

"And money."

Landy closed her laptop and said, "Okay, boys, I could get fired for this, so mum's the word. The agency takes a very dim view of moonlighting."

"Not a word," Raymond said.

"Thanks a lot, Landy."

"Don't mention it. Good luck."

She nodded and left, no handshake, no peck on the cheek of her old boyfriend. Strictly business.

Raymond crunched on some chips and said, "Fascinating, yes, but right now it's a diversion, one that we have to ignore."

Simon was bewildered by the images of Tillie and Jerry together. He said, "I don't understand. Shouldn't we tell the judge about this?"

Both defense lawyers shook their heads. Raymond said, "No, you can't simply call time-out and say, 'Hey Judge, we might have some more clues here.'"

Casey said, "It's suspicious as hell, all right, but we have no proof of anything even remotely relevant."

Simon sat down loudly, raked his fingers through his hair, and said, "This jury is going to crush me, I can tell."

Raymond took another large bite of his smoked tuna on rye and said, with a mouthful, "I don't think so. The trial is going our way, Simon. I think the prosecution is out of witnesses. The last two helped us more than Cora. Her case is sputtering to a close."

"I don't know. Casey?"

"The Commonwealth has proven the facts that we stipulated to. It has done a decent job of making you look suspicious, but it has not placed you at the scene of the crime. And I agree with Raymond—they have nothing else. I'm pretty confident right now."

"So, will I testify?"

"Do you want to?" Raymond asked.

"What I want to do is save my neck, and I'll do anything, and say anything, that will help me walk out of here a free man. Do you know what it's like to think about going to prison for the rest of your life? Carry that around with you all day long, okay? Try to get a decent night's sleep with that nightmare screaming at you. It's terrifying. I'll do anything, say anything."

The final witness for the prosecution was Sami Lu, the eighteen-year-old daughter of Tan Lu, the restaurant owner. She had worked part-time in the family business since she could walk and would soon enroll at Virginia Tech with a full scholarship. Sami did not want to get involved in the trial and would not agree to testify; thus, she had been served with a subpoena. She took the stand holding some notes, copies of which had been provided to the defense.

Cora asked her if she remembered serving the defendant and his client, Ms. Eleanor Barnett. She replied that she did not know the name of the client, but yes, they had eaten in the restaurant on three occasions the previous year and she had waited on them. Using her notes, she gave the dates and said that each meal was paid with Mr. Latch's credit card.

Almost on cue, Raymond stood, appeared to be thoroughly exasperated, and said, "Your Honor, please. Why are we wasting so much time?"

"State your objection, Mr. Lassiter," Her Honor said sharply, as if irritated by him.

"Your Honor, we have tried and tried to stipulate that Simon Latch dined there several times, then later stopped on two occasions to buy two boxes of ginger cookies. He bought them for Ms. Barnett while she was in the hospital. But he didn't poison them."

"That's enough! Overruled. Please continue, Ms. Cook."

Sami produced the credit card receipts as the prosecutor projected them on the screen. Simon used the diversion to glance at the jury. Number two was Linda Garfield, age thirty-seven, a real estate appraiser for a bank, an attractive woman with large, sad, brown eyes. If it was possible to flirt with a cute woman sitting on your jury, then Simon had been flirting. There was no way Linda would convict him.

Cora picked up two exhibits, the carryout containers for Tan

Lu's orders to go, and Sami identified them as being identical to the ones she had sold to Mr. Latch.

At first, Raymond thought about waving off the witness and forgoing any cross-examination, but decided to poke some fun at the prosecution's case. He ambled over to the podium and asked, "Now, young lady, who bakes these Saigon ginger cookies in your restaurant?"

Sami offered a lovely smile, her first of the day, and said, "Oh, everyone. Me, my parents, my sister, my aunt. The entire family works in the restaurant."

"So you can bake these cookies all by yourself?"

"Yes."

"And for how long have you been doing this?"

"I don't know. Many years."

"What are the ingredients?"

"White flour, cane sugar, brown sugar, butter, baking powder, eggs, ground ginger, molasses, a little salt, some ground cinnamon. I think that's all."

"Sounds delicious. Do you need to use a recipe when you bake these cookies?"

"No. I've done it many times."

"And they're baked fresh every day?"

"Yes."

"Approximately how many are baked each day?"

"About ten dozen."

"Did you bake the cookies purchased by Mr. Simon Latch?"

"Oh, there's no way to know. We sell a lot of them and, as I said, the entire family works in the kitchen."

"Has anyone ever complained about getting sick from eating your cookies?"

"Not to my knowledge."

"Are you familiar with a poison called thallium?"

"No."

"Have you or anyone in your family ever added thallium to your cookies?"

"No."

"So, as far as you know, when Mr. Latch bought the cookies, both to carry out and to eat in the restaurant, they were free of thallium and all other poisons?"

"As far as I know, yes."

"Well, has Mr. Latch complained of being poisoned by your cookies?"

"I don't think so. Not to my knowledge."

"Thank you."

Judge Shyam said, "You may step down."

It came as no surprise when Cora stood and said, "Your Honor, the Commonwealth of Virginia rests."

Her Honor thought for a second as she reviewed some notes. She directed the bailiff to dismiss the jury, then adjourned until 9 A.M. Thursday morning. With the early adjournment, Simon, Raymond, and Casey disappeared into an empty courtroom down the hall. Raymond was of the opinion that the Commonwealth had mismanaged its case and allowed it to end without a punch. It simply ran out of gas. The last witnesses were ineffective and Cora Cook appeared to be stalling, trying to burn some clock.

Casey was more pessimistic. Because he was not on his feet interrogating witnesses, he spent more time watching the jurors, and he was worried about most of them.

Simon was still praying for a miracle but expecting the worst. From a third-floor window, he watched the news vans close up shop and leave the courthouse. When all was clear, he said, "I'm going for a drive. Call me if you need me."

Raymond said, "What about tomorrow? Do you want to testify?"

"I don't know. I'll sleep on it. Let's meet for coffee at seven and we'll decide."

CHAPTER 49

For a moment, he thought he was being followed by a blue Impala, but it soon disappeared into traffic south of Norfolk. He zigzagged at random to be safe, and finally relaxed on a county road near Suffolk. For three hours he drove at a leisurely pace through the peanut farms and tobacco fields of southern Virginia. It was a perfect spring day and life would have been something quite pleasant, but for the horror of tomorrow when his future would be handed to twelve ordinary people, a jury of his peers.

He replayed every witness and every word of testimony he could remember. At times the past three days were a blur. A moment later, he could recall the attire of every witness and hear their voices. The Commonwealth's case was heavy on suspicion and motive, but severely lacking on direct proof. Sure, he bought the damned cookies, and gave them to Tillie who took them to Eleanor, who ate them and died. But the crucial part about the poisoning had been botched by the prosecutor and her team. They simply had no proof, primarily because there was no proof. Simon had nothing to do with her death, and the fact that he was even suspected of it still made him burn. The possibility of being convicted of it was overwhelming.

Paula had moved the kids into a three-bedroom apartment in a new complex on the eastern edge of Danville. A crowd of young singles lounged around the pool, sipping beer and listening to music. On a playground nearby, toddlers swung and seesawed as their mothers chatted.

Not a bad place and very far from Braxton.

Buck answered the door and gave his dad a hug, one he meant, and he was soon joined by Danny and Janie. Simon was determined not to get emotional and tried to keep things light. Paula was at the stove cooking pasta. For a few hours, they felt like a family again, eating slowly and talking about life—school, the new town, new friends, and old ones from Braxton. Janie asked if they were ever going back there, even referred to it as "home."

With one week left in the school term, homework was not a priority. After the dinner table was cleared, they sat for a long time and talked about the trial. Simon went through each witness and gave honest assessments. He explained that his defense would begin first thing in the morning and would not take long. He didn't have to prove anything. He was presumed to be innocent, and was in fact innocent. The burden was on the prosecution, and his lawyers thought the Commonwealth had not done an effective job.

The kids believed every word he said. Paula had repeatedly assured them that their father would never commit such a crime.

Simon asked about the media coverage and said he had ignored most of it. Buck said there was still plenty of it in the Washington and Richmond press, but nothing much in Danville. After all, it was a small town. Danny said the online stuff was terrible so stay away. Simon had no plans to take a look.

The conversation drifted to the end of school and summer plans. The year before, the family had gone camping and canoeing in the Smoky Mountains, and, in spite of the friction between the mother and the father, they had enjoyed themselves. Simon hoped they could do it again, though sharing a tent with Paula was not going to happen.

His heart ached for his children. They had done nothing to

deserve the unfairness of being forced to flee their home and listen to the crap about their father. And if he was convicted, they would be scarred for life.

They talked and talked and couldn't get enough of their time together. They were starved for his attention. At 10:45, Paula finally said, "Fifteen more minutes, then lights out."

When they were finally in bed, he said, "We need to talk."

"Okay. There's no booze."

"I don't need it."

"Do I?"

"You're okay. How about coffee?"

"Decaf?"

"Even better."

When they were sure the kids were asleep, Simon said, "I think Tillie may have been involved in Eleanor's death."

Her mouth dropped open but she didn't speak.

"It's a long story."

"I'm listening."

———◆◆►———

He slept on the sofa, the same one he and Paula had purchased on sale in Braxton years earlier when the kids were small and life was much less complicated. But sleep was only a goal. At 3 A.M., he finally got up and quietly left the apartment. Driving away, he wondered when he would see his kids again. It could be as soon as the weekend, assuming his trial ended well. Or, it could be weeks, months, or years.

In the early days of his practice, he had a court-appointed criminal client who pled guilty and went to prison. Simon liked the guy and they kept in touch with mail and an occasional phone call. The client left behind a wife and kids, and he would not allow them to visit him in prison. He missed them greatly, but didn't want them to see him in prison clothes. Six years passed before he was paroled and went home.

Six years? Simon was facing a lifetime behind bars.

Pushing the speed limit, he made it to his hotel by dawn, showered and changed, and met his lawyers at 7 A.M. for breakfast. As soon as the waitress walked away, Raymond said, "We are of the opinion that you should not testify."

"I'm listening."

"I've tried a thousand cases, Simon, and I can remember only a handful in which the defendant helped himself by taking the stand. When they do so, they become fair game for a brutal cross-examination, one the prosecutor has been planning from day one. There will be traps, trick questions, insinuations, arguments, retorts, irrelevant comments. Of course, I'll be there to object and raise hell, but in the end we'll probably wish you had stayed in your seat."

Simon looked at Casey and asked, "And you?"

"You're a lawyer, Simon, and half the jury will suspect you're not being truthful just because you're a lawyer. You're fighting for your life and you'll say anything to stay out of prison. But you've never been cross-examined like this before. Some of your actions look suspicious on the surface. By the time they're hashed and rehashed on cross-examination, they'll look even more damning. I agree with Raymond on this one. Let's play it safe and keep attacking the Commonwealth's case."

Simon looked at Raymond and asked, "If the jury voted right now, what's the score?"

Raymond took a sip of coffee and closed his eyes. "Eight to four to acquit."

Casey asked, "Who are the four to convict?"

With no hesitation, Raymond replied, "Two, four, seven, and eleven."

Casey said, "I'll take those four and add eight and nine."

For a second Simon felt like he was at a poker table with two professionals. He flashed back to those halcyon times at Chub's when he played video poker for hours while drinking bourbon and ginger ale and watching three games on the big screens.

But it was his life they were betting on.

Casey said, "I've never liked this jury. I'd say a six-six split."

"So no acquittal?" Simon asked.

"No acquittal, no conviction. A hung jury with a retrial later this year and a better jury."

CHAPTER 50

The person who acquired the thallium and added it to the ginger cookies did so either in private or in Eleanor's room when the hospital was quiet. Matilda was the only possible suspect who could have doctored the cookies either at the law office or at her apartment. But she was gone and no longer involved in the trial. There was not a speck of proof against her, only speculation. There was no procedural gimmick that would allow the defense to haul her back to court for more questions. And if there had been, why bother? She would simply take the stand again and deny every hint of culpability.

Simon still found it difficult to believe Tillie was involved, but was wavering. Her little romance with Jerry Korsak added plenty of suspicion.

What intrigued him were the comings and goings at the hospital. There was virtually no security or surveillance. Most of the doors to the patients' rooms were partially open all the time and never locked.

At his suggestion, the first witness for the defense was Loretta Goodwin, the charge nurse who supervised the east wing of the third floor of the hospital. Raymond had plenty of time and much ground to cover. He liked to roam his side of the courtroom, asking questions and listening as he gave various looks to the jurors.

Loretta had been a registered nurse at the hospital for eight years and a floor supervisor for the past three. One of her duties was to coordinate care for her patients, including Eleanor Barnett. She met with Simon Latch on several occasions and was impressed with his willingness to help his client. She got the impression he did not want to be in the middle of Eleanor's problems, but there was no one else. Loretta was in the room when Eleanor signed the advance directive and power of attorney, and, while it was an unusual event, she believed Simon was acting in the best interest of his client.

Raymond belabored this to the point of overdoing it. Simon scribbled, "Okay, move on," and Raymond must have read his mind.

Raymond talked about the security at the hospital, the visitation procedures, the flow of traffic between the floors and down the halls. As in many hospitals, there was a constant stream of health care workers in and out of the rooms.

How many? To prove that dozens of people had unlimited access to Eleanor's room, Raymond went to the big screen. He began with a large color photo of Dr. Connor Wilkes, the CEO, a witness the jury had already met. Then Dr. Samuel Lilly, the attending physician. Then Dr. Joe Huber, the chief resident. With each, Raymond asked the same questions, which were becoming monotonous. Loretta patiently explained that the doctors had unlimited access to Eleanor's room, as did the nurses, beginning with Loretta herself. She was amused to see her smiling face on such a large screen and quipped, "A bad hair day." The jury thought it was funny. Two registered nurses followed. They were followed by four licensed practical nurses and four certified nursing assistants. Raymond asked what role each nurse played in Eleanor's care, and Loretta patiently explained things to the jury. Blue Ridge Memorial had two NPs—nurse practitioners—who ranked above Loretta and periodically checked on Eleanor. Their faces went up on the screen.

By ten-thirty, it felt like the entire hospital staff had been introduced to the jury. Finally, Ms. Cook had had enough and said,

"Your Honor, this is all quite fascinating but I'm losing any sense of relevance here."

Judge Shyam said, "So am I. Mr. Lassiter?"

Raymond anticipated the interruption and pounced. "Your Honor, we have the right to prove that as many as thirty hospital employees had unfettered access to Ms. Barnett's room twenty-four hours a day with little or no surveillance, registration, or observation. We cannot prove, nor has the Commonwealth, who actually poisoned the deceased, but we can prove that her door was open at all times."

"That's enough, Mr. Lassiter. I didn't ask for a closing summation. Let's take a break and we'll continue in twenty minutes."

A cup of coffee did nothing to throttle the defense. With Loretta back on the stand, Raymond picked up where he had left off. With photos, they introduced three nurse's aides (uncertified), three orderlies who did a variety of jobs, two janitors assigned to the third floor, and five technicians who worked on every floor and could come and go as needed and for the most part went unmonitored.

Finally, Raymond pressed a button and the screen disappeared. He went to the podium and flipped through some notes as the courtroom relaxed. That ordeal was over. He addressed the witness: "Ms. Goodwin, we've just introduced to the jury almost thirty hospital employees. Does every one of them record every visit to every patient's room?"

She sighed as her shoulders sagged. "Well, not really. Every doctor or nurse who enters a patient's room is supposed to log the visit and give a brief description of the service or what happened."

"But this is not always done, is it?"

"No, it's virtually impossible. We just don't have enough time to record everything."

"What about the non-professional people—the orderlies,

technicians, janitors, repairmen? Do they keep detailed records of every visit?"

"No," she said softly.

He handed her a copy of the visitation logs and asked questions about who stopped by Eleanor's room. Mr. Latch had signed in twice, but usually skipped that requirement. Mr. Wally Thacker- man signed in once. Another lawyer had also signed in.

Loretta got another laugh when she said, "When there's a car wreck, we usually get a lot of interest from the lawyers."

She also admitted that the visitation process was not run with military precision. In fact, it was quite unstructured at times, even "porous."

She said, "Look, we're a community hospital and we encour- age visitation. We try our best to monitor things, but it's just not always possible. And, we've never had a serious problem."

By noon, Loretta was fading. Raymond and the defense had not only made the point but had driven it home with a sledge- hammer: There were dozens of people with plenty of opportuni- ties to poison Eleanor.

Cora Cook's cross-examination of Loretta lasted only ten min- utes, but was effective, at least in Simon's opinion. She reviewed the names of the doctors and nurses and asked Loretta if she was implying that one of them had used the poison. Of course not.

Loretta was excused, and as she was leaving the witness stand, Judge Shyam said, "We'll break for lunch and be in recess until one-thirty."

Raymond startled everyone when he announced, rather dra- matically and at full volume, "Your Honor, the defense rests."

CHAPTER 51

It took two hours, and all of lunch, to hammer out jury instructions and settle the lingering objections that Judge Shyam had taken under advisement. When the loose ends were wrapped up, the jurors were brought in once more and the courtroom grew quiet. Cora Cook approached the jury box. It was almost 3 P.M.

She once again thanked the jurors for their service, a needless gesture that meant nothing. By then they were weary of their service and tired of each other and no amount of false praise could impress them.

She switched gears immediately and got their attention. "According to FBI statistics, there are twenty thousand murders each year in this country. Almost forty percent are never solved. Those are troubling numbers, but let's set them aside. Of the murders that are solved, almost half, fifty percent, involve circumstantial evidence. No one saw the fateful deed. No one saw the murderer pull the trigger, or cut with the knife, or beat with the club. There were no eyewitnesses. And, since the murderer did not confess to the crime, the detectives studied the crime scene and found clues. Every murderer leaves behind evidence. Bullets and shells for ballistics tests. Blood, semen, saliva, sweat, skin, for DNA testing. Fingerprints, hair follicles, boot prints, for forensic analysis. And poison for toxicologists to examine and study."

Cora stayed behind the small podium and only occasionally glanced at her notes. She spoke directly to the jurors, looking them in the eye, an orator who was well prepared and knew her stuff.

"Eleanor Barnett was murdered in a very devious manner. She ingested a poison that has for decades been known as the poisoner's choice. Thallium has no taste, odor, or appearance. It's invisible. It can be ingested in small quantities over several days or weeks without yielding clues, often, as in this case, confounding the doctors, who so rarely confront it. Neither the doctors nor the nurses had any reason to suspect that this lovely and respectable lady, laid up in the hospital after an awful car wreck, would secretly be fed, in small doses, a poison added to one of her favorite treats, ginger cookies purchased by the defendant and delivered by his longtime and loyal secretary.

"Now, the defense evidently wants you to believe that someone other than the defendant acquired a poison that can be found only on the black market and only by someone with evil intent, and this other person sneaked into Ms. Barnett's hospital room and laced her cookies with thallium. How convenient. How original. Someone else did it. I'm sure you've never heard that one before.

"But why would someone else murder Eleanor Barnett? Ladies and gentlemen, it's a question of motive. And the motive was greed. Who could profit from her death? Oh, I suppose the funeral home could make a buck. But it's hard to imagine Mr. Douglas Gregg, the mortician you met here on the stand, sneaking into her hospital room and killing her so he could then cremate her. Are we supposed to believe that? Ludicrous. About as ludicrous as the other good and innocent people the defense has dragged into this courtroom to smear their names. The doctors, nurses, orderlies, assistants, even janitors, all those good folks just doing their jobs, trying to save her life, and now the defendant wants you to suspect them all. Pretty outrageous."

One glance at the jurors and Simon knew better than to glance again. If Raymond thought they had eight friends in the box, Simon would love to know where the first one was sitting.

"Who has the motive? Who wanted Eleanor dead?" Cora's voice was loud, incredulous, and echoed around the courtroom. She stepped away from her notes and hit her stride with a tirade of facts that could not be contested. The secrecy of the preparation and execution of the will. The obvious belief that there was big money on the table; otherwise, why would the defendant go to such great lengths to set up a trust designed to make donations to 120 charities? Why would the will leave $100,000 each to Clyde and Jerry Korsak if doing so would leave so little for the trust? Why would the defendant call his pal Dirk Wheeler, a bona fide tax and estate lawyer, and seek advice for a client with a substantial net worth? Why would the defendant insert himself as the attorney for the estate and also the attorney for the trust, with no other trustees to provide oversight? Why would the defendant award himself fees of $500 an hour, an obscene amount for a small-town lawyer with no experience in complicated estate matters? According to his own secretary, he had never been paid such exorbitant fees.

Cora stopped, looked at the jurors in complete amazement, and asked, "Who in the world is worth five hundred dollars an hour?"

Then she lowered the large white screen opposite the jurors and methodically went through the timeline, carefully listing the important dates and times: Eleanor's car wreck and hospitalization, the purchase of the first box of ginger cookies from Tan Lu's, the aggressive actions by the defendant to get his client to execute a power of attorney and living will, from her hospital bed; the purchase of the second box of cookies; the deterioration of her condition; the ventilator; her death; then, of course, the forty-seven-minute gap between her official passing and the defendant's phone call to the funeral home with the request to "come and get her."

Cora finished an hour after she began. Her final words to the jury were: "A clear-cut case of first-degree murder."

Simon tried to sit tall, take meaningless notes, and present a confident look for everyone.

———— •••• ————

Raymond wasted no time in attacking the prosecution. He said, "Well, ladies and gentlemen of the jury, once again the great Commonwealth of Virginia, with its endless resources of lawyers, investigators, experts, doctors, and money, has stumbled its way into a courtroom without bringing enough proof to overcome the presumption of innocence. The prosecution has no proof!" His voice boomed throughout the hushed courtroom.

"What the Commonwealth does have is plenty of speculation. Tons of it. Lots of suspicion too. Plenty of circumstantial suspicion. And, it has the dead body of a lovely lady who deserved better. A lady who trusted the defendant because she had no one else to trust. A lady who had once been wealthy and lost it all and was obviously mentally unbalanced in many ways. She still lived in a fantasy world in which she and her late husband were quite wealthy. She was delusional and still dreamed of the lost money. She was lost in the past.

"And how, exactly, was Simon Latch supposed to know it was all a hoax? Maybe he should have dug deeper. I don't know and it doesn't really matter right now. All that matters today is that someone poisoned Eleanor Barnett and it wasn't Simon Latch."

Raymond stopped pacing and wiped his brow with a handkerchief. "Greed? You want to talk about greed? Simon Latch never received a single penny in fees from this woman. Nothing. She didn't believe in paying her legal bills. She had plenty of cash, and he knew that, but he never pressed her for payment."

Simon kept his eyes on Raymond as he moved back and forth in front of the jury box, and in doing so he caught glimpses of the jurors' faces. Some watched Raymond and seemed to agree. Most, however, seemed dismissive.

He finished in half an hour and his timing was good. The jury had heard enough. Judge Shyam told them to go home and forget about the case until nine the following morning, Friday.

———————◆◆◆———————

Landy had been in the courtroom for most of the afternoon and was waiting behind the courthouse near the dumpsters. They made another getaway and drove for an hour west of town. She was of the opinion that the jury was split and would hang itself. Simon was too consumed with fear to say much. He certainly wasn't hungry.

They stopped at a restaurant in Williamsburg and had drinks on an outdoor terrace as the sun faded. She asked if sex might help and he said no. At the moment, nothing would help but an acquittal.

CHAPTER 52

What could be the most excruciating waits? Simon had never considered the question until then. Waiting to be executed was certainly at the top of the list. Waiting for a loved one, someone in their prime, to die, when death was imminent?

Waiting for news from a tragedy? Waiting for a killed-in-action list to be posted?

Waiting for your jury had to be in the top three.

Again, he slept only minutes at a time and he couldn't eat. He knew he looked gaunt, even haggard, and he knew the jury would see him, again, but he couldn't care about his appearance.

The jurors were sent to their labors at 9:15 by Her Honor, and the waiting started all over again. She ordered him to stay in the courthouse, so he went to an empty courtroom on the second floor and hid in the semidarkness. Then he tried to read a crime novel but the story involved a murder by poison, so he tossed it. The time was now 9:40. He removed his wristwatch. Sitting in a wooden chair, he dozed off and was soon drooling.

Judge Shyam reconvened at 11:20 and everyone hustled back to the courtroom. Simon's stomach was rolling and he was sweating. When he sat down, Raymond whispered, "No verdict. Just some question about a jury instruction."

"What does it mean?"

"Hell if I know."

The jurors filed in and everyone gawked at them, as if their bodies and facial language might tip off their deliberations. If there were signals, Simon didn't catch them, but then he was no trial lawyer. The foreman said they were making progress but were confused about the issue of motive. Was proving motive necessary to proving murder? Judge Shyam explained that no, it was not, but understood the confusion. She read again the jury instruction pertaining to motive, and in doing so only muddied the water. She said that she was not allowed to offer a more thorough explanation, and told the jurors to get back to work.

After they filed out, Simon asked Raymond what it meant. He wasn't sure.

The courtroom cleared and Raymond seemed content to sit at the defense table with his client and make small talk. Simon asked, "Is the mob still out there?"

"Afraid so. The vultures are back in full force."

"Should I say anything?"

"Let's wait. If it's a bad verdict, I'll do the talking and promise a speedy appeal and so on. If it's a good verdict, we might celebrate together for the cameras."

"I'd like that," Simon said, as he let himself dream for a second.

"If it's split, a hung jury, we should disappear quickly and say nothing. There will be a retrial and nothing we say to the press can really help us."

"Got it. And Raymond, thanks for everything. You've been great. I don't know how to thank you."

"It's been my pleasure. We gave it our best shot."

They left for lunch, ate as slow as possible, and tried to kill two hours.

———◆•◆———

The longest afternoon of Simon's life came to an end at ten minutes after five. The wait was over.

Remarkably for a Friday afternoon, the courtroom was crowded when the jurors returned to their seats for the last time. The foreman handed a sheet of paper to the clerk, who read it, then handed it up to Judge Shyam. She frowned as she looked at it, then said, "Would the defendant please rise." It was not a question.

With knees of rubber and a laboring heart, Simon Latch stood with an attorney on each side. The courtroom seemed to inhale and hold its collective breath.

Her Honor leaned a bit closer to her microphone so there would be no doubt. "To the charge of murder in the first degree, we find the defendant, Simon Latch, guilty."

CHAPTER 53

At the rap of the gavel, a bailiff opened the doors and the crowd rushed out, led by Jerry Korsak. When he was out of the building he speed-dialed Teddy Hammer, who was in his Washington office.

"They nailed him," Jerry said gleefully. "Guilty, first degree."

"You're lying," Hammer stuttered in disbelief.

"Swear. Took 'em all day."

"No way."

"All the way. You got it. Now what?"

"I don't know. Let me sit down." Hammer had watched most of the trial and left the day before convinced the Commonwealth had not presented enough proof to convict. In his opinion, the best they could hope for was a hung jury, with a retrial to follow. He said, "Let's talk tomorrow."

Jerry stuck his phone in his pocket and looked around. The sidewalk was busy with reporters either talking low or texting furiously. Cameras were waiting in an area cordoned off by bailiffs, though the defendant had not been seen all week.

The defendant sat for a long time at his table, oblivious to the noise and bustle of the crowd in a hurry to leave. The judge and jury were gone. The lawyers and clerks milled about, gathering papers and packing briefcases. Slowly, the crowd thinned on both sides of the bar.

Simon could not acknowledge the pats on the shoulder and the banal offerings of "so sorry" and "we'll get 'em on appeal." He was too stunned to respond and kept repeating to himself, "I didn't kill anyone, I swear. I know I didn't." Casey stayed by his side for quiet support as Raymond went through the forced ritual of chatting with the opposing lawyers. He also brushed off some pushy reporters.

My poor children, Simon thought, and tried mightily to keep them out of his mind.

Half an hour passed. He sat slumped in his chair, motionless, staring at something on the floor. Two Virginia Beach police officers loitered near the bench, as if waiting to pounce.

Raymond finally sat down beside him, leaned in, and said, "Look, Simon, time to go. They're taking you to the city jail where you'll spend the night. I'll be there. In the morning, some boys from Braxton will fetch you here for the drive home."

"I didn't kill anyone."

"I know you didn't. I've believed you from the beginning and am even more convinced now. But, juries sometimes do strange things and I guess this is one of them. I can't explain it."

"What's next? Prison?"

"No."

"For the rest of my life?"

"No."

"I can't do that, Raymond. I swear I can't do that."

"Not so fast. The next step is post-trial motions, then sentencing. Nobody gets in a hurry. I'll talk to the judge first thing Monday morning and ask her to allow you to remain out on bond until sentencing. That's rarely permitted, but it does happen. We'll get to the bottom of it, Simon, I swear we will."

"I can't go to prison."

Raymond looked at Casey as the two police officers walked

over. One removed a pair of handcuffs from his belt. Raymond said, "These two guys will take you to the city jail."

Simon looked at them in horror and said, "Handcuffs? And I gotta ride in the back seat?"

"Afraid so," Raymond said.

———— ◆◆◆ ————

Paula was tidying up her desk as if preparing for the weekend. The day, like the ones before it, had not been productive. It was difficult to concentrate on work with one eye on the news. While the jury was deliberating she couldn't leave her desk. A cold sandwich for lunch had gone untouched. Thankfully, her colleagues had not made the connection, but it was inevitable. They were gone for the day.

She almost shrieked at the headline on her laptop: "Virginia Lawyer Guilty in Poison Case." A live shot from *Action News* caught Simon as he was led from a side door of the courthouse to one of two fully marked Virginia Beach police cars. His wrists were cuffed at his waist and two cops held his elbows. Though his legs weren't chained, his captors still walked as slowly as possible, making the most of their brief glow in the cherished ritual of the "perp walk." Simon seemed dazed and deaf as he deflected the idiotic questions flung from the crowd of reporters. Another cop opened a rear door as Simon ducked low and was shoved inside. For some reason, the drivers of both cars needed to turn on all emergency lights and sirens as they inched away from the courthouse, as if the public should be warned that a convicted murderer was passing through on his way to jail.

Within seconds, Paula's phone buzzed. It was Danny, already in tears.

———— ◆◆◆ ————

Raymond was at the jail, threatening to sue anyone who moved. He explained, in rather coarse language that any cop could understand, that his client was not a suspect and was not under the jurisdiction of the Virginia Beach police. His stay was simply custodial, less than twenty-four hours, and there was no need to process, fingerprint, or photograph Mr. Latch. He was not going to wear faded orange coveralls that had been worn by a hundred others. He was not going to be placed in a cell with the general population. And, he should be allowed to keep his cell phone.

The jailer felt obliged to agree to all terms except the phone.

Simon was put in a single cell reserved for those in protective custody. Raymond said goodbye and left for Braxton. He was cranky, almost belligerent, and pissed-off at the world because of a shellacking in a high-profile case.

The bunk was actually more comfortable than the makeshift bed Simon had been wrestling with for the past fifteen months. He stretched out on it, closed his eyes, and tried to convince himself he was still dreaming. His moods swung sharply from despair and hopelessness to anger and retribution. He managed to block thoughts about his children.

At six, a friendly trustee appeared and slid through a tray of baked ham and boiled vegetables. "Can I get you anything?" he asked.

Simon looked around the empty cell. "There's nothing to read in here."

"Books or magazines?"

"Books."

"I'll see what I can find."

Because he was starving and had been hungry for most of the week, he played with his vegetables and managed a few bites. When the trustee returned to fetch the tray, he passed through a battered and dog-eared paperback. Simon looked at it and could not suppress a smile.

The Lonely Silver Rain, by John D. MacDonald. During his second year of law school, a good friend named Rick had loaned him a mystery titled *A Deadly Shade of Gold*. It featured a private investigator named Travis McGee, MacDonald's most famous hero. A literary project evolved as the two law students began reading, swapping, and collecting the Travis McGee series. Their goal was to collect all twenty-one books, paperbacks only, and to pay as little as possible for them. Both were on tight budgets and any excess cash usually went for beer and pizza, but they diligently searched bargain sites online, and used bookstores, garage sales, anywhere they might find a Travis McGee adventure. And the cheaper the better. During their last semester they bought the last one, for $2.25 at a flea market, and read it. When they graduated, they sold their little library to a second-year law student for $200, split the money, and had a steak dinner to celebrate old Travis.

The book was like a drug. Simon kicked off his shoes, stretched out again, and was soon lost in another world.

------◆◆◆------

As humbling as it was, jail was not the worst place for Simon to spend the weekend. Being behind bars, both in Virginia Beach and later Saturday back home in Braxton, kept him away from the news . . . and he was the news. With no access to television or internet, he was shielded from the barrage of sensational press. The main story—small-town lawyer stumbles upon wealthy widow client then poisons her to take control of her estate—was spun in a dozen different directions. The cremation scheme was a favorite—rushing her to the funeral home just minutes after pulling the plug to destroy the evidence of thallium poisoning. The tax deadline was another favorite, killing her just before January 1 to save 40 percent in estate taxes. And Eleanor's hoax was almost funny, tricking two dim-witted local lawyers into believing she was worth millions.

Experts of every stripe appeared on cable, speculating freely. Doctors and toxicologists discussed the exceptional qualities of thallium, as if it was the perfect poison for a good murder. Estate lawyers with little knowledge of the case thought Latch was scheming to earn millions in fees. All manner of legal experts dissected the trial, and the general consensus was that Raymond screwed up by not putting his client on the stand. They were shouted down by more legal experts who believed you never allow the defendant to testify. Someone found an old friend of Harry Korsak's who delighted himself by telling the story of the erupting volcano in the Caribbean and the investors getting soaked with nothing but souvenir lava.

Jail was a refuge. Simon had access to his phone at certain times, but had been warned, by Raymond, Casey, Paula, Landy, and the Braxton city police officer who drove him home Saturday morning, not to watch the news. Landy stopped by for Sunday visitation and brought him three more Travis McGee novels, slick new paperbacks she bought at a Barnes & Noble. He was starting a new collection and planned to find all twenty-one, again. Reading them not only helped him escape, it also brought back fond memories of those law school days that now seemed so carefree.

At nine-thirty Monday morning, the jailer unlocked his cell door and said, "Follow me." No handcuffs were in sight. Apparently, Raymond had threatened to sue the city, the jail, and each employee personally if Mr. Latch was not treated with enough respect. Raymond was waiting in the small attorney visitation room and seemed as cranky and aggressive as he had been on Friday and Saturday. Casey was with him and had brought a thermos of good coffee from home. He poured Simon a cup.

Raymond said, "I spoke to Judge Shyam about an hour ago. Not surprisingly, she doesn't like this verdict."

"Welcome to the club," Simon said.

"She was remarkably candid and said she was stunned by it."

"So, what can she do?"

"Well, she can do a lot but she's not willing to grant our motion to set the verdict aside for lack of sufficient proof. That takes a lot of balls and is almost never done. It would be very heavy-handed for her or any other judge. In fact, I'm not sure if I can recall a case in Virginia where the trial judge negated a guilty verdict and set the defendant free."

He looked at Casey, as if his associate was supposed to know everything. Casey said, "About ten years ago, in Rockingham County, a judge pulled a guilty verdict in a bank robbery. He was not reappointed."

"So, we can forget that. But she will allow you to go free until you're sentenced."

"When will that happen?"

"We'll find out in a few minutes."

"So, I'm walking out today?"

"This morning."

At ten, they huddled over Casey's cell phone for the conference call. Judge Shyam's clerk was recording it. Cora Cook was on the call from her office down the street.

Judge Shyam was all business. "Post-trial motions are due in thirty days, with thirty more days to respond to each other. I will rule on them at the end of sixty days. I have been informed by the defense that it will appeal the verdict to the supreme court. Of course, I don't control that schedule."

Cora Cook said, "Your Honor, the Commonwealth has no post-trial motions."

"As expected. Mr. Lassiter?"

"Several, Judge. We'll file them on time."

"I am scheduling the sentencing for Monday, August twenty-second."

Raymond said, "Your Honor, we request that the defendant be allowed to remain free on the same bond pending his sentencing."

"Ms. Cook?"

"The Commonwealth opposes this request, Your Honor."

"On what grounds?"

"Well, on the grounds that the defendant has been convicted of first-degree murder and is facing the probability of being sentenced to prison for life; on the grounds that the defendant has much more incentive to flee now than before; on the grounds that defendants are almost never allowed to remain free after being convicted. I could go on."

"Mr. Latch has been free on bond since January and has never failed to appear in court when expected. We have his passport, don't we?"

Her law clerk said, "Yes, it's in the vault."

"Thought so. I see no reason to order him to prison at this time. I'll do so in ninety days when he's sentenced. The Commonwealth's objection is overruled."

Casey whispered to Simon, "Pack your bags."

"What bags?"

———— •◆• ————

It was a beautiful spring day, everything in bloom, the town and countryside picturesque. Simon wanted a long walk to absorb the beauty and drink in the sweet smell of freedom. Walking around, though, was not a good idea. He could only imagine the excitement he would create if spotted by someone he knew, or a reporter, or, heaven forbid, one of the town's legendary gossips. Braxton was now toxic for Simon, a lost home, a place where his story would rage for years, a place where few, if any, friends would defend him, a grid of streets he could no longer walk. He wasn't sure where he would spend the next years, locked up or otherwise, but it would not be in Braxton. His family had fled to another town to start life over. His law office was deserted and his building sold. The state bar association would soon pull his license, as required by statute.

Ducking through alleys and side streets, he made it home without being seen. He entered his office through a rear door and walked around, inspecting things, as if he'd been gone for years instead of eleven days. His handshake deal with Chub allowed him to squat until July 1. After that, well, who knew? With the curtains closed he sat in the reception area and stared at Tillie's forlorn and dusty desk. The phone had been disconnected. The outdated word processor even looked like a fossil.

He still could not bring himself to believe that Matilda Clark had the guts to venture into the black market, buy a quantity of a poison she had no experience with, and lace the ginger cookies, all with the intention of killing another human being. Staring at the spot where she had dutifully worked on his behalf for twelve years, he told himself it couldn't be true.

How Jerry Korsak figured into the plot was another unknown. It certainly added an avalanche of intrigue.

One certainty remained constant: Simon Latch didn't do it; therefore, someone else did.

He had eighty-four days.

CHAPTER 54

Teddy Hammer moved quickly. The following morning, he filed a petition to open the estate of Eleanor Barnett, who, he alleged, died without a valid will. Hammer sought to have Jerry Korsak appointed administrator of the estate.

The petition was the first shot in a legal battle that would probably drag on for years, like most probate matters. Hammer believed, as did Clement Gelly, that the estate could be liquidated and yield at least half a million in cash. Teddy wanted his share.

At the same time, he filed, on behalf of the Korsak boys, two impressive wrongful death lawsuits. The first, for ten million dollars, was against Simon Latch, who had just been adjudicated as the killer. The second, for twenty million, was against the hospital for negligent care, for allowing the patient to be poisoned. Teddy was kind enough to email copies of the lawsuits to Simon, who was not surprised and enjoyed reading them. At the moment, his net worth was about $5,000 at best, most of it tied up in used office furniture and a six-year-old leased Audi that had exceeded its permitted mileage. He had almost no prospects of future income. Sue all you want!

Cautiously, he opened his laptop and began reading dozens of emails, from friends, acquaintances, old clients, and current ones who were worried about their files. He fought the urge to check social media or scan the news. Why ruin another miserable day?

He busied himself with work that had to be done. He prepared a form letter to his clients and explained that he was no longer in business and they would need to find another lawyer. Since he was not about to unlock the front door, he promised to mail or ship their files to them. He sent emails to opposing lawyers, clerks, magistrates, and judges, and apologized for the inconvenience. He struggled through a short chat with Paula. The kids were a mess and she did not want him to visit anytime soon. He loved them more than anything, but he really didn't want to face them.

A hard knock on the front door startled him. He let it pass.

Long after dark, he ventured out on foot and stealthily made his way to Raymond's office. Casey was visiting his current girlfriend and trying to make up for lost time. Raymond's wife preferred that he work at all hours and stay out of the house. He was finishing a sandwich when Simon found him in the conference room, a layer of smoke from the first cigar already hanging above the long table. They poured themselves a bourbon.

After a long pull, Simon said, "If we've learned anything, it's that we cannot assume anything. I was assumed to be the killer, and convicted because of it. We know it's not true. Now, we're assuming Matilda Clark was involved, with Jerry Korsak, and it might be a mistake to make this assumption."

"I'll play along. You got a better suspect?"

"Plenty. Let's walk through this. I bought the cookies and Matilda delivered them to the hospital. The killer had access to Eleanor's room and saw the cookies. I can't believe that the killer had the nerve or the time to remove the twenty-four cookies from the two cartons and apply the thallium while in the room. It makes more sense for the killer to notice the two cartons, go to Tan Lu's and purchase identical ones, for cash of course, then take them home or wherever and add the thallium. Then, at the right time, probably after midnight when the place is practically deserted, return to the room, and swap the cartons."

Raymond frowned as he listened and struck a match. "Seems as if I remember a similar conversation a month ago."

"Yes, but a month ago neither you nor I thought it was possible that twelve jurors would vote to convict me. And we were wrong. Also, a month ago we didn't have the time or money to investigate other suspects. Now, Raymond, things are radically different. We have to find the killer."

"I thought you were convinced it was Matilda and Jerry Korsak."

"They are the prime suspects, but what if we're wrong? We investigate them, not sure how, but we'll figure out something. At the same time, we widen the net."

"How wide?"

"You showed the jury the faces of thirty doctors, nurses, and hospital employees who had access to Eleanor's room. I thought it was a brilliant move and proved its point."

"I guess the jury wasn't impressed."

"Guess not. I've combed the records again, every page, every word, and I've found three more names. Total of thirty-three. I think we can safely eliminate the three hospital administrators and two secretaries. Down to twenty-eight. A total of seven doctors either treated Eleanor or stopped by to take a look, pinging Medicare as they came and went. Let's cut the seven. Down to twenty-one. She was a patient for two weeks and at least eight nurses are on record as having had something to do with her care. For the sake of time, let's take the eight off the list. I've found a dozen cases over the past fifty years where hospital nurses got rid of their patients, for all sorts of crazy reasons, but let's not go there now. Down to thirteen. There were three janitors on duty at various times, though they were not required to file reports. They're listed on the floor summaries. I don't want to assume too much, but let's assume these guys were not sophisticated enough to procure some black-market thallium. Now we're down to ten. Technicians and orderlies. These folks know a lot about medicine and drugs, and, same as in every hospital, they had virtually complete access to Eleanor's room. Are you with me?"

Raymond blew a cloud of smoke with his eyes closed. "I think so. Keep going."

"So, let's start with our top ten. Unfortunately, we know very little about them because we can't access all of their employment records and history. We need to hack the hospital's files."

"Come on, Simon."

"You don't have to be involved. I'll do it. Hell, what's there to lose? Convicted of murder on Friday and sued for wrongful death today. A trifling hacking charge won't faze me."

"You're on your own, pal. My firm will do whatever we can to help investigate any possible suspect, but we're not risking anything. Are you asking for money?"

"No. I'm just thinking out loud, Raymond. The person who murdered Eleanor was in her hospital room. And it was someone who was supposed to be there, someone who was unnoticed, someone who didn't care about security cameras, of which there are very few, I might add."

"What about motive? It was argued that you had motive. Perhaps Matilda and Jerry had a motive. Why would a hospital employee want to poison an old woman who's banged up anyway?"

"There's no answer to that question. Nurses who kill their patients. Serial rapists who assault random women? Active gunmen killing schoolchildren? There are no motives. Some people are just plain sick."

"Damned right about that, Simon. Look, we'll do what we can. This loss stings, you know? You bear the brunt, but it's a kick in my balls too. It's a screwball verdict that should not have happened. I'm sorry, Simon."

"Please don't say that again, Raymond. I owe you a lot, remember. You did a marvelous job and we should've won."

"Right. We should've won."

————◆◆►————

After being closed for renovation, Chub's had reopened. If the sprucing up included new paint, carpet, furnishings, and a good

power-wash to remove layers of nicotine stains, it was not immediately evident. It all looked and smelled the same, which was not
unpleasant. The clientele was accustomed to a certain grunginess.
Simon had always suspected that Chub hurriedly closed his pub
and left town to fake off the FBI, or at least cool their aggressive-
ness. At the time, Chub had given Simon too much credit for
calling off the dogs.

Now, Simon was back and needed a favor. He stopped in late
Tuesday night and managed to avoid familiar faces. At the bar, Valerie gave him a big smile and said, "Well, well, already escaped?"

"Ha, ha. I don't report for a few months."

"Rumor was they hauled your ass out in chains, took you
straight to death row."

"And how reliable are rumors around here?"

"Extremely unreliable. Good to see you, Simon. I actually
cried when I heard the news."

"So did I. Bourbon and ginger ale."

"You got it."

"I don't see Chub. Is he around?"

"Upstairs. I'll get him." She slid the drink across the bar and
disappeared. Simon kept his eyes glued to a Dodgers game and
hoped no one would bother him. He was glad it was baseball
and not basketball; otherwise, he would be tempted to place a bet.

He had never been invited into Chub's office. One wall was
nothing but blackened one-way glass that allowed the boss to
watch the floor below. One wall was framed autographed jerseys
of famous football players. One wall was covered with enlarged
photos of Chub preening next to aging sports heroes, none of
whom Simon recognized, and a few shady types who were probably either politicians or gang bosses. One wall was adorned with
autographed baseballs, basketballs, footballs, pennants, Super
Bowl game programs, Kentucky Derby betting sheets, and so on.

They sat in comfortable chairs and sipped their drinks—
bourbon and ginger ale for Simon, bottled beer for the boss.
Chub said, "So sorry, man, I couldn't believe it. Your lawyer said
you're gonna appeal and all that."

"That's the plan, but it's a mountain to climb. I need some help, Chub."

"Well, if it's your office, stay as long as you want. I'm still working on plans to renovate, probably lease it as office space, maybe retail on street level. But I'm in no hurry."

"Thanks, I really appreciate it. Right now I have no place else to go."

"A bummer."

"But that's not why I'm here." As always with Chub, Simon was wondering if someone else might be listening. He doubted it, though. And what did he care at this point? "I need some help and it involves a good hacker."

Chub whistled as if stunned by the magnitude of the crime. As if bookmaking and running an illegal gambling business for the past thirty years were nothing compared to hacking. "Can't help you, Simon. Don't know nothing about hacking. Computers, man, that's a different world."

For at least the past ten years, Chub's video poker machines had been rewired by a homemade software program that allowed him to keep tallies on his most active clients. This was not common knowledge, but the gamblers knew it. Yet he always pretended to be overwhelmed by technology.

Simon said, "I'm not asking you to get involved. I need Spade's help. Spade knows the right people."

"Yes, and he came very close to getting busted two years ago. He's gun-shy. Can't blame him."

"Here's what I'm asking, Chub. I want you to talk to Spade so I don't have to. Spade talks to a hacker. The hacker never knows my name, but he gives me a blueprint on how to hack into the personnel records of the hospital. Spade breaks no laws, neither do you, neither does the hacker. If I get caught, what the hell? I'm a convicted murderer headed to prison with nothing to lose."

"You wanna hack a hospital?"

"Yeah. I figure it's an easy job."

"Beats me, man. Not my world."

"I know, but Spade lives there and he knows the right people."

Chub took a swig from his bottle and stared at the wall of foot-ball jerseys. "What if Spade wants a fee?"

"Then remind Spade that I got the FBI off his back last December. Tell Spade that I was sleeping with the special agent, a woman, who was in charge of the investigation. You might want to remember that too."

"Oh, I remember it well." Another swig. "You were banging a Fibbie?"

"An old friend from law school. And, please, this needs to be kept quiet."

"Who would I tell, other than Spade? All of my conversations are off the record, Latch. You know that."

Of course. Either off the record or recorded by law enforcement.

"I do. Lean on Spade, Chub. I need some help. I'm rather desperate."

"I'll see what I can do."

CHAPTER 55

He met Landy at an interstate hotel near Staunton, Virginia, two hours south of Braxton. She was in the area working a case and had a few hours she could waste without raising questions. While eager to help, she had become increasingly worried about moonlighting on Simon's case. Her supervisor was pushing for arrests in some white-collar investigations and she felt the pressure. In addition to her professional problems, her divorce was now final and, while relieved with the split, she was going through the usual letdown. Simon's conviction didn't help. She had even mentioned changing careers, but starting a new one as a forty-three-year-old rookie associate at a less than prestigious law firm was not that appealing. With an endless supply of young talent, few law firms were in the market for someone like Landy.

Simon bought coffees in the lobby and took them to her room. It was not yet 4 P.M., too early to think about drinks and dinner. Not that they were in the mood. Both of their lives were upside down.

She said, "I hope you're ignoring social media."

"I am. I'm avoiding it, along with the television, newspapers, and magazines. I assume the story has legs."

"To put it mildly. It's the rage. The tabloids are out of control.

The stories border on fiction. The posts are as idiotic as anything I've ever seen. It's outrageous."

"Spare me, Landy. Things are bad enough. Paula informed me today that the kids have been outed at school. The name Latch is not that common."

"I'm sorry. And I'm sorry I brought it up. Just thought you should know."

"Thanks. I know you're concerned."

Without stepping out of bounds and violating agency rules, she had gathered some information on Matilda Clark and her boyfriend. In February, Jerry Korsak had signed a six-month lease for a one-bedroom apartment in Fredericksburg. Matilda left Simon's employment in March, said she was going to Florida, but instead moved in with Jerry. She was now working as a secretary in a car rental agency near Reagan National Airport, about an hour from her apartment. The job appeared to be full-time.

If Jerry had a job, it was not evident. He was not registered with the Virginia Employment Commission, so there was no paycheck from which to withhold taxes. He was fifty-one years old and his work history was sketchy at best. Now that he was trying to get appointed as administrator of Eleanor's estate, he would be easier to monitor. Court appearances would be required; petitions had to be filed. Judge Pointer had not yet approved his request to be appointed, but at the moment he was the only person asking for the position.

If Matilda and Jerry were legitimate suspects in Eleanor's death, there were several rather formidable problems with investigating them. The most obvious was that Detective Roger Barr had all but closed his file. He had arrested the right suspect, got him indicted, helped get him convicted, and as far as Barr was concerned the case was over. The convicted murderer could not ask the cops to keep digging into an effort to get his conviction overturned. Another problem was the lack of evidence. There was none. If Matilda and Jerry did the deed, where were the witnesses? Not a single employee at the hospital had seen them there after hours. Where was the poison? Any not consumed by the victim had been flushed months ago. Where was the proof that they had procured it? Finding a dealer in the black market would be impossible.

And where, exactly, was the black market? As Landy suspected, not even the FBI was too concerned about the illegal trafficking of a poison that had virtually no demand. The agency, along with dozens of others, was far too busy trying to stop the flow of substances much more popular.

She said, "It's a dead end, Simon. The FBI has no jurisdiction and the local boys have done their job. They got their man."

Simon nodded in muted agreement. Possessing thallium was not a crime. Producing it was. And it probably came from the third world.

He pulled some papers out of his briefcase and put them on the table. "Next project. Here are the names of some hospital employees. Were you in the courtroom when Raymond flashed a bunch of faces on the screen?"

"Yes, last Thursday, wasn't it?"

"That's right. There were at least thirty-three doctors, nurses, and other employees with access to the room. I've eliminated all but these ten. Can you dig for dirt and give me their backgrounds? Without setting off alarms?"

She flipped through the pages. Each name had a color head-shot next to it and a short paragraph about the employee. Raymond had obtained the information during discovery.

Landy looked at the list and said, "Two pharmacists, two technicians, dietitian, two nurse's assistants, three orderlies. You really think the dietitian would poison a patient?"

"No. But neither would her lawyer."

"And the pharmacists don't make the rounds, do they?"

"I'm desperate here, Landy, okay? Indulge me."

"All right, all right."

"How much information do you have?"

"Tons. The agency's database is enormous. Property owner-ship, utility services, credit card activity, marital history, education, religion, lawsuits, credit reports, rap sheets, employment history, and on and on."

"On every American?"

"Virtually every adult. But almost all of the data comes from other sources, many of them public. The agency just sort of collects and indexes everything."

"And you have access to this data?"

She kicked it for a second, shrugged, and said, "Sure, within reason. I'll see what I can find."

They finally got around to drinks and dinner. Simon did not want to drive home and shuddered at the thought of another night in The Closet. So, they slept together in her hotel bed, with thoughts of intimacy somewhere far away.

———•♦•———

After one week as a convicted felon, Simon needed a change of scenery. He was tired of living in the shadows and behind locked doors, flinching every time some jerk banged on his office door. As far as he could tell, no progress had been made in his efforts to exonerate himself. For days he had been buried in piles of hospital records, searching for more names of employees who worked on the hospital's third floor when Eleanor was there. When he wasn't digging through that monotonous material, he worked on the first draft of his appellate brief to the Virginia Supreme Court. During his career, he had appealed two cases, both dull zoning matters, to the court. In both cases he'd been the lawyer, not the client. Now, sitting in the other seat was downright bizarre. Instead of cranking out stilted legalese based on old cases, he was writing to save his neck. He vowed to do a dozen drafts until every word was perfect, persuasive, and gave the court no alternative but to reverse the verdict. If beautiful prose and clever arguments could win the day, he would somehow produce them.

Meanwhile, Landy was poking through the FBI's database. Casey was snooping around Braxton for any gossip on certain hospital employees. And Spade was dragging his feet finding a suitable hacker.

On the first Saturday in June, Simon packed his camping gear and left town. He stopped at a country store and bought canned meat, crackers, beef jerky, and a pint of whiskey, things he didn't mind carrying on his back. He picked up the Blue Ridge Parkway and enjoyed a slow, lovely drive south for ninety minutes. He entered the Shenandoah National Park and stopped at a rest area with a dozen other vehicles. It took a few minutes to adjust the backpack and get it as comfortable as possible, then he was off on a five-mile hike that would take two hours. Hawksbill Mountain rose four thousand feet above the valley and was the highest peak in the park. He had hiked it for years and loved the views, and the solitude.

On a clear day a hiker could see for fifty miles. Everyone stopped at the peak for a rest, a photo, lunch, a nap, maybe even to sketch or paint. Danger signs were conspicuous. According to a guidebook, at least seven people had taken one step too many since the hike was opened in 1936. Three of the bodies were not found until months later, after the snow had melted and the coyotes were finished. Two of the dead people had left notes behind.

With less than ninety days to go, Simon was thinking of his future, grim as it was. Assuming his efforts to clear his name went nowhere, the direction they seemed to be headed, he would take command of his final matters here at the peak of Hawksbill Mountain. He would leave notes in his car, take a shot or two of bourbon, trot to the edge of the rock, and launch himself into the air.

He sat on a bench, sipped water, breathed the clear air, absorbed the panorama, and was at peace with his decision. The more he envisioned his flight, the more he wanted it.

CHAPTER 56

As usual, Simon was refusing all calls from unknown numbers. If they deemed themselves important, the callers left voicemails. Occasionally, he was interested enough to return one. A voice said: "Simon, Spade told me to call." Female, slow, precise, with a slightly husky tone.

He immediately called back and said, "This is Simon Latch."

"Hello Simon. I'm Zander. A pleasure."

A woman of few words. "So you know Spade?" he asked.

"Oh yes. We were once close. A long story. He wants me to meet you and get some background."

Since she was a complete stranger, and since she existed somewhere in Spade's orbit, Simon told himself to be careful on the phone. Someone was probably listening. Then again, what the hell? What could the authorities possibly do to him that they had not already done?

"Where would you like to meet?" he asked.

"I assume you're keeping a low profile these days."

"Yes, as a matter of fact."

"There's a tea shop near the college on Kitt Street. Meet there in an hour?"

"See ya."

Herbal teas were not the rage in rural Virginia. The shop was

tiny, only six small round tables, and there were no other customers at ten-thirty in the morning. Zander was seated in a corner and
gave him a half-hearted wave, as if she was being forced to indulge
him. But for the bright-teal spiked hair, collection of facial pierc-
ings, and rampant mascara, she might have been attractive. Inde-
terminate age, probably between eighteen and thirty-five. Simon's
first thought was: *I'm trusting my fate to a flake like this?*

He sat down without shaking hands, not that she offered one.
He nodded and said, "Nice to meet you, Zander."

"And nice to meet you as well." He wasn't wrong about the
slow, sultry voice. It almost made up for her initial appearance.

"How do you know Spade?"

She smiled. Beautiful teeth. No metal stud through her tongue.

"My mother is one of his ex-wives and we lived in the same
house for a short period of time, back when I was sixteen or so."
She made it sound like a long time ago. "Then they split and we
moved out. But I've always liked Spade. He inspired me to find
nontraditional work."

Simon was not about to open that door.

She asked, "Would you like some tea?"

Her cup was almost empty. "Do they have coffee?" he asked,
looking for a menu on a wall.

"Sure. Anything special?"

"No, just black."

She said loudly, "Lois, a black coffee and another mint tea."

From somewhere on the other side of a curtain behind the
counter, Lois either grunted or passed gas. Either way, the order
was acknowledged.

"So, you know something about the darker side of the web."

She smiled again and said, "How much has Spade told you?"

"Nothing."

"Sounds like him. I've read about your case, still reading actually. There's quite a lot of stuff buzzing around. Do you keep up
with it?"

"Oh no. I've sworn off social media and all that crap for the
time being. Too depressing."

"I live online. Twenty-four seven. It's all I do. My boyfriend and I made some serious dough a few years back, shut down the entire department of transportation of a certain Midwestern state. They paid the ransom."

"You're still in business?"

"Sort of. Laying low. We got caught doing the next job. He took the fall and he's serving time. Gets out in four months and I guess we have some decisions to make."

Lois appeared through the curtain, put two cups on the table without saying a word, and vanished.

Simon ignored his and said, "I'm trying to find the killer. Maybe it's someone who works for the local hospital. I need personnel records, everything in their files. Of course it's confidential."

"Everything's confidential, Simon. Unless you know how to penetrate confidential files."

"And you can find it?"

"Sure. This is easy. Hospitals only think they're secure. Patients' rights and all that crap. The problem with hospitals is that too many people have access. And now you have all this see-a-doc online, Zoom consultations, teletherapy. They make it easy for pros to wiggle in and have a look."

"I'm interested in ten people who work there."

"No problem, but I'm not sure what you expect to find. I mean, look, if someone, say an orderly, likes to poison people, there probably won't be anything about it in his or her personnel file."

"Got it."

"I mean, like, it's just common sense, you know."

"Maybe so, but I have to start somewhere. I have a list of the ten names."

"Hard copy, nothing online, nothing in your computer. Every-thing leaves a trail, Simon, and I can find it."

Simon handed her a folded sheet of paper with the ten names. She took it, laid it on the table, then ignored it.

"How long will this take?" he asked.

"Are you in a hurry or something?"

"Damned right I'm in a hurry."

"Same time tomorrow?"

"Sure. That easy, huh?"

She dismissed him with a look that said, *Don't doubt me.*

He wondered if the metal in her eyebrows somehow kept her from blinking. Her gaze was not altogether unpleasant, but he was finding it unsettling. Whatever pill she was taking to remain so calm and unconcerned was the one he wanted.

From one criminal to another, he asked, "Do you worry about getting caught?"

"Not really. It happens, but rarely. We're light-years ahead of the cops. And if you get caught, like Cooley, my boyfriend, then you go to a nice federal camp and keep working in prison."

There was so much he didn't know, and even more he didn't want to know.

———◆◆———

The following morning, they met at the same table and ordered the same drinks. Zander handed him a sealed manila envelope, eight-by-eleven, and said, "I'm afraid there's not much there. Just the usual stuff—generic job applications, references, education, payroll information, a few disciplinary matters, all minor. Nothing that piqued my interest."

She spoke like she was now in charge of the investigation, which was fine with Simon. She worked in a world foreign to his, and if she wanted to dig in and help, go girl. "But what did you expect?" she asked.

"I don't know. There's a level of desperation here, you understand?"

"Sure, but you won't find anything in the personnel files. If a bad actor works for the hospital and might have been involved in a poisoning, you won't find anything useful in his file. What's he gonna admit to? Favorite hobbies—mixing poison compounds? Collecting banned substances in the black market? Education— bounced from college chemistry for blowing up a lab."

What a smart-ass! Simon tried to suppress a smile as he admired her sarcasm and nerve. She was thoroughly unintimidated. He said, "I get that. I'm just beginning, okay? Gotta start somewhere."

"Well, you're off to a bad start."

"I'm digging in other places." He drank some coffee and tried to hold her gaze. She flicked her lazy eyelashes and asked, "So where would you look?"

"Someone inside the hospital had the thallium. That person is a sicko who likes to poison, probably done it before."

"And you think that'll be in the file?" she asked.

"No, not at all. Are you always such a smart-ass?"

"It's likely. I talked to Cooley last night."

"Cooley has a cell phone?"

"He has three, all contraband of course. You'd better bone up on this prison stuff. The guards smuggle in phones and sell them to the inmates."

"That's nice to know."

"Some of the guards make a ton of money smuggling goods."

"I'll remember that. What's Cooley up to?"

"He's intrigued. Took him two hours to find a dealer for thallium, guy in Singapore. If you want, I can order some. Five hundred bucks for fifty grams."

Simon had to catch his breath as his thoughts scrambled.

She continued, "You can't order it because you'll leave a trail. We don't."

"Okay, but I think it's too late for that. Let me think about it. It's that easy?"

"Oh no. It's hard as hell. Far too complicated for the average hacker and impossible for a guy like you. It's the dark, dark web, Simon. Don't go there."

"Don't worry."

She finished her tea and asked, "Are you in a hurry?"

"Not at all."

She looked at an opening that apparently went to the kitchen and said, "Lois, more coffee and another tea, please." Lois did not reply.

Simon believed her but asked himself if he should be more cautious. It sounded so easy: an inmate in a federal prison with three cell phones and a computer, all contraband, goes into the dark web and locates a source of thallium in about two hours.

They sat silently for a while, waiting on the refills. When Lois was gone again, Zander said, "Judging from what I've read, and again I'm suspicious of everything, it looks as though you bought the ginger cookies, your secretary took them to the hospital, and at that point everything was still okay."

"Assuming the secretary didn't doctor the cookies."

"Is that a possibility?"

"Remote."

"Okay, so your theory is that someone on the inside did the deed."

"Correct."

"We have work to do."

For some reason, Simon felt safer with a criminal like Zander on his side than with the FBI.

CHAPTER 57

Simon felt no loyalty to Eleanor Barnett. Her deceit had caused more problems than she could possibly have foreseen. However, the last will and testament he prepared for her was properly executed and legally valid, unless, of course, it could be proven that she was not mentally sound. That fight now belonged to someone else. But he would not sit idly by and allow Teddy Hammer and his bogus clients to plunder what was left of her diminished estate. Plus, he was about to be disbarred and sent away, so what the hell? He decided to thoroughly muddy the water and go out in a blaze of glory.

He filed a petition to probate Eleanor's will, along with the affidavits signed by the Larsons, plus one signed by him in which he attested to the "sound and disposing mind and memory" of the late Eleanor Barnett. Since there was no way Judge Pointer would appoint him as the executor, Simon asked the court to appoint Clement Gelly, who was still acting as the conservator. In a phone call, Judge Pointer was pleased to hear from Simon, even claimed to be concerned about him, and welcomed him, and Eleanor's will, into the fray. She scheduled the initial probate hearing for June 17 and notices were sent. As expected, it drew a crowd of reporters and other courthouse regulars.

Simon knew his days in the courtroom were numbered. He

would be forced to appear before Judge Shyam on August 22 for his sentencing, and he assumed that would be his last time in court. For the initial hearing in the probate matter, in his home courtroom, he was determined to look sharp and act as if life was swell. He had told Paula and the kids that his chances on appeal were excellent and his conviction would be set aside soon enough. He had refused to say a word to any reporter. He avoided them and entered the courthouse through a side door, then hurried upstairs to the main courtroom.

Judge Pointer called things to order, welcomed the large crowd, and thanked everyone for their attendance and their interest in making sure the judicial system worked properly. Of course, the crowd had no such interest. They were there to have a look at the lawyer who poisoned his wealthy widow client and got convicted of her murder. Everyone was working on a story. Simon knew all eyes were on him. The locals—lawyers, clerks, courtroom regulars—were, as a group, dumbfounded that Simon Latch, one of their own, had managed to get himself in such hot water. They found it difficult to believe that he was headed for prison. The others—reporters, journalists, true-crime hucksters—were there because they smelled blood and wanted a fresh angle.

Wally Thackerman sat low in the back row, curious as hell but still unwilling to step forward with his version of Eleanor's will, primarily because he had no idea what would happen if he did so. The chances of him cashing in on his scheme seemed remote. The chances of getting embarrassed seemed rather high.

As the petitioner, Simon was allowed to speak first. Without referring to his problems, he explained to Judge Pointer that on March 27 of the previous year, the decedent, Eleanor Barnett, signed a last will and testament that he had prepared himself. It met all of the statutory requirements. He offered it as Exhibit A and she accepted it into evidence. In quick order, Simon called Tony Larson to the stand and quizzed him about his involvement in meeting Eleanor Barnett and witnessing her signing the will. His wife, Mary Beth Larson, was next, and explained that their good friend Mr. Latch, the lawyer next door, often asked them to step over and witness wills. She was quite impressed with Eleanor Barnett and had no doubt that she was in her right mind and knew exactly what she was doing. They even walked around the corner and had a nice lunch together afterward.

Once the will was admitted for probate, the question became: Who would serve as the executor or the administrator? The will named Simon as the executor, but that did not seem feasible. An administrator was needed, and Simon argued that Clement Gelly should be appointed. Clement took the stand and agreed to continue with the estate.

Teddy Hammer wanted Jerry Korsak to have the job and to control the estate's affairs. However, he was afraid to put him on the stand. At that point, Simon would be allowed to grill him, and the results would likely be disastrous.

Teddy said, "Your Honor, we have confidence in Mr. Gelly and will agree to his appointment as administrator. The much larger issue is the validity of this will. We plan to file an objection to it and demand a trial."

"On what grounds?" Judge Pointer asked.

"On the grounds of undue influence. Ms. Barnett was under the complete control of Mr. Latch when she signed her will. At trial we plan to prove that at the time it was drafted, Mr. Latch was laboring under the false assumption that his client was quite wealthy. The language of the will gives him extraordinary power, along with the opportunity to earn substantial fees for representing not only her estate, but also the trust it created. He was after her money, Your Honor, plain and simple."

The last thing Simon wanted at that point in his life was to sit through another trial, especially one where he was the sole target. And he would not sit through the will contest. He really didn't care who got the money or how much was actually out there.

He managed to mute Teddy Hammer and tune out everyone else. For a moment he was pleased to be making his exit, albeit a rather unexpected one, from the legal profession. The lawyers—they do go on and on.

Let the vultures fight over Eleanor's remains.

Chapter 58

The airtight conviction of Simon Latch began to crack late one summer night in Raymond's office. Cigar smoke boiled from the open windows. His staff was long gone. Soft bluegrass echoed through the speakers. It was almost 10 P.M. and Raymond was reading the latest decisions from the state supreme court, a boring habit he had not broken in almost fifty years. He still loved the law and kept abreast of its changes.

He heard a knock at the front door. Normally, he would have ignored it and waited for the person to go away, but for some reason he was curious. Something told him to check it out. With a cigar in his mouth and a drink in his hand, he waddled to the front and opened the door. Standing there was a young lady he recognized from somewhere but couldn't immediately place.

"Good evening, ma'am," he said, always the gentleman, especially around women.

"I'm Loretta Goodwin, a nurse at the hospital. We met at the trial last month."

His plans to shoo away the visitor changed quickly. "Of course, of course. Please come in."

Hit with the aromas of smoke and bourbon, Loretta stood her ground. "No, I'll just be a minute. I'm trying to get in touch with

Simon Latch, but he won't answer his phone and I have no idea where he is."

Raymond knew immediately that something was up. "Well, I'm sure I can find him. Is this about his trial?"

She glanced around, hesitated, and answered the question with her eyes. "I need to talk to him."

"Okay. I'm happy to make contact, but he'll want to know what's up. For a lot of reasons, he stays buried in his office these days. Talks to very few people."

She was nervous and uncertain. Raymond said, "Look, if it's about his case, we don't have time to play games. If it's not about his case, he has no interest."

"It's about Ms. Barnett."

"Come in and have a seat. I'll call Simon."

Fifteen minutes later, Simon appeared. His shirt was damp with sweat and he said he'd been out for a long walk. Always after dark.

Loretta was uncomfortable, but also resolved. She began by saying to Simon, "When we met in the hospital last December, I already knew who you were. Several years ago my uncle had a boundary dispute with a neighbor. We live out in Beeno, a whole slew of Goodwins out there. Kind of a clannish bunch. Anyway, my uncle hired you to represent him and you got things settled in a proper way without charging a lot of money. He had good things to say about you. It's not easy hiring a lawyer when you don't know much about the law and don't know how much it'll cost. So, anyway, I knew who you were when you came to take care of Ms. Barnett. We, the staff, were suspicious when you got her to sign those papers while she was in bad shape, but we were surprised when they accused you of the poisoning. We figured the police knew what they were doing."

"Who is 'we'?" Simon asked.

"The staff, everyone around the patient. As you know, a lot of people come and go at all hours."

"I tried to sleep there one night. Impossible."

"By the time the trial was over, we assumed the police and prosecutor got things right. We talked about how sad it all was, nice lady, our patient, being killed like that, and you, a nice law-yer, guilty of it. But I always had a nagging doubt. Something told me it was somebody else."

A long pause. Finally, Raymond asked, "Was it somebody else?"

"I don't know. But there's a guy."

———— •♦• ————

She talked about him for a long time without giving a name. He was an X-ray technician who'd been at the hospital for a cou-ple years. There were three technicians in his group and they worked all wings of the hospital, so he was not limited to the third floor where Eleanor was a patient. He was thoroughly nonde-script, the kind of person you would never notice in any situation. Said little, not the least outgoing, wouldn't speak unless spoken to, sort of edgy though. Since the nurses and their assistants rou-tinely gossiped about everyone else who roamed the halls, they had mentioned him a few times. He was single and got pretty low marks on personality, even lower on good looks. But, she now remembered three events that might be relevant.

One day in the lounge the staff was lunching on free pizza from a local restaurant. About a dozen were there in a relaxed atmosphere. This guy was on the fringe, eating, listening, saying nothing. It was the week before the trial and the gossip centered around nothing else. The mood was clearly against Simon Latch. Everyone was buying the same greedy-lawyer narrative that had been plastered in the newspapers the previous weeks. They had a mock verdict, with each person allowed to chime in. Most voted for guilt. A couple were undecided. This guy wouldn't say, but it was clear, at least to Loretta, that he didn't think Simon was guilty. Throughout the discussion she noticed him several times, always shaking his head and rolling his eyes.

She flashed back to Christmas, when Ms. Barnett was a patient and not doing well. Loretta saw the guy leave her room late one afternoon, all alone and carrying nothing. She checked the charts and saw that the patient had not had an X-ray in three days. There was no reason whatsoever for this guy to be in her room. It was unusual, though not that suspicious.

Then, a week or so after the trial, some of the boys from the hospital were in a bar late on a Friday night, drinking beer. Saturday was an off day, and they decided to break bad. The guy was with them, though he rarely hung out with anyone at the hospital. The bar closed, they were still thirsty, and they ended up at the apartment of one of the male ER nurses. The beer was losing its effect so they switched to vodka shots. Somehow thallium became the topic and they talked about the poisoning of Ms. Barnett. The guy knew a lot about various poisons, their prevalence, legalities, histories, and effects on human bodies. He claimed that thallium was not that difficult to find. At some hazy point in the early hours of Saturday, a bag of pills hit the table and was passed around. Bennies, Mollies, mud, cubes, who knew what else? There was also cocaine, and someone said something like "Gee, hope it's not thallium we're snorting." As the hellraisers began passing out, someone heard the guy say, "I promise you that lawyer didn't poison the old gal," or something to that effect.

Around noon Saturday, as they staggered forth in their stupors, they realized the guy had already left. They could not imagine him leaving in his condition, and they spent an hour or so chugging coffee and talking about some of the things he had said.

Loretta was quick to acknowledge that most of her information was secondhand at best, but she believed it anyway. Why, other than being drunk, would the guy know so much? Her source was the ER nurse, a trustworthy pal she had known for about five years. He was bothered by some of the things the guy said, at least as much as he could remember.

At work the following Monday, the guy kept away from his drinking buddies and fell into his usual routine of saying little and acting detached. The ER nurse described him as being "downright weird."

His name was Oscar Kofie. Simon remembered meeting him in Eleanor's room not long after she was admitted. He and another technician were in the process of returning her after more X-rays. She had referred to them—Bill and Oscar—as her new friends. Oscar Kofie, an unusual name, and one that Simon had run across digging through the hospital's records.

As lawyers, Simon and Raymond immediately recognized the potential danger facing Loretta and her story. If it led to the investigation and, hopefully, conviction of Kofie, the hospital would be liable for the death of Eleanor Barnett.

At that moment, they didn't care. Finding the killer was far more important. And Loretta was a confident professional who gave every indication of being able to fend for herself.

Simon managed to suppress his excitement and thanked Loretta for coming forward. Raymond puffed away, poker-faced, and said they would check out the new suspect. He said, "We'll keep your name out of it."

Loretta said, "Thanks, this is all secondhand stuff. I don't have any real proof."

CHAPTER 59

Time for more tea with Zander. Her wondrous hacking skills had yet to produce anything useful, not that Simon was ungrateful. Since she had already found her way into the hospital's system, running down another name was no problem. She opened her laptop on the little breakfast table and pecked away. "Got him."

She turned the screen to Simon who was suddenly staring at the face of Oscar Kofie, one he vaguely remembered from last December. Early thirties, chubby cheeks, clean-shaven, drug-store eyeglasses, receding hairline. Nothing noticeable or distinguishable about the face. Nor the bio—associate's degree from a community college in Dayton; certified X-ray tech in Ohio, Maryland, Pennsylvania, and Virginia; eleven years of experience in various hospitals, public and private.

"What makes him a suspect?" Zander asked casually, as if she didn't care. Simon had learned that she really, truly didn't care about anything, except perhaps her incarcerated boyfriend and the problems he might cause them after he was paroled.

"Just some new gossip. How deep can you dig into this guy?"

"Deep as you want."

"How about prior places of employment?"

"Give me a day or two."

Simon drove to Charlottesville to meet Landy for lunch. She was appearing before a grand jury there and wasting the day, in her opinion. In her spare time, and Simon reminded her repeatedly that in his world there was no such thing as "spare time," she had put together profiles of about forty hospital employees, with no red flags. Oscar Kofie was not one of them.

They were eating outdoors on the downtown pedestrian mall, under the shade of an oak, with dozens of other young professionals, shop owners, office employees, students, and tourists. It was a splendid day. Simon was eating with a pretty lady, one he had known in every way since they were twenty-three years old. As fine as the moment should have been, he found it impossible to enjoy anything about it.

"You look miserable," she said.

"Well, maybe prison does that to a person. Don't know. Plus I got the letter from the state bar yesterday, yanking my license without so much as a hearing."

"I'm sorry."

"You keep saying that and I wish you'd stop."

So she said nothing for a long time as they suffered in silence. He hardly touched his food and finally said, "I'm spending twelve hours a day digging online. I have piles of research, most of it useless. I've gone back twenty years and tried to find every murder-by-poison case in the country. There are about twenty a year, confirmed, but probably hundreds that go undetected. I need more help from the FBI."

"I'm doing all I can, Simon, and I'll do whatever is possible."

"The FBI collects more crime data than any other agency, but many cases go unreported and fall through the cracks."

"A lot of crime in this country."

"I know. Is it possible to go behind the published statistics? Is there more data that the FBI doesn't publish, for whatever reason?"

"You're talking about poisonings, right?"

"What else?"

"Don't snap at me. I'm on your side, remember?"

"Sorry. Yes, murder by poison."

"I don't know, but why would we, the FBI, hide those statistics?"

Simon took a deep breath and didn't answer. He tried two bites of a pan-fried trout and put down his fork. "I know I'm being difficult."

"Not at all, Simon. I'm trying to understand."

"It's just that we expect miracles out of the FBI and I know that's not realistic. But I have a hacker pal who's finding more stuff than the FBI."

"Hacking is a crime. We can't go in without a warrant."

"I know."

"Are you violating the law?"

He laughed and said, "Who cares? I'm fifty-eight days away from prison. Indict me! Convict me! Hell, give me the needle."

"Not so loud, Simon."

"I'm sorry."

"I'll see what I can do. Just hang on, okay?"

"Easy for you to say."

"I know, I know."

At four-thirty that afternoon, Simon walked into an Avis car rental office in Pentagon City near Reagan National. Three women worked the counter, one of them was Matilda Clark. She wore a smart navy pantsuit uniform with AVIS above the right pocket and her new name, MADDIE, above the left. It fit her nicely. He wore a cap and sunglasses, got in line, and sort of hid behind the large man in front of him. When it was his turn, he yanked off the cap and sunglasses, leaned on the counter, and was face-to-face with Tillie. She appeared as though she might faint.

"Hello, Matilda," he said in a low voice. "Oops, I see it's 'Maddie' now."

She was still struggling to speak and glancing nervously around.

"Don't worry. I need to rent a car. No problems from me."

She pecked her keyboard as if just doing her job, gained some composure, and asked, "What do you want?"

"A drink after work. Down the street at O'Malley's. Five P.M.?"

"Sure," she said with a smile. "Make it five-thirty."

"Okay, please be there and don't run. I know where your apartment is in Fredericksburg. Unit 614. And I know where your roomie hangs out these days. The FBI is watching him."

Her mouth fell open as he turned and left.

At five-thirty, Tillie walked into O'Malley's and Simon waved her over to his booth. They had a lot to talk about, not that she was planning on saying much. He sipped a beer as a waiter took her order for a diet soda.

"What, no asparagus smoothie?" he joked but it fell flat.

If she had been rattled to see him, that had now passed. She was unmoved and quite collected. "Why are you here, Simon?"

"Just passing through. I'm looking for the person who poisoned Eleanor Barnett, Tillie, because I damned sure didn't do it."

"And you've found me. You think I did it?"

"That thought crossed my mind. In fact, when I found out that you were shacking up with Jerry I got real suspicious. But if I've learned anything lately, it's not to assume too much."

"Why did you hide her will from me?"

"Because I got greedy and wanted her money, and to get it I had to draft a lopsided will that gave me complete control of her estate and assets. And I didn't want you to know about it because you're a good, honest, decent person who would have questioned me over such a will. I didn't want a fight. I wanted the money. My marriage was falling apart. I was sick of the office and its overhead. And Eleanor Barnett was my way out." He slugged some beer and wiped his mouth with a sleeve. "There. Is that honest enough for you?"

"I suppose."

"Let's be honest, Tillie. Cut the crap. I've been convicted and I'm headed to prison, so I can afford to be brutally honest. I didn't poison Eleanor."

"That makes two of us."

They studied each other for a long time, neither daring to blink. Simon took a sip, wiped his mouth, and asked, "When did you first get suspicious?"

"Three days after she signed the will you typed. Then you lied to me and tried to cover up. You're not a deceitful person, Simon, and a lousy liar. You were sneaking around, taking her to lunch, ingratiating yourself. I knew what was going on. Then we did the living will that gave you full control. The cremation angle was a nice touch. Face it, Simon, there was plenty of red flags."

"Well, my jury certainly thought so, didn't they?"

"They did."

"And you agree with them? You think I'm guilty?"

"No, I don't. I was very suspicious, but I've changed my mind."

"Why?"

"I know you too well. I watched you in the courtroom and I saw a man who was bewildered by the accusations, a man who would never harm another person."

Her soda arrived and she ignored it. Simon drained his beer and ordered another. They stared across the table for a long time, both wanting to believe the other.

Finally, he asked, "How did Jerry enter the picture?"

"Is that really any of your business?"

"Let's say it is."

"Simple enough. He stopped by the office one day when you were gone. He called a week later and we had a drink. One thing led to another. He's had his ups and downs with romance. I certainly have."

"He doesn't seem like your type."

"What is my type, Simon? I've tried them all." She managed to smile.

"You want advice from me? I can't remember the last time I made a smart decision. Got a question."

"I'm an open book."

"December thirtieth, the day she died. I called the funeral home to come get her, but an anonymous caller alerted the Braxton police. The cremation was stopped. I'm assuming that call was made by you."

Her jaws clenched slightly and she glanced away. Dead guilty.

"Why did you do it, Tillie? I'm being perfectly honest with you, so return the favor."

"Jerry wanted me to do it. He wanted an autopsy. By then Teddy Hammer was calling the shots and he was very suspicious of you."

"And the fact that you, and Jerry, stopped the cremation is pretty clear proof that you didn't poison Eleanor. Otherwise, no one would have ever known, and I would not be facing prison."

"We didn't do it, Simon, I swear we didn't."

"Nor did I, regardless of what the jury said."

"So, who killed her?"

He rubbed his temples, then shook his head. "If it wasn't me and it wasn't you, then I don't know. I suspect someone entered her hospital room after she'd been there a few days. You know how casual hospitals are. Doctors, nurses, and staff come and go at all hours."

"An inside job?"

Simon would only say so much. She would repeat everything to Jerry.

"Possibly. Why did Jerry sue me?"

"I begged him not to, told him you were broke. But Hammer said it had to be done."

"I'm worse than broke."

"Can I help?"

"Hell no. The last thing I need is for you trying to get involved. Just leave it alone. Things are bad enough and you're sleeping with the enemy."

CHAPTER 60

Evidently, Cooley had plenty of free time in prison. He was actually finishing his time in a federal "camp," a fenceless low-security joint where violence was not tolerated. Simon tracked him down online and learned that he had been convicted in Maryland three years earlier and would be released on parole in early September. It was his first offense, a federal violation, something complicated to do with internet theft. Further sleuthing revealed virtually nothing about his girlfriend, Zander.

Simon's curiosity about them paled in comparison to their interest in him. According to Zander, Cooley had easily trespassed into Simon's virtual world, and not only thumbed through his office files, a mind-numbing waste of time, but also accessed his longtime personal email account at Google. Simon was momentarily irritated by this, but then figured what the hell. For years he had assumed that someone somewhere was seeing every email, shopping order, calendar entry, and personal note, so he had always been careful. He was floored, though, when Zander informed him Cooley had hacked into the secret email account Simon had opened over a year earlier, primarily to hide his gambling.

"Why'd you stop gambling?" she asked over a drink in a student bar, two doors down from the tea shop.

"I made too much money."

"Doesn't appear so."

"Look, the FBI had me on its radar and I got a tip from an old friend. It was time to quit."

"Just curious."

"Okay, I have something important for you. Can you guys take a look into the virtual world of Oscar Kofie, the X-ray tech I mentioned last time?"

She giggled, a little teenage snicker, and said, "Cooley's already on the trail. It's not going to be easy, though. Kofie really likes his privacy and he knows his way around the digital world."

"Not sure I follow." When it came to technology, Simon was often on thin ice, and usually felt like a moron when talking to Zander. She could roll her eyes like a know-it-all kid or she could flash a warm, reassuring smile that exuded patience.

She smiled and said, "He's obviously paranoid and protects himself with some pretty impressive firewalls and gates. But Cooley loves a challenge. He'll get in soon enough."

Simon was once again amused at the idea of a federal inmate with his own contraband laptop, holed up in the prison library wreaking havoc in the virtual world. It was also sobering to know that somewhere out there in the vast universe of the web there were people who could find and watch everything. Why couldn't those people work just for the intelligence agencies and leave the common folk alone? If he could do it, and he knew it was impossible, he would toss his computers and retreat to the Stone Age where people wrote letters with pen and paper and had long chats on old-fashioned telephones.

She said, "Cooley's working on something for you."

"I can't wait."

"Are you being a smart-ass?"

"Yes."

"He has developed his own home-brew software that cannot be hacked or penetrated. Calls it Teflon."

"Original."

"Smart-ass again. I have it on my computer. He's customizing a program for you that'll keep your systems thoroughly secure.

That way, he and I, and anyone else for that matter, can send you stuff without leaving a trace."

"And what are we afraid of? I've already been convicted, Zander. I'm going to prison."

"Congratulations, gold star for you. I, however, am not a felon, not yet anyway, and I prefer to keep it that way. I'll install the software for you at no charge and you'll never know it's there."

"Whatever. I wonder if Kofie likes girls. He's thirty-six, single, never married. Maybe he cruises through the dating sites looking for love."

"I couldn't care less. But if he does, Cooley will know soon enough."

———————•••———————

Loretta Goodwin reluctantly agreed to meet for coffee after work. She was the mother of three, happily married, and unwilling to risk being seen talking to Simon in a bar or some other shady place. She chose the cafeteria in the basement of the hospital, a place that was always deserted at 6 P.M.

Simon bought two cups of coffee and they hid at a corner table, his back to the entrance. Loretta could see those coming and going, but there was hardly anyone to notice. She was not eager to talk but willing to listen.

"We don't have a solid suspect," Simon said. "Our list is rather short, but Kofie is at the top of it. I'm not accusing him, yet. But Kofie is the most promising. How much do you know about him?"

She shrugged and studied the floor. "Not much at all."

"Does he have a close friend here at work? Does he date anyone? Straight or gay?"

"I don't know and don't care. It's none of my business. I have enough to worry about, Mr. Latch."

"Please call me Simon. How often do you see him?"

"Once a week maybe. He's the kind of person you see but don't see. Like a piece of furniture."

"But there has to be someone here who knows him."

"Maybe, but I don't know who. We work in different worlds, Simon. When I'm here I'm very busy caring for my patients. I don't have time to socialize. That's not part of my job."

"I understand. You told the story about Kofie out drinking with his buddies from work and running his mouth. Who were the friends? I believe there were three of them, right?"

"I think so."

"Can you get me their names? And the names of his supervisors?"

She took a deep breath, reluctant to say yes.

"Please, Loretta. I'm not asking you to do anything illegal or unethical. I'm desperate, okay?"

"I'll see what I can do."

"Thank you. Any scrap of info could be crucial, not only for me, but for the hospital as well. Imagine for a moment if Kofie is really the killer. The legal aftershocks for the hospital would be horrendous. An employee, one supposedly vetted, poisons a patient. There's not enough money in the Commonwealth to pay for that lawsuit."

"I get it."

CHAPTER 61

Meticulously researched, beautifully written, and thoroughly persuasive, the *Defendant's Motion to Vacate the Guilty Verdict and Grant a New Trial* was filed by Raymond Lassiter on time. It was a 38-page masterpiece, at least in the opinion of its author, the defendant himself. Raymond and Casey read it carefully and did not suggest a single change, not even an extra comma.

With that chore out of the way, Simon returned to the monotonous task of tracking murder-by-poison cases over the past forty years. Landy received clearance from her supervisor—crime data was not exactly classified material—and was passing along links to more crime statistics than any one person could read and filter. The previous year there had been twenty-two cases, or at least twenty-two people had been indicted for such murders. Four had pled guilty. The others were still awaiting justice. The troublesome trend in the past decade was that about a third of the persons accused walked free with not-guilty verdicts. Murder by poison was hard to prove. This, obviously, was not comforting to Simon. He had been nailed by a screwball jury, and the more he dwelt on his verdict, the more he was convinced he had been convicted because of the greedy-lawyer theme the prosecution had used so effectively.

His phone pinged at 2:38 in the morning, and of course it
was Zander, who slept past noon most days because she roamed
the internet all hours of the night. Simon was at his desk, sipping
strong coffee, wide awake, and digging through crime statistics.

"Bingo," she said.

"And?"

"A major breakthrough. Just wormed my way into the hospital's archives and found the employment application for our boy."

"Congrats. I will not ask how you did it?"

"You wouldn't understand if I drew pictures for you."

"Thanks, as always."

"Oscar Kofie applied to Blue Ridge Memorial in 2013. His
previous job was the same, an X-ray tech at the University of
Maryland hospital, where he worked for two years. Before that,
a system in Scranton. Before that, a hospital in Columbus, Ohio.
Seems he moves around every two or three years. I'll send you
the data."

"Any reasons for his departures?"

"Don't be ridiculous. He applied in an effort to get a job, not
lose another one. Why would he include anything even remotely
negative?"

"Got it." Simon once again chastised himself for throwing out
useless questions when he knew damned well they would draw a
sarcastic retort.

"I'll send it over."

"Can you take a look at his HR files at previous hospitals?"

"I'm on it. So is Cooley."

"Thanks."

Simon fell asleep on his sofa, which was more comfortable
than his cot, though between them they were wreaking havoc
with his spine. He slept a few hours and woke up with the sunrise.
He went to the reception area, peeked out the front window, saw
no one and no traffic, and at 6:15 sneaked out the back door into
the alley and went for a long run. Day 51, more than halfway to

his sentencing date when Judge Shyam would be forced to send him away for a long time.

After a shower, he packed his gear and drove three hours south to a state park in the Appalachian Mountains. Paula had spent the first night with the kids in a rustic cabin on a lake, and she was eager to hand them off and get away. She and her old girlfriends from Braxton had a week of partying planned in the Outer Banks. The family ate hot dogs together for lunch, then Paula made a quick exit.

Simon was in charge of the kids, so there were no rules. They swam in the lake for hours, fished the mountain streams, canoed and kayaked, ate junk food at will, and watched old movies until they fell asleep. No one said a word about the future, though it was always there, hanging over them like a distant cloud. Buck and Danny knew far more about the case than Simon could imagine. It was not clear how much Janie knew because she said little. All three ignored the mess their father was in, or at least did a fine job of pretending to.

The only unbendable rule for the week was no devices. The vacation was offline. They awoke early, went nonstop during the days, and at night played old-fashioned board games and cards when they were not watching movies. Simon taught them poker, though it was obvious the boys had played it before. He taught them gin rummy, bridge, and blackjack. Before long they were betting with plastic poker chips, and all three kids seemed to have a knack for the table. Little Janie did especially well and suggested they up the ante to real pennies. Simon worried about the example he was setting, but let it pass. He admitted to himself that he missed the action at Chub's. It was harmless fun, right? By the third night, Janie was up a hundred and ten cents at blackjack.

After the kids crashed, Simon sneaked to his car for a shot or two of bourbon and a quick check of phone messages. On the fourth night, he finally returned a call. Zander had texted: *Call. Important. Could be very important.*

Without hesitating, he violated The Rule and called her.

She answered with "How much are you paying your lawyers?" Always with something random.

"I don't know. Is it really any of your business?"

"Could be."

"Not much. Actually, they're not getting paid. It's called pro bono."

"I've heard of that. It means for free, right?"

"I thought this was urgent."

"Well, your pro bono hacking team is kicking ass and finding more dirt than your pro bono legal team."

"I'm listening."

"Cooley and I are making a wild hunch that our boy Oscar Kofie is a serial killer."

When Zander was wired and on a roll, small pauses in the conversation were usually filled by another shot from her. "You there?"

"Uh, I don't know."

"He moves around and leaves dead bodies behind."

Cell service was sketchy at best. He lost the call, tried again, and couldn't get her. He quietly walked through the cabin, to make sure the kids were sound asleep. They were, and he returned to his car and drove away. There was a picnic area on an incline with great views of the lake and the service was better. He parked there and called Zander. It was almost midnight and the full moon seemed touchable.

"Sorry about that. I'm in the mountains. The part about leaving dead bodies behind."

"Yeah, just a hunch, something to work with, but Cooley and I like it. Three years ago Kofie worked in a hospital in Baltimore. While he was there, three people, all geezers, died of unknown causes, which, as we're learning, is unusual. Unknown causes is rare these days. The docs always find a cause, you know, makes 'em look better. Kofie left two months after the last one died and showed up in Braxton. The kicker is in Pennsylvania. Kofie worked at a hospital in Scranton for three years. There were two mysterious deaths—both of unknown causes. However, I've seen the records and the victims suffered severe headaches and nausea, internal bleeding, skin rashes, etc."

"Sounds like thallium."

"You got it. What's intriguing is that the personnel file goes blank. Zilch, nada, as if someone tried to wipe it clean and bury it. But they got a bit sloppy and missed a few sheets of paper. One was a letter from a lawyer, guy named Victor Mulrooney. From Scranton. Ever heard of him?"

"No. You have the employees' files and the patients' records?"

"Come on, Latch, you think I'm just making this shit up? I told you. Hospitals are a piece of cake. They store everything in the cloud and just dare people like me to take a peek. Get with it. You wanna talk about Kofie or you wanna marvel at the brilliance of your pro bono hacking team?"

"What's his name? Victor Mulrooney?"

"Yeah, looks like a legit lawyer. We thought we'd let you dig through his dirty boxers since you're a lawyer and all, or at least you used to be."

"Thanks. So there was a lawsuit?"

"Don't know but the lawyers got involved. I've rummaged through the court records for the Scranton area and can't find a case with either patient's name."

"Just guessing, but there probably wasn't a lawsuit, I mean, nothing that was filed in court. If they caught Kofie with his chemicals, the hospital was probably extremely eager to settle the matter and keep it quiet. So they bought off the victims, or the victims' families, and the lawyers, and tried to wipe the file clean."

"Can you talk to Mulrooney?"

"Sure, if he'll talk. Let's slow down a bit. I need to chew on this. There are plenty of angles and dangers."

"Okay, Latch, you're the lawyer."

<hr />

For breakfast, the kids wanted pancakes and sausage, and Simon managed to whip out a batch in the small, spartan kitchen. By the time they were finished, every dish, pot, and pan in the cabin was dirty. He ran them out of the cabin and to the lake where they jumped into three kayaks and took off. It was their last full day of vacation and they were already griping about leaving. Simon treasured the moments, but he was also eager to get home and meet with Zander and his lawyers.

With the kids disappearing in the distance across the lake, Simon opened his laptop. Victor Mulrooney was a board-certified member of the College of Trial Lawyers, an elite group of courtroom studs with at least a hundred jury verdicts under their belts and a minimum of one billion dollars in recoverable damages. He was sixty-four years old, Rutgers undergrad, Penn Law, founding partner of a firm with at least thirty lawyers who did nothing but personal injury litigation, with a specialty in medical malpractice.

Simon called Raymond and asked if he knew Mulrooney. He did not, but would check him out. Simon relayed the latest news from Zander, and Raymond was stunned by the suggestion that Kofie might possibly have a history of poisoning patients. "A complete game-changer," he said more than once.

No kidding.

An hour later, as Simon was finishing the dishes and keeping an eye on the lake, Raymond called back. The cell service went south. Simon got in his car and hustled up the mountain.

"I talked to Mulrooney," Raymond said. "Nothing is easy. He can't talk."

"What do you mean he can't talk?"

"NDA. Nondisclosure agreement, one with plenty of teeth. Are you familiar with them?"

"Somewhat. There are various types."

"Yep, and Mulrooney signed a tough one, which means the hospital, and I'm assuming it's the hospital in Scranton where Kofie worked, was horrified by the allegations and threw a lot of money at a settlement. A very confidential settlement."

"Would he confirm that there was a claim against Kofie and the hospital?"

"No, he wouldn't confirm anything. But, he did say something interesting, almost as an aside. It was a brief conversation, and at the end he said something like, 'This is the phone call I never wanted to get.'"

"Meaning?"

"Maybe he was afraid Kofie would kill someone else. Maybe he took the money and went home instead of destroying the hospital and Kofie in a civil lawsuit, then handing him over to the police for a criminal prosecution. Maybe Mulrooney was bought off and thus allowed the killing to go on."

Simon's brain was spinning and he couldn't speak for a moment.

"Must've been a lot of money."

"No doubt. Casey ran a quickie on the hospital, third-largest private system in Pennsylvania. Tons of cash, tons of insurance, and plenty of competition. Thus, reputation is everything."

"Okay, Raymond, contact Judge Shyam and tell her I need to leave the state for seventy-two hours. I'll drive straight to Scranton, pester Mulrooney until he talks, then drive straight home."

"What if she says no?"

"I don't care, Raymond, I'll go anyway. I'm a convicted murderer. What else can they do to me?"

"Okay, okay. But what if Casey goes with you?"

"No, I don't need babysitting."

CHAPTER 62

Three days later, on July 18, Simon drove four hours non-stop to Scranton, Pennsylvania, and found Mulrooney's law firm in a nineteenth-century warehouse overlooking a river. The massive redbrick building was as long as a football field and had once been a foundry before being abandoned for decades. Now it was bustling with shops, offices, and condos. The firm's expansive suite occupied one corner of the second floor and was beautifully decorated with subtle paint colors, Persian rugs, local art, and hidden lights. The old, worn floors had been refurbished. The steel ceiling beams were exposed. The place reeked of money, of big verdicts and even more lucrative settlements. Its opulence reminded Simon of Marshall Graff's spread in Virginia Beach, and that reminded him of his trial, a nightmare he tried to avoid. It also reminded him that he had practiced law in another world, one far away in his quaint little office at the corner of Main and Maple, downtown Braxton. Former office.

Victor Mulrooney was old-school and still wearing dark suits and silk ties, even around the office. His associate, Hilary, wore jeans and sneakers. They met Simon in a small conference room with three walls of glass and impressive views. They sipped coffee for a moment, but only as a formality. Hilary, a senior associate, was allowed to speak whenever she wanted to.

"We've gone through your file, Mr. Latch," she said. "Quite a lot of press."

"It's Simon. You've probably seen more news reports than I have. I've been dodging reporters and their outlets for many months. I know it's all bad."

"I had a nice conversation with Raymond Lassiter. He says the defense was surprised by the verdict."

"Still stunned. I didn't testify because we were confident the Commonwealth did not prove its case. That was a miscalculation. I'd rather not talk about the trial. You know why I'm here."

Mulrooney said, "Yes. Raymond and I discussed it. He seems quite the character."

Simon nodded politely but had no interest in talking about Raymond, regardless of how colorful he might seem. "Can you answer a few basic questions?"

"We'll see. You understand our situation, Mr. Latch."

"Yes, and you understand mine. In a month I go before the trial judge to be sentenced to prison for something I didn't do."

"I believe you're innocent, Mr. Latch."

"Then help me."

"It's not that easy. We have an agreement with the defendant—"

"Fendamar Health."

"Yes, and we cannot discuss the matter. There are some rather harsh penalties for violating the nondisclosure agreement."

"Got that. Did your client have a claim that involved an X-ray technician by the name of Oscar Kofie?"

Mulrooney looked at Hilary. The answer was obvious. He said, "Yes."

"Was your client either Mr. Herbert Grasskie or Ms. Ruth Abercrombie? Both died here in Fendamar Hospital under mysterious circumstances. We have their medical records and we know that Kofie was at the hospital when they died."

"You have their records?" Hilary asked.

"Yes. Enough piles of paper to cover this desk."

"But how?"

"I have secrets too. But the answer is easy. Just hire the right people and turn 'em loose. Illegal as hell but for some reason I really don't care right now. If I have to break a few more laws, what's the downside? I'm looking for the truth."

Mulrooney's facial expressions were almost noncommittal, but he absorbed this with a hint of admiration, even satisfaction. He said, "We represented both families."

"Were they poisoned?"

"Here's the way we'll handle this, Mr. Latch. I'm not willing to run the risk of violating the nondisclosure agreement. Wouldn't be fair to me, this firm, or our clients. But there might be a way around it, a way to give you what you're looking for while keeping us safe. The hospital has some very tough lawyers and will not hesitate to seek damages from a breach. But, sir, you are indeed on the right track."

"I'm listening."

Hilary cleared her throat, flashed a conspiratorial look at Mulrooney, and said, "There is a person who might talk. His name is Alan Teel, and he was a junior partner in this firm until he left three years ago. He burned out, to put it mildly. If you need to know more about that, ask him. Alan was our colleague and a truly gifted trial lawyer, very hard worker, very committed, some would say overly zealous. When he crashed and burned he quit the law. Resigned from the firm, surrendered his license, the works. It was a fairly dramatic exit from the legal profession."

Mulrooney said, "We tried to help him, paid for therapists and doctors and such. And he got better, but he was completely fed up with litigation and the law."

Simon asked, "Was he a member of the firm when it settled the cases and signed the nondisclosure agreements?"

Mulrooney said, "No. He knows everything, but the NDA is not binding on him. That's why he might talk."

"Where is he?"

"A small town about an hour from here."

"Do you mind calling him?"

"He knows you're coming," Hilary said.

Simon was eating a BLT in the town's only diner when Alan Teel walked in, twenty minutes late. He wore a beard, shorts, a T-shirt, and hiking boots, and nothing in his appearance suggested he had ever been a star in the courtroom. They were the same age—forty-three. Simon offered to buy lunch but it was already 3:15.

"Sorry I'm late," he said. "We had a fire call and I'm on duty."

"You're a fireman?"

"Volunteer. Town's too small for a professional department."

"Mind if I ask how you picked this place?"

"How much did Mulrooney tell you about me?"

"Some of the basics. I assume your story has many chapters."

Teel laughed and asked the waitress for some coffee. "I try to avoid Mulrooney, another long story. I'm still friendly with Hilary and she made the call, gave me the heads-up. I went online and read about your recent adventures. Quite the media star these days."

"Thanks. Had you seen the story before now?"

"No. I don't read newspapers and I ignore the television and use the internet only when necessary."

"That's enviable."

"You flamed out of the profession with headlines. I left it in the middle of the night." The waitress placed a cup of steaming coffee on the table and Teel took a long drink without the slightest grimace.

"I'm facing prison for the rest of my life, Alan, and I haven't killed anyone. I need some help."

A long slow minute passed as Alan stared at something on the floor. Simon finished his sandwich and drank some tea.

Alan asked, "Ms. Barnett was poisoned, right?"

"Yep. Thallium."

"Was Oscar Kofie working at the hospital when she was a patient?"

"He was."

Alan glanced at his watch and said, "Look, I can't talk right now. My son has a baseball game at six and I have to get the field ready. I'm the grounds crew. Pays as much as a volunteer fireman. Come to the game and we'll sit together, have a long talk."

"How old is your son?"

"Ten. My youngest."

"I have a daughter who's ten, a soccer star."

"Can you handle a weed-eater?"

"Haven't had much practice but I'm sure I can."

"Let's go."

———————◆◆◆———————

At six, they were sitting in lawn chairs just beyond the left-field fence, under the shade of an old tree, sipping cold lemonade and admiring their handiwork. The field was pristine, and Alan took full credit for its perfect condition. He did everything, from fertilizing the grass, trimming it three times a week, grooming the dirt infield, raking the mound and batter's boxes, and pulling and cutting weeds. He had even painted the dugouts and repaired an old scoreboard.

After three hours together, Simon was still uncertain as to what, exactly, the man did for a living, if anything. He appeared to be a full-time volunteer.

And he was content to get out of the way and let others do the coaching. Once the field was ready and the perfect chalk lines were down, he retreated to his favorite spot in the shade, far away from home plate. He had yet to mention a wife, either current or ex. Simon figured they would never meet again and didn't press for details. Hayden, his son, played second base for the Marlins and struggled at the plate. When he struck out to end the first inning, Alan, showing no disappointment at all, began talking.

"A secretary in the law firm got an anonymous phone call about the death of Herbert Grasskie, age eighty-one, lived somewhere around Scranton or Wilkes-Barre. Said his death was not caused by pneumonia. Rather, he was poisoned. Mulrooney assigned me the case and I started digging. Autopsy, toxicology tests, the works. Took about two weeks to confirm the cause of death was thallium. I'm sure you know all about the toxin."

"More than enough."

"The perfect poison to kill with. More digging and we found another case in the same hospital. Two months earlier a seventy-two-year-old woman named Ruth Abercrombie died a similar death. We really opened the bank at that point, eventually spent over three hundred thousand dollars on the investigation. Mulrooney took charge, as only he could do, which wasn't a bad thing. He's brilliant, both in court and out. And we knew that Fendamar Health has very deep pockets. It's owned by a private equity fund out of Boston that's worth zillions. You can imagine how valuable the cases were—two wrongful deaths caused by a demented hospital employee who likes to play with poisons. The cases were pots of gold and we were all losing sleep with excitement. For various reasons I won't waste time with, our suspicions soon centered around an X-ray tech named Oscar Kofie, a truly strange character."

"Slow down. How did you choose Kofie?"

"Bribery and espionage. Mulrooney managed to keep the cases away from the police because he didn't want to frighten the killer. We found a nurse who claimed she saw Kofie in Ms. Abercrombie's room when he had no business being there. We paid the nurse cold cash to dig some more. And we hired a technician from another hospital, a spy really, to get a job at Fendamar. He did and it worked beautifully. We were in no hurry, you see, because another poisoning would only bolster our case. Pretty sick, really, looking back now, but at the time we were out of control and terribly excited. Our spy befriended Kofie, which wasn't difficult because he didn't have many friends, and they became drinking buddies. Then they did drugs. Kofie liked to talk about poisons and toxins. We also hired an ex-DEA guy, called himself a consultant, to poke around in the black market. Thallium is not that hard to find because it's not illegal to possess. It's just against the law to produce it. Our consultant found a broker in a shady lab in New Jersey and was able to track a shipment to Scranton, to a post office box rented to a guy with a fake name. The trail ended there, but the shipment confirmed our suspicions. Our spy finally got inside Kofie's apartment, which had security alarms and cameras at both exterior doors, but nothing more inside. The boys from the hospital, three or four of them, including our mole, had a late-night vodka and coke binge while watching porn videos. Keep in mind these are the people we entrust with our health care. The spy managed to stay somewhat lucid, and when the others passed out, he looked around the apartment. Wasn't much to see. Two small bedrooms, a den and a kitchen. One bedroom door was locked solid but there were no visible alarms. A weekend trip to watch a Steelers game materialized, with our guy suddenly in possession of four tickets, plus he found cheap rooms. He said that Kofie admitted he'd never had so many friends. When they were at the game, a security team entered his apartment, disabled the alarms, opened the locked bedroom door, and found two metal boxes, similar to toolboxes. They removed them from the apartment and rushed them to a hotel room where their technicians were waiting. Got one open and found enough coke and assorted pills to put him away for years. In the other they found a little pharmacy, with several plastic bottles of poisons—arsenic, cyanide, strychnine, aconitine, and of course, thallium. They were not labeled and the team was not equipped to identify them, so they took a small sample from each container and, later, ran them through a lab. Everything was put back in order, and, as far as we could tell, Kofie never suspected the break-in."

Teel's son made a diving catch at second and doubled-up the runner at first. It was a spectacular play for a ten-year-old, yet Teel showed no reaction. He was lost in his story.

"At that point, we made a strategic decision. 'We'? It was really Mulrooney, the one and only boss. I didn't like the way the case was going so I took a back seat, though I was still in the room. Mulrooney decided to deal with the hospital directly and not involve the police. He demanded a huge settlement in hush money. If Fendamar would pay him the fortune and get rid of Kofie, he would not file a billion-dollar lawsuit, nor would he go to the cops. The hospital's lawyers were tough, but so is Mulrooney. They beat each other up for a few months then reached a settlement. Pay the fortune, sign a nondisclosure in blood, bury the story, run Kofie out of town, and everybody's happy. That was about the time I left the firm."

"Why?"

"Why? Because I was disgusted with Mulrooney. He was agreeing to take the money and in return allow a murderer to walk away unpunished. We fought and I remember asking Mulrooney what he would do one day when he heard that Kofie had killed again."

"And that day is here."

"It is."

"What was his response?"

"Nothing much. A shrug that said, 'So what?'"

Simon's mouth was dry and he sipped some lemonade.

Teel had a dip in his lip and spat on the grass. "I had two allies in the firm who wanted to stand our ground, file a big suit, and go the distance. We wanted Kofie brought to trial and sent to prison. We wanted to expose Fendamar, though, in all fairness, the hospital is well-thought-of around here. But we were no match for Mulrooney. He just wanted the money."

"How much?"

"I can't say because it's in the NDA."

"Bullshit. Everything you've just told me is covered by the NDA, which you're not subject to, right?"

"That's far from certain and it has not been tested. It's a thick and complicated document that, believe me, nobody on our side wants to litigate. I could get in trouble for talking."

"You're obviously not afraid of it."

"No, I don't care. I have few assets and have no plans to acquire anything else. Life is simple. I like it this way."

"Mulrooney's life is not simple."

"No, he's quite complicated. But he's struggling right now

because he knows his own greed has led to more killings. The man's got a soul, buried deep somewhere."

"He also got a lot of money."

"Yes, he did. He got a huge slice of the deal and took his fee offshore, tax-free."

"How much?"

"Lots of rumors around the firm. No one in the firm knows for sure because Mulrooney routed the money through Singapore and parts unknown, but the best guess is that Fendamar paid around fifty million."

CHAPTER 63

Alan did not inquire about his overnight plans, and Simon didn't offer because he had none. He found a room at a motel that appeared to have been constructed in the past thirty years, and would have felt better if the rate for one night had been more than $45, but he was in no position to be selective. The other two motels along the highway were far older, cheaper, and had yet to pave their parking lots. He had corn chips and beer for dinner, and at 9 P.M. called Raymond, who, of course, was at the office. Simon could almost smell the cigar smoke.

Raymond's customary crankiness vanished after Simon's opening. The old windbag was speechless and allowed Simon to deliver his narrative for at least twenty minutes before uttering a sound. It was, "Hang on. I need another shot."

———◆◆———

Alan agreed to meet for breakfast at the same diner at seven-thirty before he took his boys to school. Still no mention of a wife or woman in his life, not that Simon cared.

He was only ten minutes late. Simon had just taken his first bite of oatmeal—prepackaged—and flagged the waitress over for more coffee. Alan ordered wheat toast and honey.

"Get any sleep last night?" he asked with a grin.

"No, not much. A lot to think about."

Alan pulled a folded sheet of paper from his shirt pocket, and thanked the waitress for the coffee. "I have three priorities, in order of importance."

The small sheet of notebook paper had scribblings on both sides.

"Number one: I want Kofie off the street and locked away somewhere. I can't help with that because I'm not a direct witness to his crimes. And you can't trust our local boys because they've already solved the crime and got their conviction. This is a matter for the FBI."

"How'd they get Kofie out of town without raising suspicions?"

"Another sad part of the story. They suddenly had some layoffs at the hospital and he got his walking papers. Since no one filed a complaint against him, he kept his technician's license. Pretty sick, huh?"

"Yeah. His license to poison others."

"And, apparently, that's what has happened. May I continue?"

"Proceed, sir."

"Number two: I want to help you walk away from this. I see where you've filed a motion to vacate the guilty verdict. What are the chances of getting before the judge on this?"

"Quite good. So far, she's held hearings on all motions from both sides. We consider her to be sympathetic."

"She should be. She presided over a trial that convicted an innocent man. As a believer in our system of justice, I'm appalled by any wrongful conviction. You're innocent and we know who's guilty. Let's nail him."

"Will you testify at the hearing?"

"I knew this was coming and the answer is yes, with conditions. I'm not sure of the procedure in Virginia, but around here it's possible to have a closed hearing, on the record, of course. If we can have a closed hearing to vacate—empty courtroom, no press, no spectators, no one there who's not supposed to be there—then I'll testify. The Fendamar file is under lock and key and it must remain buried. Which goes hand in hand with number three: I have to protect the NDA. The hospital can never know about my involvement. If it finds out it will come after me and the entire Mulrooney firm. That would not be pleasant. The NDA has some clawback provisions that allow the hospital to recoup some serious money should the lawyers develop loose tongues."

"How do we get the file?"

Alan smiled and pulled out a thumb drive. "It's all right here. I kept copies and recorded everything, even have the video of Kofie's apartment. Surprisingly, not a very cool pad."

"Are you offering that to me?"

"No. I'll bring it to court and share it with the judge."

"Okay. My lawyer will start pushing for a hearing right now."

"You told him?"

"Oh yeah, had a long talk last night and we'll have another when I leave here and drive home. This changes everything, Alan. I can't thank you enough."

"You're an innocent man, Simon."

"I know."

———◆◆———

He would have called Zander with the news but it was not yet noon. He should be in Braxton by then. Perhaps he could buy her lunch.

He called Raymond, who was far more talkative now that he'd had some sleep and time to digest the news. Raymond was full of ideas about legal procedures and maneuverings Simon had never heard of.

He called Landy and they discussed the FBI's involvement. She was certain a file would be opened and an investigation would be ramped up soon enough. She would call her supervisor as soon as she hung up.

As he drove past the sign for the city limits of Braxton, Simon asked himself, and certainly not for the first time, why he was returning to the town. It wasn't home anymore. For the past nineteen years, ever since he finished law school, Braxton had been the center of his world. His home and office, real estate he'd once owned, were there. His three children had been born in the very hospital where Oscar Kofie was still working. He and Paula had raised the kids in the public schools and rarely missed a teacher conference, a play, a concert, a graduation, or a game. His church was there, though over the years the family had attended less and less. The Latches were now considered Easter Christians. His friends still lived in Braxton, though he felt abandoned by all of them.

The only thing Simon wanted from Braxton at the moment was a clear name. He had been wrongfully convicted by a jury far away but harshly condemned by the people closest to him. He wanted to be able to walk through the courthouse and then down Main Street, his final walk on his way out of town, with his head high as he looked down on all those who doubted him. He wanted them to feel rotten for misjudging him. He wanted retribution.

It was a sad commentary on his life that the only acquaintance he could meet for lunch was a young, talented criminal with hair that was the color of a tangerine this week and lavender last week. Zander managed to pull things together by 2 P.M. and meet at her favorite tea shop, where the antisocial chef/owner was advertising ginger cookies as a special.

"Let's skip those," Simon said, but Zander missed the connection. She ordered a breakfast tea loaded with caffeine and slugged it down. She was emaciated and needed to add at least twenty pounds. So did Simon, and he ordered two sandwiches. As he devoured them, he gave her a sanitized version of Alan Teel's story, careful to avoid the sensitive areas.

He thanked her again, and she again waved him off. It was just something she and Cooley did for fun, sometimes for profit.

CHAPTER 64

He loathed the prospect of returning to his dark, empty office and The Closet with nothing to do but dig through more research. Hadn't he just solved the mystery, or had it been solved for him? Had he not found the killer? His phone buzzed as he pulled into the alley behind his office. Landy said, "There's an FBI office in Charlottesville. Can you be there at nine in the morning?"

"I have nothing else to do. What's up?"

"The FBI and the U.S. Attorney."

"Is that all? Sure I'll be there."

"Bring your research. Bring everything."

"I have at least three boxes of files. And umpteen gigabytes on my laptop."

"Zip me that stuff tonight and bring the boxes."

"So you and your pals are interested?"

"The investigation is now open. Congratulations."

He didn't feel like celebrating, nor did he feel like working. He fell asleep on the sofa, napped for an hour, then jogged for another one. He talked to Paula and the kids for a long time and got the latest scoop on their back-to-school adventures. Buck was entering his senior year. With some luck, Simon would not miss it.

When the sun faded, he changed into jeans and slinked through the alleys and back streets, and entered Chub's a few minutes after nine. Valerie brought him a drink, then a cheeseburger. Chub was not around and that was okay. Simon didn't feel like discussing his problems. He played video poker for two hours, won thirty-one dollars before finally quitting, and left a twenty-dollar bill on the bar for Valerie.

———◆◆———

Landy pulled an all-nighter and put together a ten-page memo, a very rough draft of Mr. Oscar Kofie's adventures with thallium. She had plenty of facts on the Eleanor Barnett case, but fewer on the others.

It was an all-girls show, except for Simon, who sat on one side of the table with Landy as they faced Carmen Riddle, the assistant U.S. attorney (AUSA), and Shelia Wycoff, supervisor in charge (SIC), FBI. Once Simon had the alphabet untangled and some-what clear, he was ready to proceed.

He explained that he possessed an extensive collection of materials regarding the suspect: his personnel, employment, HR files from the four hospitals where he had worked in the past decade; the voluminous medical records of patients in those hos-pitals who had died either by poisoning or similar, though undi-agnosed, symptoms; along with a mountain of materials regarding the claims of two deceased patients in Scranton, Pennsylvania.

Shelia Wycoff asked, "How did you obtain the personnel records from the hospitals?"

"I paid a hacker. I don't know anything about hacking, so I found someone who did."

"Did you violate statutes?"

"Oh hell yeah, and maybe I'll do it again. What are you gonna do, indict me? Look, Ms. Wycoff, I've already been convicted, wrongfully, you see, and I'm headed to prison for a long time. I really don't give a damn about breaking laws at this point. Pile it on. I don't care if you indict me."

Carmen Riddle asked, "Okay, what about the claims, the law-suits, in Scranton. Where did that information come from?"

"It started with the same hacker, you see. A young lady with a boyfriend who's in a federal prison camp with two laptops and three phones, all contraband. They're a great team, unless they get caught. You guys should really tighten up security at your camps. Anyway, they picked up the trail of the Scranton claims and located a lawyer who was involved. I went to see him three days ago and I learned all we need to know about Oscar Kofie. He's a serial homicidal poisoner with at least three dead bodies notched in his belt, maybe as many as five more. But you don't have to prove those. Prove only one. Prove only Eleanor Barnett, and send him away for life."

It was obvious Simon was miles ahead of them, not only on the facts but also with strategies. Carmen Riddle was curious about the role of the local police.

Simon dismissed it immediately. "Don't waste your time. Their case is closed. They got the killer, the wrong one, and they'll probably defend their bogus investigation until hell freezes over. Standard procedure for law enforcement. Sorry, but that includes the FBI. In wrongful convictions the stakes are too great, and the mistakes are so catastrophic, that no one can ever admit getting the wrong guy. Forget the locals. Nice boys and all that, but you don't need them. I'm handing you the case, okay?"

"Got it."

Carmen Riddle looked at Landy and asked, "Should we put Kofie under surveillance?"

Simon barged in with "Why? He's not going anywhere, unless he gets spooked. Play it cool, don't tip him off, grab him one day at work, then trash his apartment."

Riddle said, "We'll handle that part, Mr. Latch. For now, I advise you to stop your illegal monitoring of his email."

Simon shrugged as if he'd think about it. "Will you get a warrant and watch the apartment?"

"That's what we usually do. We'll tap his phone and his computer."

Simon found it funny and said, "Well, if your boys need any help, just let me know. My hackers are already there."

The three women seemed startled and glanced at each other. Carmen Riddle took a deep breath and asked Simon, "Do you know the medical director at the hospital in Braxton?"

"Yes, quite well. Dr. Connor Wilkes."

"Well, how should we approach her?"

"Simple. The most urgent matter right now, other than me saving my own neck, is to make sure this guy does not poison anyone else. Right now the hospital has no clue. They think the Barnett murder is solved, life goes on as usual. Though I've heard through the grapevine that they've banned all carry-in food. No more cookies and brownies for Grandma. Which is a shame because they should ban all the food from their own cafeteria."

Simon paused for a bit of laughter, or at least a nod to his quick wit. Nothing.

"And I've also heard that Tan Lu's Vietnamese restaurant can't give the damned ginger cookies away these days. Too bad."

Carmen said, "If we could get back to the issues."

"Sure. If I were you, I'd have a powwow with the hospital brass soon, tomorrow if possible, and make sure their lawyers are there. Tell them the truth. Tell them that Eleanor Barnett was not poisoned by me. Tell them they have a probable serial killer on their payroll, and that the FBI has the place surrounded.

"Their exposure is enormous. A trial lawyer's dream. A public relations nightmare that could easily bankrupt the hospital. Who would want to go there for critical care? Make sure someone inside is watching Kofie to keep him away from the patients. You need the hospital's cooperation right now, at least until he's in custody. Once that happens, the shit hits the fan. It's front-page headlines and the hospital turns into a bunker. I don't really care. Kofie is their employee. He'll go to prison and the hospital will be mired in lawsuits for years."

Riddle and Wycoff scribbled furiously. Landy looked at some notes. To Simon, the silence indicated they would like to hear some additional thoughts from him. He continued, "Once you meet with the hospital and drop that bomb, you lose control of the story. You can't trust everyone to keep quiet. If I were in charge, I'd move quickly but carefully. Get your warrants, go through his apartment, where you're probably going to find one or two locked toolboxes where he keeps his little pharmacy, his collection of poisons. I've seen pictures. It's quite impressive. Includes thallium, which appears to be his favorite. When you find that, you have probable cause."

Riddle asked, "And what's your schedule?"

"As you know, I'm trying to set aside my guilty verdict. We have a hearing next week, a closed one. You should be there. Let me know and I'll get you front-row seats."

CHAPTER 65

Judge Shyam made the wise decision to hear the defendant's motion several days before she was to sentence him on August 22. That day was on the record, well known and publicized, and thus on the calendar for the reporters, journalists, news crews, and other tabloid junkies. Justice would be better served if those people were not watching. She personally called the lawyers and arranged a closed hearing a week earlier, on August 16, in Virginia Beach. She cautioned them to keep it confidential and wanted no leaks. She even drove home the point by threatening sanctions.

Before the hearing, she put three deputies at the main door to check the guest list she had screened. Only a handful of people were allowed inside. When they were seated, she entered the courtroom and greeted her invitees. She began with "Mr. Lassiter, it's your motion to vacate. Please get things started. Feel free to keep your seat."

There was no way Raymond could speak properly to a judge while seated. He stood, fiddled with his silk tie, thanked her properly, and said, "Your Honor, my client, Simon Latch, was found guilty in this courtroom on May the twenty-seventh. I was shocked at the verdict, as was Mr. Latch and many others. Since then, we have worked desperately to solve the mystery of who poisoned Eleanor Barnett, and through the rather heroic efforts of Mr. Latch himself, we now know. Our first witness will testify under a pseudonym. His identity must be protected. After he testifies, I will tender to the court an affidavit with his real identification along with an explanation of need for secrecy. This affidavit should not go into the record."

"Very well, Mr. Lassiter. You have briefed me and the Commonwealth's attorney on this. You may call your first witness."

"John Doe the Third."

"How original," Simon whispered to Casey.

Alan Teel took the witness stand with all the confidence of a seasoned trial lawyer who'd had a brilliant career in courtrooms. After being sworn, and after a slight prompt from Raymond, he was off and running. He began his story eight years earlier when a secretary in his unnamed firm got a tip from a nurse about an unusual death at a local hospital, also unnamed. This happened in Pennsylvania. The tip led to more information, then to an investigation by the law firm.

Cora Cook stood and said, "Your Honor, I hate to interrupt, but are we ignoring all rules of procedure and evidence here? Are we allowing the witness to use hearsay and irrelevant facts and anything else he wants?"

Judge Shyam said, "Yes we are, Ms. Cook. I want the entire story and I'm the sole decider at this point. There is no jury in the box. I'll filter the testimony and decide what's relevant. Thank you."

The prosecutor shrugged in defeat and sat down.

Alan hardly missed a beat and continued with a narrative that he obviously enjoyed sharing with the sparse crowd. He was a wonderful raconteur, like most trial lawyers, and his audience was rapt.

Simon sipped coffee at the defense table and casually looked around the courtroom. Landy and her boss, Shelia Wycoff, were in the front row. On the far side of the courtroom, Detective Roger Barr sat alone, listening and not taking notes. Then, the usual cast: court reporter, two clerks, one bailiff, the judge.

After Teel had rambled for an hour, Raymond thought Judge Shyam might be getting bored. So, he decided to liven things up with a video. Casey tapped keys on his laptop and an image appeared on a screen in front of the jury box.

Teel said, "This is a video of the search inside Oscar Kofie's apartment. The date is May third, 2009. There are the two metal toolboxes, locked. Our technicians took them to a makeshift lab." The video continued with footage of the metal boxes being opened, the bottles removed, the samples taken. An unseen voice narrated the action. The video stopped after seventeen minutes.

Teel described some of the toxins and substances found in the boxes. Then he returned to the lawsuits, the negotiations with the hospital, and so on. He whitewashed his departure from his firm as simply a misunderstanding and did not disparage his former partners in any way. He never mentioned their names. When he finished, some two hours after he started, his small audience was still hanging on his words.

Judge Shyam said, "Ms. Cook, any cross-examination?"

Cora appeared flustered, even shell-shocked, as if she was beginning to understand that her conviction was in serious jeopardy and that perhaps she had prosecuted the wrong man. She stood, fumbled with a legal pad, and said, "So, Mr. Doe, your law firm did not prosecute Oscar Kofie when it knew the truth, is that right?"

"That's correct. My ex–law firm. I quit by the time the settlement was complete. But yes, they took the money and remained silent."

"And that's why you left the firm?"

"The main reason, yes. They allowed the killer to walk away without a word to the police. They were hoping that maybe Kofie had learned his lesson and would change his ways, but the problem was that Kofie never knew he'd been caught. It was buried from everyone. His job got cut with several others and he left town, none the wiser. It was a cowardly move by the law firm. And they were praying that he would not kill again. Well, they were wrong.

The man is a sociopath, like most serial killers. He works in health care, a place where homicidal poisonings are prevalent. He enjoys watching his victims die, it gives him a perverted sense of control. He eventually showed up in Braxton, Virginia, and here we are."

Cora's questions were getting more answers than she cared to hear, so she sat down. Raymond rose and said, "Your Honor, the defense calls FBI special agent in charge Ms. Shelia Wycoff."

Simon glanced at Landy in the front row and gave her a grin. She crossed her legs and smiled in return. It was odd how much better a pretty woman looked in an empty, stale, dusty old courtroom.

Wycoff testifed that the FBI received information regarding a possible murder, or murders, ten days earlier, and opened an investigation into one Oscar Kofie. He had worked in the hospital for three years, and left under the cloud just described by John Doe the Third. From there he went to a hospital in Baltimore for two years, then to Braxton. At each hospital, there were mysterious deaths that could have been caused by poisoning, and the FBI was investigating.

At the moment, the FBI was concentrating on the suspect, Oscar Kofie. In fact, the day before, the FBI had obtained a warrant to raid his apartment in Braxton. The raid was successful and yielded a number of poisons, including thallium.

Simon enjoyed a long look over at Cora Cook, whose face was ashen in disbelief. Her world would only get worse.

Luckily, the suspect had just received a package containing 25 grams of thallium. It came by U.S. mail from a bogus address in Durban, South Africa. There was a video of the search if the court wanted to view it.

"Maybe later," Shyam said, leaving little doubt she had seen enough and had little curiosity left.

Then the bomb landed, and Simon could almost feel himself sprinting from the courtroom, a free man.

Wycoff said, "Yesterday at approximately seven-twenty P.M., the suspect was taken into custody as he left the hospital, and he is now locked away in an undisclosed location. He will be charged with one count of first-degree murder. His case will be presented to a federal grand jury next Tuesday."

It was the perfect stopping point. There was really nothing left to say. Raymond read it nicely and said, "We tender the witness." As if Cora could possibly undo any of the damage with a brilliant cross-examination. Instead, she shook her head in defeat.

"You may be excused, Ms. Wycoff. Your next witness, Mr. Lassiter."

"I believe the court has heard enough, Your Honor. The real killer has been arrested by the FBI and will be indicted next week. The Commonwealth made a grave mistake in prosecuting Simon Latch, an innocent man. You should vacate that conviction and set him free."

"Ms. Cook."

She stood slowly, searching for words. "Perhaps not so fast, Judge. A jury of twelve informed citizens heard the proof and returned a unanimous verdict of guilty. We can't just ignore that and sweep it aside. The defendant got a fair trial in this courtroom and, at least in my opinion, there was no reversible error. A clean, fair trial."

Judge Shyam leaned forward and held some notes. "Ms. Cook, are you familiar with the case of *Commonwealth of Virginia versus Herman Dungee?*"

It came from left field and Cora was at a loss. "Maybe. Sounds somewhat familiar."

"Mr. Dungee spent thirty-one years in a prison for a rape and murder committed by someone else. Three years ago he was cleared by DNA testing and exonerated. His trial in 1985 was in this very courtroom. The jury returned a unanimous verdict of guilty. The jury got it wrong. Are you familiar with the case of *Commonwealth versus Boyd Keenan?*"

"I don't think so."

"A case out of Norfolk, just down the road. Mr. Keenan spent eighteen years in prison for a bank robbery that did not go as planned. Two bank tellers were killed. When the crime occurred, Mr. Keenan was working in South Carolina. Nevertheless, the jury convicted him. The jury got it wrong.

"Are you familiar with the case of *Commonwealth versus Harlan Miller,* another local screwup?"

"No." Cora sat down.

"Mr. Miller served twenty-eight years on death row and came within six hours of being executed. DNA cleared him. The jury, again in this courtroom, found him guilty and recommended death."

She laid down her notes and glared at the prosecutor. "I could go on. In the past thirty years, at least forty-one people in this Commonwealth have been convicted by well-meaning juries, only to be exonerated years later. Across the country, over three thousand innocent people have been cleared, and virtually all of them were convicted by unanimous juries."

If Cora had had a white flag, she would have waved it.

Judge Shyam said, "Would the defendant please rise?"

Simon was startled, but nonetheless managed to get to his feet. Raymond stood beside him, suppressing a grin.

"Mr. Latch, on behalf of the Commonwealth of Virginia I apologize for this miscarriage of justice. I was surprised when the jury found you guilty. Fortunately, our rules of criminal procedure allow me to correct a wrong decision. I hereby grant your motion to vacate the verdict of guilty and dismiss the charges against you, with prejudice. I will instruct the Commonwealth's attorney to close this file and disavow any notion of a re-indictment. You are free to go."

Simon's knees went soft and he fell back into his chair. He covered his eyes with his palms and began to cry.

———————◆◆◆———————

They drove south for an hour until they came to the Outer Banks. Simon was lost in another world and said nothing. Landy drove with no destination in mind, just happy to be out of Virginia. She glanced at him occasionally to make sure he was okay. His eyes were closed but he was not sleeping.

What a waste. Of time, money, emotions, lives. What needless suffering. There was so much to say, but no energy to say it.

They stopped at a convenience store in Currituck because she needed something to eat. Simon saw a picnic table under a tree and said, "I'm going to walk over there and call my kids, and tell them that their father has been declared innocent."